THE
NAVIGATOR

THE
NAVIGATOR

MICHAEL POCALYKO

FORGE®

A TOM DOHERTY ASSOCIATES BOOK

NEW YORK

THE NAVIGATOR

A Forge Book
Published by Tom Doherty Associates, LLC
175 Fifth Avenue
New York, NY 10010

www.tor-forge.com

Forge® is a registered trademark of Tom Doherty Associates, LLC.

Library of Congress Cataloging-in-Publication Data

Pocalyko, Michael.
    The Navigator / Michael Pocalyko.—First edition.
        p. cm.
    "A Tom Doherty Associates book."
    ISBN 978-0-7653-3224-0 (hardcover)
    ISBN 978-1-4299-5539-3 (e-book)
    1. Investment banking—Fiction.   2. International business enterprises—Fiction.
3. High technology—Fiction.   4. Suspense fiction.   I. Title.
PS3616.O26N38 2013
813'.6—dc23

                                                                    2012043862

Forge books may be purchased for educational, business, or promotional use. For information on bulk purchases, please contact Macmillan Corporate and Premium Sales Department at 1-800-221-7945 extension 5442 or write specialmarkets@macmillan.com.

First Edition: June 2013

Printed in the United States of America

0 9 8 7 6 5 4 3 2 1

To Walt, Paul, and Jim Pocalyko
my father, brother, and son

Und geht es draußen noch so toll,
Unchristlich oder christlich,
Ist doch die Welt, die schöne Welt,
So gänzlich unverwüstlich!

—Theodor Storm, *"Oktoberleid"*

THE
NAVIGATOR

PROLOGUE

April 1945

As darkness edged the empty dawn, the navigator inhaled violently. The Lucky Strike stub burned both his thumb and his lip. He chased the cigarette smoke with a shallow gulp of thick air then held his breath tentatively. The nicotine swirling in his lungs provided no relief. He flicked the tiny butt with a *hrsssp* into the thick mud at his feet. Nothing helped. The stench of death screamed, outshouting the senses. His head hammered hard. His heart raced in the comfortable tobacco rush as his stomach and bowels clenched in irregular spasms. Unable to hold the smoke in any longer, he exhaled and panted involuntarily, wishing for the hundredth time tonight that he could have stayed with the damn plane.

"Lieutenant?" The voice, kind and firm, called out to him. "Come on over here." It was the tall captain from air intelligence. "Stay with me. We have to talk to this Kraut. He may be what I'm looking for. He wants to say something. How about lending a hand? Can you make me understand him?" The navigator slogged through the rain-bred swamp. The mud, ankle-deep, stuck like paste to his flight boots. He approached the German soldier. Christ, he thought. How old can this one be? Sixteen? Seventeen? He studied the German intently. The young face was drained and quite pale, sweating despite the chill night mist. He had no facial hair except an uneven bristle of black stubble on his chin. A wild panic flushed in the boy's eyes. It was the instinctual fear of a trapped animal.

The navigator himself was twenty, and he suddenly felt very old.

But he felt not one bit of sympathy for the German soldier. It was time to get in character. He braced. Striking quickly with both hands, he lunged and grabbed the young man roughly by the shoulders and neck, shouting and spitting the coarsest rage into his face. "*Wer bist du?* Who are you? *Was machst du denn hier?* What do you do here?" The American's swift and perfectly accentless *Hochdeutsch* German using the familiar form took the young man quite off guard—its precise intended effect. The soldier sputtered and began to speak rapidly.

I have been in the camp less than three weeks and have never had the disposal duties. Never. Nimmer. They did not let me there. The young man made his assertions with an imminent fear of death, providing the purest distillation of truth. So they called it the "disposal duties." That was the term he used for the operation—*die Verfügungschuldigkeiten*. The navigator had to think about the unusual word for a moment. *I am a perimeter guard. That is all I am. I am begging to make you understand. I am only a man with a sense of loyalty. I have the strength of duty to my family and to the country of my fathers. I have never met Americans before, but naturally you must understand my position. Look at me. I have no control over what goes on here.*

The German soldier spoke on, babbling in a distinctive *Schwarzwalder* accent, wavering on the brink of tears. His voice, deliberately or not, conveyed increasing urgency pleading conviction. But the navigator was hearing less and less of what the boy said. He was finding it terribly hard to concentrate. The stench was simply too distracting, painted thick on the inner walls of his skull. He could taste it, feel it dripping down the back of his throat. The burnt hair and fat, the putrid flesh, the thick air fetid with thousands of human remains in their many strata of destruction and decay. They were forgotten souls in a forbidding place. The navigator took several shallow breaths. I am choking here, he thought. So this is how the war ends. I would never have believed it.

"Nothing here, Captain," he told the officer from air intelligence. "This is just one more of them who never had anything at all to do with this." His sarcasm rang flat. There was no longer any contempt left in his voice. No matter who he questioned the theme never varied. He was by now well beyond disgust. The navigator felt a heavy tightening in his chest, a thick knot clenching below his sternum. A wave of heat flushed his ears as his body reacted with more unfamiliar mechanics. He began to wonder if he could take much more.

"Thanks," the tall man replied. "But don't get too far away from me, okay? I'm still looking for something. I need you to talk to them." The navigator understood. It was why he was ordered here in the first place, yanked out of his regular B-24 crew from the stand-down in England.

The native German language ability that he possessed came courtesy of his immigrant father, who called it *ein Geschenk:* a gift. The navigator's German was an enablement of beauty and value that had come from a place abandoned shortly after the Great War. This night was the homecoming of an American-born son of the Fatherland. Before today the navigator had passionately hated the Nazis. But it was all done from a distance and through an iron bombsight. He used to despise them for everything they had done to his father's home—a thought he allowed himself with every weapons release over Köln, Bremerhaven, Dresden, and Berlin. But in this moment he hated all Germans. He even hated himself.

"It's so much easier when we do it to them from the air," the captain stated with sincere gravity. "We never have to see the killing we do. It's cleaner. Nicer. Technical. Not like this. Fucking unbelievable." The navigator shook his head slowly. He tried very hard not to breathe. Despite the captain's instructions, he moved away.

No, it wasn't like this. Nothing was ever like this.

As he walked, he continued to feel dizzyingly ill, more lightheaded, but he was managing. He was already quite numb to the sights—a reality darker than his imagination would dare. The carnage without blood. The genderless nude bodies stacked with neat precision at the base of the piles, then strewn haphazardly toward the top as the British infantry forces had advanced and the death camp's liberation inched nearer. The thick bile liquefied and mixed into the mud at his feet. And all around him, there they were: the standing, breathing dead, grateful skeletons of thin opal-gray skin draped over atrophied muscles. The navigator wondered if they might envy those who had died. And then there was the other most disquieting image he saw everywhere he turned—the faces of the Englishmen and the other Americans, flattened beyond belief in frozen stares that must, he recognized, exactly mirror his own.

Rounding the corner of a barracks, the navigator noticed the first dull sunlight brighten the eastern sky. This was usually his favorite time to fly. He stopped short of the air intelligence captain, who was deep in conversation with two German officers. One of them gestured, attempting to communicate energetically in shards of broken English. He watched and strained to listen, comprehending only part of what the German said. A mute crowd of prisoners, all of them men with deep sunken eyes of unlit rage, gathered.

"Shoes! All shoes, *ja*," said one of the German officers to the captain, who watched the slowly advancing crowd. The captain was silent and could not understand.

"*Juden*," said the navigator, enunciating clearly. Both Germans turned toward him and nodded. "Jews, Captain, not shoes. He's trying to tell you that these prisoners are all Jewish."

So there it was. The stories were true.

The tall American was no longer listening. Now intent on the prisoners, the captain walked into the small crowd and began to study each man's face, one at a time, moving slowly, occasionally glancing back at the Germans. He was searching.

In the new dim sunlight, all of the faces looked alike to the navigator. The two German officers stopped talking and also watched the captain among the prisoners. The air intelligence man took his time. For his part, the navigator wanted desperately to light a smoke again, but he could not bring himself to move. In the center of the crowd, the captain leaned over a prisoner. Their conversation became a lengthy exchange which the navigator could not hear no matter how hard he tried. Then gently, courteously, the captain took the man by the arm and led him from the group to where the navigator stood beside the German officers.

The prisoner's clothing hung on him loosely. A dull gray threadbare tunic full of holes. Ragged black trousers. One pant leg was cut off above the knee exposing a thigh rotten with filth and sores. The prisoner was barefoot and bare headed, his scalp and heavy beard shaved in uneven cuts. He could be twenty-five or he could be fifty, the navigator thought. Who could tell? The air intelligence officer whispered to him once more and the man nodded. Wordlessly, the captain unhooked the holster of his service revolver and withdrew it, turning it around to hand to the prisoner. The navigator froze in panic and disbelief as the man calmly took the weapon and cocked it, lowering the gun and pointing it at the chest of the nearest German officer. Suddenly, the prisoner became a man transformed. The navigator saw in that sallow face the instant serenity of total control. His mind raced with the realization that he had better unholster his own pistol right now.

He was fumbling for his .45 when the first shot cracked into the nearest German officer's chest. The prisoner followed the man's collapse to the ground with the gun barrel, firing his second shot even before the German had finished falling. There was almost no pause before the third round, which hit the other German officer in the side of the head, instantly obliterating most of his skull. Now the navigator had his weapon drawn—a gun that he had carried on bombing runs for two years, but which he had never fired in anger. In the distance, he could hear soldiers running through the mud and shouting, trying to discern where among the many rows of barracks the shots had come from.

The prisoner fired a fourth time, into the trunk of the second German officer. The navigator kept his eyes fixed on the man. He was terrified, stock-still, unsure how to act. The prisoner's next move made the decision for him. Carefully, the pistol turned directly toward the navigator and for a fifth time the prisoner took aim.

The navigator was never exactly sure what happened next.

He had a sensation—that was all it was—that he had lived. He never knew how many shots he fired or where they hit. Prisoners crowded about. Many American soldiers appeared and converged. Men stood over him, armed statuary arrested in place. There were wide stares, orders barked with cracking voices, cries of disbelief. Permeating everything was the smell. The navigator's last conscious memory from the camp—and from the war—was of the blooming sunrise. When the medics finally arrived they found him sobbing loudly and incoherently, sitting cross-legged in the thick mud and rocking rapidly back and forth, his whole mind and what little was left of his soul thoroughly shattered.

CHAPTER 1

The tenth-floor offices of Carneccio & Dice LLC were in an aggravated state of disarray when the elevator opened into the firm's usually well-appointed reception area. This morning about a dozen workmen from the construction trades stood around being busily unoccupied. Most were wearing coveralls and grubby clothing. With them were a few building engineers distinguished by their short-sleeve polyester shirts and loosely knotted neckties. Some looked impatient. Others were just plain bored. To one side, hunkered behind her circular desk, a single harried receptionist eyed them warily.

People who did business with Carneccio & Dice—and even some of the seventeen partners, associates, and employees who worked there—were not entirely sure precisely how to categorize the firm. Occupying the top floor of Class A office space in a building on 19th Street Northwest, a few blocks from Washington, DC's K Street power corridor, it wasn't exactly a venture capital firm, a corporate financial advisor, a government marketing advisory firm, or a personal asset management firm. But it would admit to being partly all of these. Mostly what the company did was move money. For the large part, it was OPM: other people's money, scads of it, fueling private deals of all kinds. The firm's prosperity was a legacy of the post-9/11 homeland security business boom, now a distant memory of glory days before the big recession, but still roaring as far as the dealmakers at Carneccio & Dice were concerned. As Washington business languished, a few spots flourished in the desperation to seed economic recovery. This place was an anomaly, and a good one. The people who circulated through here were flush with cash. If they wanted more of it, and of course they all did, a firm like this would be pleased to accommodate them.

There was only one man on the elevator. Slim, fair, his sandy hair just beginning to thin, he was impeccably groomed in a new blue Ermenegildo Zegna suit and knotted Hermès silk tie. Rick Yeager was just handsome enough to get himself noticed in an executive suite. He scanned the scene quickly, approving the appearance of the office. He was entering a firm doing exceptionally well. He liked the corporate image: building, growth, renewal. Stepping from the elevator into what was obviously soon to be chaos, he paused at the display of three easels holding architectural drawings of the new office design. It was an aggressive expansion of which he was personally a part, beginning today.

There is a moment in every man's life when he becomes conscious, in varying degrees depending on the individual, that he really has arrived. At the age of forty-one, Richard Montgomery Yeager was convinced that he had now found his moment. For the past couple of weeks, Rick had fantasy-practiced this day of arrival at Carneccio & Dice. Prior to today, the firm had never brought aboard a new partner as a direct hire. He carefully pre-considered the message he should convey. Confidence and competence, professional reserve and near distance, the light touch of a heavy hand. None of these traits came naturally to him, but he knew how to project an image. In response, what he expected were a few deferential young associates being courteous to a fault. Maybe there would be a hint of gently flirtatious flattery from the women on the clerical staff. He could handle that.

What he got were the suspicious stares of the assembled construction workers, all of whom seemed precisely to record his arrival. He made his way to the receptionist, who smiled and greeted him by name.

"Mr. Yeager, it's so good to see you. The very first thing I was told this morning was to expect you in today." Rick vaguely remembered meeting the woman. "I'm sorry about all the confusion. Didn't they tell you? July first," she said, waving the back of her hand at the room as if the date explained the lounging construction crew. "It's the new fiscal year. Today's the day they start to take us apart."

"Thanks," he replied. "I knew that. Lois Carneccio called me this weekend. She told me to plan on attending her first meeting this morning."

He turned to glare pointedly at one of the workmen who was listening with great interest and no attempt at discretion. Unaffected, the man gazed right back. So much, Rick conceded to himself, for the confidence and the heavy hand.

The receptionist nodded. "Except right now, she and Mr. Dice are tied up with some men who aren't on the calendar. I don't know who they are. And your client is waiting."

"My client?"

"She's a rather sweet older woman. I like her. I asked her to wait in the small conference room—that's the second door over there. She didn't want to give me her name, but she told me that the two of you were friends and that you always handled her accounts personally."

Rick Yeager glanced at his watch: 8:40 A.M. From that description, he thought, the client could be anyone.

"Even for private finance," Lois Carneccio commented over a Cobb salad in the wood-paneled Taft Dining Room at Washington's celebrated University Club, "you've had one hell of an eclectic career."

"I don't deny that it's been kind of a wild ride."

"And not at all linear."

"When you called, you told me that wasn't a problem. You said that my background is attractive to you . . . ?"

"Absolutely. Who you are makes you all the more valuable to this firm, especially the way we've built it. Rick, in my firm we embody the entrepreneurial spirit. Carneccio & Dice seeks out exactly the qualities that you possess. Our clients will relate to your career more than you can imagine. You've got to trust me on this."

Rick Yeager began that career in the finance departments of two information technology firms, federal systems contractors. He subsequently worked with varying degrees of success and occasional failure in a commercial bank financing federal government contracts; in a small-fund to the resources of a larger firm now. I am going to need a great deal of assistance with something which will become immensely complicated. And I will need to trust you much more than was necessary in our professional relationship up until now."

Rick nodded. It was not uncommon for older clients to believe that their estates were unbearably complex. This was not the first time that Hannah Geller had shown a tendency for overstatement.

"I'll help," he said. "But we'll need to find a time to meet in a few days, after I'm settled in here." He began to think of a way to extricate himself gently from this conversation, aware that he was due to meet with his new senior partners just about now.

As he stood, the commotion in the hall began with two loud crashes. Doors slammed hard against non-load-bearing walls. The thud of heavy running surrounded the conference room. Muffled shouts quickly followed, then the sound of women shrieking in genuine panic. Rick made his way quickly to the door, which was slightly ajar. As he reached for the handle, it came bursting toward him with a swift kick. He found himself face-to-face with four members of the construction crew, all with pistols drawn and held with both hands in combat shooting stance. Two of the crew trained their weapons directly at him. All four of them shouted in clear voices.

"Move! Move! Turn around! Hands behind your head, fingers interlaced! Do it! Move!" He had no time for rational thought as he was grabbed, pushed, manhandled, and spun about to face a thoroughly shocked Mrs. Geller. One of the construction men pushed Rick forward roughly, bending him at the waist over the conference table. Another punched him with a closed fist to the middle of his back, low between the shoulder blades, while kicking his feet apart and jamming his stomach into the table's edge. He was still attempting unsuccessfully to interlace his fingers behind his head as the men grabbed both of his wrists and twisted. The four of them all seemed to swarm on top of him at the same time. He was immobile, his face pressed hard into the top of the conference table.

"Tell me your name!" one of the men ordered.

"Richard Yeager."

private equity firm backing information technology plays; in distressed debt lending; and then made a foray into commercial real estate development before the day he started his own company. Terrific timing. Just before the financial crisis. RMY Personal Financial Inc. was headquartered in Arlington, Virginia, across the Potomac River.

"I'll have to close my firm."

"Rick, to be blunt, you ought to. At—what is it? RMY?—what you've got is comfort, pitifully low risk, and small reward. You may make what you *think* is a nice living, but frankly you're just chugging along. You'll never get any respect from the financial big leagues. You won't even come close. We can fold your company and your clients into ours. I'll make it painless. Joining us is the one best way you can overcome your background. Use your advantages and your strengths. With us it doesn't matter where you worked or where you went to business school. All I care about is how goddamn much you deliver, and I wouldn't have invited you here today if I wasn't convinced that you can."

As Rick Yeager now dipped his toes into the waters of middle age, it was getting harder than ever to overcome majoring in fraternity at Washington and Lee and then copping a "distance learning" Internet MBA from a school that he had never visited—one that advertised prominently in Google's sponsored links as "accredited in California."

"The Wall Street boys"—Lois Carneccio practically spit out the words as she continued—"care only about your damn pedigree even when they say they don't. *Especially* when they say they don't. People like us, Rick, we're the mutts of finance. And we scare the shit out of the big dogs. I know I've come to terms with it. For me it's about the money."

Rick Yeager always hoped and assumed that someday he would catch this one good break. The only part that surprised him was that it came from Lois Carneccio, whom he barely knew.

"And I got your attention," he said.

"You did. Rick, you can do something I can't. You have a way of making people connect with you and trust you. It's a remarkable skill. Be glad that you work in investments and you're not a con man. Although there are days when I swear I don't know what the difference is between those two. I know what you can do. Now I intend to put you in touch with people who are a hell of a lot more wealthy." Lois Carneccio put down her salad fork and tossed back the remaining half of a Grey Goose martini, her second of this lunch. Her reputation for aggressive risk-taking was widely known. She had a knack for bringing in the hot players, no matter where they came from. Provided, of course, they could deliver. Rick Yeager was sure that he could, now that he was moving up to the kind of firm where he belonged all along.

Stepping over some tarpaulins, careful not to bump the fine art prints piled haphazardly near the reception desk, he made his way to the small conference room, site of his first two interviews at Carneccio & Dice. There, demure and dwarfed by the large round conference table, sat a small woman of somewhat more than eighty very well preserved years. Impeccably groomed and perhaps overdressed for a sweltering Washington July, she was visibly uneasy. Her snow-white hair was pulled back into a small bun. She watched through gold-rimmed glasses as Rick Yeager entered and recognized her.

"Mrs. Geller," he said. The old woman brightened visibly and nodded at the mention of her name. Rick was excellent at remembering names and faces. You had to be if you were in the personal asset management business. Hannah Weiss Geller. Net worth exclusive of her house in north Arlington—owned clear—possibly $155,000, most of which had been invested by Rick in the past three years. Pocket change, considering where he was headed now. Yet he was incapable of any discourtesy to a paying client, no matter how small the opportunity. One never knew. "How are you, my dear?"

"I'm fine and I'm impressed," she answered truthfully. "This is an extremely nice office you have now." RMY Personal Financial had storefront offices in a forty-year-old strip mall in Arlington. Mrs. Geller had been a walk-in.

"Well, it's hardly mine. Here I'm just one of the hired help." Yeager tried out a bit of self-deprecating humor, which was a new style he had been considering. "How did you know where to find me?" he asked as he took a seat next to Hannah Geller at the conference t[...] even started work here yet, officially."

"Your new company wrote to me," she explaine[...] purse to produce a letter, which she unfolded and ha[...]

"And here you are on my first day."

"Should I have made an appointment?" The old [...] denly chagrined.

Rick saw that her chagrin was feigned. He smile[...] about it. You know that I'm always delighted to see [...] ward, conspiratorially, squinting slightly. "And wher[...] bring in clients? So what can I do for you? Can I h[...] thing?"

"Richard," she said, "it's time. We haven't talked [...] I have resisted the matter for quite a long while. But [...] ent to me that I should place some priority on plan[...] have a will, but there is a very serious financial matt[...] tend to. For several reasons no one but you is appro[...] Hannah Geller still spoke with the thinnest hint of [...] cent, from where exactly Rick Yeager had never asce[...]

"I'm flattered," Yeager said. "Is your health——"

"No, nothing particular," she said, anticipating h[...] age that is finally getting my attention. I'm slowin[...] I want to. It's harder for me to see, and it's harder [...] know."

"I'm sorry to hear that," Yeager said, and he go[...] would be very routine, he thought. What could b[...] sion to liquid instruments, a pitifully small commi[...] billable time. Not the strongest start out of the blo[...] Dice.

"I don't even drive anymore, Richard. Now I take [...] that in the next year I'll sell the house and the car an[...] to stay here in the area of course, but I do need to go[...] nancial holdings in order." She hesitated, pointing t[...] C&D letterhead. "This is good. I was pleased to see t[...]

private equity firm backing information technology plays; in distressed debt lending; and then made a foray into commercial real estate development before the day he started his own company. Terrific timing. Just before the financial crisis. RMY Personal Financial Inc. was headquartered in Arlington, Virginia, across the Potomac River.

"I'll have to close my firm."

"Rick, to be blunt, you ought to. At—what is it? RMY?—what you've got is comfort, pitifully low risk, and small reward. You may make what you *think* is a nice living, but frankly you're just chugging along. You'll never get any respect from the financial big leagues. You won't even come close. We can fold your company and your clients into ours. I'll make it painless. Joining us is the one best way you can overcome your background. Use your advantages and your strengths. With us it doesn't matter where you worked or where you went to business school. All I care about is how goddamn much you deliver, and I wouldn't have invited you here today if I wasn't convinced that you can."

As Rick Yeager now dipped his toes into the waters of middle age, it was getting harder than ever to overcome majoring in fraternity at Washington and Lee and then copping a "distance learning" Internet MBA from a school that he had never visited—one that advertised prominently in Google's sponsored links as "accredited in California."

"The Wall Street boys"—Lois Carneccio practically spit out the words as she continued—"care only about your damn pedigree even when they say they don't. *Especially* when they say they don't. People like us, Rick, we're the mutts of finance. And we scare the shit out of the big dogs. I know I've come to terms with it. For me it's about the money."

Rick Yeager always hoped and assumed that someday he would catch this one good break. The only part that surprised him was that it came from Lois Carneccio, whom he barely knew.

"And I got your attention," he said.

"You did. Rick, you can do something I can't. You have a way of making people connect with you and trust you. It's a remarkable skill. Be glad that you work in investments and you're not a con man. Although there are days when I swear I don't know what the difference is between those two. I know what you can do. Now I intend to put you in touch with people who are a hell of a lot more wealthy." Lois Carneccio put down her salad fork and tossed back the remaining half of a Grey Goose martini, her second of this lunch. Her reputation for aggressive risk-taking was widely known. She had a knack for bringing in the hot players, no matter where they came from. Provided, of course, they could deliver. Rick Yeager was sure that he could, now that he was moving up to the kind of firm where he belonged all along.

Stepping over some tarpaulins, careful not to bump the fine art prints piled haphazardly near the reception desk, he made his way to the small conference room, site of his first two interviews at Carneccio & Dice. There, demure and dwarfed by the large round conference table, sat a small woman of somewhat more than eighty very well preserved years. Impeccably groomed and perhaps overdressed for a sweltering Washington July, she was visibly uneasy. Her snow-white hair was pulled back into a small bun. She watched through gold-rimmed glasses as Rick Yeager entered and recognized her.

"Mrs. Geller," he said. The old woman brightened visibly and nodded at the mention of her name. Rick was excellent at remembering names and faces. You had to be if you were in the personal asset management business. Hannah Weiss Geller. Net worth exclusive of her house in north Arlington—owned clear—possibly $155,000, most of which had been invested by Rick in the past three years. Pocket change, considering where he was headed now. Yet he was incapable of any discourtesy to a paying client, no matter how small the opportunity. One never knew. "How are you, my dear?"

"I'm fine and I'm impressed," she answered truthfully. "This is an extremely nice office you have now." RMY Personal Financial had storefront offices in a forty-year-old strip mall in Arlington. Mrs. Geller had been a walk-in.

"Well, it's hardly mine. Here I'm just one of the hired help." Yeager tried out a bit of self-deprecating humor, which was a new style he had been considering. "How did you know where to find me?" he asked as he took a seat next to Hannah Geller at the conference table. "I haven't even started work here yet, officially."

"Your new company wrote to me," she explained, reaching into her purse to produce a letter, which she unfolded and handed to Yeager.

"And here you are on my first day."

"Should I have made an appointment?" The old woman acted suddenly chagrined.

Rick saw that her chagrin was feigned. He smiled. "No, don't think about it. You know that I'm always delighted to see you." He leaned forward, conspiratorially, squinting slightly. "And when is it ever wrong to bring in clients? So what can I do for you? Can I help you with something?"

"Richard," she said, "it's time. We haven't talked about this, because I have resisted the matter for quite a long while. But now it's very apparent to me that I should place some priority on planning my estate. I do have a will, but there is a very serious financial matter that I have to attend to. For several reasons no one but you is appropriate to that task." Hannah Geller still spoke with the thinnest hint of some European accent, from where exactly Rick Yeager had never ascertained.

"I'm flattered," Yeager said. "Is your health—"

"No, nothing particular," she said, anticipating his question. "It's my age that is finally getting my attention. I'm slowing down more than I want to. It's harder for me to see, and it's harder to get around, you know."

"I'm sorry to hear that," Yeager said, and he genuinely was. This would be very routine, he thought. What could be simpler? Conversion to liquid instruments, a pitifully small commission, maybe some billable time. Not the strongest start out of the blocks at Carneccio & Dice.

"I don't even drive anymore, Richard. Now I take the bus. I anticipate that in the next year I'll sell the house and the car and relocate. I'll want to stay here in the area of course, but I do need to get some personal financial holdings in order." She hesitated, pointing to the letter with the C&D letterhead. "This is good. I was pleased to see that you have access to the resources of a larger firm now. I am going to need a great deal of assistance with something which will become immensely complicated. And I will need to trust you much more than was necessary in our professional relationship up until now."

Rick nodded. It was not uncommon for older clients to believe that their estates were unbearably complex. This was not the first time that Hannah Geller had shown a tendency for overstatement.

"I'll help," he said. "But we'll need to find a time to meet in a few days, after I'm settled in here." He began to think of a way to extricate himself gently from this conversation, aware that he was due to meet with his new senior partners just about now.

As he stood, the commotion in the hall began with two loud crashes. Doors slammed hard against non-load-bearing walls. The thud of heavy running surrounded the conference room. Muffled shouts quickly followed, then the sound of women shrieking in genuine panic. Rick made his way quickly to the door, which was slightly ajar. As he reached for the handle, it came bursting toward him with a swift kick. He found himself face-to-face with four members of the construction crew, all with pistols drawn and held with both hands in combat shooting stance. Two of the crew trained their weapons directly at him. All four of them shouted in clear voices.

"Move! Move! Turn around! Hands behind your head, fingers interlaced! Do it! Move!" He had no time for rational thought as he was grabbed, pushed, manhandled, and spun about to face a thoroughly shocked Mrs. Geller. One of the construction men pushed Rick forward roughly, bending him at the waist over the conference table. Another punched him with a closed fist to the middle of his back, low between the shoulder blades, while kicking his feet apart and jamming his stomach into the table's edge. He was still attempting unsuccessfully to interlace his fingers behind his head as the men grabbed both of his wrists and twisted. The four of them all seemed to swarm on top of him at the same time. He was immobile, his face pressed hard into the top of the conference table.

"Tell me your name!" one of the men ordered.

"Richard Yeager."

"Do you work here, Richard Yeager?"

"Yes, but—"

"That's all I need. Mr. Yeager, we are special agents of the Federal Bureau of Investigation." The man held up to Rick's face a small rectangular leather badge holder strung from a dog tag chain around his neck. "Pursuant to warrants issued yesterday in the United States District Court for the District of Columbia, you are under arrest."

CHAPTER 2

Yasuo Tondabayashi, managing director of Roppongi Securities (USA) Limited, shifted uncomfortably in his chair, hoping that the man seated across the big glass desk from him would not be able to detect his discomfort. What he was about to do would require some degree of delicacy and diplomacy, but he felt well prepared. He wished that he could have held this meeting on his home turf. Protocol dictated, however, that he should come to the visitor's ballpark. Tondabayashi favored baseball metaphors. The game was his one true passion. He had even played a half season as a catcher in the Japanese minor leagues during a severe flight of personal irresponsibility thirty-one years ago.

Tondabayashi searched the face of his counterpart at Compton Sizemore and Company. After Wall Street's serial implosions and the fall of the House of Lehman, Compton Sizemore had become by default the final remaining true partnership among Wall Street's reigning investment banks. But compared to Roppongi, Tondabayashi considered this to be an infant of a firm, born in the dealmaking boom of the late 1990s.

The man in whose office he was seated, Warren Hunter, reclined in an immense chair, feet crossed at the ankles on the glass desk, talking into a Bluetooth telephone headset that he wore on his right ear. The office decor was stunning, as was the view—a fifty-sixth-floor corner suite looking south on lower Manhattan and east to Brooklyn and Long Island.

Warren Hunter was a warm, outwardly ruddy man with finely drawn dark features, fierce in his style and dress, favoring Bengal stripes and SoHo art-print ties like the one he wore today. He had waved Tondabayashi into his office, continuing to chat as if the man from the Japanese bank was not even present. In the six minutes since Tondabayashi was seated, his conversation had been about tennis, the implied senility of an unnamed senior at a rival investment bank, and a woman whose particularly spectacular oral sex skills both Hunter and the other party to the conversation had apparently independently experienced.

Tondabayashi writhed inwardly, but he was certain that on the surface his expression was one of utter calm. The American investment banker's tactic of manners, this making him wait, was a deliberate act of incivility. However unfortunate, it was typical of the way so many Americans postured.

"Yaz," Warren Hunter greeted him as he punched a button on the phone and threw the headset to the desk, "thanks sincerely for coming by." He rose and smiled in a very winning way, just like a slick American politician, even bowing his head ever so slightly. Tondabayashi also stood and extended his hand across the desk, certain that Hunter had only risen to accentuate the height advantage he enjoyed over the Japanese banker.

Despite his genuine distaste for the man, Yasuo Tondabayashi knew that he needed to be most careful here. Few international bankers in New York commanded as much respect as his counterpart here, which was all the more amazing when one considered his age. He was not yet forty. How had this man managed such a glorious rise? Tondabayashi consoled himself with the thought that Warren Hunter, partner for less than a year and heir-apparent to the chief of investment and merchant banking at Compton Sizemore, would only enjoy American-style respect, the kind that comes with rapid wealth and achievement. He would never in his life generate the Japanese version of deep and genuine respect, an innate regard bred of the highest personal character and lifelong accomplishment.

Warren launched right into business. There was no use wasting time.

"First off, I have to report to you what I just got done telling our Canadian national partner. ViroSat is perfectly on track and on time. You and your boys in Tokyo were wise to issue the letter of intent and join up when you did. We should be closing later this month, first of August at the latest."

Tondabayashi waited before responding. "You are correct, Warren, about the purpose of my visit. There are a number of important matters concerning ViroSat that we should discuss." Even after a turbulent decade on Wall Street, Tondabayashi still had trouble with the use of first names and the fiercely frontal approach favored by the American bankers. "I have been in lengthy conversation with my home office, and I am here to report that there are now a number of substantial obstacles with the project. They will, in my judgment, face the most extreme difficulties to be resolved."

Warren nodded. He knew this code. The Japanese participation in the deal was in serious trouble. They were pulling out.

Sometimes putting together an international deal was like herding rabbits into a pen. Each time you caught one and put it in, another one of them already inside hops out. That was exactly what Tondabayashi and his bank were attempting to do.

"I'm not sure you understand what's at stake in this deal."

"A Compton Sizemore deal."

"Also a Roppongi deal. ViroSat has taken us all almost three years to develop, and I don't have to tell you what it took to survive this economic mess. Last time I counted we have thirty-seven countries involved, with major financial institutions like yours in each one of them. You know as well as I do that this is really too big to be considered one deal. By the time we're done, ViroSat will be the most significant technological venture ever created from scratch. And it's exactly what this economy needs right now."

"The concept," Tondabayashi offered, "does not give rise to these difficulties. What does is our view of the execution, the systemic risk, and the long-term capital needs."

ViroSat's execution would be awesome: a worldwide system of satellites and remote receiving stations, all digital and optical, all integrated. It would dwarf both the Internet and the existing international telecommunications system in scope and size. It would be the first communications infrastructure able to move information faster than the human perceptual limen. Communication would be instantaneous as far as the brain could tell. And all of it would be privately owned. Like the operating system of a computer network, ViroSat promised to be the foundation on which everything else in the future history of telecommunications and computers would have to be built. The obvious benefits to the global economic recovery would be profound.

Warren Hunter was unmoved by Roppongi's difficulties.

"What is unique about the project, and I've said this from the start, is its legal design and the basic economics. They're fucking awesome. There is never going to be any one nation with controlling authority over this project, or any international body able to tell us what to do. But every government, at least in any country that actually matters, gets a customer stake in the venture." Warren, having punched his tickets at Princeton and JPMorgan Chase, now nine years out of the Harvard Business School, had put all of this together. If you took the time to add up all of the pieces, ViroSat would be Wall Street's first trillion-dollar private deal.

And now here was the principal Japanese venture partner telling him that his bank had cold feet.

"So. The extent of these difficulties . . ." Warren mused. "Do you envision a possible resolution?" He could play the Japanese game.

"To be frank, I do not."

"Well, I do."

"I am not sure that I understand." Tondabayashi was genuinely puzzled.

"Yasuo, do you think it was by accident that Compton Sizemore selected your bank as our Japanese investor partner? Do you actually think that your own presentation swayed our decision? With no disrespect intended, there are a number of factors that went into our choice. You are not completely aware of them. The last thing I need is your capital position in ViroSat. Really. I have more goddamn leverage available than I know what to do with in this deal, and even if I did require a Japanese player, don't you think that I could replace your participation tomorrow with any of a number of Tokyo banks? Come on. In this unbelievably weak economy all of your banks have to invest here. What I needed, and frankly still do need, is Roppongi on my tombstone."

Tondabayashi found the morbid humor of Americans to be curious.

They called the printed notice of an investment banking transaction a tombstone, the marker of death. He held his ground and spoke firmly. "That would remain exceedingly difficult. It is truly without a possible resolution," he said. But what other factors was Hunter talking about?

"There are political considerations," Warren was saying, as though he had read Tondabayashi's mind—a thoroughly unsettling thought for the Japanese banker. "Given your corporate structure and the composition of your board of directors, ViroSat requires Roppongi's participation. That's as simple as it gets."

"For that very same reason, our participation will not be possible."

The board of directors at Roppongi had five former cabinet ministers from the current ruling party in the Japanese Diet. One of them was the only recent prime minister not to have resigned under a cloud of suspicion. Two of them were former finance ministers. Roppongi Securities, though certainly not the largest or the most prestigious Japanese investment bank, was at this moment without question the most politically influential. That influence was profound. The five former government officers had been *sempai*, mentors, to more than half of the leaders in elected or civil office in Japan. With Roppongi on the team, the legendary Japanese regulatory hurdles would not even rise to the level of speed bumps. And they both knew it.

Warren Hunter stood and walked to his south-facing window, his back to Yasuo Tondabayashi. He pulled his jacket back, hands on his hips, and studied the Manhattan skyline with a theatrical delivery not lost on Tondabayashi. Today it was clear enough that you could see the Jersey shore. When he spoke, it was to the window.

"Please make certain," he said slowly, "that you understand the complete extent of the consequences if Roppongi withdraws at this time."

"I cannot imagine that there would be any real financial consequences," Tondabayashi replied, but his voice betrayed that he was nervous now. "You as much as said so yourself. You have the capital."

"I am not talking about financial consequences." Warren turned around, and Tondabayashi sensed a vast ugliness creeping into his voice beneath the gentlemanly courtesy. "Listen carefully, because what I am about to say is not a negotiation point. It is a statement of fact that you would do well to communicate immediately to Tokyo. Long before the day of your initial involvement in ViroSat, our equity arbitrage unit here at Compton Sizemore began carefully assembling a portfolio of Nikkei equity futures contracts and stock options. This was done at very little actual cost to us, you understand. That portfolio exactly mirrors the positions in your own directors' personal stock portfolios, as well as certain blind trusts that you manage on behalf of ninety-one officeholders in the current government of Japan. Do not be concerned with how our knowledge of these portfolios was developed." Hunter leaned forward. "These individuals include your prime minister and every serving cabinet minister. When the markets open in Tokyo tomorrow, we will sell either puts or calls on those options with an intent to increase exponentially the gross market capitalization value of the undergirding stocks. This action will of course make all those men immensely wealthy instantaneously. The margins will be extreme.

"The arbitrage movements will take place through a large number of international venues, quite geographically diffuse. They will all be impeccably legal and just as untraceable. But the effect will be shocking to the markets and incredibly evident. The net result, Tondabayashi-san, will be one of optics. How will things look?"

Warren smiled benignly at the Japanese banker.

"You will never be able to identify where the leak originated to either the opposition parties or to the *Nihon Keizai Shinbun* and the *Asian Wall Street Journal*. The use of public office for such an immense private gain is so greedy, so unseemly, so . . . *American*. There will no doubt be calls for the immediate resignation of your directors after trading in certain issues on the Nikkei Exchange is suspended after a few hours. This will happen tomorrow.

"But those are the insignificant consequences. Really. You may be aware of some of our groundbreaking work here with artificial securities and the linkage of foreign exchange rates to equity positions. Shall I connect the dots for you? These same securities also just happen to undergird all of Compton Sizemore's distributed yen positions in the Tokyo, Seoul, Shanghai, and Hong Kong money markets. Those positions are enormous, Yasuo. We hold more than your own central bank. With the profit-taking that naturally will follow such a huge rise in the equity share values, I would expect nothing less than the bottom falling out of yen prices throughout Asia as well as here in New York.

"And all of *that* will happen," he concluded, "later this week. By this weekend, it's doubtful to me whether Roppongi Securities as constituted now will continue to exist. The government will almost certainly fall in a vote of no confidence. Neither the yen nor your ruling party are doing that well right now, are they?"

Tondabayashi's mouth was dry. Warren reached for a folder on the credenza beneath his window.

"In order for you to know that this is no bluff, please take this list of securities and money market positions—yours and ours—back to your office." He opened it and glanced down at the folder as he handed it to Tondabayashi. "Not too imaginative, is it? But I think you'll find the information quite comprehensive."

"I am not certain," the Japanese banker answered, "how to respond."

"No problem," Warren said pleasantly. "I'll tell you how to respond. Here's what's going to happen." He reached for another folder and opened it. Tondabayashi could see that this document was written in Japanese. "This is a binding letter of commitment with conformal copies produced in English and in Japanese. Sorry about this, buddy, but your play here this morning just cost you big time. Before the markets open tomorrow Tokyo time, this is going to be executed and on my desk. You do not get to make any changes. That'll be by eight P.M. New York time. I'll be sitting here waiting for you.

"Oh, and one more thing. That letter of commitment provides that you will also arrange for the full capital contribution of Roppongi Securities for ViroSat to be deposited by electronic funds transfer by the same time. Today. All seventy-one four. No notes, no escrow accounts, no stalling. Cash."

Was the American crazy? Seventy-one billion dollars? Tondabayashi could no longer find the words in English to speak.

"Put your analysts on it." Warren Hunter walked around the glass desk. "And Yaz, settle down. I'll see you tonight. We'll go out to dinner and celebrate. This is not something you can concern yourself about. It's just something you have to do. As I said, there is a cost. One way or the other."

Warren Hunter took Yasuo Tondabayashi by the arm gently and looked into his face as the Japanese banker silently calculated a month's interest on $71.4 billion, which would now be Compton Sizemore's to use until the ViroSat deal closed. The American leaned in to his ear and said softly, "*Bijinesu izu waru*, Tondabayashi-san." Business is war. "*Yaru ka yarareru ka.*" Kill or be killed.

As Tondabayashi retreated without a word, Warren leaned against his desk and exhaled. All that preparation and in the end, that one had been way too easy, he thought. Tondabayashi came in just as his ViroSat team had expected, and almost on the exact date they figured. The Japanese, Roppongi Securities in particular, were predictable. Now they were caught.

This deal, more than any other, was about control. Roppongi's position amounted only to a minor annoyance. All of the rabbits in ViroSat had to be kept in the pen. Nothing had better interfere.

"Warren?" He looked up to see his executive assistant Jenny Lau approaching him with some urgency.

"Problem?"

"Yes. I'd certainly call it that."

"What?"

"You should know by now that you only get in trouble when you keep secrets from me. You never told me you had a brother."

"And what has my brother got to do with—"

"He's on your direct line," she said dryly. "It seems he's been arrested."

North of Georgetown, the Potomac River splits the nation's capital from the woods of northern Virginia. On the west bank of the river is a thin ribbon of road ledged into a nice high ridge. There the George Washington Memorial Parkway follows the water's natural path. The few homes in the woods are some of America's most exclusive real estate. There is very little pedestrian traffic.

At midday a solitary wiry old man trekked through these woods, pausing in the shade of maples, cedars, and poplars. He considered himself to be in superb physical condition for his age. At the moment he was drenched with sweat. He paused during his rest both to wipe his brow with his wide-brimmed hat and to draw a long drink of warm water from the Nalgene bottle slung at his side. He sat, then took his bearings. No one from the big houses could possibly notice him here unless they were looking. Even then, finding him in the privacy of this brush would be most difficult. He knew that he had not been followed. It may have been some time since he had actively employed these skills, but they were fundamental tools of personal survival that one never forgot. They were also skills that for so many years had kept him alive.

From his new vantage the man watched and waited, scrutinizing every car passing below him on the parkway. He had a remarkably clear view and was quite satisfied with his chosen spot. He checked his watch, careful not to miss a single vehicle, although traffic was very sparse. This was exactly what he had been counting on.

Seven minutes. Not late enough to give him major cause for concern, but certainly enough to make him more sensitive to the situation. When he had learned this trade decades ago, one of his instructors in the field had told him that a *little* bit of nerves was good for him. It would keep him sharp. Feeling his adrenaline level rise gave the old man a rush of many dormant emotions that he had tucked away. He surprised himself with the joy he experienced upon their return. His breathing quickened.

There. Unmistakable. It was a big old land yacht, a 1996 Chevrolet Caprice Classic, long and fat, a faded hunter green. The car approached him, northbound on the river side of the road at a very high rate of speed. It rounded a gentle curve in the road to turn toward him, accelerating uphill as it approached a scenic overlook opposite his position in the woods. As the old man watched, eyes fixed as though recording each frame in his memory, the Chevy slowed almost imperceptibly. It swung wide past the scenic overlook, and with a balletic grace crashed through the low barricade separating the road from the Potomac River below.

It was all he could do to keep from wincing. He strained to hear the series of continuing crashes and the crackling of trees snapping as the car plunged deeper down the embankment before stopping. No one traveling on the parkway slowed or stopped. As far as he could tell, no one even saw the accident. He stood, stretched, and began to retrace his path through the woods.

CHAPTER 3

Independence Day. In a wallow of depression, Rick Yeager contemplated what would be more applicable now, rude irony or bitter cynicism, as he surveyed the detritus of his life and business. He sat in a wobbly molded chair missing the end tip of one leg, head in his hands, elbows propped on a chipped pressboard folding table, alone in the empty corporate head-quarters of RMY Personal Financial Inc. A few naked phone and Internet cables snaked from the walls well-banged by the movers. The filthy indus-trial carpet was thick with office litter, bent paper clips, and dust dogs. It still bore deep indentation marks from the filing cabinets. The carpet was a shade of mustard that Rick really hated, but he had always concluded that it was adequate whenever he considered the cost of a replacement.

All of it was gone now. His move to Carneccio & Dice had required him to close the business and sell the client base to his new partnership in a transaction handled by C&D itself. After tax, his take came to around $270,000 and change, every buck of which (plus a five thousand dollar personal check) he immediately used to purchase his $275,000 partner-ship share of Carneccio & Dice. One settlement, neat and precise. At the time it seemed to Rick like a very prudent investment. Of course that was the theme song of every financial loser who ever gambled big and went home broke. At his age, he was getting pretty tired of starting over. But what other possible option was there? Rick made a quick calcula-tion, chin in his palms, fingertips rubbing his temples. A year and a half after an expensive divorce and now there were more lawyers to pay. Negative net worth about sixty grand, he figured. Upside down, any way you want to cut it.

It took almost three full days, including two miserable nights spent at the District of Columbia Department of Corrections, before the investigators from the FBI, Treasury, the Department of Justice, and the United States Attorney's office released him. Among the eighteen suspected financial felons brought in during the sweep of Carneccio & Dice, he was the only one not charged and booked. Even the secretaries were covered by name under the RICO indictments. For the C&D partners and professional staff, the charges were piled on: conspiracy, money laundering, fraud, securities violations, racketeering. The interrogations were relentless. Rick Yeager was twice reduced to tears for the first time since childhood. Gradually the FBI agents' unhinged aggression gave way to incredulity. What was worse, they settled on pity and contempt as his involvement—actually, the total lack thereof—became clear to them. He could read it on their smirking faces. *This loser wanted to throw in with them. He deserves everything he got.*

The phone call to his brother could not ease the pain, but it did result in his meeting two new lawyers within forty minutes of hanging up. In hindsight, Rick thought, their arrival and ruthlessly brutal defense probably delayed his release rather than hastened it. That was certainly in keeping with Warren's style. The suits he sent behaved like legal flamethrowers, frightened no doubt of failing the great Warren Hunter. They were probably more desperate not to lose the vast Compton Sizemore legal business that was in his brother's direct power to control.

Rick stifled a sob. He was fully aware of the depth of self-pity he was approaching, but entirely unable to muster any meaningful way to halt his psychological descent.

In the parking lot of the strip mall, barely visible around the partially papered glass front window of the office, a small crowd was gathering for the morning's community Fourth of July parade.

It had been weeks since Rick had talked to his kid brother. Their reunion was not what he had planned. He wanted to arrive in New York with a Carneccio & Dice deal in hand, magnanimously presenting the opportunity to Compton Sizemore. It would have been a complete surprise, and for once Rick could have met Warren on the level. It's never the level of achievement that makes you fall so hard, Rick knew. It's the level of expectation. Expectations die harder than dreams.

"But at least all that's taken care of," he said out loud to the empty room. "Now I don't have either."

"You really ought to hear it from me." Warren Hunter spoke loudly over the measured manic pulse of the techno-funk music. He leaned in to Rick Yeager's ear. "It would probably be easier for all of us if he was just dying. But he's not. His body is fine. Better than fine, actually. Physically, he's healthier than a goddamn horse. That makes all of this a lot worse. The trouble is, now we know for sure that his mind is going. And it's accelerating."

The two of them sat behind drinks in a plush maroon horseshoe at Augustino's, one of the few remaining mid-Manhattan "gentlemen's clubs" to have survived both the Times Square renewal and the recession. Two very nude dancers, girls of slightly less than modest beauty but spectacular architecture, swirled nearby in full anatomical accuracy. Warren had selected their meeting place.

"So there's no way he'll be able to stay at his apartment anymore," Rick responded.

"Not a chance. I don't want to do it, but we have to move him this week. You should be there. His doctors are calling this the early part of the intermediate stage. There are times when you can talk to him and he's completely lucid, totally normal. Nothing's wrong. Other times he just drifts off, or worse, he shuts down. It's scary. The other day I think he forgot who I was. He started talking about how Mom was getting ready to go on some last big march on Washington—how he was worried she had to be careful now that she was having another baby."

"The year before you were born," Rick said.

"Yeah." Warren was atypically quiet.

"Does he have any problem recognizing people yet?"

"Not so far. But his doctors told me that we ought to be prepared for that. Soon. Eventually."

"Warren, how long . . . ?"

"You can't tell with Alzheimer's."

"Okay. It's your call, of course." Rick sighed. "You were always closer to Dad."

"Yeah," Warren agreed. "But Mom always liked you best." He smiled and grabbed his glass of scotch from the table, gulping half of it, thoroughly intent on the dancers.

"Mr. Yeager?" The woman's voice was sweet and solicitous, and woke him with ease. She had entered the empty office without Rick noticing. "I'm sorry. Is this a bad time?"

Of course it's a bad time, Rick almost said. The drums from the high school band—the drum and bugle corps style, not the military kind— were playing a syncopated cadence in the parking lot outside, hammering up for the Fourth of July parade. His head hurt mightily in time with the beat, and he was fairly certain that his personal grooming could use some work. "No, not at all," he lied.

She approached the folding table as Rick stood. "I'm Lauren Barr," she said, extending her hand. "And I've been trying to reach you by phone for two days. This morning I thought I'd come here to leave you a note, but now I'm glad we're finally able to connect."

Rick became aware of how she was sizing him up as he shook her hand. Analytical, but calm. She conveyed a fine gentleness and resolve as he stared. Her honey-auburn hair was pulled loosely back into a braid, and she wore oval, dark, wire-rim glasses—a little out of fashion—setting off lustrous deep green eyes. Lauren Barr was dressed for business on this hot holiday in a gray linen suit and white blouse. She had a radiant charm about her. She was slightly moist from the humidity. For the moment he was uncertain what to say.

"And you were calling me because—?"

"It's about my aunt. Well not actually my aunt. She was some sort of cousin to my mother, but we all called her Tante Anna when we were growing up." Lauren Barr was a fast talker. She pronounced the woman's name with a soft A."

"Again, Ms. Barr, you were calling me because—?"

"Please, it's Lauren. And I'm getting to that."

"Okay, Lauren." Rick was finding her mildly annoying but in an engaging way. Like he wanted to be annoyed right now.

"My mother is in California," Lauren continued, speaking rapidly. "She called me three days ago when my aunt died and asked me to handle all of the arrangements, mostly because I'm here and she's not. Otherwise, and believe me, because I know my mother, she'd be doing it all. According to Mom, there may be a few other distant cousins, but we're the closest family that my aunt had. She lived with my mother's family in the forties in New York when Mom and her sisters were girls and Tante Anna had just come to this country and needed a place to stay.

"Anyway—" she caught her breath, "Do you have any idea how difficult it is to find an Orthodox Jewish women's burial society in Virginia? There's one in Maryland on the other side of the District, but tell me, have you ever tried to move an unembalmed body across state lines?" Lauren Barr paused, not expecting an answer. Her voice slowed. "She was buried the day before yesterday. I'm here because, according to Mom, my aunt didn't have a lawyer. She didn't like them or trust them. Hey, who can blame her? And her friends are gone already. Yours was the only name that my aunt ever mentioned to my mother. It was in a letter she wrote about a year ago. Funny, some people still actually write letters."

Lauren sat sideways on the table, which Rick hoped would not collapse. "Forgive me. I'm babbling. Maybe this is a little bit of grief. Tante Anna told my mother that you handled her financial affairs."

"That's entirely possible. You haven't told me her name."

"Oh, I'm terribly sorry. I was sure that I did. Hannah Geller. She was a wonderful lady."

His name was Horvath, and despite the general thickness of his waist—heavy, packed hard, not fat—he prided himself on his size and brute strength. He stood no more than five eleven, but with his broad shoulders and stunningly ugly countenance, the overall effect, which he actively sought, was that he appeared huge.

He threaded his way through the haphazard organization of the parade. He was gentle and even courteous to the people in the crowd, and avoided all contact and conversation. He picked his spot carefully among a clutch of minivan moms waving at their patriotic children as the procession formed. Horvath was unconcerned about being conspicuous. From here, he had an unrestricted view of the place that was important to watch: the closed financial office. He saw the man inside. He looked like shit from the farm. He saw the woman enter. Now they were talking. This was good. He could wait.

"Mrs. Geller?" Rick Yeager's question was unintentionally flat, devoid of emotion. "I saw her on Monday."

"When?" Lauren Barr was suddenly almost accusatory.

"Around nine in the morning."

"She was killed early that afternoon."

"Killed?"

"In a car crash on the GW Parkway," Lauren explained. "She apparently just ran off the road. They didn't even find her until rush hour, when a traffic helicopter spotted the wreck. It was on TV. Didn't you see it? My mother's beside herself. Tante Anna promised her more than once that she'd quit driving, given her age and all."

I don't even drive anymore, Richard, he thought.

"She was driving?"

"Of course she was. And of course she shouldn't have been. But you know how important getting around is for anyone at her age. So I can understand why she would want to. To continue, I mean. She was an unbelievably independent soul. She wouldn't give up mobility."

"No, I suppose she wouldn't," Rick replied. *Now I take the bus*, he thought. "Lauren, you and your family have my sympathy. I really liked your aunt. How can I help? I don't see what I can do. Look around. This office is closed. How did you even find me?"

"Your business card."

"From this office?"

"Do you have another one?" she asked, glancing around. "I'm sorry. I didn't mean for that to sound unkind. Here. Yours was one of two cards that the park police found in my Tante Anna's purse when they got to her car in the woods. They had to rig nylon ropes and wear safety harnesses to get down there." Lauren Barr fumbled in her own purse, a smooth Ann Taylor model of real patent leather. She dealt the cards onto the table for Yeager to see. "And do you by any chance know this other guy? My mother didn't."

Rick stared at the small congressional seal in raised gold on the card, in the simple style favored by the Senate staff. He read out loud. "J. D. Toussaint, Legislative Affairs. Not a guy," he said, looking at Lauren Barr and faintly smiling. "The 'J.D.' is for Julia Diana. And yes, I do know her. Or I did. We were married for six years."

CHAPTER 4

Senators have secret offices. Warrened away in unmarked locations inside the main Capitol building, they are among Washington's best-kept secrets. But unlike policy secrets or national security secrets or especially political secrets, these secrets actually get kept. There are real consequences if they get told. Secret offices give senators the one thing that they value most on the Hill. They get privacy in the middle of the public maelstrom. There are not nearly enough secret offices to go around. Therefore seniority for their assignment and deepest discretion about their existence rigidly prevail. It is the rare legislative staffer who ever gets to visit a senator in her secret office.

On a particularly heavy tourist week Julia Toussaint made her way through the summer crowd. A gaggle of T-shirted and ball-capped kids with their parents strained to see into the museum display of the Capitol's Old Senate Chamber as she clutched tightly onto her leather padfolio and shouldered her way through the crowd. No one paid her any attention. Julia, always keenly attentive to situation and progress, considered that a good thing. When she first arrived in the national capital, African-American women were exceptionally rare on the Senate side of the Hill. They were less rare today but definitely not the norm. Julia at thirty-four still looked so young that most of the staffers took her for an intern. Thin, blessed with what her grandmother in Newark always called "good features," she had the fairest skin tone among her sisters, contributing both to her self-awareness and, perhaps with some measure of guilt, to her evident confidence in white Washington. She was gorgeous and at the moment unsmiling. Her hair was pulled back into a severe ponytail. She would look determined if any of the tourists had bothered to notice.

Casually dressed on this Fourth of July morning, she wore a wide khaki skirt and a light off-white sweater in an air-conditioned Capitol chill that bordered on arctic. A right turn into a wide unmarked passageway, a left past two blank doors on either side of the hall—no more crowd back here—and Julia arrived at the secret office of Senator Tenley Harbison, Democrat of New Jersey. She paused, took a deep breath, and knocked on the thick wooden door.

"Please, come in."

"Good morning, Senator." Julia smiled tentatively, entering. This was only the second time in her four years as senior legislative director for the senator that she had been invited to this office. Most of her time—pretty much all of her waking hours if she took the time to think about it—was spent in the Russell Building, across Constitution Avenue from the Capitol.

"Relax, J.D. Have a seat. I'm pretty sure that we're the only ones here today."

"I'm quite certain of that, Tenley."

When Tenley Harbison first ran for Congress, her political consultants struggled to create a brand identity for her. The unusual first name was a double-edged sword, they said. Her mother, a figure skating fan, had named her for the most famous American skater at the Olympics in 1952, the year she was born. Even now in her second term, not everyone recognized that Tenley was a woman's name, which was fine with her. The confusion frequently worked to her advantage, first as the Bergen County prosecutor, then as the United States Attorney for New Jersey, and finally in the Senate. Now completely gray, she still had the oval face, gentle eyes, and wan smile of a Ford model, which she actually was for a brief time while working her way through law school.

"We should get to it. Run it down for me, please. What were you able to find out?"

"ViroSat," Julia Toussaint began, "seems to have been designed so that it's fundamentally beyond our regulatory reach."

"I know—not that I accept it, but I understand. I think that we have a good enough perspective on the telecom regulation," the senator said. "The Commerce Committee staff produced an excellent paper for us on that point. But I'm less interested in that aspect than I am in its financing. I can't even understand the scope of this project, much less who's paying for it. I learned a long time ago as a young prosecutor that the real story isn't told by who benefits from a deal, but by knowing who provided the money in the first place. Let's start with the federal component. Are there tax issues? Any government contracts involved?"

"Unclear right now, but probably not," Julia responded, referring to her file. "As far as I can tell, Compton Sizemore isn't building this specifically for any kind of tax advantage. Remember, this project began long before the recession. They're proceeding in two directions. The strategy appears to be very basic. First, they're assembling a research and development conglomerate for ViroSat that essentially forms the project infrastructure. They have a large number of companies and joint ventures. They're called 'enterprise units' and are spread worldwide. A good number of them are publicly traded. We don't know exactly where all the rest of them are. Here in America the primary companies are in California, Virginia, Florida, and Texas. They range in size from start-ups that Compton Sizemore owns outright to subsidiaries of our largest defense contractors—but there doesn't seem to be a link to any federal research and development funding. The joint ventures are on the commercial side of Lockheed Martin, Northrop Grumman, and General Dynamics. All of them have formed their enterprise units as new stand-alone companies.

"Elsewhere, it's pretty hard to tell where the companies are, what they do, or whether they are foreign government entities or privately funded. We know that the ViroSat team is busy marketing to federal agencies. They're pushing hard for commercial business—with the government as a customer—once the system is built. We may have an angle there.

"Second, Compton Sizemore is amassing cash, and they are very good at it. I'm amazed at how they've been able to pull this deal together in *this* economic environment. It appears as though they have commitments and actual payments from international investors all over the world. I'll give you an example: almost seventy-five billion was transferred from Japan to a Compton Sizemore house account in New York just two days ago."

"Political motivations?" The senator was following Julia's narrative closely.

"Not that we can determine. I asked over at State, Treasury, the FCC, and the Agency. I called the Internet registry people in Marina del Rey, too—and yes, I was very circumspect. They were all interested, of course. One way to understand ViroSat is that it's a private Internet that goes technologically way beyond anything we can even envision today. The catchphrase—we've all heard it—is 'Internet Next.' But to answer directly, no, it doesn't look like there are any international political incentives involved. This thing is just too big."

"How big?" Tenley Harbison asked.

"I don't know. Treasury says the investment will be more than a trillion dollars. That's probably a guess."

"And we don't know the sources of equity."

"I'm not sure I follow you." Julia consistently admired the ability her boss had to stay one step ahead, especially when they were both trying to figure something out.

"I used to prosecute financial crimes. There are always two parts to the money that backs a deal like this. There's equity from the investors and debt from the lenders. You don't get any of the loans without significant cash in the deal. That's the equity. What is the source of equity?"

"We haven't determined that yet," Julia replied.

"Yet," Senator Tenley Harbison repeated, nodding, thinking out loud. "Well, that's only my first question. The easier excursion is where that debt is going to come from. Who's providing leverage? And then, who does Compton Sizemore propose to sell this to? They're not going to hold onto ViroSat, that's for sure. Where is *that* cash going to come from, once they sell? Who gets the profits? You know that they're going to be huge."

Julia looked up from her notepad, where she had been writing furiously. "A lot more questions than answers," she said. "I believe that I have the scope of the tasking."

"Let's concentrate on the financial side."

"I will," Julia said. She paused. "And I know how careful you need to be here."

"We both need to be careful," the senator replied. "You know that's why you're handling this all alone, J.D."

"I appreciate your confidence." Julia scrawled a few more notes. She paused again, thinking. "Tenley, do you know about—"

"Your brother-in-law. Warren Hunter. Compton Sizemore's guy behind this deal."

"*Ex* brother-in-law." Why had she even considered that Tenley Harbison would not know?

The senator smiled, which Julia read as confidence. She was good at her game. "J.D., you're probably thinking conflict of interest. I've considered that. I'm thinking instead that you have a deep knowledge of the people involved. That factor is going to be critical here. And besides, you're just gathering information for me."

Julia nodded and thought, deliberately slowing down the conversation. Nothing about Tenley Harbison's ViroSat interest seemed normal to her. The subtleties, the holding back, the solo inquiry, even this meeting in her Capitol building office on the Fourth of July. This was all quite unlike her senator's usual style. She was usually much more—what was the word she liked to use with the staff?—*communitarian*. Best to address this obliquely.

"I was surprised when you called and told me that you were still in Washington on the Fourth," she said.

"I had some really pressing family business," the senator replied, "and I'm due at an event in Asbury Park this evening, so I have the usual trudge up I-95 ahead of me this afternoon."

"I'm going to bet that you're the only senator left in town."

"That's a very safe bet." Tenley Harbison laughed lightly, picking up a pen, and Julia thought that the laugh was genuine. Family business? She has two grown sons, Julia thought, and if her husband left Teaneck twice a year she'd be surprised.

"I'll let you know about everything I find."

"Um-hmm." Senator Harbison was busy sketching lines and circles on a tablet, already lost in some new concentration. The *New Yorker* once ran a brief profile of Harbison entitled "Famous Focus," and Julia Toussaint, like all of those closest to the senator, knew the moment it was turned elsewhere. The meeting was over without a formal punctuation. Nothing else she said now would penetrate. She stood and departed wordlessly, shutting the heavy door as she stepped into the cold stone corridor deep within the old Senate wing.

In nine years on Capitol Hill, Julia had learned more than a few verities. First among them was that the senator always controlled the flow of information, giving or receiving. She had just leaned over the edge of that rule, risking not only senatorial wrath but her job and reputation. There is no sinecure for political staff, she reminded herself. Then again, Tenley Harbison had provided her with the perfect opening to say no more. The senator already knew that Warren Hunter had been her brother-in-law. That was enough.

There was no reason to let her know that Warren was also responsible for ending her marriage.

Senator Tenley Harbison stared at the tablet, doodling, retracing lines. Three circles in a vertical row on the left, two directly opposite on the right. A fork above the columns joined in a point at the top. How did this work again?

Lucca, old country she wrote at the apex, *Nonna Cristina/her brother Giulio*. On the right side, next to the first circle, *Mama*. Just below, alongside the second circle, she scrawled the stylized initial-signature *TH* that Julia and her entire senate staff knew extremely well.

On the left, top circle, *Giulio's son—??—died in Italy, never left*. Next circle down, *Zio Salvatore*. Uncle Sal. In the lowest circle on the left she printed *LOIS*.

Second cousins, once removed, she concluded. When her mother was still alive, this used to be easy. Mama was brilliant, had total recall about family, and kept it all in her head. Tenley only had to ask.

Now that Mama was gone, her daughter could never work out all the cousins without drawing an abbreviated Carneccio family genealogy.

CHAPTER 5

Lauren Barr paced back and forth at inconstant speed, walking the entire length of the closed storefront office of RMY Personal Financial Inc. She was a dynamo of nervous energy. Watching her made Rick Yeager tired and slightly fascinated.

"No, Rick, I don't have the letter that Tante Anna wrote to my mother—the one where she talked about you—but my mother definitely read it to me on the phone two days ago. Well, she read part of it to me, the part where you were mentioned, not all the rest of it where Tante Anna was writing about personal stuff that the two of them always share, because that's really not my business. Although now that she's gone maybe it's *all* my business since my mother has made it very clear that I have to take care of her personal matters."

"You don't slow down," Rick interrupted.

"Pardon me?" Lauren Barr stopped walking and turned toward him.

"Please. Let me catch up here."

"I'm very sorry," she said, nodding in understanding. "It's the way I deal with grief and stress sometimes. I babble."

"Ms. Barr—"

"Again, Lauren, okay?"

"Lauren, understand, it's not all that unusual for my clients, especially if they're retired and a little bit older, to make sure that some family member knows where to find me. I'm fairly certain that must be why Mrs. Geller mentioned my name. You said she didn't have any other close family. I didn't know that until now. I'll try to help you in any way that I can. But look around. This office is closed now, and given some recent circumstances, it's going to be quite a while until I'll be able to access any of your Tante Anna's records." Rick was not about to get into any conversation about the purchase of his firm by Carneccio & Dice.

"Good," Lauren replied, smiling. "I was hoping you'd offer. I'm glad you were here. I'd like you to go with me to her house."

"I've never been to her house, and I'm not sure—"

"Truth told, Rick—please tell me I can call you Rick—I haven't been there either. And as far as I know, there isn't anybody else here in Washington other than you who knows her." She paused. "Knew her. Remember what my mother said. Essentially, she outlived her friends here."

"Lauren, I did not know her that well."

There was a visible change in Lauren Barr, all of the conversational energy dissipating. Softly, hesitating, she said, "We share that, too." For a moment that lingered long enough to reach the edge of awkward, she stood still and stared at Rick. Her face was searching for expression as she sought the right words. "Could you please accompany me—as her financial advisor—to find and go through her papers? I do not want to do this alone."

He was terribly conscious that his most recent business decision was based on instinct and on trusting a woman he did not know very well. But Rick Yeager felt compelled by and drawn to Lauren Barr. Maybe this opportunity to help her was an inflection of Providence beginning to right him. It could be like inching a knee forward to crawl out of the depth of his own personal mess. Wherever it goes, he thought, let the rest of my miserable professional life begin with an act of kindness.

"We just met. Are you . . . comfortable with me going along?"

"Tante Anna knew you and trusted you."

"And that means you do, too?"

"I suppose it does. That's the way it works in our family."

Horvath knew how to be inconspicuous. He knew how to conceal himself. He considered himself a man of proud legacy. Pride was all that sustained him now. It was resident with the secrets in his mind and if he had one, in his soul. He was still unsure about the immortality of the soul, but at his age he realized that he definitely did think about this matter much more than he used to in Europe in the old days. His kind comfort was that he would take the secrets to his grave. Horvath had joined *Allamvedelmi Osztaly*, AVO—the state security department—in Budapest in 1951. Today he knew of only eight men and one woman from those great days still alive.

He smoked a fine cigar. It was his "nice detail," *szép részletességgel*. That was the term they used when he was a student at the clandestine State Security Academy in Komárom-Esztergom. A bit of tradecraft always remembered: The one who gets noticed is always the one who is trying not to get noticed. Include an element that makes you stand out, but only the slightest bit. Your presence is far more credible in that way. The concept worked consistently well in America. No one smoked cigars very much here, certainly not in the morning in a shopping center parking lot in Arlington, Virginia, on the Fourth of July. He scratched his face with the thumb of his hand holding the cigar. He looked at the letters on the band of the cigar, smiling at his own private nice detail. This was a beautiful Dominican maduro belicoso handmade by . . . Avo.

Horvath huffed his cigar twice, exhaled fully, and watched the woman step out the front door that was held solicitously, almost formally, by the man. The man locked the door. They walked to her car. Horvath walked to his.

Lauren drove a pale green Prius. Rick Yeager directed and navigated the Arlington streets familiar to him and foreign to her, using for reference a MapQuest printout that Lauren had prepared.

"If I ask you something a little bit sensitive," she began, "would you promise not to think that it was too weird?"

"Hasn't that train already left the station?" Rick grinned weakly, more than slightly surprised that he could muster up some humor here. Lauren smiled back, her eyes still on the road, but it seemed like a nervous smile to Rick.

"This may be just nothing at all," she began, "but I need to ask. You're not Jewish, are you?"

"No. Registered Lutheran. And not at all good at that."

"Okay. I thought so. That was obvious to me. I don't mean the Lutheran part. The not being Jewish part."

"And this matters because—"

"Because I've been wondering about something. How long have you known my Tante Anna?"

"I'd say three years. No, maybe a little longer. It was spring when we met, right around the end of tax season."

"How did you meet her?"

"She came to see me at the office we just left."

"Who referred her?"

"I don't think that anyone did. It was a weekday morning, before lunch. Mrs. Geller came into the office, asked for me, and we started talking. An hour later she filled out the paperwork and became a client."

"And you didn't find that odd?"

This time Rick did not answer. "Lauren, you keep asking a lot of questions. I just finished days of answering questions—and don't ask. What do you mean odd?"

"Please don't take this the wrong way, Richard Yeager. You must be a very excellent financial planner, or my Tante Anna would not have hired you. But truthfully, have you ever had any other little old Jewish lady as a client?"

"I don't know. I'm certain I never thought about it."

"Exactly my point." Lauren pulled to the curb in front of the tiny Craftsman-style house now owned by the estate of Hannah Weiss Geller. The Prius glided silently to a halt, and she threw the shift into park. She turned to face Rick, looking both kind and puzzled. "You didn't consider it, but my mother did. And I agree with her. Women of their generation— Mother and Tante Anna—don't hire a gentile to handle their personal finances. That just wouldn't happen."

Rick Yeager exhaled. "And yet it did."

"Quite apparently."

"Does that bother you?"

"It *will* bother me," Lauren said with determination as she stepped out of the car, "until I find out why."

* * *

Rick watched her fret and dig into her purse, standing at the front door of the small house. Typical for this old neighborhood, he observed, the structure was trim and scarcely bigger than a standard apartment. It stood alone on a small circling apron of grass and lightly ornamental shrubbery. No driveway, no garage. Lauren dug in her purse, finally located a ring with two keys, studied the lock briefly, selected and inserted one of them, and pushed open the door.

"My mother lives out in the Mission District in San Francisco. She overnighted these."

Rick had expected a little more order. Hannah Weiss Geller's home was not exactly untidy, but it was cluttered. The two of them walked in silence, stepping slowly in the place brightly lit by the midday sun. The front room comprised most of the house and was filled with bookshelves. The bookshelves were overfilled with books. Even the spaces above the vertical volumes were crammed horizontally with books. The spines and dust jackets were sun bleached. Rick saw that not many of them had been published in the last thirty or forty years. More than a few of the books were in German and in some language that he did not recognize, but that had a lot of diacritical marks in the titles and authors' names.

"It's Magyar. Hungarian." Lauren had been watching Rick carefully. "She grew up in Győr. Near Bratislava and Vienna." As if anticipating his question, she continued, "My mother's parents were from there, too. That's where our family connection comes in. The word 'cousin' in that part of the world has a legion of meanings—there's lots of nuance in the Hungarian language. So I'm still not exactly sure how my mother and Tante Anna are related. They both grew up speaking Hungarian and Slovak and Yiddish and high German. Apparently learning multiple languages wasn't that big a deal for them in that part of the world. There was a rather large and vital community of Hungarian Jews there before the war, before—"

"I know," Rick said.

"Mother is a lot younger than Tante Anna. She was eight when she arrived in New York right after the war."

"Considering all of the wars since then," Rick Yeager offered, "I find it interesting how, for their generation, it's always simply 'the war.'"

"Except in Israel," Lauren replied. "There you have to specify."

"I've never been there."

"Yeah. I could have figured that," she said. Rick could not tell if that was a lighthearted comment or if it had an edge.

She walked into the kitchen and Rick followed. On the round kitchen table—two chairs only—was a vase with very dirty water and cut flowers now deeply wilted. Four days at the least, Rick thought. Hannah Geller walked out of here expecting to return that afternoon. Lauren stood in the arch between kitchen and dining area, silently surveying the dining room table. From appearances, it had not hosted a dinner party in years. More clutter, but this stuff was quite neatly arranged. Clearly Mrs. Geller was a woman who in the Internet age still managed her entire life in paper. Most of it was laid out in a dozen stacks. Some letter-sized pages were piled in flat organized groups. Others were in number ten envelopes. Lauren Barr rapidly took to the task of discovering what was there and how it was arranged.

"When she and I last met," Rick said, "she talked about putting some priority on estate planning. It was on the day she died."

"What was that?"

"I said, when she and I last met—"

"No, I don't mean what you said. Did you *hear* something?" Lauren was holding a fat pack of thick white envelopes in her right hand as she walked quickly to the staircase central in the house. "Quiet. Listen. Upstairs."

Horvath watched the house, assessing. No good approaches. No good place to stay and continue surveillance. No way to be inconspicuous. *Alig észrevehető*, it was called in the service. Hardly noticeable. He concluded that this was not a particularly good place to be, but then again, everything was very quiet in the summer heat. People were either inside or away on holiday. He could wait here. This was an entirely acceptable risk. His tasking—one he completely agreed with—had been most clear. Watch, understand, report, do not engage. Assessment concluded, he settled back into the driver's seat of his two-year-old Buick LaCrosse and stared unblinking at the front door of the house.

Horvath genuinely loved America. For decades he had lived here. He raised both of his boys as Americans. He buried his wife here. It felt very good to be practicing, to be an artist again. One last time, and finally for the kind of rewards that he knew his American grandchildren deserved. Horvath permitted himself to think about them briefly before forcing his concentration back to the small house. He loved his grandchildren most of all.

Lauren looked up the stairs. As Rick Yeager walked to her side she shrieked loudly and jumped backward in his direction. He practically caught her as she began to yell and quickly regained her footing.

"Who *are* you? What are you *doing* here? How did you get *in* here?" She was screaming, her questions coming rapidly, like a chant.

"Please," came a calming man's voice. "I was about to ask you the same thing." He was walking down the stairs.

Lauren ignored his response. "You have no right to be here—*none*!"

"I'm a lawyer . . ." he began, as if this would explain everything.

"You have no right to be here! Get out! And I'm calling the *police*," Lauren shouted at him, louder, truly disturbed.

"Won't be necessary." Another man's voice came clear and controlling from upstairs, but Rick thought it sounded slightly tentative. "I'm a deputy sheriff here in Arlington County."

"Then show me a *warrant* or a *court order*!" Lauren's voice increased in shrill intensity as the two men reached the landing of the stairs and stepped into the front room, which Rick Yeager suddenly found quite confining.

"There's no warrant," said the man who had identified himself as a lawyer, "and no need for one. It's not that kind of visit. I'm here because Mrs. Geller was my backyard neighbor. She was also a client of mine. And Deputy Duncan—" he visibly glowered at the other man, an imposing red-faced giant, head shaved bald for intimidating effect "—is merely assisting me. He is off duty and he is not here as a law enforcement officer."

Lauren Barr was anything but calm, but she did manage to hold back. Her words were measured. "Start," she said with exaggerated enunciation, "by telling me your name."

"Daniel Ter Horst." He extended his hand, which was pointedly ignored.

"My name is Lauren Barr. Mrs. Geller was my aunt. This is her financial advisor, Richard Yeager. We are here at the request of my mother. Mr. Ter Horst, I have never heard of you." Her hands were on her hips and she leaned in his direction with an unpleasant assertiveness that intrigued Rick Yeager and that was clearly unexpected by the lawyer. The deputy sheriff moved quickly in her direction. Lauren wheeled to face him, bounded in his direction, and moved into his personal space.

"You. You're slow, you've just proven that you're not very bright, and you're relying on the only thing you can remember from the academy right now—*take control of this situation*. Am I right? By stepping forward, Deputy, *after* I told you to leave, you've committed criminal trespass under the color of law enforcement authority. While armed, incidentally. As though I would not notice? He's wearing a polo shirt"—she hooked a thumb at Ter Horst—"but you put on a sweatshirt on the Fourth of July in ninety-degree heat? Come on. If you wore something that fit you correctly after gaining forty extra pounds, maybe you'd do better at weapon concealment.

"Counsel," she said to Ter Horst, "think very carefully what other lies you want to tell me next about my aunt being your 'client.' Remember that old joke about the small town whose only lawyer was starving until another lawyer showed up? That's what we have here. I think we can call this *a situation*. I am here to represent my aunt. Her estate. I may be from Maryland and I certainly don't practice, but I still have a Virginia bar card."

The two men stood stunned and speechless. The deputy sheriff held back a fountain of rage. Rick Yeager noticed his fast shallow breathing. Why hadn't he asked? In Washington the question *What do you do?* was immediate and natural with any casual introduction. He had been too steeped in self-pity to inquire when Lauren Barr walked into his life an hour ago. Now he smiled. She was finally starting to make sense.

"Deputy," she calmly ordered, "step outside."

CHAPTER 6

"You're her backyard neighbor." Lauren began with the clear inflection of a cross-examination. She and Ter Horst were seated on the two chairs at the kitchen table. Rick Yeager stood watching, arms crossed, leaning against the countertop.

"Yes." The man was tentative, cautiously confident. He was assessing, knowing he was not playing the dominant role here.

Lauren tapped the table top with the fat pack of number ten envelopes rubber-banded together. "Why did you tell me that she was your client?"

Ter Horst hesitated, holding back and thinking. "Because technically that was correct. I did do legal work for her and I did advise her, although I certainly never billed her. For example, this subdivision had a property issue with the county a little more than two years ago. I wrote the letter we sent—a coordinated response. And there were other matters. Ms. Barr, please, I apologize, I did not know that anyone was coming. My visiting here today was a genuine good faith—"

"You were about to begin a coordinated search. I am going to assume that fact because you brought that deputy with you. Where did you get a key?"

"Hannah gave one to my wife. She has one of our keys here somewhere, too. We're neighbors."

"And you were looking for something, neighbor."

"I am able to assist in some estate matters. One of the more prominent areas of my practice is elder law and estate planning for—"

"Oh. Did you ever do that kind of work for my aunt?"

"Ms. Barr, I was only trying to—"

"I know what you were only trying to do. You were only trying to get a good look around in here."

She was extraordinary, Rick observed. She was advancing her own line of inquiry without permitting Ter Horst any chance to set the hook into his version of the story.

"Again, I apologize." His words were now a gesture of total resignation. The silence with which Lauren greeted his admission drifted far off the edge of uncomfortable.

"Now," she continued, "I'm going to suppose that you were looking for *this*." She flopped the package of envelopes on the table. A square yellow Post-it Note was affixed to the top envelope, a single word written on it in a beautiful hand that was part cursive and part printing. *Estate.*

Always the observer, Rick knew what she was doing. He was also certain that Ter Horst did not. Lauren was intent upon seeing his reaction, looking for the *tell*. And there it was. The lawyer tried to hide it, but his reaction was immediate, autonomous, involuntary. The slightest, nearly imperceptible movement of trunk and shoulders, a visible and serious attempt not to move any facial muscles, his dry mouth opening slightly, and just the quickest movement of his eyes in the direction of the package. Confirmation. He was in Hannah Weiss Geller's house seeking information about the estate.

"Did she ever discuss this with you?" Lauren Barr's question was now almost kind, pitying.

"Ms. Barr, I am not prepared to share with you any of my conversations with Hannah."

"You're here because you're acting for another client." She followed his kindness with bluntness. It was apparent to Rick and to Ter Horst that she was not asking a question this time.

The lawyer put his two hands together, palms flat, and brought them to his face, tapping the paired forefingers lightly on his nose. To Rick he looked judicial. Daniel Ter Horst said nothing.

Lauren Barr continued. "I understand, Mr. Ter Horst. And I don't think that any of us has to wonder what would have happened if you had picked this up before I did." She took back the packet of envelopes and held them. "You told me where your home is," she said, "but would you have a card?"

Ter Horst reached into a deep front pocket and pulled out a fat round wallet from which he managed to extract a cream-colored business card worn at the edges. He placed it on the table and wordlessly slid it across to Lauren.

When the lawyer left, Rick Yeager took the seat he had occupied. Streaks of natural light lit the kitchen. The reflection from the table illuminated Lauren's face, and Rick noticed how her hair appeared so much lighter in the sunlit wash. She glanced over her glasses at him before pushing them back into place.

"That wasn't me," she said.

"Then who was it?" Rick Yeager smiled.

"Let me answer you this way. I have a partner who always laughs and accuses me of being the 'three faces of Lauren.' Do you know about a movie called *The Three Faces of Eve*? Multiple personalities? It was something like fifty years ago. I didn't have any idea what he meant until I looked it up on Wikipedia."

"Lauren, what do you do for a living?"

"Area director in a real estate investment trust. We're called Kehina Alliance Partners, with offices in Bethesda, Maryland. We are also in London and Tel Aviv."

"Acting is your method of negotiating."

"Precisely, Richard Yeager."

"Do you do a lot of that? Negotiating, not acting."

"I do as much as required, which is more than I'd like. Kehina is what we call a fund of funds in the real estate finance world. We invest in other investments. You would have no idea how difficult our business has become in this last couple of years, especially when the recession hit commercial real estate. The financial upheaval we're experiencing has been utterly world-changing. We've had investors pull out of our financial operations, we've had whole cityscape projects come to a crashing halt, and we've handed the banks the keys to any number of distressed properties."

"What I just saw there—"

"Is what I've learned dealing with project developers and the kind of

people who finance them. And I don't care if they're in Washington, To-
peka, or Jerusalem. Every one of them thinks that they can roll over *the
girl*. Maybe they teach that skill in some kind of developers' academy—
although my experience is that their attitude is pretty common in finance generally. However, I rarely run into one who's armed."

"You are disarming in a number of ways."

"Thank you. I don't doubt that. But," she said, standing and turning
to face the dining room table stacked with papers, "we have a chore here."
She put both of her palms flat on the table's edge, leaned into it, and
scanned the stacks, thinking, organizing. Rick walked to her side and
watched.

The view from their detached vantage, uncomfortable as it was for
Rick, was soon clear enough. Hannah Weiss Geller had been planning.
She was intending to close out the segment of her long life that was cen-
tered here in Arlington, Virginia. One group of papers documented her
down payment at an elder-care facility near Leesburg, forty minutes farther away from Washington, DC. Another stack was a tightly organized
financial package concerning her house. Rick's memory had been correct.
She owned it clear, having paid off the mortgage almost twenty years ago.
There was a huge tax pile, with income tax returns dating back to 1974.
A large, well-worn red accordion file was marked simply *Ben* in that neat
half-cursive handwriting. When Lauren pulled out its first page Rick
could see that it contained the remnants of a life. The document was an
original Commonwealth of Virginia death certificate for Mrs. Geller's
late husband, dated 1991.

"I never met him," Lauren remarked, anticipating the question that
Rick did not ask.

"She never mentioned him to me," he responded, "except to say that
she was widowed."

"Mother knew him, but not well. The way she tells it, he was considerably older than her. He married late in life. There were never any children. When I was talking to her last night, Mother remarked how that
fact made for such an enduring sadness as well as a sad endurance in
Tante Anna's life. Children, generational renewal, progeny . . . all of that
had such overarching importance to them."

"Hannah and Ben."

"No, not just them specifically—but I am certain that it must have been there. I mean to all of them. The survivors. No matter what they survived."

"There was a corresponding imperative that I think I saw in my father," Rick said, "and he was also older than my mother."

"No," Lauren Barr said. She was suddenly icy, definitive, punctuating. "It was *nothing* like it was for her. Don't say that. And we are not continuing this conversation." She returned to the papers on the dining room table.

Two fanned-out stacks of printouts and one thick pile of envelopes, slit open and loose, bore the RMY *Personal Financial* logo and provided a general record of Mrs. Geller's investment holdings. Together they examined the papers in strained silence. The details emerging were pretty much as Rick had recalled at their last meeting, except that he had mis-estimated the market value of the portfolio. Hannah Geller's investments had been ravaged as the wildest demons of the market had their way with her life savings. It would take some work to figure out exactly what she was worth.

"I'd say that you did better for her than most of our limited partnerships have done for Kehina Alliance," Lauren observed.

"Worst market, worst financial environment in my professional lifetime," Rick said. "In my *entire* lifetime."

"Not much consolation in knowing you're not alone, is it?"

Rick let it pass. She had no idea the extent to which he did feel alone. He was suddenly and quite unexpectedly hit with a renewal of the wave of the self-pity in which he was swimming when Lauren arrived at the closed offices of RMY. Where did that come from? He shook his head, imperceptible to her, in order to concentrate.

"That's it. Nothing else here."

"No. One more—over there, the first one I picked up."

Estate. Rick handed her the package, and Lauren unbanded it.

Two envelopes with inventories, one listing personal property, furniture, and jewelry and one containing a thick sheaf of handwritten book lists. Four envelopes of old investments predating Mrs. Geller's engagement of Rick Yeager.

"Those are not included in the RMY Financial packages," he said helpfully. "They may make the estate a bit larger."

"Uh-huh." Lauren continued flipping through and opening the envelopes.

One yellow manila envelope, slightly larger than the others, containing a few old photographs.

A half-dozen or more letters bearing this house's address written with what Rick thought was a typewriter. Lauren said, "These must be from my mother."

The last envelope was white and unmarked, unsealed, holding four or five folded pages. Lauren opened it and pulled out the contents.

"She made a *will*." Rick Yeager could not tell immediately whether she was shocked, disappointed, or angry. Some combination of all three was most likely, considering her tone. He got the distinct impression that this document was not what Lauren Barr had expected. She was reading rapidly.

"She *downloaded* it." Lauren's hands were tight, and this was now definitely anger. "Right here. From freevirginialegalforms-dot-com. And then she had it *notarized*. At a *bank*. And I suppose that *you* are going to tell me that you had no way of knowing about this, right?" Her tone was now accusatory with a decidedly ugly edge.

"Lauren, I encourage clients to do proper estate planning, with counsel, of course. I agree that it may not be particularly advisable to download your will from the Internet, but for a simple estate, I'm not sure how improper—"

"Stop. You don't think that *this* is improper?" She had the harshest edge yet in her voice.

Rick read in silence.

```
I do give, devise, and bequeath all of my personal
effects and all of the property which I may own
at the time of my death, real or personal, tangi-
ble and intangible, of whatsoever nature and
wherever situated, including all property and in-
```

```
terests which I may acquire or become entitled to
after the execution of this Last Will and Testa-
ment, and including all lapsed legacies and de-
vises, to Richard Montgomery Yeager.
```

Lauren's words came from what seemed like an echoing great distance as Rick's peripheral vision condensed, his diaphragm tightened, and his mouth dried.

"Congratulations," she announced with high irony and flat emotion. "You are now the executor, trustee, and beneficiary of her entire estate." Each word was shoved in his face with a grudge.

Rick Yeager held the will tentatively, speed reading and then re-reading the text. He could feel Lauren's burning stare intent upon his face looking for the *tell*, but he could not bring himself to meet her eyes. She had already scanned the three printed pages. The last page bore the unmistakable signature of the late Hannah Weiss Geller overstruck with a notary's raised seal and the stamped name and address of an assistant branch manager at her bank. Rick slid the three pages back and forth along the two folds.

In the hasty rage of discovery Lauren had missed the final page, a piece of lined tablet paper. She peered now as he separated it from the will, laid it on the table, folded it out flat, and slid a finger slowly down the left-hand side of the page.

He counted eighteen organized lines of numbers written in the same beautiful script as the signature.

CHAPTER 7

The hour between 5:30 and 6:30 A.M. was Warren Hunter's particular favorite. Around two years ago he was named managing director and the number two to the head of investment and merchant banking at Compton Sizemore. For a few weeks the members of his staff stumbled over each other in a comical attempt to beat him to the office every morning. One by one they gave up that goal, resigned to granting their improbably young boss his treasured solitary first hour of sanctuary. This was what Warren intended. He relished the early time to be alone and productive. Time to collect his thoughts. Time to prepare. Time to strategize.

When he arrived this morning just before sunup, a waxing anticipatory purple glow bathed the Brooklyn horizon. His office was organized so that his chair fit between the immense desk and a thin parallel credenza running the entire length of one windowed wall. He turned to the enormous flat screen on the credenza—it was never to be turned off—and began to scrutinize the usual hundred or so overnight e-mail messages from London, Europe, the Middle East, and central Asia. There was no Fourth of July holiday for these markets. More than the usual activity had to be accounted for on this morning that the American markets would reopen after a one-day holiday break.

The brutally persisting economic morass in which he was operating was the first down market of Warren Hunter's storied career as a financier. Compton Sizemore, as the last investment bank standing as a real partnership, maintained a strict and wise division between its bankers and its traders. The bankers did deals, large transactions for the benefit of wealthy corporate clients. Mergers, public offerings, recapitalizations, leveraged buyouts, commercial debt, and debenture issues, all of it the lifeblood of modern global capital finance. The traders only swapped back and forth the fruitful harvest of the bankers' real work, at least in the general perception of everyone on Hunter's side of the firm.

He had recently named this mess the Great Wallow. The term was beginning to catch on. The research department at Compton Sizemore traced its inception to a *Wall Street Journal* article quoting Warren Hunter: "This economy is not headed for depression, and any banker who says it loses his license to predict the market. What we have instead is a great wallow, credit constipation coupled with extreme risk aversion. It is a fundamental realignment, not just a huge recession."

Warren enjoyed being Compton Sizemore's current king of the bankers. It was an especially good time to be king because at present he had no counterpart among the traders. Four heads of the consolidated trading desk at Compton Sizemore had come and gone during his tenure at the firm. The position was at the moment vacant. That whole side of the business was presently in utter turmoil and hemorrhaging cash. This unsettling fact—known to few at the firm and fewer on the Street—only made Warren glad that there was no disclosure or answering to public market shareholders for Compton Sizemore's performance.

Warren particularly liked the traders, even while his entire small world in midtown Manhattan would clearly have pegged him as a banker from birth. The traders themselves, the guys on the desks (they were still overwhelmingly guys) were for the most part ethnic white, crude, blue-collar studs with vowels hanging onto the back ends of their names. Their demeanor never varied in this down market; the long run for them was this afternoon or tomorrow. More than a few of them had no college degree, and those that had them certainly did not share Warren's Princeton-Harvard pedigree. They were his favorite people in the firm. By contrast, his own department of high Ivy bankers, despite their much greater and much-heralded diversity, consistently harbored ambitions exceeding their abilities, in Warren's considered judgment. They could do well by learning more from the traders about meeting the demands of near-term discipline, micro-focus, and the realism of expectations. That's what made a good investment banker.

* * *

The day he arrived at Compton Sizemore, the minute he first met August Compton, he was asked a most unusual question: "Bean counter, gearhead, or poet?" Warren had no idea what Compton was talking about. The founder of the firm explained. This was his way of sizing up a new hire. Every business school graduate, Compton said, came from one of three types of people. Bean counters were the accountants and economists, balance sheet wizards, believers in ratios and rules. Gearheads were the engineers and mathematicians, the dominant modality of Wall Street entrants Warren's age—quants, builders, lovers of the practical, doable, and pedestrian. Poets were the humanities people, English majors and linguists who migrated into the profession once they discovered the elegance, creativity, and baroque complexity of modern finance.

"Poet," Warren answered honestly, expecting opprobrium. Instead August Compton smiled at him broadly. "So was I," he offered. "And you're the only other one here. Now get the hell out there and go run the world."

Wall Street was not strictly speaking contained on Wall Street anymore. Wall Street wasn't precisely American anymore either. Conventional wisdom prevailing during Warren Hunter's decade-and-more in the industry held that the island of Manhattan was basically the new Wall Street. Compton Sizemore itself was a good example of that, with seven floors in the famed Citigroup Center between Lexington and Third Avenue, midtown on the East Side. Most of the Compton Sizemore partners, Warren certainly included, could barely remember the last time that they had been on the *actual street* named Wall Street. In the same article where he invented the Great Wallow neologism, Warren was also quoted concerning this phenomenon, priding himself at recognizing a trend. "Wall Street," he told the reporter, "has not only gone to Washington during the economic crisis. Wall Street has gone global. Where we are in the physical world no longer matters. How we work is

all that counts. Our industry, battered and demoralized as we are, is still fundamentally about the movement and placement of capital, just as it always has been. That movement happens everywhere and constantly. 'Wall Street' is simply how we describe the collective group of professionals who move that capital."

The news article was all about Compton Sizemore, its genesis in the nineties, its triumphs following the last big meltdown, and its enviably solvent position in an otherwise deconstructing industry. Other firms, the *Journal* wrote, were looking to replicate the Compton Sizemore model the way they once aspired to the Lehman Brothers template. August Compton had been incredibly pleased with what it said. He especially noted what the reporter had not asked.

There was nothing in the entire piece about ViroSat, Compton Sizemore's biggest deal, now and in the history of the firm.

It was 6:27 A.M. Warren Hunter glanced at his watch—a Patek Philippe Nautilus in rose gold, the understated version. Time to get seriously into role. He stood up from his seat at the screen, shook his head slowly at the FTSE index in London taking a huge midday dive, and tightened the knot on his necktie. Purposefully he walked around the big desk, out of his inner office, through his empty staff office, and into the main corridor of the fifty-sixth floor. A dozen fast strides, each accelerating until he reached the door to the big conference room.

The bankers on the Compton Sizemore ViroSat team, *his* team, all fourteen of them, were already in place. While a few were standing, most were already seated around the big conference table. Starbucks cups, laptop computers, iPads, iPhones, and BlackBerrys were scattered about. There was no evident deference when he entered, but it was clear how hard they were all working to look productively occupied and that his arrival was anticipated. Not one of them was older than forty. Warren Hunter took his seat at the head of the table.

"Time for details. You all know the drill here." Not a word of greeting. This morning he was going to be all about productivity.

Johnny Shen, a pleasant quant who came out of Chapel Hill, spoke

up first. His given name was not Johnny; that was his English name. His Chinese name, Warren recalled, was something like Jen-Nan, but after six years here in the States, Zhejiang Province was far behind him. The young banker preferred Johnny. The name only emphasized his impossibly boyish looks.

"In aggregate, the debt and commercial paper from the various enterprise units are all in place," Johnny Shen began. "Our infrastructure plan is fully funded. With respect to the enterprises themselves—there are now one hundred and twelve of them—they're set to begin cash flow generation as soon as we close the major financing."

"How many begin cash flow positive on day one?" Warren asked.

"Ninety. That's over eighty percent of them cash flow positive."

"Aggregate cash flow to debt service ratio?"

"Six point two to one."

"And the twenty percent of the enterprises that are going to be cash flow negative?"

"They are all build-out related. Let me provide an example. The worst case for the worst one of them is the mess in central Asia, that satellite trunk line to Dushanbe, Tashkent, Bishkek, and Almaty. And even that is going to be cash flow positive less than twenty months from inception."

Warren mulled over the implications of the cash flow information. The best financing, he always maintained, came from within—the cash that the businesses generated themselves, not the catalytic cash that investment banks provided. This was huge. It was unexpected by the markets, but in a very good way. When it came time to sell ViroSat, or to sell the pieces of ViroSat, the financial buyers would not yet be expecting much in the way of profits or free cash flow. Delivering positive cash flow would mean a value and a sale price far beyond expectations. In this market, with nothing but unmet expectations and negative cash flow, what he had created was the architecture of a major win.

"Okay. Good work." That was as much of a platitude as Shen could expect from Warren Hunter, and while the young man was immensely

pleased, he tried not to show it as his boss moved on. "Capital foundation."

"I have the final breakouts." This answer came from Dawson Mac-Neil, the oldest member of the staff and as thoroughly unlikeable as he was spectacularly competent in technical finance. Privately August Compton and Warren Hunter referred to him as "the fucking weasel from Brown," shorthanded in their e-mails as "FWB." He possessed absolutely no intuition, social or management awareness, or deal sense. He lacked completely the ineffable ability to read a transaction and run it to closure. He nonetheless wanted to *be* Warren Hunter, knowing that his accounting skill was unsurpassed. But he gleaned no clue that he would never progress professionally past the seat he held at this exact moment in time.

"One point three seven, all totaled." MacNeil didn't even know enough to set up the delivery of the most important figure of the entire deal. Warren took the number and repeated it for dramatic effect.

"One trillion, three hundred and seventy billion dollars." He drew out the words carefully. "Gentlemen and ladies, you are now working on the biggest deal in the history of world finance, and we're less than thirty days from closing. This deal is being locked down on August first. That's the day of closing. Mark it carefully, because it's the most important day of your life. I don't have to remind you that in this economy, our worst ever since they invented capital finance, Compton Sizemore's success is going to have an effect far greater than any of you could ever have dreamed. I hope you've all figured that out."

"Isn't it good"—MacNeil smirked—"to be master of the universe." Cricket moment. No one laughed.

"Bullshit," Warren responded in two very distinct syllables, his annoyance clear to everyone but Dawson MacNeil. "I am not exaggerating when I say this: the level of responsibility in this room is now greater than that held by the United States government. We are the private sector of telecommunications and 'Internet Next.' ViroSat has taken on a global life and power beyond governments. Some of you will recall, that was our entire intention. This project is a triumph of the free market.

God knows, the nation needs a success like this. But I don't want to hear a word about our running the world. Leave that nonsense to the conspiracy theorists. We are investment bankers. We are managing this transaction because it cries out for our unique skills and because the project itself is as incredible as it is incredibly necessary. We are building this project to sell it. That's what we do here, and if you lose sight of that fact, you should find some other way to engage your time.

"Now what's the possible variance on that total?"

"Less than one-one hundredth of a percent, including any currency variations."

Warren watched the room calculating the decimal places. The possible *slop* in this deal—and it was infinitesimal—amounted to a hundred and thirty-seven million dollars.

"Good. That's within the—"

"We still do not have the equity picture completed." Slow-motion head-turns from the whole conference room as Dawson MacNeil had the temerity to interrupt Warren Hunter.

"I see." Warren's words were ice.

"Yes," continued the oblivious MacNeil. "I have a very good vantage on the source of all debt issues, and you know that they come in a wide range of legal types, especially in the European and South American markets. But I do not yet have the equity sources."

"And you will not." Four syllables stabbed Dawson MacNeil.

"Warren, I am really going to have to press you on this point—" MacNeil began, stopped by Warren's palm spread flat and shoved in his direction in an ugly dismissal of the way his question was going.

Warren Hunter rose and paced the length of the conference room, an exemplar of absolute calm, which his assembled staff of bankers knew meant exactly the opposite: the man was furious. He walked to the conference room window, a wide southern-facing vista, and stared at the tip of Manhattan Island, gazing in the direction of the spot where the Twin Towers once stood. The city was now fully bathed in summer sunlight. When he spoke, every man and woman in the room, including Dawson MacNeil, was paying peak attention.

"This deal breaks out to be twenty-one percent equity, making our leverage ratio less than four to one. The number is two hundred eighty-seven point seven billion in cash equity at the closing valuation. The remainder is in the debt issues, comprising all of that wide range of legal types you're so concerned about. The debt encompasses the national contributions and the big bonds. Equity ownership of ViroSat, however, is more closely controlled. All of the required cash is in the assembly process. It will be aggregated in our house account through a rather elegant limited partnership arrangement. So it's appropriate for me to review with you how we do a limited partnership here at Compton Sizemore. The limited partners hold limited partnership shares. They own the entire economic interest of the partnership, which is just a fund, a collection of cash. The general partner—who is here *also* a limited partner—manages the fund, investing it, charging just a minimum fee until the project is harvested. In this case, that harvest will happen when we sell ViroSat, because our limited partnership will own one hundred percent of the equity in this deal."

He let that part sink in. The gang of fourteen here, as the entire investment banking team at Compton Sizemore called them, had not yet heard about the equity funding, the ownership of ViroSat. Until this moment, Warren Hunter had brushed aside all inquiry.

"The moment ViroSat closes," he continued, "we begin immediately to execute our harvest strategy. No hesitation. After the sale—and I expect a significant run-up in value—we distribute the proceeds. First the limited partners get paid back their original investment. Then the remainder, the gain in the investment, the value we create, is split eighty-twenty. Eighty percent to the limited partners, twenty percent to the general partner.

"This is *precisely* why ViroSat is and will remain a private transaction. This is also why our present structure of closing this preliminary financing, rather than making a direct offering to the public, is critical. No one needs to know the least bit of information about the composition of our ViroSat limited partnership. It is immaterial.

"You may, however, want to know one important feature about the management of this funding mechanism. The general partner, especially with skin in the game, has an incendiary motivation to do well. He also controls each of your personal destinies in the entire financial services industry. That general partner would be me."

The news took a long moment to digest.

Warren Hunter, limited partner and general partner, was backing ViroSat himself. The deal was brilliant, innovative, and amazing to all of them, it was perfectly legal. He was right. Whoever else he might have in the deal was immaterial. He was not only running it, he was also owning and controlling the biggest deal on the Street. And the Street had become a planet.

CHAPTER 8

Julia Toussaint always enjoyed the downtime of midsummer Congressional recess precisely because downtime was so rare. What she could never manage was sleeping in. She allowed herself time to daydream this morning as her MacBook Air notebook computer booted up and connected to the Wi-Fi portal at the King Street Starbucks in Old Town Alexandria, Virginia. At a quarter to seven, the two-block walk from her apartment to here was probably going to be the coolest fifteen minutes of the day. She was half attempting to decide whether a trip to the office later on this morning was called for. Her initial thought was that there is always some immediate value to be gained from a day alone in the Russell Senate Office Building, where Tenley Harbison's elegant public offices were located. She could clear her desk uninterrupted by phones, the constant stream of e-mail, eager summer interns, pressing issues, happen-by lobbyists, über-arrogant committee staff, and of course the senator. As one of only two "politically" designated staffers for her senator, she was in constant demand. This situation was brought about by the self-imposed general inaccessibility of Harbison's chief of staff as contrasted to Julia's easily evident approachability. Her second thought was that it could all wait. She quickly decided to go with that.

"Grande cinnamon dolce latte." Julia heard the clear announcement delivering the overindulgence of caffeinated sugar that she was permitting herself this morning. She turned from her notebook computer to recover the cup from the raised counter and smiled at the barista, a severe young Latina with a startlingly asymmetrical haircut and six or eight facial piercings. The young woman beamed back flirtatiously. Julia, a total empath, recognized the grin with brief eye contact and turned her back a little slower than she really had to. It's perfectly okay for the barista to believe that we had a moment there, Julia told herself. She was feeling quite progressively magnanimous while settling onto the tall stool and looking over her screen at the developing morning rush hour on King Street. She sipped the latte and clicked on the e-mail program.

Her usual glut of messages contained only one this morning that would require any attention.

04 July   23:27.04 EDT
From: Senator Tenley Harbison [harbi01@harbison.senate.gov]
To: Toussaint, Julia [toussaintjd@harbison.senate.gov]
Subject: virosat
jd further to our earlier conversation this aftn can u drill down on 2 areas. first what possible tech advantage is there with vs? and can we make best est of what likely numbers are going to be after sale? tks! th
Sent from my BlackBerry Wireless Handheld

Julia always wrote best when she had time like this to think, when these small strokes of public policy were able to come together in lightning bursts.

MEMORANDUM - Eyes Only for Senator Harbison
JDT 7/5
Subject: VIROSAT BACKGROUND AND FINANCE

Executive Summary
You inquired concerning three points:
  • The structure of ViroSat, including possible federal contracts
  • Technical advantages conferred by the project
  • The value of ViroSat after its presumed sale

This memorandum confidentially addresses these inquiries.

Background

ViroSat is the commercial outgrowth and realization of a concept first suggested in 1994 at a technical conference in Berne, Switzerland. The suggestion attracted little notice at the time. Accounts vary about who exactly first made the proposition. This ambiguity gives the genesis of ViroSat the quality of an urban legend or at best, a Wikipedia argument. The essential story is, however, not in dispute. Someone at the conference forwarded the assertion that the technical structure of the Internet as it then existed (and is pretty much the same today) was outright inadequate or unacceptable for commercial use. Recall that in 1994, commercial applications online were either just being imagined or were in their infancy. This was long before the mad dash of the dot-com bubble. In the years since then, and even with our extraordinary advances in information technology and systems engineering, everything about the Internet has essentially been "cobbled together." This troubling fact, even after the warning in Berne, keeps being ignored. The original Internet systems are now said to be so aged, so "clunky," with the infrastructure itself so overtaxed, that it is no longer worth fixing. The theory behind ViroSat is that this situation presents an opportunity. Prior to the inception of ViroSat, open-source literature called the opportunity "Internet Next."

Our "old" Internet, our existing systems, can be thought of like a neighborhood gone bad. Very bad, in some cases, if one considers the worst excesses available online, from child pornography to phishing scams. The theory behind "Internet Next" or ViroSat is that the neighborhood is not worth rebuilding, that any new engineering applied on top of the current structure would be only further burdening a terribly shaky foundation.

ViroSat is like a whole new neighborhood, a planned city with the latest technology, especially cognizant of the human-computer interface.

General Structure

It's fair to say that the project would never have been commenced in the current economic environment. There is some criticism on investment blogs that big-deal technology plays have "gone out of style." Estimates of its cost and scope are all just that: estimates. ViroSat is a private enterprise, or more correctly an enterprise of enterprises, all building to an "Internet Next" of massive scale and scope. There is no overarching or nationally controlling legal authority other than the commercial laws of the various venues in which ViroSat has contractual arrangements. These are reliably reported to be one hundred or more. I have inquired of action officers at Defense, Commerce, State, and two intelligence agencies through our legislative office contacts at the Office of the Director of National Intelligence (DNI). All of them are closely tracking the progress of the project, as has been the case over the past couple of years since the enterprises began being formed worldwide and the first satellite was launched.

A sidebar worth noting: ViroSat takes its name from two Latin roots, *viro* for *man* or *mankind*, and *sat*, meaning *to please*. The few early press reports and at least two blogs tracking the project's progress have this wrong. They aver that the name derives from "viral" and "satellite."

ViroSat's financing and corporate structuring are all resident at Compton Sizemore, specifically at the New York headquarters. We do have a legitimate New Jersey constituent interest here, because as you know, about 90 percent of their trading and clearing operations relocated to Jersey City after 9/11. That part of the business is at the Goldman Sachs Tower on Exchange Place.

Treasury provided us with the best guesstimates of ViroSat financing. A consensus view is that the entire infrastructure cost will be "not less than $1.25 trillion." You had inquired about the mix of debt financing and equity capital to build ViroSat. All that Treasury can say is that the bulk of the project will be in debt issues. There are no public filings, no review or oversight by the Securities and Exchange Commission, and the sources of equity capital are likely to be as varied as the distribution of capital to the various enterprises that comprise the project at large.

Technical Advantages

In a word, ViroSat is secure. Any computer system within or connected to the new structure is basically inside that planned city, and the city is technologically "gated." Moreover, a lot of the research engineering that has gone into ViroSat has been in languages, cognitive and psychological processes, improving the human-computer interface, and especially in what the National Institute of Standards and Technology has called "computational velocity." (Note: You cosponsored the NIST supplemental appropriation this year, and it was a significant increase even in the overall cost-cutting environment.)

This "computational velocity" issue is the key to ViroSat's implementation. It is an outgrowth of something known as "massively parallel processing" or "distributed array processing." Any ViroSat-related computer system moves faster than the human mind is able to perceive, faster than the limits that biology imposes on us. What this means is that all computing is now going to be instantaneous—and interestingly, it does not have to get any faster, because any further increases in speed will be "wasted." This is an enormous technological leap, and even people quite familiar with the systems architecture contend that we have not even begun to understand the overall technical implications. What we do know, and assume, is that the commercial demand for the system will be extreme. ViroSat represents an entire new dimension beyond what we know today as "online." It is the fulfillment of "Internet Next."

Valuation

This is the most difficult inquiry of all, and frankly, any estimate is a sheer guess. We have valuation guesses across wide ranges, encompassing hundreds of variables. Among these are the various currencies in which the ViroSat enterprises are valued, the

timing of any potential sale, the profitability of each discrete enterprise, the amount of growth in ViroSat demand and the rate of
growth in that demand, and many, many others.

As a consequence, I am most reluctant to place a value on the
"likely numbers . . . after sale," as you require. No number I provide you will have any high degree of veracity. With that disclaimer,
however, I can report to you what I believe to be the most reasonable valuation reported to me. By "reasonable," you must not take
this to mean that the value is reasonable; on the contrary, it is so
enormous as to tax the imagination. "Reasonable" only means
that rational analysts have at least concurred, and that if you elect
to use this number in public discourse, you are not likely to be em-
barrassed.

ViroSat will probably be worth $12 trillion or more when com-
pleted globally, producing a valuation of almost ten times what we
believe the initial investment assembled at Compton Sizemore is
going to be.

Senator, that number, for your reference, is about equal to 75
percent of the gross domestic product of the United States.

Julia sat back and read her last four paragraphs over again, considering
whether that change to the first person hit the correct level of emphasis.
She concluded that it did.

July on the Potomac was definitely heating up outside the Starbucks.
Her latte was now down to just half an inch of muddy swirl. She adored
this part of Old Town Alexandria.

"You're married to that man?" The tone was accusatory and the question
was not a question. He was a huge black man, their potential landlord.
Rick Yeager had gone in ahead of her and was walking around the bedroom of what was to become their first apartment, in an older mid-rise
building off South Washington Street.

"Yes," Julia Toussaint responded firmly. She crossed her arms so that her left hand and the new gold wedding band were visible. She wanted to look defiant, not defensive. She knew to expect this reaction and thought she was prepared for it. They had talked about it—God knows how endlessly they had talked about it—but such an overt disapproval from an African-American man, a man approximately her parents' age, had the unanticipated effect of shifting her significantly off-balance. And the landlord knew it.

The man pressed his advantage and did not seem to care if Rick heard him.

"You have a daddy?"

"Yes, but I don't see—"

"And was he particularly happy when you brought that white man home to meet him?"

"I mean to be courteous," Julia replied, sounding like she was on firmer ground than she really was, "but this is not a conversation that is appropriate to have with you."

"I think," the landlord said, nodding, "that I have your style."

"You know nothing about me," she responded, and on that count she was very sure.

"Marry anybody you want to," he said with a dismissive curve of a half smile. "That's a big part of what the movement was all about. But don't expect everybody to approve when you set out to marry up. That says something about *you*, missy."

"How can you . . . ? Is that what you think . . . ?" She was still trying to formulate some kind of question as the landlord turned his back and shut the door to the apartment.

Julia knew how unlikely a couple they were. She knew the odds against them going in. So did Rick, perhaps even more than she.

They met on a blind date. It was a situation created out of a prank on the edge of cruelty, one that solidified into an attraction beyond manners.

Julia was set up. She was new to Washington, a Jersey girl who arrived on Capitol Hill from Clinton Hill, conscious of how she was suddenly a long way from Newark and a new bachelor's degree from Fairleigh Dickinson. There were two other roommates, three miniscule bedrooms, and a common area in their DC apartment. The girl from Jacksonville, the one she did not know so well, said she could find someone for Julia, who had just begun to use the contraction of her names to "J.D."

"Date? What do you mean *date*? Don't you realize that no one *dates* in the twenty-first century?" Miss Florida—that was how she thought of her—seemed incredulous, though Julia believed at the time it was an act.

"It's the twenty-first century in New Jersey, and I *dated* there," she replied, but her laugh was forced.

"I think I know just who you should meet, J.D.," the girl said assertively. "He *dated* a friend of mine from back home."

"As long as this isn't a staffer. No Hill types."

"Finance, I think. Something not government. Definitely not Hill staff."

Their first meeting was at Mr. Henry's on Capitol Hill, where they had each arrived fifteen minutes early and then waited patiently separate for almost thirty-five minutes—Rick expecting a white woman, Julia certain that she was meeting a black man.

"You wouldn't be J.D.?" were his first words to her.

"Yes, I would," were hers to him.

They ate the bar food, hamburgers with slaw, cheese fries, jalapeño poppers, Sam Adams White Ales. Julia, the close observer, perceived an unassuming charm and quietude in Richard Yeager. She found it difficult to concentrate on their conversation because underneath it, she was trying desperately to figure out why on earth she was so attracted to him. She eventually concluded that it was because Rick, at his dangerously charming core, was not a terribly complicated man. That and he had such a handsome calm about him.

"This—us—probably couldn't happen in Newark," she told him tentatively at the end of the evening. "Well, it could, but it doesn't. Not actually." It was the first time either of them mentioned race, even obliquely.

"It never does in most of Virginia," Rick said. "And you don't even want to ask about the way some Germans think about race."

"Everybody has family," Julia answered.

"Yes we do."

"And nobody is responsible for what family thinks, or how they act."

"Yeah. I like you, J.D."

"Julia."

"Okay. I like you, Julia."

Chin in her palm, elbow on the counter, Julia glanced back down at the MacBook's screen then swished a finger on the trackpad to un-blank it. She reread the memorandum to Senator Harbison, considered it, observed that it held up pretty well, and made a few corrections. She clicked the print icon then selected "create PDF." After a few seconds, the electronic file was ready. She hit "reply" to the senator's e-mail from last night and attached the finished memorandum. "Per your request and as discussed— JDT" she typed, selecting "send." She closed the e-mail program, terminating the connection to her senate account.

With the mouse pointer, she swung to the bottom of her screen, pulling "Gmail" from the horizontal dock of programs. The page was up in an instant. Julia quickly logged in with the familiar letters of her personal account: JayDeeTee22314@gmail.com. There were six new messages in her inbox; she ignored them all. She opened a new e-mail and clicked on the open long white rectangle of the "To" line and typed again, this time a little slower: warren.hunter@comptonsizemore.com.

CHAPTER 9

It had been a most thoroughly miserable night. He got no sleep, no rest. There was no way to make his mind stop whirling. After his sojourn in the system of federal detention and his afternoon with Lauren Barr, Rick Yeager was more than looking forward to coming home to Reston, Virginia, in the heart of Washington's western suburbs. That was before he saw the place. His first reaction: he should have known. The FBI had been here, too. Not a single millimeter of his garden condominium was untouched. Furniture was tipped over in deliberately reckless piles, drawers were spilled out, clothing was everywhere, his mattress was cut open, the box spring of his bed thrown against the bedroom wall so hard that its wooden frame was smashed through the wallboard. The computer was on the floor, and it appeared to Rick as though its connecting wires had been ripped from the wall rather than unplugged. Both the refrigerator and freezer doors were wide open, food in various stages of thaw and spoilage strewn about the kitchen. That one he understood, because he'd read about it: when a federal investigation turned up ninety thousand dollars in cash in the freezer of a crooked congressman a few years ago, dumping the box became standard procedure for any federal raid. In the bathroom, every bottle, whether it held liquid or pills, had been opened, contents dumped into the bathtub. That, he was certain, was for one reason only—because they could.

All night long, after he partially assembled what was left of his bed, Rick had rolled about violently, unable to beg any sleep no matter how desperately tired he knew that he was. Lauren Barr had dropped him off back at the RMY Personal Financial Inc. offices in the late afternoon without much else to say. She was sputtering furious, her mood telegraphing to Rick that his legal problems would increase now. Twice he had attempted apologetic conversation, and both times the otherwise engaging Lauren had cut him off summarily. "I am thinking and planning," she told him finally and firmly, "and right now you are not part of those plans. I will inform you when you are." Rick believed her.

All night long, she haunted his sleepless thoughts.

The bedroom television was still operative. He watched the orchestra concert and the Fourth of July fireworks on the National Mall in silence approaching catatonia, not bothering to eat, not even remembering to be hungry, which he finally realized at about 3:15 A.M. Somewhere he recalled that these could be symptoms of clinical depression. He shook off that avenue of thought by rationalizing that he had just been through an unnatural trauma. If he recognized what was going on, he believed, then he would be less affected by it and eventually he would be okay.

But therein, Rick reasoned—his first coherent thought-to-the-point in many hours—lies the problem. He could not recognize or understand these events.

"Outside perspective," he said to himself out loud at precisely 4:12 A.M. He knew the time because it was announced by the pale blue numbers on the bedside clock.

The federal searchers did leave a working landline telephone in the condo. Rick found it in a damp cardboard pile of unfrozen microwave entrées in a corner of the kitchen. His mobile phone was still in federal custody. As morning and clarity both began to dawn on him, Rick was thankful on two counts. First, that he was very good at remembering telephone numbers. Second, that he had not just gone completely mobile in lieu of keeping a home phone, something he had seriously considered coincident with his big move up to Carneccio & Dice.

A few minutes before 8 A.M., he placed the call, betting that his outside perspective would be at his desk and would answer his own telephone. He was correct on both counts. Rick heaved a terribly exhausted sigh, genuinely grateful for the first break that he was able to catch in days. His mind, however, wouldn't or couldn't stop this merry-go-round whirl, wouldn't permit him to reach a cognitive end point. He tried, continuing to fight for meaning, perspective, and the uncompromising

clarity of focus as he cleared out the pile in the bathtub onto the tile
floor and turned on the shower. He made do for soap with the goopy remnants of a shampoo bottle.

His appointment was for 10:30. By 10:10 he was seated in the small waiting room outside Sanford Tuttle's private office, looking up at the framed
cover of a three-year-old *Washingtonian* magazine—the year that Tuttle
had been inducted into the Washingtonian Business Hall of Fame.
"Powerhouse IT for the 21st Century" was the bold proclamation headline
under Tuttle's photograph. He was smiling a natural smile, arms crossed,
leaning into the camera with a jaunty stance, very evidently posed. Behind him, only partially obscured, was the brushed-silver logo GT3 on a
blue wall flecked with silver—the same receptionist's station that Rick
had walked past forty-five seconds ago, at the exact center of a stunning
office campus in Chantilly, a part of ex-urban Virginia not far from Dulles
Airport west of the District of Columbia.

Tuttle was a quiet legend in Washington, northern Virginia, and the
entire mid-Atlantic region. Wall Street and Silicon Valley knew him
well, too; he maintained offices on Park Avenue and in San Jose. GT3
was only his latest business incarnation. ("It's like the 'S' in Harry S. Truman," he told the *Washingtonian* writer about the then-new company.
"It doesn't stand for anything.") Since the mid-eighties, Sanford Tuttle
had been the most successful serial technology entrepreneur outside of
California—and maybe in California, too. Each success seemed to build
on its predecessor. All of them had been in federal contracting for information technology. "Duke of the Beltway Bandits" announced another
magazine cover adjacent the *Washingtonian*. Rick took note of the mast-
head: *FedTech*. A casualty of the dot-com bust, the magazine had chron-
icled the rise of the industry before going under a year after 9/11, two
years after its Sanford Tuttle cover. "Integration, Internet, and Federal
Information Technology" read the subtitle.

There is one particularly honorable avenue to wealth in Washington:
federal contracting. The formula had not changed much over the quarter century since Tuttle practically invented it. "Our method," he liked

to say, "is totally open-source." It always began with the foundation of a new company with a minimum of investment capital and eager, future-incentivized young professionals. Next came the federal contracts, as the government's insatiable appetite for outsourced information technology services spread far and wide. Then recapitalization, more investment, and an expanding technical staff to handle the work. A few acquisitions of smaller firms are added until critical mass is achieved, followed by a rapid sale to one of the federal government's preferred "IT solutions providers," the multibillion-dollar behemoths that seemed constantly to be in the process of transitioning from defense contracting to a network-based service economy. The whole process was largely immune to recessions, even the Great Wallow. After a decent hibernation, the beneficiaries of the acquisition would simply do it all again, each corporate reincarnation bigger and stronger, more refined and more adaptable than the last.

No practitioner was better at it than Sanford Tuttle.

There were times during his more-frequent moments of deep self-doubt when Rick Yeager wondered why Tuttle would even bother with continuing their friendship. He consistently concluded that the continued existence of their connection said more about Tuttle than it did about him.

Rick's first job out of college had been for a start-up that Sanford Tuttle was backing and running, a story that could be told by dozens or maybe hundreds of folks in the business. Tuttle had already pocketed the first two fortunes and was working on his third. At the age of twenty-two, Rick was hired as "badge number seven"—the seventh employee—of QUATECH Federal Systems. "Qua, as in quality, *sine qua non*, and the Quakers of the University of Pennsylvania," Tuttle explained to him during the job interview over a folding table with two laptop computers. The man loved to play with names. Rick stayed for two years and nine months at QUATECH. He was the number two and the spreadsheet wizard in the finance department (a department of two). He left for another tech start-up with Tuttle's generous thanks and reluctant approval—this time, he would be the lead financial manager and earn a major stake when that firm would be sold. But Rick's new company promptly folded. The reasons were its desperate lack of funding, its corresponding lack of any federal IT contracts, and the rampant narcissism and arrogance of its CEO, whose off-putting manners certainly drove away every single investor in the heady days that *FedTech* magazine called "our best only getting better."

Sanford Tuttle's QUATECH eventually sold at a multiple of twenty-four times its earnings in its initial public offering. To this day Rick was afraid actually to calculate what his small, cavalierly abandoned QUATECH stake would have been if he had stayed. A few million? It didn't matter. There was a rule of business that Rick Yeager frequently shared with his investor clients in later years: You cannot count as a loss something that you never had in the first place.

The tech company that he did ride ended up yoking him to a little more than three thousand dollars in credit card debt, the sum total of his unreimbursed expenses. The founder added "Richard M. Yeager, as an Individual" to the list of trade account payable creditors in the bankruptcy filing. He never saw a nickel.

That was the time during which his true friendship with Sanford Tuttle began. Rick's inner hope was for Tuttle to take him back into QUATECH or the company he started after that. He did not make that offer, but he did offer advice and generous laudatory introductions. They were more than enough to get Rick a solid foothold in a new network, not of the electronic kind.

Tuttle became his wedge into the quiet, private cadre of banks and financial service providers that supported the federal information technology industry, just as the commercial Internet began to take root again following the dot-com meltdown. This was a lucrative, symbiotic relationship from the wellspring of lubricating capital that kept Tuttle's serial entrepreneurship going.

Once RMY Personal Financial Inc. came into being, Rick did ask Sanford Tuttle if he could manage his personal account. Tuttle declined, but it was a good talk and not too hard a turndown. That conversation recently gave Rick some decent hope that once he was fully established at Carneccio & Dice—part of the Washington web-ring of Internet and information technology financiers—he would be able to ask Tuttle again with better results.

"Another extraordinary opportunity," Rick Yeager said aloud—this time making a mental note that he had to stop this habit of talking to himself. He reached inside his suit jacket and tapped with his fingers the white unmarked envelope containing four tri-folded pieces of paper. From the moment that Lauren Barr handed it to him, Hannah Weiss Geller's last will and testament had never been out of his reach.

"Let me guess," Rick offered with a slightly nervous smile, "this time it's Homeland Security." Sanford Tuttle was in a wingback chair perpendicular to the couch on which Rick was seated. The office, with windows on three sides, overlooked a placid man-made lake and an expanse of green grass, ornamentals, and old-growth trees that would have been magnificent on a championship golf course.

Tuttle was great with eye contact. He looked right at Rick. "Not even close. That IT market is too dissipated. The federal contracts are too small, too demanding, and too short-term to make the exit play worthwhile."

"Defense and Intelligence?"

"You know I never liked them. They're all security clearance divas. In this economy it's nothing but severe cutbacks. Never expand into a declining sector." Tuttle was beaming and enjoying the game.

"Cross-agency systems integration, then. You went back to your roots."

"Now you're getting close. Our business plan for the next fiscal year projects cross-agency work to become about fifteen percent of new sole-source business and a little less than that percentage in bid responses."

"You got me. I can't figure out what else there is."

"Neither can most of our competition. GT3's client is now the Treasury Department. Not Treasury *per se*, but a neat public-private venture that's solving a lot of Treasury's problems. And we're solving *their* problems. The information technology market in finance is expanding explosively. Government is touching practically every area of business. Our client—that's right, just one—can't buy enough of GT3 services for one simple reason: we're the only place that specializes in their exact needs. Rick, today commerce is all about the government and banks—how they communicate, how they share data, and how they manage oversight in real time. This is a frontier that is as wide open as the broadband spectrum market used to be, and our business is downright wonderful. All of it is sole-source. We don't even have to bid."

"I'm envious, Sandy."

"You don't want to be envious. You want new opportunities."

"A week ago I would have agreed with you." Rick struck a wan smile.

Tuttle leaned closer to him, with the effect of making the eye contact seem even more intense and enduring. "I'm glad you came out here. I heard all about what happened to you at Carneccio & Dice. This advice is going to sound a bit counterintuitive at the moment, but in the long run, your standing is only going to be enhanced by that unfortunate series of events. Right now you feel like you took a major hit, and you're going to spend the next couple of years banging out the dents in your reputation. Maybe you will. But Yeager, you walked away from it. You're the only one still standing. You come off looking like one of two possible alternatives. Both of them are positively mythic in Washington. You got shot at completely without effect. That makes you bulletproof. Or you were indeed at the edges of whatever Lois Carneccio was attempting and you got away with it. That makes you powerful."

"Neither perception is exactly the truth."

"Doesn't matter. You are annealed and hardened by this one, my friend." In the early years at QUATECH, Sanford Tuttle favored steel metaphors. Rick found this odd for an info-tech entrepreneur. "There are people who think that reputation is like a bank account: once you begin to use it, it gets depleted and it's difficult to replenish. That's a completely wrongheaded perspective. Thinking like that will keep you from taking new risks. Instead, reputation is more like armor plating. If it gets banged up, repair it. Restore it. Make it tougher and stronger. There's your opportunity."

"I appreciate your confidence."

"I'm not wrong very often. I know that I have this one right. It's only a matter of perspective."

"Thank you for saying that. Perspective is what brought me here."

"You said that when you called me this morning."

Rick began his narrative. Sanford Tuttle listened intently. Twice he pulled a small leather card holder out of his jacket pocket and scribbled notes—the first time when Rick was explaining his offer and the terms of the deal from Carneccio & Dice, the second time when he talked about the arrival of Lauren Barr at his old office and how he heard the news of Hannah Geller's death.

"So help me understand," Tuttle asked at the conclusion of the story, "why would she make you her executor and beneficiary?"

"Not a clue. That's exactly what I am trying to figure out."

"And with the will—"

"Is a numerical list." Rick reached into his own jacket and withdrew the envelope. He took out the folded document and separated the page of lined tablet paper, handing it to Tuttle, who studied it without any visible reaction.

"You were thinking some kind of bank accounts."

"That was my first idea."

"They are not that. At least not any that I've ever been familiar with. They don't match up with the IBAN system. We're the only contractor using Fedwire, so I can at least recognize the system of domestic bank accounts, and it's definitely not that either. However, I'm no expert. Do you want me to hang on to a copy of this and ask somebody here who is?"

It was not an unexpected question. "Would you?" Rick responded.

"If your list turns out to have any kind of significant value," Sanford Tuttle said, "then you can finance my next company." It was dry humor and Rick knew it was well-meant. Tuttle reached for the phone, punched a few numbers, and asked his executive assistant to step in. When she arrived, he asked her to make two copies of the tablet paper then stood at the window wordlessly watching the green space until she returned.

"Here," he said, handing the original and a copy to Rick. "I'll work on your numbers. You should speak to Ms. Barr again. There's a reason you got this estate. You'll never know it until you find out more about your late client. I don't know any other way than to ask."

"Neither do I."

"Congratulations. You now have a way forward."

For the first time in four days, Rick Yeager felt the slightest slackening in his companions, the twin toxins of fear and uncertainty.

Sanford Tuttle leaned over his desk, studied the photocopy, looked once more for a pattern in the numbers, and found none. He straightened and paced, exactly once down-and-back, the length of his office. He picked up the phone and again punched the number for his assistant.

"I know that this is an unusual request—yes, they're all unusual. At that display next to your desk, do we have the tombstone for my QUATECH IPO? It says 'initial public offering' right in the text across the top." Gallows humor from the investment bankers, a "tombstone" was the announcement of a deal's closing, including all of the public details, a Lucite block with the printed announcement embedded. The writing on them looked like grave markers, and when a bunch of them were lined up, as in the display outside Tuttle's office, they did look like a little cemetery. "Good. Can you bring it here to me, please?"

When it arrived, he studied the chunk of Lucite. That was his fourth initial public offering, a particularly good one coming at a peak moment in the business cycle. The number announced was a boldfaced $245,000,000, the amount of capital that the QUATECH offering raised from investors. That much he easily remembered. What he wanted to confirm before his next phone call was the lead market maker, the broker-dealer who first sold QUATECH's stock. He was right in his recollection.

Compton Sizemore.

Tuttle looked up the number on his computer screen and punched it in himself, waiting and listening to the rings, thinking as the call rolled to voice mail.

"Warren, good morning, it's Sanford Tuttle in Virginia."

CHAPTER 10

Jenny Lau occupied the elegant redoubtable office space immediately outside the door of Warren Hunter's suite in Compton Sizemore's global investment banking center. The designer of her workstation had produced it to be open and free-flowing, with southern sun and a good though limited view of lower Manhattan to her right side. Visitors actually reached Warren's office door before passing Jenny's desk, resulting in a slightly intimidating effect: the architectural layout essentially dared people to walk in before checking with her. No one ever did, including Warren Hunter, who now stood at the desk of his assistant in khaki chinos and a stylishly wrinkled black polo shirt bearing an orange Princeton "P."

"You don't golf," she scolded gently, "and I know you are not visiting any clients who would require you to dress like everyone used to in the dot-com bubble. Then you ask me to clear the calendar at four and get you a car but not a driver. Are you trying to be unsettling? You really can't hold out on me like this."

"Sure I can." There was the smile, the confidence, the crystalline self-possessed charm. Warren was not giving away anything.

Shrugging, knowing better than to press the issue, Jenny handed him a Compton Sizemore form to sign bearing the boldface title "Livery Ticket" across the top. "The car should be already there waiting for you at the curb on Fifty-fourth. They said to call ahead at least forty-five minutes prior to the pickup at your apartment tonight. Here's your car tag. And this card has the telephone numbers you'll need."

In ten minutes Warren Hunter was behind the wheel of a dark blue

Ford Explorer driving uptown on Third Avenue. The summer traffic was particularly light. Warren, who unquestionably enjoyed driving, caught the first seven lights, counting each one, his competitive soul dominant even when he was alone. When he stopped somewhere in the east Sixties, still getting the feel of the vehicle, he tried to recall the last time he had driven a car.

He ended up remembering the last time and the first.

In the empty middle of the parking lot at their high school near Trenton—from which Rick had already escaped and where Warren was still a student—Rick glided the four-year-old Nissan to a stop, flopped the gearshift into neutral, and set the parking brake. They were alone and unobserved on a cloudy Sunday afternoon. He unbuckled his seat belt and opened the door, nodding sideways with a grin for his younger brother to do the same on his side. Warren eagerly complied. They switched sides, crossing behind the car and settling into each other's seat.

"Pop would want to be teaching you this, Warren, just like he did for me," Rick said. He meant it as a kindness.

His brother noticed the way he pronounced his name, monosyllabically: *Warrn*, with the slightest tint of genteel Southern accent. Rick was going on three years in Lexington, Virginia, after a childhood during which he almost never left central New Jersey. Warren, already supremely perceptive at the age of seventeen years and three days, wondered if that change in diction was a mindful affectation or whether the Southern-prep-fraternity environment he was living at Washington and Lee was changing his brother unconsciously. Warren was oddly troubled by that thought, at a time when he was busy playing the role of spectacularly troubled young man—and he knew it.

"Do you know when he's going to come home this time?" Warren asked.

"No. No way to tell. Aunt Elli and Uncle Dan have been up to see him. They said that he was really in a bad way."

"What the fuck does that mean—bad way?" Warren buckled his seat belt and moved the seat back a notch. He was already taller than his older brother.

"You don't have to fucking swear at me," Rick said, again with kindness and predicting wrongly that his own profanity would diffuse some of his kid brother's anger. To Warren's ear, "swear" came out *swaar*.

"You even think that this shit is a real illness?"

"It's real. *Warrn*, it doesn't get any more real than it is for him."

"I am just so fucking sick of going back and forth between the two of them. Now he's gone away again for who knows how long."

"As his family we ought to be glad that it's not permanent."

"Yeah. I am *so* incredibly glad for *that*. And how do you know that, anyway?" Warren meant the question-as-scorn to be a challenge. He could tell how much it hurt his brother and felt, for an instant, the lightest touch of guilt. He just wished that Rick could get as pissed off as he was about the situation.

"I don't know, Warren. No one does." This time Rick articulated every syllable.

"Health issues" was their euphemism for their father's deep depression, dysthymia, and the advancing stresses, including a broad variety of other mental illnesses that periodically caused these hospitalizations. The health issues were the grace notes of their childhood—a growing-up that was by turns happy then maintaining, followed by joyless, load-bearing, demanding. As younger boys, Ricky (who became Rick on the day he entered the sixth grade) and Warren each tried in his own way to be a good son.

The two good sons always called him Pop. He was born in Trenton in 1924, a first child, only son of German immigrant parents. His mother and father were once desperate refugees. They sought the American promise and economic stability during the hyperinflation of the *Weimarer Republik*. The move to America was an enormous leap of faith. Pop's mother was nineteen and pregnant at the moment of her arrival in *die Vereinigten Staaten*, both hands gripping a young husband's sturdy arm on the unsteady walk down the gangway to the Port of Elizabeth. Lotte, diminutive for Karlotte (a Christian name in her family at least since the Reformation) spoke no English. Wilhelm Jäger—immediately "Will Yeager" upon reaching the American shore—knew some rudiments of the language. He had left *Universität* after only one year of study during the Weimar depression. They determined to maintain their lives in two worlds, one old and one new. They always spoke German in the household. *Nur Deutsch, immer Deutsch.* Their pledge was absolute to each other: culture and history would prevail in *die Verwandtschaftskreis*, in family relations. Their children, the boy and then much too rapidly thereafter the girl, were named for the Protestant hero of the Thirty Years War, a Swede and his royal German wife. This was Will's reach back to family legacy in Breitenfeld *nahe* Leipzig, where he was born. He could never have predicted how extraordinarily unfortunate his selection of the boy's name would become.

In a Lutheran church using the German liturgy he was christened Gustav Adolf Yeager. He was thereafter called only by his middle name, Adolf.

His sister, Maria Eleanora, was likewise Elli. Lotte saw to it that their German was perfect, and that they were perfect and simply happy American children. Will found excellent employment in manufacturing. He prospered in the pride of steady work, a life of the mind and reason in two languages, and an American family. Where they lived in New Jersey was a superb place to be from in the 1920s, and less agreeably, later in the Great Depression. This was nothing, Will Yeager would opine, compared to Germany.

In January 1942, Pop, Adolf Yeager—now "Dutch" to everyone outside his family—had completed one semester of mathematics and engineering at Rutgers. Exactly like Will and to his father's vocal regret, that would be the extent of Dutch's college education. It was, however, more than enough to qualify him for entry into flight school in the United States Army Air Forces.

He gained the rank of first lieutenant and had a genuinely—but, he would always humbly insist, not uniquely—distinguished tour in a B-24 squadron of the Eighth Air Force based in eastern England. In the service a cheerful Dutch Yeager (who even had a sense of humor about his Christian name) was a man quite in demand beyond his own flight crew.

In the nose cone of a B-24 *Liberator* he truly found his center, proving to be a most precise and gifted navigator.

"Ease out on the clutch. No, not like that. Easy—easier. It's a coordinated movement. Try swapping your feet back and forth like that. Start out slowly until the clutch grabs, then when you find the right coordination you can speed up your movements. There. You're getting it." Rick's patience had the effect of only adding more fuel to Warren's frustration.

"Is that the way Pop taught you?"

"Not exactly. Pop yelled a lot."

"Dutch is a dick," Warren declared, laughing meanly at his own creative alliteration—the kind of laugh you only hear from a seventeen-year-old boy.

"He's our father, and I think that means we have to love him. And yeah, I admit he can be a dick, but that's only when his health issues fire up again. You know it's not all of the time."

"Fuckin' may as well be."

"Again with your swearing, Warren. What is it, you think it makes you sound more mature? It doesn't. It works the other way, brother. You come across as more adolescent, and I know you don't want that."

"Since when does anybody in this whole fucking family care what I want?" Warren observed the sadness that washed over his brother, because Rick knew that he meant it. That was the effect Warren had been seeking. Now he was in control.

Dutch's diagnosis, rendered at an army hospital on Long Island in December 1945, was "psychoneurotic disorder and severe stress reaction incident to combat fatigue." Gustav Adolf Yeager, 1/Lt USAAF, was mustered out of the service on Christmas Eve with a disability discharge. He spent New Year's Eve 1946 quietly reading at the Veterans Administration

Hospital in East Orange, New Jersey. And he built back. That was the term of art that his psychiatrist employed. Dutch was grateful for the fact that he was being treated by a veteran. The doctor walked with just the slightest limp from a rifle shot to his right leg that he took at Chateau-Thierry in June 1918.

"You have a wound," the psychiatrist explained patiently. "It's a fairly serious one. It is not, however, in any way unrecoverable or appreciably different from the shot I took as a Marine. So you have scars. We all do. The important thing is, you survived. You are already past the hard part. Now bury it deep and build back."

Dutch found himself reassured by the psychiatrist even though the doctor and the medics assisting him at the VA could not seem to understand why he was so rattled by the basic notion of receiving psychiatric care.

There was a day—spring was breaking with bright lateral sunshine—when his doctor smoothly demanded that Dutch assess and provide a catalog of his comforts.

"I am comforted by you," he responded quietly, lighting a cigarette.

"This is called transference," the doctor answered. "Why do you feel comforted by me?"

"Because you are damaged."

"I've told you before, we all are. I'm well repaired. You will be, too. Is there anything else?"

"You don't seem like you're pushing me."

"No one should. You're safe. The war is over."

"I am not sure that my war is over. You keep 'affirming' me, and I suppose that's supposed to be comforting, too. It is. Even when I do not believe you for a moment."

"Don't you think that you will come to that belief?" the doctor asked, jotting a note.

"No. I never will."

"Don't be so sure. You're very young. You heal. Things will change a lot over the course of your lifetime."

"*You* shouldn't be so sure. Things already have changed a lot for me. You, too."

"What do you mean by that?"

"You're Jewish." The doctor's name was Olkiewicz.

"No. Roman Catholic."

"I'm very sorry."

"You have no need to apologize. You made an assumption based on my name. It's what we call an inductive generalization, and it's quite normal. People do that." The doctor smiled quite parentally. "Could I ask you why you thought that my religion was important?"

"No, you can't."

"We'll come back to that."

"No, we won't."

The doctor, compassionate, liberal, and knowledgeably progressive in his practice of medicine, nodded and made another note—something to the effect of *German sensibilities about race* and repeated the advice that he assured Dutch would sustain him.

"Bury it deep. Build back."

That was, of course, terrible advice.

He was released from the East Orange VA Hospital in June of 1946 to begin burying and building back in Trenton. There followed more than a decade with a rapid succession of various employments. None lasted longer than eighteen months. He began as an hourly wage machinist at the factory where Will Yeager still worked, but from which his immigrant father would soon retire. Then a painter, a mechanical draftsman, salesman in a men's clothing store, grounds supervisor at the municipal golf course, production engineer at an aspirin factory—the last position coming almost solely as a consequence of his having held an officer's commission in the war. Sometime in the late fifties (he was always memory-vague), he took the New Jersey state civil service examination. He tested extremely well, and with the marginal benefit of his veteran's preference, became an examiner in the enforcement division of the Division of Taxation, Department of the Treasury.

There he found his place in the world.

The hospitalizations in East Orange became less frequent. Bury it deep. Build back.

Of course there were affairs, and one spectacularly failed engagement that he would never speak about once it ended. He was well past forty by the time he married. Gloria, his only wife, was more than twenty years younger, although always most circumspect about her exact age. A teacher of elementary school children, she was a radiant woman of understated beauty, an intellectual curiosity that exceeded her formal education, and a passion for very few things other than a certain general brand of politics: activist, left, confrontational. Orphaned in an automobile accident that took her parents while she attended state teacher's college in Pennsylvania, she was widowed in the same manner before her twenty-third birthday. The improbability of this story in her young life intrigued Dutch. Gloria was likewise fascinated by him. Their mutual love—they both knew it was real—and their shared loneliness seemed to exist in roughly equal proportions.

This proved a stubbornly difficult foundation for their marriage.

Dutch found himself incapable of explaining the raging violence within that he experienced when each of his sons was born. The feeling was anger, and yet it was not. *Der Zornglühen des Innenlebens* he characterized it in his own way, a concept better expressed in German than in English: a glowing rage of the soul.

"Why would you be sad like this?" his sister, Elli, would ask. "A wife, two young and healthy boys, good work—*Adolfi, was jetzt?*"

Dutch could never formulate an answer.

The marriage lasted nine years. It ended during the summer after Will and then Lotte died gently—he of congestive heart failure, she of a broken heart, both in their sleep. Dutch's two boys, both smart and creative, were thereafter shared between their parents' households from early age, in a family life sloppily divided.

Rick walked his mother's difficult path. He was the pleaser, always starting over, ever adrift but quietly coping.

Younger Warren favored his father, although he would be loath ever to admit this inclination, especially upon turning seventeen. He was tough, full of wrath, careful never to show the world that he was barely holding together.

*   *   *

"That's a little fast . . . *more* than a little fast!" Rick Yeager found himself almost shouting at his younger brother, who had accelerated to almost fifty miles an hour in the high school parking lot. Warren grinned widely as he jammed hard on the brake, throwing them both against the shoulder straps of their seat belts and locking four tires into a skid.

"Upshifting. Did you see how smooth I did it that time?"

"Congratulations. You now know just enough to be dangerous."

"I *live* for fucking danger." Warren was clearly enjoying himself.

"Man, you have to go easy on the danger, at least in cars," Rick said. Warren recognized it as a plea. "The one thing that you cannot do is off yourself in a car wreck. That would kill Mom."

"Yeah, I get that," Warren replied as he shifted into reverse for a K-turn to point the car back in the other direction. "Ironic, isn't it? Her worrying about me wrecking a car. With all that shit she still puts up with from Pop. Health issues, my aching ass."

Rick thought that his brother's contempt was both artificial and most uncalled-for, but he let it pass.

"You really shouldn't have done that, you know."

"Then she shouldn't have told me what it is that fucking sets him off. It's partly her fault. Shit, I didn't think it would fucking send him to the VA hospital again for goddamn Christ's sake."

"You aren't going to quit this swearing, are you?"

"You fuckin'-A got that right, brother."

"Well, it's quite big of you to recognize how this time it's at least partly your fault."

"Ooooooh. More irony."

"Sarcasm, Warren. That was sarcasm."

"Fuck you. Double fuck you with your own fucking pencil dick." Warren jammed the gearshift into first, jumped the clutch out too fast, and promptly stalled the car in a two-stage bucking jerk.

Rick watched as his brother screwed up his face hard, eyes jammed tight, and let out three rough sobs before he broke down completely and cried. He tentatively put his left hand on Warren's shoulder fully expecting his brother to pull away. Instead, Warren leaned into Rick, pulled close into his torso, and sobbed—long, deep, and with the blameworthy pain of a soul bearing much more guilt than he could possibly admit to anyone else.

Dutch's torment often turned brutal. He was prone to smashing objects large and small, kitchenware, furniture, glass, appliances, and especially gypsum wallboard walls. He never struck his wife or his boys. He never even threatened to do so. This tension made the episodes as weird as they were scary in the boys' childhood. Weeks or months of calm and likeable decency were followed by moments or days of the most expressive rage, *die Tobensüchtig*. Sometimes he would regain control slowly, in staged and measured advances. In other rages he returned to calm instantaneously.

Ricky—Rick—found it all most fearsome, always off the mark, unpatterned, and unpredictable.

Warren was fascinated by his father's violent moods. When Pop was at his center and okay, which was most of the time, he wondered exactly what provoked his father.

They were very different sons.

Rick, with his mother's obliging encouragement, found peace in academic successes, but not without much structure and study. Warren achieved incredible grades with stunning ease, but his academic life was always a trial—one inflicted upon his teachers. A patient struggle for Rick, effortless A's without a moment of study for Warren. Rick a conformer, Warren a rebel. Rick a citizen, Warren a delinquent. Rick an Eagle Scout, Warren a not-infrequent visitor to the juvenile court of Mercer County, New Jersey.

Warren tutored at the output of Dutch's rage and learned it well.

The marital split may have been exaggerated by the difference in age between Dutch and Gloria, but all four of them, parents and sons, knew that it was Dutch's behavior and the health issues that broke them up. The boys did not always live together as they adjusted to living between two households. Gloria liked to describe her older son as contemplative and caring, her younger son as "rambunctious," an archaic word that Warren hated. He grew only more aggravated whenever he heard it.

"How was it," the already hyper-perceptive Warren asked his mother, "that you just broke apart your marriage like that with no fights, no girlfriend for Pop or boyfriend for you, no money problems? Especially when you were the only one who knew how to deal with his trouble?"

"We hit the expiration point," she rationalized, feeling for the right words. "He simply used up all of the love and tolerance that I had in me."

Gloria once dutifully attempted to instill an empathetic spirit in Warren—a quality that came naturally to her older boy. This excursion proved to be a very bad prospect.

It changed her son forever.

"Pop has some very distinctive triggers," she explained to Warren. "Things he can't talk about, places he just won't go."

"What places?"

"Not geographical places," she explained. "Places inside himself. There are elements of the war that are yet within him."

"And you know what to say to send him there?" Warren was curious, engaged, which his mother took as a good indicator.

"Not exactly. For Pop it's more often loud sounds and certain images from the war. This is difficult, both for him to experience and for me to talk about, son. He does not know completely or exactly what will cause his health issues to resurface. We do know that his sense of smell is the worst trigger. He told me that this is because he once smelled burning human flesh, but he refuses to say anything else. I only know about it because I saw him screaming and vomiting when he smelled burning feathers. We were still married and he was doing a field audit for the state at a poultry processor near Camden. I got a call and had to go get him. He was still deeply affected an hour later when I arrived. Smell provides the most powerful ignition of our memories, son. Especially your father's. His doctors told me that. You really must be aware of this and attempt to be more tolerant of your father's reactions. None of us knows how we might react if we had seen or known the same deadly horrors that he had to experience. Be understanding, Warren. Please."

"Fuckin' sucks to be him."

"Watch your mouth, Warren. Please."

Two afternoons later, alone after school in his father's town house, Warren partially, carefully, disassembled a feather pillow with a pair of scissors. When Dutch came home—not a word passing between father and son—he ignited the feathers inside a deep pot placed on the kitchen stove. The smoke was dense and putrid, the reaction from Pop's room more violently immediate than he could have imagined.

Dutch's hospitalization meant that he would renege on his promise to teach Warren how to drive.

"I didn't want to fuck him up, I really, really didn't," Warren wailed. Rick knew how very uncharacteristic this display was for his brother. The crying, Warren out of control, scared him with the same sensation of panic that he normally associated with Pop. For the immediate moment he maintained his composure.

"I know. Mom does, too."

"I . . . just . . . wanted to see . . . what would happen."

"You did." Rick instantly knew that this was the wrong thing to say, as his brother devolved into rapid shallow breathing and smaller sobs. He tried again. "You had no way of knowing what it could cause. Pop has a lot going on that only exists in his head and nowhere else. You are not responsible for that. No one is, Warren."

"I need to quit being such a fucking dick." Warren, wrung out, was now beginning to regain a semblance of self-possession, face red and eyes still wet.

"I thought you said Dutch was the dick."

"I'm worse. And I gotta fuckin' change."

If there can be a *Schwerpunkt* for a young man's fury, this was Warren's: a laden moment. Rage channeled into focal discipline. Thereafter he prospered in school and in the next year achieved the impossible in New Jersey, becoming a local student early admitted to Princeton with a full scholarship. It was a further contrast to his brother's collegiate flight to the gentility of the Shenandoah Valley.

Late in the summer before he took the twelve-mile drive on Route 1 to settle into his freshman year at Princeton's Holder Hall, Warren returned to the Mercer County Court. He acted as his own lawyer, presenting the judge with a petition to alter his surname. "Pop," he spoke calmly, explaining, in a conversation he had long considered, "your pop did the same thing. Jäger"—he overemphasized the long *a* as his grandfather would pronounce it in German—"became Yeager. It's the same thing as Hunter in a different language. I'm only finishing what Grandpop started—no more German, just American English. That's all I'm trying to accomplish."

He spoke not a word about his enduring shame and deeply conflicted worry. He was sure that his love and tolerance were only growing for the old man.

Dutch had smiled approvingly, proud of both his sons, the Yeager and the Hunter.

Warren Hunter loved to drive. He now recognized just how much of an infrequent joy it was, and how much he missed it while living in Manhattan. Crossing the George Washington Bridge eastbound into New Jersey, he came to both this realization and a resolution. He would definitely spend more time behind the wheel. Maybe he would buy a car again.

The simple act of driving is the most culturally American of tasks, easily learned by any teenager, even the mean and angry young man in the parking lot of his high school on a long-past but unforgotten Sunday afternoon. That guy wasn't around anymore. For Warren, then or now, seizing the wheel meant that he was required to increase his attention and concentration. It was like doing a deal. Deliberate focus kept you very sharp. He was nothing like the drivers in the Jersey suburbs who did this every day so casually and reflexively. He was unable to be relaxed about it, particularly when he drove only a few times a year.

Paying attention this afternoon, however, was inordinately rough, nearly impossible.

In his wide universe of expectations about Pop, there was one call he never thought he would get from the elder-care facility in Fair Lawn. He was prepared for a greater onslaught of the Alzheimer's dementia and memory loss, with its slow-rush erosion of being and spirit. He was certainly prepared for a sudden return to the violence and burning visions of his father's war. He thought that he was prepared to hear that Pop had died.

But he was entirely unprepared to be told that his father had now forgotten how to speak the English language and, in sparse moments of slightest lucidity, was able to communicate only in word-burst remnants of German. The other language of his earliest youth.

CHAPTER 11

Horvath grunted. He sat on the bench alone staring at the low-slung building across the old divided road that ribboned the public park in Fair Lawn. The design of the structure was pleasing to him. For a moment he felt a twinge of the old socialist jealousy. While most of his life had been spent here in America, his first observations still compared the architectural prosperity of this country with what he left behind in Hungary. The comparison was never with regrets, however. He certainly *would* regret being one of the old men in the home. For that much he was thankful. This got him thinking: thankful to whom?

He was an old-Europe atheist, of course. No respectable man growing up in his generation and profession could be otherwise. His wife had been a believer and both of his sons were now churchgoers. Horvath had even been at the baptisms of his grandchildren, ceremonies that he found most pleasant and agreeable. So why, at this late age in his life, was he wondering about these things, this concept of a God? Twice before he briefly allowed for the possibility of a deity. The first time was when he became an American, sent to work here clandestinely by the service, with near-unbelievable independence and free reign. The original assignment provided him with degrees of freedom that rewarded his extraordinary loyalty and his even more extraordinary operational competence. The second time was when communism collapsed in Hungary. Good riddance, he had remarked at the time to his wife. He was particularly grateful then because the entire system in its deconstruction completely forgot about his existence—confirmed consistently over the next twenty years, even when all of the old state secrets were published on the Internet.

Horvath, you are a shitty communist, his top-control at the Hungarian embassy stated to him on many occasions. The last Horvath knew, the man was part owner of the Five Guys burger franchises in Fairfax. A good move. Horvath heard he was going to retire with reasonably decent American wealth even in the middle of this global economic mess.

It was nothing like the wealth that Horvath—more correctly his sons—would share.

So this would make the third time that Horvath was grateful again, maybe grateful to God. He wondered if intellectually allowing for the prospect of a God made him a shitty atheist. Perhaps advanced age and the reality of his own mortality were corrupting the absence of deity. Death was something that he accepted as a fact of the natural world. This was the kind of intellectual dialectic that he used to enjoy in his youth but for which he had no time now. He needed to concentrate. He had a job to do. Now there would be no more observation, no more fatigue, no more boredom of watching and waiting.

And there would be no more screwing up his back like that roll on the Potomac slope he took when he drove the old lady off the cliff.

The nice detail that he carried this afternoon was a cane, all the better not to be noticed once inside the home. He caught himself. This was an elder-care facility, a retirement community, an assisted-living environment. Call it anything but an old folks' home. He was now so American that even in his private thoughts he was politically correct. Horvath was very used to this psychodynamic. It was the first thing that the service taught you. When you are in role, even your thoughts must be in role, in the mission. He pulled the cane across his lap and checked its head, finely carved in the form of a diving duck native to the upland swamps near Lake Balaton. It was screwed on tight. He stood up from the park bench and planted the cane, watching as the blue Ford Explorer with New York license plates pulled into the circular driveway. Horvath observed that the driver seemed hurried and somewhat exasperated as he stepped out and slammed the vehicle door. Horvath watched him enter the facility's front entrance. He began to cross the road, remembering of course to lean into the cane properly as he walked.

*   *   *

"Pop? Pop, it's me, Warren. I wanted to see you this afternoon—I drove out from the City. How have you been?" Warren sat down in a chair next to his father, grinned, and hoped that if the words were not immediately getting through, Dutch could see his facial expression. He also hoped the full extent of his concern would not be evident. Dutch sat silent and expressionless, eyes locked on his son.

Warren thought that he detected a brief smile, but he wasn't exactly sure. "I love you, Pop. I love you and I will always take care of you."

Warum vergesse ich? Vergesse . . . forget. For. Getting. Why?

"Ich Vergesse," said Dutch.

"I know, Pop. It's difficult to remember. I'm Warren. You don't have to try so hard. I'll help you."

Fin. Finden. Wo finden wir . . . wo finden wir ihn? Find him.

"Wir finden." Dutch looked quite strained and confused.

"Do you need me to help you find something? How can I help you, Pop?

Anhalten. Stop. Lassen sie ihn nicht das tun. Don't let him do that! Dieser Krieg ist jetzt zu ende. This war is now . . . end. My son, mein Sohn, der jüngere. Die Wörter running zusammen together, Englisch und Deutsch Sprachen. Warum?

"Warum?"

"Why what, Pop?"

"Warum tat, schiessen Sie?" Dutch spoke very clearly now.

"Pop, I don't understand."

"Pop, Ich verstehe nicht," Dutch said.

"Do you recognize me, Pop? I'm Warren."

"Kennst du mich, Pop? Ich bin Warren." Dutch pronounced his name with the hard "V" of German, not the soft "W" of English.

"You're translating, Pop."

"Übersetzen."

Can you make me understand him? The voice, die Stimme, vor langer Zeit, long time ago. Wo? Where? Hier, immer hier, always right here. The shots, Schüsse. Wo ist Stauber? Dieser.

"It's okay, Pop."

"Stauber."

Warren startled. "Stauber?"

"Ja, Stauber." Dutch grinned.

"Yes," Warren said. "Stauber."

"Warren." With the soft "W" this time.

"Yes, Pop?" He was incredibly pleased to be recognized.

"Er hat die Zahlen."

"That's right, Pop. I'm the one on Wall Street that works with the numbers."

"Doctor, it's innate to my profession. I deal with trade-offs of risk on a daily basis, and I'd like to know the ground truth. I've also done a whole lot of medical transactions as an investment banker. I'm more than capable of understanding what's going on. And I'll understand if you don't know. Really." Warren attempted not to sound plaintive in his plea to his father's attending neurologist. He knew that he was not succeeding.

"You're very much on track. We aren't completely sure what's going on with him, other than the obvious. The Alzheimer's, even in this stage, has caused some fairly significant ongoing degradation in the language centers of the brain."

"Centers, plural?"

"There is almost no neuroscience research in this area at the present time. We know some things about multiple-language processing from MRI and PET scans of people who have suffered brain damage. There's also quite a bit of new data from the traumatic brain injury patients that the military has seen come back from Iraq and Afghanistan. I know of other cases where patients who speak multiple languages and have advancing forms of dementia can't speak spontaneously in one of their languages anymore. But the evidence is anecdotal. Translating is a complex skill—it involves several areas of the brain that have to coordinate together. We do know that it's very different from just speaking one language or the other. We are pretty sure that your father does understand us when we speak in English. He simply cannot express himself verbally other than in German. I assume that was the language he grew up speaking."

"As far as I know he spoke both languages equally well, from birth."

"Hmm. That could actually be the complication here. Neurologically he's what's known as a natural multilinguist. He is experiencing the most significant confusion now, and it would be difficult for me to tell you how much of it is the Alzheimer's and how much of it is specific to the organic degradation in those areas of his brain that process the two languages. We also do not know if this unusual kind of language dysphasia is going to be temporary or permanent. It may improve and then recede. His double fluency in this case can actually become a hindrance. It is possible that his brain is conflating the two languages, but that only German, and only a small bit of German, is all he can express in speech."

"You do know that my father has a significant psychiatric history . . . ?"

"I do. And that's an entirely different complication." The doctor paused.

"What?" Warren asked.

"Gustav is a—"

"It's Dutch. Please. He's never been called by that name."

"I apologize. Dutch is a very difficult case. He is suffering—and I use the word suffering very advisedly—from some of the most advanced and long-term post-traumatic stress disorder that any of us have ever run across. PTSD, combat trauma, and the effects of elder depression are prominent within my own practice. What I need to share with you is just how horrible this affliction can become for him as the Alzheimer's progresses."

"More horrible?"

"We have experience with cases of capture trauma victims in advanced age. Their symptoms of dementia return them to the events that caused their PTSD trauma in the first place."

"What is capture trauma?" Warren had never heard the term before.

"Think of it this way. For one kind of PTSD survivor—that's our preferred term—there is always a single central event. Nine-eleven is the perfect example. Or an airplane hijacking. A terrorist bombing. A rape. The moment in time that changed everything, where a person's life narrative is disrupted forever and permanently.

"For another kind of PTSD survivor—and we are just coming to understand this now—the trauma was sustained. It was delivered to him over a long period of time. Think about Holocaust survivors, casualties of the African genocides, or political prisoners who endured years of imprisonment and torture. In that manner of trauma, the victim—another word I use very advisedly—cannot escape the causation of the trauma. The environment of his life itself continues the trauma. He's captured. He has lived the trauma continuously, for years and maybe decades, before it ends. Only then does the PTSD begin."

"But my father," Warren said, "seems to be the first kind. In the family we never knew exactly what happened to him in the war."

"That makes sense," the doctor said, nodding. "When survivors of shock trauma turn these events into an interior reckoning, even with proper therapy, they create a profoundly capturing environment within themselves. It becomes no different in its effect on the mind and body from the physically traumatic environment."

"Is that what my father's done?"

"Possibly. What we do know, and this is what you have to prepare for, is that in this kind of PTSD, and especially where a clinically significant history of depression is involved, his retreat can take him right back to the environment where the trauma occurred. Mr. Yeager, he will begin to relive it all over again. He has perhaps already begun to do this."

Warren did not bother to correct the doctor's erroneous assumption about his surname. He sighed, crossed his arms, and thought for a long moment. "Is there any good news?" he finally asked.

"Again, possibly. His core memory seems to be failing most rapidly. In instances like this, he may recall very little of his original trauma. Or it can come back to him in pieces. This kind of organic deterioration is always the most troubling thing that a family has to go through with a parent. But in Dutch's case, it is a very mixed blessing."

"I can appreciate that. Thank you." Warren felt positively drained, not a bit of emotion left. There was too much for him to process here.

"Could I ask you—do you understand him? In German?"

"Not much. I do understand him on a number of other levels, though."

Warren believed that he had lied convincingly to the doctor on both counts. He almost convinced himself.

The doctor reached out to shake his hand. "I'm sorry."

"So am I," Warren said.

This time he was telling the truth. *Die Wahrheit.*

The cane was proving to be a real pain in the ass but magnificently effective for Horvath. He literally felt a sharp pain in the ass with every other step. This was easier when he was a young man. The cane was one of the implements of tradecraft that he had brought to Washington from Hungary so many years ago, now pressed into service one more time. Horvath was not usually one for nostalgia, any more than he had use for the deistic metaphysical wanderings going on in his head. But both had their place. No one in the entire facility even gave a second look at him when he entered.

He had done his operational preparations well, professionally. This place was one of the nation's most expensive and exclusive, so he had better dress the part he was playing—and he did. He liked the beautiful new windowpane-plaid linen summer sport coat and perfectly tailored gray slacks that he wore. If he had been twenty years younger—walking in as an obvious visitor—he would, no doubt, have been stopped. Instead he followed the fundamental rule: Look like you know what you are doing, look like you belong here, and no one will ask. Carry it forward and carry it off. He had the run of the place. He was pleasant when greeted by the staff, never avoiding them, never becoming too memorable, never looking like he was steering clear of anyone. This was how one managed the perfect blending-in.

Horvath had memorized the location of every surveillance camera in the place. He had to stop himself from making his on-camera shuffles and head-nods—always down—from getting too theatrical. He was enjoying the operation. Well, he enjoyed this part of it.

He never trusted agents who actually enjoyed the part that was coming. One needed to keep his fundamental humanity intact in order to be effective. As far as Horvath was concerned, if you enjoyed the harshest task in a spy's toolbox too much, you surrendered your right to be human. He knew too many who did. Almost all of them were Russians.

When he reached the room, the old man was sitting alone. To look at him, you would never know there was anything wrong. He was sitting and smiling lightly, as if he was thinking and working on something. Horvath knew that was not the case. The man's mind was going, maybe already gone.

"*Grüss Gott*," he said. The greeting comprised the entire extent of his German vocabulary. It was what he had been told to say. Nothing. No response. He sat in the chair that was already conveniently pulled up close to the old man. If anyone looked in, it would appear that the two were just having a conversation—that the younger old man was doing a kindness. Maybe, Horvath figured, he was.

He laid the cane across his lap with the duck's head to the right side. Carefully he unscrewed the top. The service's equipment fitter in Budapest decades ago called it a Toulouse Lautrec cane. The guy snorted socialist contempt for French decadence when he said the name. In the original, he explained, the artist kept a long thin cylinder of his absinthe. This one is different. Look what it holds.

Horvath withdrew a syringe.

The first time he ever used this cane, the syringe was glass and steel. The injectable chemical was a neurotoxin developed at a laboratory somewhere in Novosibirsk Oblast, seconded to the Hungarians. Medical technology advances however, and Horvath was as well prepared now as he had been then.

Dutch Yeager watched intently as Horvath withdrew the plastic composite syringe. He was surprised, just as he had been when he placed it in the cane back in Virginia, at its size and the volume of its contents. Horvath knew what was in it. That was part of his preparation and planning. This is an extremely purified, very concentrated blood glycoprotein, he was told. It is called Von Willebrand factor, and it is used medically to induce blood clotting. The compound is perfectly naturally occurring in the body—nothing like the stuff we used in the old days. It will cause a stroke. Okay, so even this, Horvath had joked, is natural. "Going green."

Horvath removed the cover from the long needle of the syringe. He lifted it vertically, pointing it up and depressing the plunger slightly, snapping its side with a fat forefinger. Then he wondered why on earth he was worrying about a bubble, now. He reached out to take the old man's arm. This would be the only difficult part. Not in the muscle, he was cautioned. You have to find a vein. Horvath extended the old man's forearm and squeezed his bicep with a strong left hand. There. A good vein. He carefully inserted the needle.

"*Ech, ach,*" said Dutch Yeager, looking Horvath in the eyes without comprehension. But no words would come. Horvath pushed down the syringe's plunger, steadily and slowly until it emptied.

He reassembled the cane, stood, and left the old man still sitting and staring. Just as he planned, Horvath did not look back, so as to keep his fundamental humanity intact.

CHAPTER 12

The walking paths of Reston, Virginia, are famous and special. They are particularly special to the residents of Reston, who style themselves as stewards of the nation's preeminent planned community. Built beginning in the 1960s in what were once the forest and agricultural wilds of northwest Fairfax County, the "new town" was constructed with meticulous planning and a fierce local bureaucracy. In the beginning, everything was laid out. Zoning reigned with rigidity rivaling Soviet central planning. The result was stunning. Everything about Reston *was* special, parklike, and visionary. It was Rick Yeager's home. Frequently he thought this was the only place where he ever felt completely at home. While the location was admittedly inconvenient to his old office in Arlington, he was the beneficiary of an unusual commute, bailing out of the highways before the massive snarl of traffic that attended commuters going all the way into the District of Columbia. The walking paths of Reston were Rick's favorite part of the place, winding among the trees and along the golf course near his condominium.

This morning he was thudding along a forested Reston walkway, making good on his resolution to get back to jogging. He had concluded that this particular discipline was missing in his life. There was a time when he had been a dedicated runner. He even completed the Marine Corps Marathon once, half a dozen Octobers ago. Lately he had fallen severely out of the habit. At the moment his lungs, upper calves, and lower back were all harmonizing a symphony of pain to remind him of that fact. The beat was heavy and the crescendo was increasing. He knew this part. If he could sustain the run through this pain, he would hit a sweet spot, a well-worn groove. It would not be as good as when he was actually in shape. But it would get comfortable. He looked around, trying to occupy himself with something other than the pain. You couldn't beat the scenery here. Reston had suburban forestry of the first order. A run like this always helped him to shake things out in his mind.

When Warren called last night, Rick thought that he didn't sound completely like himself. He was in the car, on Route 4 headed back to the City. Rick made a weak joke. Since when did you have a car? Watch yourself, he warned his brother—in Jersey they're cracking down on anybody who doesn't use a hands-free headset. Warren had not responded, instead remaining silent on the phone for much too long. When he did speak, his voice was calm and sad.

Pop was losing it much faster than anyone had figured. You and I might have already said our good-byes. Pop is never going to be the same. This isn't even Dutch you're talking to anymore. At this point he can only speak to you in German, and that's not coherent. He can recognize you. He is deteriorating. He looks healthy, but he's not at all good.

Health issues again. Only this time it's the big one.

Rick thudded and leaned forward in the run against the spreading pain creeping tightly up his back. He made a left turn onto a wider expanse of trail that looped alongside the back nine of the Reston National Golf Course. The midday heat of northern Virginia in July—with no sign of abating this week—had not yet hit this morning. The greens were a dewy silver, wet. No golfers had advanced this far on the course this early. Rick took a shortcut across the fairway, aware that he shouldn't be doing this.

The legal case in the Carneccio & Dice arrests was now in the process of clearing. Rick had had two more extended meetings in two consecutive days with the United States Attorney for the District of Columbia. Not the AUSAs this time. Rick got to meet the man himself, who was clearly not amused that he was obliged personally to participate in the sit-down. He was highly disturbed to be put in a defensive stance as Rick's team of lawyers—Warren sent six of them—methodically extracted his promises of public apologies to Mr. Yeager and written assurance of settlements and legal fees. Rick was in awe of their skill. At the end of the second day of conference he also knew more about the inner workings of

Lois Carneccio's firm than he could have gleaned from years of actually working there. Rick let the lawyers do all of the talking. It proved to be the right move, because Sanford Tuttle was correct once again: the United States Attorney regarded Rick Yeager as the man in the room with all the power. This was a new feeling for Rick, a marvelously uncomfortable emotion. He considered whether he should like it or not. Lois herself, he now knew, was out of the federal lockup, no doubt doing major damage to the prosecution's case with her own legal team. Rick decided that he wouldn't bet against her survival. But her firm was dead.

His, too. There was no going back to RMY Personal Financial Inc. It was time for reinvention again.

Reinvention, he thought, is always such an easy thing to recommend—happy, generous, optimistic. It's much more difficult when you're required to do it yourself and you're almost completely out of cash.

He realized now that he was in that zone on his run, the stage when he was no longer very conscious of the pain anymore, when his concentration was accelerating, when his levels of understanding were about to get very good.

Now it was time to work on Mrs. Geller.

He'd settled an estate once before, in the Court of Common Pleas of Northampton County, Pennsylvania. Not too far from Trenton, bordering Jersey, that was where his mother had died, in a hospice near her family home. She had brothers and sisters there. None of these uncles and aunts were ever close to Rick and Warren—another legacy of Dutch's health issues. A difficult time: Dutch inconsolable, Warren angry, Rick practical, Julia brokenhearted. The last time they were still sort of a family. When Mom died, Rick thought, we may have all been a mess, especially Pop, but at least she didn't die alone, like Hannah Weiss Geller did.

As he slowed and wound down the run, approaching the driveway to his condominium cluster, his exercise-clear mind fixed on his next course of action: finding a solid estate attorney and disposing of this matter. Mrs. Geller had financial assets to be sold, a decent piece of Arlington real estate to be put on the market, all of those books and a house full of modest possessions to liquidate or give away. Wherever his personal reinvention was going to take him, he had to close out this matter first. Or at the very least, put it all on autopilot. He slowed to a walk and stretched his back hard, clasped his hands over his head, then bent sideways and back and forth as he reached the courtyard of his home. He stepped onto the flagstone patio flanking his front door.

Lauren Barr smiled at him.

"That is," he panted while embarrassingly wiping snot from his nose with the side of his thumb, "the second time you've done that to me."

"Well good morning, Richard Yeager." Lauren spoke quite pleasantly, unfazed by his mild accusation. "Done what?"

"Showed up unexpectedly. I don't know if I should be flattered or disturbed."

"Maybe I planned it that way. Showing up unexpectedly, I mean." She was being both flirtatious and matter-of-fact, Rick observed, which he found completely maddening at a little past seven in the morning. "And your answer is 'flattered,' I hope. I like you, Rick. Listen, I came here to apologize. I know that I reacted pretty badly there at Tante Anna's house, and when I left you I am sure that I offended you. For that I am sorry."

"You did not offend me, and there is no need for you to apologize."

"Thank you for that. So are you and I okay?"

"Lauren, we were never *not* okay. You were the one who was angry. I was mystified. "I still am," Rick said. He wondered where this conversation was going.

"Good. We have work to do. I'll wait for you here." She motioned toward the patio table, where two large Starbucks cups sat in a square carry-container. "I was hoping that we could tackle this estate together."

"And . . . you didn't think that it would be better to call me or to send an e-mail?"

"Would you have answered?"

"Sure."

"Liar." Lauren grinned. "Once I'm here it's difficult for you to ignore me."

"No. It's impossible."

"My point exactly."

Ten minutes later, showered and dressed—he did not invite Lauren Barr inside the place, which was barely more put together than it was after the FBI's search-tossing—he rejoined her on the patio. Again, Lauren spoke first, passing him the now almost-cold cup of coffee.

"Rick, I have no way of knowing what my aunt was thinking, or how deeply she felt about you, but I do know that if she wrote her will in the way that she did, she considered you family. I've talked to my mother a lot in the last couple of days—she's out in Sonoma County, she and her husband have a weekend place there—and we just want to help. None of us needs the money—it's not about that—although with the state of this economy, anything additional that comes your way is always appreciated." She paused. "I'm sorry again. I didn't mean it that way. You're the beneficiary of her estate, period. I'm curious about why, but I have no cause or reason to doubt her decision here. She trusted you, she obviously thought highly of you, and I trust you."

"There's a 'but' coming here, right?" Rick was warming to her, still reserving some judgment.

"No. Two requests, and Rick, they're up to you to decide, completely. First, may I be involved when you go to probate her estate? I know just the bare minimum about that area of the law in Virginia. But I do know that whenever someone dies leaving an estate with assets, the executor has to qualify with the court in the county where she resided at the time of her death. And you have to probate the will, since there is one. Have you done anything with it yet?"

"No. What's the other request?"

"Could my mother have anything of Tante Anna's that has no real value, but might be of sentimental value to the family?"

Rick couldn't think of anything objectionable in either request. "I can't refuse that. Lauren, all of this came as something of a shock to me. All I want to do is get it settled as fast as possible—I have my own family stuff to deal with right now."

"I appreciate that," she said. "Your agreeing to let me help, that is. Thank you."

"You're welcome, I think."

"Were you able to figure out anything concerning that list of numbers with her will?"

"No. I did ask around. I talked to a friend of mine who's positively a genius in information technology."

"What do you think—banking? Secret accounts?"

"Sandy doubts it. So do I."

"Sandy?"

"Sanford Tuttle. He's a tech entrepreneur."

"You *know* Sanford Tuttle?" Lauren was impressed. "Important guy."

"Yes. I was one of his very first hires at QUATECH, when I was right out of college. Do you know the company?"

"Of course. QUATECH had contracts in Israel when I worked in Tel Aviv. They were everywhere in the information technology sector through-out the Middle East. Highly regarded, cutting-edge. And Kehina Alli-ance Partners, remember, the real estate investment trust where I work, owns the three buildings that GT3 leases over in Chantilly. Small world—no coincidences, huh? There's more, but I have to say that you are constantly surprising me, Rick. I would not have figured that you played in Sanford Tuttle's league, and I mean that as a compliment."

"I don't play in his league. And right back at you on that being sur-prised thing. I wouldn't have supposed you had even heard of him."

"I wonder," Lauren said, "how he can help. He may have a range of resources that we can't access."

Rick thought for a moment, looking kindly at Lauren, his mind wrapped around a lot of possibilities. The word "we" had caught his attention. She was much too interested in Sanford Tuttle and his company. He recalled something that Tuttle himself had warned back in the early days of QUATECH, when a venture capital firm made an offer too early in the dialogue. When something proposed in a deal catches your attention, like it was going to slip by you, always ask the fundamental question: *Now why was that?*

"He might," Rick answered, his voice deliberately trailing off to signal her that he was deep in thought. Better not to let her know that Tuttle was already working on this. How well did he know Lauren Barr, any-way? "And there might be other resources."

"I know a lot of folks who could help us."

"Us?"

"Help you. Sorry. We covered that already. I truly don't want to presume on you, Rick. My mother tells me that I do that. Especially to men."

"Who am I"—he smiled—"to disagree with your mother?"

Usually Rick Yeager drew closer to people the longer he knew them. He trusted them more as he came to understand them. Time is an infusing catalyst for confidence. It was rare when he sensed that the opposite was happening. This was one of those times. He sincerely wished at this moment that he had his brother's natural spot-on accurate intuition about people. But then he might have to live with Warren's demons, too.

"She had a suggestion. We talked about you. We talked about Tante Anna's will and about how I treated you. I'm sorry again, by the way. Mother said I should make it up to you, and that I should introduce you to Jonas. Same place, different angle."

"Who is Jonas?"

"My brother. Jonas Barr. He's a systems engineer on some kind of serious government secret squirrel project. You may already know him."

"I'm certain that I don't. Why would I? That's not my world anymore."

"Well, he worked for QUATECH. Sanford Tuttle hired him personally. I know that he wasn't there on the ground floor, but he still made a bundle in the IPO. And now he's at GT3."

CHAPTER 13

"Jaaaaay Deeeee, well hellooooo." The voice with the drawn-out vowels was lightly mocking with too much saccharine overtone. Julia looked up from her desk to see this summer's most annoying intern, Allen Dorn, smiling and approaching her with a copy of the *Washington Post*. Dorn was a black preppie, son of two Camden medical doctors, who had just completed his sophomore year at Duke as a political science major. He ached for a career in partisan politics. Julia could not stand him. She was certain that Dorn, easily Senator Harbison's most highly self-regarding intern in the entire time she'd worked here, didn't have a clue how much of a stereotype he was. That's what annoyed Julia most about him. This guy, she had said to the senator in June when he arrived, probably already has the bullet points drafted for his second inaugural address. And he thinks that because he hasn't written out the full text, that's humility. Tenley Harbison replied simply that when ambitions exceed abilities by this much, Washington has its own special ways of evening the score. The manner in which political life will eventually treat this guy will be ugly, but he'll learn. No, he won't learn, Julia remembered thinking at the time. Allen Dorn hadn't done a thing to change her mind since then. On the other hand, he'd only be here another few weeks. He was a distraction, nothing more.

"Have you seen? Our girl did great, don't you think?" The grin was wide, the attempt at flirtation was unconcealed.

"Our girl?"

"Our girl Tenley. Have you read it?"

Senator Harbison, in welcoming chats with new staffers and interns, told them all pro forma to please call her Tenley. Julia had not done so for her first three years with the senator. The worst thing about Dorn's extent of presumption, she thought, was that he had no idea what bad form this was. Or that Julia would write for the senator's signature the law school recommendation he would inevitably demand.

"Allen, I haven't had time to read anything except legislation this morning. We have the first budget markup later this afternoon and it's about as complex as a bill gets. The senator is always in the paper. You should talk to Stephen if you're interested in a press matter. He handles all media."

Dorn was not going away. "Jaaay Deee," he said, "this one's about your favorite issue."

"I don't have a favorite issue, Allen. That's all, thank you."

"'ViroSat Heaviest Bet in Economic Recovery,'" he read from the business section, folding the paper down and placing it on her desk. "Tenley's quoted extensively. Her depth of knowledge positively amazes me. That's why I'm privileged to work here. I want you to know that."

"I'll read it."

"Do you have lunch plans?"

"Yes. Please go."

"I'll check back with you," he said pleasantly.

Once the intern left her office, Julia picked up the newspaper. She normally made it a practice to read a number of newspapers online, but had missed this headline in her haste and preoccupation with the budget bill.

ViroSat had become a national story. At least half of the article was comprised of direct quotes from her memorandum to the senator. She was immediately faced with a binary choice—feel flattered or be outraged. There was no paraphrasing. This was verbatim reprinting. "In a word," the article began, "ViroSat is secure." Julia scanned the piece quickly. Senator Tenley Harbison was quoted extensively, explaining the technological imperatives of ViroSat and the broad outlines of its financing. The senator opined about how the ViroSat transaction—scheduled to close in New York in less than three weeks—would give a needed boost not only to the struggling American economy but to the world at large. "The ViroSat enterprises are the new sparking dynamos of the global economy, providing

a service base that will undergird the kind of growth and prosperity that
we have sorely missed and may just now be commencing again." The *Post*
also included a brief profile of "master dealmaker" Warren Hunter,
"slightly secretive, reserved, and presumed to be utterly ruthless. A colleague familiar with his work who requested anonymity because he was
not authorized to speak publicly about the transaction by the investment
bank Compton Sizemore, admiringly described Hunter as 'a gentleman of
Wall Street's old school, where old school means 1995, a time when market makers were daring, compensating for risk in the return an investment
could generate rather than in the depth of its derivative financing.'"

Julia picked up the handset of her desk phone and punched in a
three-digit extension, then waited for a pickup. "When," she inquired,
"is the senator coming back from that Democratic caucus breakfast?"

"I read this morning," Julia began dryly, knowing she might be treading
on some shaky ground, "where you've decided that ViroSat is the best
thing we have going for the economic recovery."

"Good," Senator Tenley Harbison replied. "I'm glad you saw it. What
did you think?" She walked from behind her desk. The senator's office in
the Russell Building was long and thin. Three of its high walls were covered floor-to-ceiling with photographs, framed news clippings from the
senator's prosecutor days, and every manner of New Jersey memorabilia,
capped by a dozen rectangular college and university banners. She motioned for Julia to sit with her on the leather sofa.

"I think that you're personally depicted quite well. It's a positive en-
hancement to your political capital. But I think I would have held back
some more on that memorandum if I knew we were going to read it in
the *Washington Post*."

The senator nodded. "That wasn't planned. I met with the reporter
on background. ViroSat was not even our main subject, at least not the
subject that we agreed to meet about. You know how this goes, J.D. We
were supposed to be talking generally about the effects of government
funding constraints on industries in the mid-Atlantic region. I had your
memo with me. When he brought up the ViroSat deal, I pulled it out to

use as my talking points. We spent half an hour on the deal and the federal role in it. After that, he already had everything, so I gave him the paper. The story turned out accurate and didn't give anything away. No national security secrets. No harm at all."

Julia elected to say nothing about the difficulty she would have the next time she talked to anybody at Treasury, let alone in the intelligence community, concerning ViroSat. She knew that there would be a brief but meaningful interval during which she would be shut out, paying penance for her senator's indiscretion. That was par for the course in Washington. The penalty box would amount to an additional pain during a summer budget season in which she had already used up far too many favors.

"There is going to be an altered legislative landscape now," Julia said. "Additionally, we'll have other senators and a lot of congressmen on the House side who will try to grab a leadership role regulating ViroSat. Or they'll want to take credit for it, depending. Once the project's profile has been raised this high, there's no telling where it might go politically."

"I thought about that," Tenley Harbison said. "It was a trade-off. I made a judgment call. If I hadn't responded to the *Post*'s inquiry, they would simply have found someone else who was more willing to comment. That's never difficult here in Washington, which you know as well as I do. The reporter would have found someone with far less knowledge about ViroSat, with far less at stake, and who didn't have the benefit of your research—which was positively brilliant. And for which I thank you. I should have said that at the outset. I rely on you more than anyone else here, J.D. Truly. And I do not say that often enough to you."

"Thank you." Julia wondered what she meant by having far less at stake, but chose again to say nothing. Some questions are better left unasked when you are dealing with political risks and gambles.

"I've given consideration to our next move," the senator continued. "You are spot-on in your concern about others—not just in our party, but on the Republican side—trying to take a leadership role here. To take it away, I mean."

"You have an idea." Julia brightened. Strategy, her favorite part of the legislative game.

"I do. Daylight," she said wryly.

"Daylight?"

"Daylight is sunshine inside, but not too much of it—moderation in all things. We don't want anything getting out of control, and we certainly don't want to impede Compton Sizemore. They employ over twelve hundred people in Hudson County, so let's be careful. Do you recall that old aphorism from Justice Brandeis, the one about sunshine being the best disinfectant? Well, we don't want a whole sunburn dose of sunlight here. Just a little daylight."

"You want to hold a hearing on ViroSat."

"Exactly."

"Better if it's not the whole Commerce Committee, Tenley."

"I agree."

"You chair the subcommittee on Communications, Technology, and the Internet. Now that the *Washington Post* has broken the story about 'Internet Next,' I can make a supremely good case to the committee professional staff that ViroSat is squarely in that jurisdiction. Still, that's twenty-two senators. More if the full Commerce Committee's chairman and ranking member decide to sit in."

"That's the reason why we schedule the hearing for the last week of July."

"Pressing business in their home states will keep most of them away."

"Our thinking is clearly in alignment, J.D. Go on."

"It may not be easy. You'll have to get Velez on board," Julia said, naming the ranking member on Harbison's subcommittee. The Texas Republican was distinguished in the Senate principally for his legislative caution. Julia could not think of a single issue or piece of legislation where he had ever stepped out in front before gauging all possible reactions and consequences.

"Let me handle that personally. This one is worth my owing him a favor."

"Have you thought about an executive compensation angle?"

"Yes, I have. Okay. Let me turn the question back to you. Is there one?"

"I seriously doubt it. The significant payout for ViroSat is in the out years. No one at Compton Sizemore is going to be making a killing on this deal, in this political environment. ViroSat is not about fees, either for the investment bank or for the dozens of international debt sources that they seem to be using. I've checked around. Whoever the equity investors are, they are assuming the risk. Seems kind of old fashioned, doesn't it? They will benefit when this ViroSat is operational—from the revenues it will generate—and then again when it's sold, from the profits on the sale."

"Do we know," the senator asked, "when those out years are going to be? Or who all of those banks and investors are? Can we find out?"

"Excellent questions," Julia answered, "for you to ask at the hearing."

"You know my rule. I never want to ask a question to which I do not already know the answer." She had repeated this injunction hundreds of times, beginning with her first trial as the greenest prosecutor in Hackensack more than thirty years ago.

"I understand."

"I am going to need you to take the lead here, J.D. I have an opportunity for some great positioning."

"When ViroSat becomes a global technological and economic success."

"Or," Tenley Harbison said, "in the event that it doesn't."

"And do you have a preference there?"

"No. My only preference is to be identified as the first senator to track ViroSat. Closely. For that, I have a lot of reasons."

Julia knew better than to ask. "Did the *Post* ever get around to asking you about the recovery and the use of federal funds for banking institutions?" she said.

"Sure. The backgrounder wasn't all about ViroSat. We talked a great deal about the use of Treasury funds, how advanced technology industries are just now seeing their first loans from the long pipeline, and how all of it ties into a severely strained information technology infrastructure that's kind of bulging at the seams. That discussion is what brought us around to ViroSat. That reminds me. What do you know about a business entity called the Financial Systems and Services Corporation? He asked me about it—some kind of public-private venture."

"There are a hundred of those ventures, senator. They are all part of the economic recovery effort. We're up to what? Phase four now? It's difficult to keep track of them all."

"Look into it for me, please. He asked me what I knew about it. I pled the usual senatorial overload."

Julia made a note. "I'll find out."

"You have some pretty good sources for us to use on ViroSat, don't you?"

"The best," Julia said smiling. "They really are."

On the return to her own office, Julia found her way blocked by a group of constituents being ushered around by Allen Dorn, holding forth about how "Tenley respects all of our views and our collective judgment when we work together to develop legislative priorities, always for your benefit as her constituents. That's why every one of us is working here. We are imbued with an ethic of service, a deep public trust." They were just more July visitors to Washington. She wondered how many of them found Dorn as oleaginous as she did, decided that it didn't matter, and pardoned her way through the group. At her desk, she typed a quick e-mail to the office manager reminding her that constituent walk-throughs of the senator's offices were not supposed to wander into the legislative working spaces.

The red light on her phone set was blinking, of course. She hit the voice mail button to recover the messages. There was only one.

Message received at . . . nine . . . forty-one . . . a.m. Then a scritch of static from a mobile phone. *Call me. Please. As soon as you get this.* That's all it said. The voice was plaintive, pleading, deeply distressed. The tone was intimately familiar. Julia found her purse, took out her iPhone, and located the number. She walked to her office door, closed it, then punched the touch-screen with her thumb.

Warren Hunter answered before the first ring ended.

"Julia?"

"Warren, are you all right?"

"No. All right is a far-off place for me right now."

"What?"

"It's my pop. He's just had a stroke. He's still alive, but they don't know for how much longer. I thought I was ready for this, I really, really did. You have to help me. Do you remember . . . ? I couldn't call anybody else—"

"I'll help. Have you talked to Rick?"

"No. Can you call him?"

She hesitated. "Could you?"

"I will but I can't right now! You have no idea what I'm facing *right now*!"

"Calm down. Where is your father?"

"Bergen Regional Medical Center. And I can't get there until I finish here."

"I know the hospital. And Warren?"

"What?"

"If you need help yourself, they have it right there for you, okay?"

"I do *not* want to hear that!"

"I know. But it's an option."

"No, it isn't. Not for me. Why do you think I called you?"

"I understand. I'll see you in the morning. We can figure it all out. Call me tonight, no matter how late."

"Thank you."

The budget markup meeting later today, perhaps the most important legislative work she did, would have to be delegated. Julia Toussaint quickly packed her briefcase and grabbed her purse. She breezed past the constituents in the outer office just as they were politely listening to Allen Dorn holding forth about Duke and Rutgers basketball.

Once more, Julia told Warren, and only once—if it's your father.

Warren Hunter, dynamic, gregarious, and constantly surrounded by intelligent people (including plenty of sycophants) was in reality a desperately lonely man, holding on. His achievement was real and the power of his role in international finance was quite valid. He was a giant intellect and a man to be admired. There are some people for whom this measure of towering strength means great brittleness. Warren was one of those.

This had happened before, when Gloria died. Clinically, as Julia later discreetly inquired to discover, it was called a major depressive episode.

It began on the evening of the burial in Pennsylvania. Death from ovarian cancer gives a family time to plan the logistics. They traveled north in two cars. Rick would be taking Dutch back to Trenton, watching after him, continuing home to Virginia. Julia would be heading to see family in Newark. Warren would be going back to the City. Julia offered Warren a ride.

The breakdown happened in her car on Interstate 78 at seventy miles an hour. The wailing, kicking the dashboard, raging, guttural moans, grief beyond consolation, the rant about his worthlessness. She pulled off the road at a Holiday Inn Express and checked in.

Don't leave me here, he pleaded. If you do I'll kill myself. He cried for hours.

She stayed with him for nine days.

When they parted, he was functionally recovered but not even close to being himself. Warren consistently refused any other assistance. He kept saying, "I will build myself back." He made two plaintive demands of Julia. In retrospect, she regretted agreeing to them.

You can never tell anyone what happened here, especially my brother.

And when Dutch goes, you may have to help me again.

She thought that Rick would understand. He did not, especially given her circumspection.

Not what you think.

You don't know what I think.

That was the beginning of the end.

At the lawyer's office where they signed the final divorce settlement she asked for a private moment with Rick. She kissed him on the cheek and whispered in his ear that she still loved him, but that this is the right thing to do.

Julia's strength, it occurred to her as she walked out of the Russell Building, was that she always knew the right thing to do. Her weakness was that she always tried to do it.

CHAPTER 14

Warren Hunter thumb-crushed the red button on the face of his Black-Berry, ending the call to Julia. His face was flushed. He took at least a dozen deep breaths and gazed out his window at the thickening clouds stumbling up over the southern tip of Manhattan. His sense of calm was returning. He felt relieved. If he could continue this trajectory, and he was sure that he could, he would soon arrive at the utter composure that he needed this morning. Warren was proud of the levels of calm that he could muster. After exceptional moments like this one, he could feel the serenity roll over him in waves. But these waves were not like big water lifting him, carrying him limp and happy-hopping to his boyhood Jersey Shore. These waves behaved like light in particle physics, sometimes undulating, sometimes bombarding in stinging particles. It all depended on the circumstances. The transition from particle to wave hurt, but he knew that after it was completed, he could do some of his best work. This morning his best would be required.

Jenny Lau tapped on his open office door. "It's time."

"Good." He glanced at his watch: 10:02 A.M. Warren always arrived at a meeting a few minutes after the appointed time, but never significantly late. At the Harvard Business School he had a management professor whose academic research area was the application of senior military leadership to business. Admiral Louis Mountbatten, whom the professor interviewed in the 1970s, always made it a point of honor to arrive a few minutes late to staff meetings. Warren learned Mountbatten's point and employed it ever since: a leader should never embarrass his charges by arriving early. If the staff arrived precisely on time, they would be late by virtue of the commander's premature presence. Beginning on the day

Warren took over as the firm's deputy chief of investment and merchant banking, he arrived at every meeting precisely four minutes after the appointed starting time. August Compton completely approved.

Compton Sizemore's big boardroom was two floors down from Warren's office on fifty-six. He took the stairs. Today was the long-scheduled meeting of the entire ViroSat senior management deal team, including a select few managing directors—MDs—of associated investment banking firms. The outsiders all had either significant financing in the ViroSat deal or fees at stake. Three of the outsiders were responsible for bringing in a sum total of two hundred and ten billion dollars— more than a hundred billion from one publicly traded house alone. Two other firms, neither of them household names on the Street but extremely well positioned and well regarded, were the advisory valuators. They would forgo an investment in ViroSat in order to write the advisory reports, draw up the valuations and the fairness opinions where required, and negotiate a myriad of side deals. Most of the deals were with foreign governments, not all of whom were friendly or explicitly ethical. Warren appreciated these auxiliary skills and was glad to pay the premium fees required for them. The rest of the meeting's participants would be from Compton Sizemore, including every managing director on the investment banking side of the house and a fair number of the MDs from the traders' side.

More than seventy people were gathered in the big boardroom when he arrived. His small ViroSat team, the "gang of fourteen," was positioned closest to the head of the table and already seated or standing at their seats. For this meeting a few handshakes and greetings were required. Warren worked the crowd. No one went without his personal acknowledgment. He came across as efficient, visibly carefree, good humored. He was keenly aware that every professional in the room was both taking his temperature and contemplating his or her best power-angle, not just for this meeting but for every future encounter with him, real or imagined. He positively loved this element of the i-banking game. This morning was good therapy for him. His movement around the room and his positioning—heading to the chairman's seat at the table—signaled that the meeting was about to begin.

"Now which one of you magnificent sons of bitches actually thinks that I am a gentleman?" he began.

A third of the men and women at the table laughed loudly. Almost all of the middle managers ringing the room, now seated in chairs against the walls, looked at each other quizzically. They wondered what the inside joke was.

"Warren," said one of the trading-side managing directors, "nobody here reads the *Washington Post*. Have you fallen into the habit of believing your own press now?"

"Oooooooo," came the predictable response, a fine adolescent gloss of sarcasm and light humor. The Compton Sizemore insiders knew that the zing was completely cost-free, because the MD who spoke didn't report to Warren and happened to be a guy who was a year ahead of him at Colonial, the eating club they shared at Princeton. Warren smiled, thereby establishing the tone: He expected today to be a work-hard, play-hard meeting. Dissent would be encouraged and was likely to be rewarded.

"Let's look at the financing presentations first," Warren said as they all settled in. He opened a leather folder and referred to a bulletized list on a single piece of paper. "Then the political risk assessments, our currency float data, hedge positions, cash management of all the ViroSat investment assets we're actually holding here inside the firm, the transnational subsidiaries, the federal regulatory picture, that special study about ViroSat and the economic recovery, and where we are on business development and revenue for the operational enterprise firms. Then I want to see the technical and engineering data, followed by roadblocks and wild cards. The equity team is last, and that one's mine. We need to get to work, people. There's a whole lot of ground to cover here. We're only a week from setting up the war room that will close this deal."

The financing presentations went smoothly enough. There were seven separate PowerPoint slide shows to slog through, each with spreadsheet data and detailed sensitivity analysis to consider. For the early part, Warren held back. He observed the rapid-fire deliveries approvingly and spoke up with regular praise. His questions—tough, thorough, either embarrassingly easy or embarrassingly difficult depending on the preparation of the presenter—made several points overwhelmingly clear to the team. Closing the deal for ViroSat was not going to be like mortgage-world, the credit default mess, or derivative quant-land. Everyone here must approach his or her role with deep preparation and penetrating knowledge. ViroSat, a complex technical system backed by a correspondingly complex financial system, must be brought out fully formed. It would all happen simultaneously on August first. No mistakes.

A photographer circulated around the boardroom, anything but unobtrusive, snapping digital photos. His presence had the effect of making the presenters and the participants look sharper, aware that they were on stage. Warren ordered this addition knowing that when the staff was acting for the camera their professional focus and clarity improved markedly.

Before the political risk assessments began, one of the outsiders—a woman who did double-duty as a professor of finance at the NYU business school and the creative valuation guru at a small advisory firm—flagged his attention with a raised hand. Warren nodded in her direction.

"Bio break," she said, turning up two hands.

"That, my friend, just cost you a hundred bucks," Warren replied. The younger Compton Sizemore people hooted and applauded.

"What?" she asked, not exactly pleased to be at the center of whatever was going on. "You're going to charge me?"

"Here's how it works," he said, addressing the crowd, not the offender. "A hundred-dollar fine every time anyone in my meetings uses consulting jargon. We hate it here, and by 'we' I mean me. A lot of people, however, follow my lead. You want to use consultant-speak, go to work for McKinsey. This is i-banking, baby. There's a difference. We're the operators. We work the levers. We finance. We take risk. We sell actions, not words. Thirty years ago there was a distinct difference between what the Brown Brothers Harrimans and the Goldman Sachses of the world sold to their clients and what the *consultants*"—his contempt for the word deliberate, clear to all—"sold to theirs. All of that changed around the time that most of us here began in the industry. The lines got way too blurred. The consultants thought that what we produced wasn't unique, wasn't that valuable, and that anyone who'd read the books and took their MBA exams could do our jobs. Not so incidentally they wanted to charge our kind of fees. That was what the conflation of the two industries was really all about.

"The way I tell the two apart is when consulting words start leaching their way into our deals. 'Benchmarked.' 'Right-sized.' 'Deliverable.' 'Operationalizing.' 'Liaised'—I especially hate that one. So you, my friend, get a speeding ticket . . . it's just a hundred-dollar fine. Show of hands: Who's already had one?"

Every Compton Sizemore hand in the room went up, including Warren's.

"Now who's actually *paid* one?"

Not a single hand went down.

"Thank you, folks. In response to your request, no breaks. We push right through. If you need to stand up or go to the can or do anything else, just go. We're not stopping. I think I made my point. I want real information and straight talk. Now, political risk, starting with the Americas."

Lunch was brought in. The presentations and discussions did not slacken at all. They accelerated. Warren on his A-game was a controller of the first order. There was nothing oblique about him. He knew it and they knew it. He had successfully harnessed once again the respect of everyone in the room. And the friendship of none.

In retrospect the conflict was inevitable. So was the provocateur.

Warren Hunter began the discussion of what he called ViroSat's "equity undergirding" at around 4:15 P.M. The morning's energy in the room was certainly dissipated. Attention spans were shorter. So were the limits of polite tolerance, including Warren's.

Warren was not particularly fond of PowerPoint, judging stand-up slideshows to be necessary nuisances. When his own time on the agenda rolled around, he stood, stretched, and walked the length of the boardroom.

"Many of you know August Compton, my boss and the only guy I answer to," he began. "Some of you do not. Those of you who are acquainted with him, or who observed him when he started this firm, will probably agree with me that he is the original metaphor man."

There were more than a few smiles. A couple of the most senior MDs chuckled. The experienced Compton Sizemore bankers noticed that Warren was now slowly pacing the length of the room, reversing, and repeating the slow walk in the other direction. This was Compton's habit. Was he mimicking it intentionally or unintentionally, especially while talking about metaphors?

"When August Compton and Mr. Sizemore founded this firm—using only cash capital out of their pockets and not a lick of debt, I have to add—they envisioned that we would be financial architects. We are designers. We create. We begin by drawing structures, rough and conceptual. We do not start with an idea, we build ideas as we produce those structures. As ideas are completed, as they take shape in multiple dimensions, we must make certain that the structures in which they are expressed are resounding, robust with compositional elegance. That's what successful architecture does. That is precisely what financial architecture has to accomplish. The better our design, the higher our returns on invested capital.

"The greatest American architect—the greatest, period, in my judgment—was Frank Lloyd Wright. Wright's deepest failing was that he was a terrible structural engineer. A Wright building is foremost a thing of beauty, a creation of wholeness and wonder following Wright's Organic Commandment: Decision is the virtue of the will. Here is the problem: Wright buildings cannot be relied upon to be structurally sound or secure for the long run. You cannot count on their foundational strength, their ability to hold up over time, or even their materials. They have a propensity to crack.

"Wright's work is a perfect analogue for ViroSat. We are designing and creating something entirely new, but using tools of the last century—like Wright working for Louis Sullivan in Chicago a hundred and twenty years ago. Some of our structures for ViroSat are incredibly basic, with design elements dating back to the 1940s. Other elements are constructed deliberately to avoid the mistakes that have got us stuck in this Great Wallow— and yes, that's my metaphor. Our charge here, what we've been talking about for the last six hours, is essentially what clients tell architects. When the ground needs difficult preparation, not unlike our markets today, your imperative is endurance. Build this for permanence. Build it for decades. Build it so that no one can take it apart. Build it, above all, for two-dimensional profitability. Right now *and* in the long term."

Warren Hunter stopped his pacing at the middle of the great table and looked about the room, turning about slowly. He met every eye.

"Enough metaphors. Please take all of that as a review of our funda-mental charge. We are deeply into the building phase now. ViroSat will launch financially on the day that this transaction closes, August first. That launch is going to be more consequential than the eleven actual launches of ViroSat satellites that we've already paid for and successfully accomplished."

"Yeah. More consequential for the equity chain, perhaps." Dawson MacNeil spoke, challenging. "And after all of what we've heard today, that's the single area, the one critical accounting that we haven't heard about. If you don't intend to be more forthcoming about the equity chain, you're raising the risk profile of the whole deal. I have to contend with that. Substance, Warren. Disclosure."

"I understand—" Warren began.

"No, I don't think that you do understand," MacNeil said.

The pronouncement was his fatal mistake.

"You're holding out twenty-one percent of the deal's value in equity. More than a fifth of this deal price is in stock, from that limited partner-ship you run. You haven't opened even the smallest window inside. That's where the first distributions of investment returns are going to be made. I do not intend to give on this point. The limited partnership fi-nancing brings two hundred and eighty-seven billion dollars and change to this deal. Its composition is materially relevant. It is more important to this group than an unctuous lecture on architecture."

Warren Hunter sat in his chair, put two palms flat on the table, leaned back slightly, and stared silently at Dawson MacNeil. The ViroSat crowd watched intently, wondering if they were about to witness one of those Wall Street confrontations (a frequent occurrence) that become legends (most infrequently). No one expected the volcanic eruption of rage to come instantaneously from Compton Sizemore's famously well-controlled head of investment banking.

"Materially relevant to *you*," he screamed violently, as the entire boardroom drew a collective breath, "or to *others*? Not to our debt providers. Not to our clients. Not to the governments. And you don't intend to *give* on this point? *Give*? Nothing is yours to give!" He fell silent, suddenly back in check, the meeting now reeling in shock and wonder.

"I know about your media conversations," he said quite pleasantly to Dawson MacNeil. His change in tone scared the assembly. "And you should know that newspapers are not only unreliable for gleaning information, they are also unreliable when they promise you anonymity in our age of technological imperative. They are also going out of business."

"I have never had any media contacts," MacNeil replied confidently.

"I thought you would say so. That statement just sealed your departure from Compton Sizemore, Mr. MacNeil. If you believe that there is actually such a thing as an anonymous prepaid mobile telephone, you've been watching too much television."

McNeil blanched.

"You're not just fired, Dawson." Warren's voice was rising again. "You're out of this industry and you're going to be facing criminal charges. You signed the same confidentiality documents that all of us did, the ones about the law enforcement and national security implications of ViroSat. You've also violated a broad range of securities laws and certain political corruption statutes. Disclosing information illegally to the press is part of Washington's culture. It is not part of ours.

"Don't believe for a moment that your dismissal is the result of challenging me here. I won't permit you to craft that narrative for your own comfort. You simply don't comprehend the concept of boundaries.

"So comprehend this: I hope that you are going to have a long and healthy life. One where you wonder, all the time. 'Why is it that every opportunity from which I attempt to benefit suddenly dries up? Why is it that those reporters, even those bloggers, don't take my calls anymore? Why does the world think that I'm deranged and spinning conspiracy theories? Why can't I find *any* professional venue that will accept me?' Good luck with all of that. I mean it, Dawson. Good luck. You will need it."

Warren Hunter looked at his watch. He stood, walked to the boardroom door, and opened it. Four private security guards, all wearing sidearms and each standing at least six foot four, were waiting. With a nod he invited them inside.

"You remember Darlington Global Security. I believe you worked on their IPO, Dawson. These men are from a company that's both client and vendor to Compton Sizemore. Unlike you, they have a sense of loyalty. They will escort you out, and they will do so with courtesy." To one of the security men he asked, "The documents?" Wordlessly, the man handed a fat manila envelope to him.

"Here," Warren said, slapping the envelope on the table and sliding it to Dawson MacNeil. "Some reading to keep you up at night. Letter concerning your termination for cause. There's also Compton Sizemore's civil suit against you, your girlfriend, the law firm where she works, and her parents. You think we didn't track how you got and used the prepaid mobile? You will note that the Attorney General of New York State and the US Attorney for the Southern District of New York, in behalf of the government of the United States, have both joined us as civil plaintiffs. There's also a restraining order providing certain geographical restrictions on your movements. Citigroup Center is at the head of the list. Consider yourself served.

"Dawson, when an insurrection is begun, it is death to fail."

MacNeil, mute, dry-mouthed, his jaw moving wordlessly up and down, stood and walked with the security guards, shoulders back, attempting to display the last ounce of dignity and defiance left in him.

"He called me a gentleman. Complimentary as he attempted to be, he had no authority," Warren said to no one in particular, "to speak to the *Washington Post*. He didn't even have enough judgment to inquire about our media strategy. If he did, he might know that we are sourcing New York and financial outlets exclusively. That particular piece of information, by the way, was not on the agenda for today.

"Of course," he said with a wide grin, again meeting every eye in the room, "I wouldn't think that anyone left here is anxious to share it."

CHAPTER 15

The empty shell that was once Dawson MacNeil shuffled and stumbled. He turned north on Lexington Avenue, then crossed in the middle of the block to the west sidewalk. Two taxis swerved around him with horns blowing and a scream, unmistakably a curse, in a language he did not know but thought was probably Arabic or Farsi. He clutched in his sweaty right hand the manila envelope that Warren Hunter had handed him. His mind was unable to function. His stomach struggled against the nausea, knotting and unknotting.

Between 54th and 55th Streets, at the foot of the stone stairs leading up to the Lexington Avenue façade of Central Synagogue, an unshaven old man reclined. His clothes were thoroughly grimy and he wore too much clothing for July, including an old fedora, large and full of holes, pulled far down on the crown of his head. He gripped under his lower arm a cardboard boxed piled high with clothing. Before him was placed a cardboard Payday candy-bar box containing two crumpled one-dollar bills and some assorted loose change. The man stared at Dawson Mac-Neil, who reached into his right front pants pocket, withdrew a handful of coins, tossed them into the box, and then did not move.

"You look terrible," the old man said.

"It did not go the way you said."

"Not here. Around the corner on Fifty-fifth. By the trees. Wait."

Dawson MacNeil walked away from him very unsteadily and turned left at the corner. The old man began counting. He was using a method that he first encountered in excess of six decades ago—measure time, a decent interval of time, by integers. Eleven minutes passed.

He stood and stretched his lanky frame, his acquired-this-morning bum clothing (that was how he thought of it) hanging on him. The movement and the sartorial presentation had the aggregate effect of making him look quite emaciated. Viewing video of him in this outfit would lead one to the conclusion that he had once been hardy and much more filled out, but was now decrepit among the homeless, very likely in the terminal stages of AIDS. Overclothed with the fedora, not just his face but his race would be obscured. He too was skilled in the subtle art of making people look at him but not see him. As he stretched, it occurred to him that the aches and pains resulting from that reclining position were harsh, a function of his advanced age—notwithstanding his physical agility and remaining strength.

He permitted himself to grow nostalgic for the briefest instant. The reclining beggar was how he observed os Magyar forradalom, the Hungarian revolution of 1956. The American ambassador thought it was most unseemly for his CIA chief of station to look and smell so horrible for days at a time—while extravagantly praising the quality of his reporting.

In this location, on Lexington Avenue, he was certain that his begging sojourn and the interaction with MacNeil had been filmed. On 55th Street, however, at midblock in the stand of trees, no cameras could possibly capture them. He leaned over to pick up his Payday box, collected the larger box, and walked to the corner, crossing the numbered street with the light before turning left.

That move was for the street-level cameras on Lexington, a bit of insurance. With the time difference and crossing to the opposite side, no photo interpreter would likely put him and MacNeil together after their smallest initial interaction. In all of spycraft, you had to play the odds, so you had better take every opportunity to improve them in your own favor. Cameras could be tricky but were usually manageable. New York City in the age of Homeland Security had nothing on the communists.

He allowed himself another reverie. There was the tour at Langley, with the window office in the Old Headquarters Building overlooking the park, when he headed photointerpretation. He'd resisted at first. The assignment proved to be most positive, an inflection moment of career acceleration. Six weeks into the job the director handed him Project PSALM and sent him to the White House to brief Bobby Kennedy personally on the aerial photos of the missiles in Cuba. He told Bobby that he first did this back in the war. Berlin, Bremerhaven, and Dresden were not all that different from San Cristobal.

He was pleased that all of his great old skills were proving fungible over the decades. They were timeless techniques made new, ironically, by the advance of technology. Like weird old carpenter's knives and chisels from a century ago, nothing could fundamentally improve upon them and none of the new stuff was definitively better.

When he knew that he was clear of the cameras, he caught a break: there, a fat pile of construction garbage awaiting pickup. He dumped the larger box of clothing on the trash and glanced up the street. Dutifully following instructions, Dawson MacNeil stood slumped in the shade of the trees on the other side. The guy looked stunned, which was good. He wondered just what the hell happened up there at Compton Sizemore. Then he crossed the street.

"It went bad," said MacNeil. "It went very, *very* bad."

"You shouldn't take that judgment on yourself," the old man said softly. "Run it down for me, please."

The courtesy made MacNeil calm down enough for him to narrate the broad strokes of his firing from Compton Sizemore and the legal morass that Warren Hunter had promised him. He waved the envelope for emphasis.

"May I see that?"

The old man pulled the legal papers from the envelope, tipping his head so that Dawson MacNeil could not see him smile. Everything—*everything*—was electronic today, and here he was successfully hiding from cameras on a cross-street and reading paper documents that weren't his, that he wasn't supposed to see.

"I'm afraid," he concluded, "that you are in very deep trouble."

"What do you think I've been trying to tell you? You told me to provoke him at the big meeting."

"I said gently. Provoke him *gently*. I did not tell you to talk to a newspaper. That's a major issue now. Your conduct was outside what we agreed."

"You told me that you would take care of me. Now what?"

"I did. And I will. Let's get back to the substance of your meeting. Tell me what Mr. Hunter said about the equity sources—inside the limited partnership."

"Nothing. That was the point at which he exploded."

"Mr. Hunter does not explode. He is controlled and calculating."

"You weren't there. I've worked with him for three and a half years, and *this* was out of control."

"He was acting."

"Believe that if you want to, but the result was the same. He never said anything about the composition of the limited partnership. I asked before. He's just not giving. I thought it prudent to push this time."

"Your role was to gather information, to listen, not to push. This"—the old man held up the documents—"now presents a problem."

"You fix problems." MacNeil said it like a plea rather than a statement.

"Yes I do. Again, Mr. Hunter said nothing about the sources of equity?"

"I told you. Not a thing. Why do you keep asking? You apparently know Hunter and his goddamned limited partnership better than I do."

The old man was quiet. He looked down at MacNeil. "You may have misjudged the situation here. Have you called anyone about your firing and the way you were just treated?"

"No. They took my mobile, too. It was a Compton Sizemore phone. I walked out then I found you at the temple, just as we agreed."

"Thank you."

"I know that you were not explicit. But you held out the possibility that I could displace Hunter in this deal. Now what do I do?"

"I apologize if you got that impression. We may both have made some misjudgments."

"And I have to pay for them, apparently."

"No," said the old man, at his comforting best. "We'll bring you in."

From a distance of thirty yards, illegally parked in a battered white panel van with very illegal windows darkened almost black, Horvath sat and watched their conversation. He had stolen the van this morning in Spanish Harlem after choosing carefully. Targeting the scruffy construction crew of Dominicans, almost certainly illegal immigrants, meant that the theft would not be reported quickly, if at all. The license plates (purposely, they did not match) were both lifted from New York cars in the most remote long-term parking lot at Newark Liberty Airport, where he flew in three days ago from Dulles Airport in Virginia. He had blackened the windows himself. Horvath was unconcerned about fingerprints or forensic evidence. His prints existed in no database system anywhere in the world.

There. The hand on MacNeil's shoulder blade. The slow nodding. Signal and double-check. Horvath turned the key—the Dominicans actually left it in the ignition on First Avenue at the Metropolitan Hospital Center—and put the van in gear. He drove forward, crossed to the side of the trees where the two men were talking, and pulled up alongside them. Horvath leaned over and rolled down the driver's side window, a manual crank in the old van, as the tall old man spoke again.

"My colleague is going to assist you," he said. "We have an explicit trust, and you can rely on him as much as you rely on me. On this you have my word."

There is no resistance left in this guy, Horvath thought.

Dawson MacNeil extended a hand through the window. "What should I call you?"

"Szekeres," said Horvath with a firm grip. He silently laughed. The name was Hungarian for "coachman."

"Zeck—" MacNeil attempted to repeat.

"Close enough," Horvath replied with a disarming smile. "Get in. We're going to New Jersey." MacNeil did as he was told.

The passenger side door slammed shut and the old man watched as they drove away. Deliberately he crossed the street at midblock, backtracking to the trash pile. As he walked he shed the fedora and his long-sleeved shirt. He unbuckled the belt cinched tight on the trousers that were at least three sizes too large. As he reached the discarded construction materials, he quickly dropped these oversized overpants and pulled them down over his shoes. He tossed the hat and the rest of his bum clothing on the pile. In seconds he was transitioned, wearing khakis and a striped polo shirt. He was wrinkled but dressed perfectly appropriate, and perfectly unremarkable, for a man his age walking in midtown east in July. Next he pushed aside the top layer of clothes in his abandoned cardboard box, withdrawing a compact leather duffel bag, wraparound sunglasses, and a dark blue New York Yankees ball cap. He put on the glasses and pulled the cap low over his forehead as he strode purposefully west toward Park Avenue—watching as Horvath's van made the left turn headed downtown.

Definitely not according to plan. MacNeil's utility was now zero. The part that troubled him terribly was Warren Hunter's apparent loss of composure. He would have to spend some time thinking about this carefully and closely.

As he made his way to the west side and the Lincoln Tunnel, Horvath whistled. There was no radio in the Dominicans' van. His whistling was calculated. It was an excellent way to keep from making conversation with Dawson MacNeil, who did not exactly seem too talkative himself.

"You're worried," Horvath finally said, his first words since MacNeil got in the van.

"That is a tremendously perceptive observation, Zeck."

"Don't be such a douche bag," Horvath told him. He liked that expression and thought that it applied to MacNeil, who did not react at all. "What did he tell you?"

"He said that you would be bringing me in."

"And what am I doing?"

MacNeil said nothing. He stared straight ahead as the van crawled to a stop, right into the messy funnel of traffic that fed into the tunnel.

"Relax," Horvath said. They were going nowhere—total traffic constipation. He put the van's gearshift in park and reached over to place a firm right hand on MacNeil's shoulder, gripping him paternally, manfully. MacNeil responded with a shallow breath, exhaling and tipping his head back very slightly. It was all the opening that Horvath needed.

His two huge hands were as swift as they were deadly, belying his age.

Horvath grabbed his neck and crushed down fast and menacingly hard on MacNeil's windpipe and larynx with thick thumbs, crossed for maximum killing effect. The banker struggled, more from shock than from any conscious effort to save his life, eyes wide, reddening, and bulging. His hands futilely gripped Horvath's forearms. Horvath kept up the pressure as the throat cartilage gave way quite easily now, moving his hands outward without releasing the pressure, constricting his fingers around both carotid arteries. In seconds Dawson MacNeil lost consciousness, but Horvath continued to choke unrelentingly, not loosening his lethal grip until he was absolutely certain that the biology of death had progressed beyond the point of no return. When he loosened his grip MacNeil was probably not clinically dead yet, Horvath figured, but he was definitely not breathing. He would expire on his own in a couple of minutes. He reasoned that this was not at all a bad death, as these things go.

Horvath arranged him in a generally upright position in the van's front seat and fixed the seat belt. Then he stretched and relaxed his hands several times while rotating his wrists. When he first learned anatomy and was instructed in this technique—truly, a whole lifetime ago—he did not have to contend with arthritis. The method, he observed, was quite as deadly now as it had proven to be during his operational days.

Strange how some things in the business change and others never do. Here was a situation he never could have imagined in the old country: Horvath's partner now was his enemy then.

No, he corrected himself, that was definitely incorrect. They had been adversaries with enduring common respect, never enemies. They always liked and trusted each other. Now it was good to work with him in common purpose. He shifted the van into drive and lurched forward a few feet as traffic finally began to move into the Lincoln Tunnel feeder.

Horvath had some disposal duties now in New Jersey, bringing in Dawson MacNeil.

CHAPTER 16

Throughout Warren Hunter's presentation on ViroSat's equity under-girding and dynamics, no one in the boardroom at Compton Sizemore said a word. It was now evident to the group why he had begun with a discussion of financial architecture and Frank Lloyd Wright. The equity structure was compositionally brilliant, its surface simplicity only made possible by its underlying complexity. It did not take much figuring on the lined tablets scattered about the room (with corporate logo and "Compton Sizemore Conference Room" printed across the top) to see what Warren had accomplished. Here was the "view from the balcony," as he called it, apologizing for his brief return to the metaphors. The eq-uity structure—the actual cash in the deal—elegantly provided the most efficient means to the most rapid return on investment *and* the highest return on investment. It was all quite remarkable. As he spoke, it gradu-ally dawned on each of the meeting's many participants that the proj-ect's financial speed-and-maximization result held true whether or not the ViroSat investors were providing debt for the deal's huge leverage or basic equity through the limited partnership.

There was a surprising amount of financial intricacy in Warren's dis-cussion, which slightly puzzled the big deal team assembled here and the Compton Sizemore gang of fourteen (now thirteen with the depar-ture of Dawson MacNeil). He knew as well as they did how unusual it was for the soon-to-be head of investment banking at one of the world's top financial institutions to produce and then lay out such deep detail. Warren Hunter had anticipated their unasked question, *Why?*

"You may remember that I was a quant once," he said, concluding his presentation and hoping that he could end the day on a light note, "although I could not begin to approach the quality of some of the minds in this room. I began my life in investment banking as an equity analyst. I wrestled with the toughest of the tough math. A couple of you know why."

"Poet." One word came from the trading-side managing director, the guy who had known Warren since Princeton.

"Exactly. I had to prove what I could do. In a way, that's why I did this by myself. To prove to each of you the strength of this analysis, to demonstrate my deepest personal commitment to it, and to show you that it comes from me individually and not from the Compton Sizemore team that I am privileged to manage. That is a measure of how highly I regard all of you.

"And I present it," he said, glancing around the room, "with what I hope you will come to regard as humility, notwithstanding the unfortunate events earlier this afternoon." He glanced at his watch. A half-dozen other people in the room took this as a signal that it was now acceptable to do the same. It was 6:18 P.M. "It's been a pretty long day. I said at the outset that we had a lot of ground to cover, and unless there are any pressing matters outstanding, that should just about conclude our time together."

Johnny Shen, the most highly regarded quant in the room and the intellectual leader of the Compton Sizemore gang of thirteen, raised an open palm. Warren made a motion of recognition and nodded. "You asked me to bring up our next steps before you adjourned," he said.

"Right," Warren responded, then addressed the room again. "Dr. Shen, managing director and our head of structured finance, will be taking the lead on all ViroSat matters for the next few days while I'm out of town. Before we enter hardcore deal-closing days I have very pressing family business to attend to. Before you all wonder, it's my father—we have no secrets here. Then I'll be in Washington meeting with some of our principal investment stakeholders. Don't be too surprised at hearing that last part, people. We are operating in a financial environment where the goodwill of our federal government is critical, where cooperation from us now results in cooperation from them later, when we will certainly need it. Why else do you think that the Justice Department was so willing to work with us in that delicate matter concerning Mr. Mac-Neil?"

The bankers in the room had spent the last two hours trying to figure that one out. They were amazed at Warren Hunter's anticipatory powers.

"You've taken an awful lot on yourself, Warren," said Johnny Shen softly.

"I don't disagree with that," Warren answered. "If you see that it becomes an unmanageable load, I expect you to speak up."

"We will," Shen promised, his considered use of the word "we" not lost on anyone in the room. "Everyone here supports you, Warren, and we are committed to this enterprise. Our personal stakes couldn't be higher. Still. Two hundred and eighty-seven billion dollars. No one before you has ever pulled in that kind of equity alone. It takes some real stones, especially when you're at risk yourself. We admire that."

"I appreciate your confidence," Warren said. "I know better than anyone how much is riding on this deal."

"Yeah. You do." If this simple truth had been offered by anyone else on the team at the conclusion of a brutal workday, it would have sounded like the most blatant sucking up. Johnny Shen's core simplicity and sincerity gave his words weight beyond their own measure. Warren Hunter, whose degree of conscious eloquence was often an indication of his seriousness, was clearly moved.

"Let's not ever lose sight of the fact that our closing the ViroSat deal is going to be the one thing that pulls this country—and other free market economies around the world—out of its worst recession since the end of World War Two."

The substance of that statement was the last bullet on his outline notes prepared for the meeting. A *nice symmetry*, he had written in the margin. And a fearful one.

Warren flopped his leather folder closed, stood, and began to shake hands around the boardroom. It was an indisputable signal that his meeting was terminated.

An hour and forty minutes later, Warren Hunter stepped out alone from his spacious office suite. No one else remained on the investment banking group floors of Compton Sizemore except the two janitors, whom

Warren greeted pleasantly in Spanish, *buen' noches*, as he waited for the elevator. When it arrived, he punched the button for the ground floor—not for the exit lobby, but for the landing in the atrium of the Citigroup Center. The descent was rapid, straight down with no intermediate stops. As he walked through the atrium, his steps echoed in the wide expanse. The food court was empty. He looked about, then took the escalator up and crossed diagonally to the Lexington Avenue side. Making certain that he was entirely unobserved, he moved quickly to a well-worn double door of light-colored wood and pulled open its right half. His heart raced, his breathing accelerated. Not until the door closed behind him did he permit himself to relax, relent, and calm down.

A solitary figure, a placid middle-aged man, sat quietly reading a gray Kindle at the circular reception desk of Saint Peter's Lutheran Church. As he entered, the man looked up and greeted him warmly. "Good evening, Warren."

Warren knew only a little bit about him. His first name, Sheridan, that he was gay and partnered, and that he used to work in the capital markets group at Lehman Brothers before its sudden bankruptcy. One of the deeply faithful, this was what he did now. The man was outwardly at peace with this station in life and inwardly at peace with all things. Warren admired much about him.

"I need a little time alone," he said.

"We have all that you need," replied Sheridan with simple kindness.

Warren stepped into the small chapel, the one at street level that he always preferred to the big sanctuary one level below. Its bounded confines gave him a huge measure of comfort. So did the variant tones of white, the modernist vertical Louise Nevelson sculptures on the walls, and the few spare blond wood pews.

He took a seat, inhaled and exhaled deliberately, folded his hands together, leaned forward, and began to pray very hard.

The western sky was beginning to purple into darkness by the time Horvath finally approached his destination. His drive had been delayed by the acute angle of the setting sun, which slowed traffic considerably as he made his way from the tunnel to the New Jersey Turnpike, west on Interstate 280, and then Interstate 80. He wondered how people could do this every day. As he crawled along in traffic, Horvath made a running comparison to the congestion at his home in northern Virginia. After he exited the highway at Mount Hope, he concluded that New Jersey had the better deal in this regard, but that it was a very close call.

Heading into Dover, truly the established suburbs, he stopped the van at a red light. Horvath reached over and poked at Dawson MacNeil's face. Rigor mortis starts there, he recalled, and sure enough, the body was getting pretty stiff. He picked up the left arm and noted that the shoulder and elbow were also getting very tight. His timing could have been better, but this wasn't bad. It was manageable.

His instructions were precise. He was content to be compliant. He located the red-brick industrial building adjacent to the cemetery just as the last rays of sunlight were waning. A slim macadam driveway led alongside and around the back of the low-slung structure. He drove slowly and arrived at a paved lot facing three garage doors. He blinked the van's high beams and hit the horn once. Then he waited. Horvath had been here before, but it had been years. This place was his connection, one of his own contributions to the operation. He spoke to his cousin, *unokabátya*, very often, especially now. This was the only man living, other than his partner, with whom Horvath could share every manner of secret. But he figured that it must be fifteen years since he had last visited his place of business. It was a crematorium.

A windowless garage door, the one on the left, rose. Horvath drove inside, stepped out of the van, and stretched his back.

"János!" he yelled. "*Hogy vagy!*" He pronounced the words "*hodge vudge.*"

"Horvath *Basci,*" came the shouted reply using the Hungarian honorific. "How *you* doin'?" János—John to everyone but Horvath—affected an overexaggerated New Jersey Italian accent as he stepped forward and they embraced.

On the drive out from the City he had worked out their relationship in his head, an exercise in recollection to keep his brain in gear. János came to America in Horvath's first cousin's daughter's belly. She was pregnant when she fled Budapest with her husband after *os forradalom*, the failed revolution. The Party briefly permitted some people to leave for Austria. She took advantage of the opportunity. His parents arrived just before baby János was born. The two cousins met only after Horvath came to America permanently. There ensued a deep friendship that transcended mere bonds of biology. A man like János, an everyman, was extremely useful to someone in Horvath's line of work—his old line of work, that is. János in return deeply appreciated Horvath's mentorship and instruction as he built his own entrepreneurial presence on the edges of New Jersey's ever-nascent culture of organized crime.

"You know, I had to request and receive permission to do this."

"You did."

"Absolutely. They are good people, and they are trustworthy. I've been filling them in on our progress all along. I can't hold back on them."

"No, you can't." Horvath understood this dynamic more than János could possibly understand, but he was not entirely pleased that his younger cousin was sharing information. "You told them everything?"

"Most of it. Well, yeah. Everything. They were 'intrigued.' That was what my guy said. But they don't have a play here. My guy told me that, too. They were interested in receiving some of the service income."

"Tell me more about that," Horvath said. He was beginning to be concerned.

"I have to give them ten thousand," János said. "It's a simple tax. For this." He hooked a thumb in the direction of Dawson MacNeil's body in the van.

"You're correct," Horvath said. "*You* have to give them the money. I never agreed to anything like that."

János brooded for only a few brief seconds before he agreed. "Okay. You can owe me a favor."

"You," said Horvath. "Not them."

"They know that. Hey, did you know that my guy knows your guy? My guy's old man, I mean. The one who's ninety-three and retired down in Coral Gables—he still walks a mile and smokes four cigars every day. The two of them worked together in Cuba. You understand why I trust them?"

"Shut up, János," Horvath said with tolerance in his voice. "You are talking too much. We have work. Here, I'll get him out. You don't touch anything in that van."

Horvath hauled the body out while János rolled a mortician's gurney over, then helped his cousin lift the body onto it. The rigor mortis was not too far developed, although they did have to lean together on his knees to straighten MacNeil out at the waist. Horvath closed the van's door and caught up to János as he was wheeling the gurney into a freight elevator. He pulled on the frayed web strip that brought the two halves of the doors together and they began to descend. They reached the basement and exited the opposite side. Horvath instantly felt as if he had stepped into a wall of heat emanating from the oven that his cousin had prepared in advance of his arrival.

"We've been busy today. Pull him over here," János said, indicating an industrial conveyer slide on which was already mounted a thin wooden box, not quite a coffin, but sufficiently long and wide enough to support the body. He adjusted the temperature upward in preparation for the cremation. They lifted the body into the box and Horvath watched as János worked with precision and efficiency, methodically going through every pocket in his clothing. He withdrew MacNeil's wallet and handed it to Horvath.

"Burn it," he said.

János replaced the wallet in MacNeil's jacket pocket and smoothed the clothing over the corpse. He folded MacNeil's hands flat across his chest and stepped back. "This part gets real hot," he said. "We have to step back."

They both withdrew to a small shielded area of the crematorium containing a simple control panel. János pressed a wide collared button with one thumb and flipped a switch with the other hand. The oven door rose and Horvath felt an additional wide blast of heat, making him thirsty. He tried not to breathe too deeply. János now flipped the cover on another switch and held it as Dawson MacNeil's mortal remains began to be conveyed into the flames.

"You can watch over there if you want to," he offered, indicating a small window where the operator could observe the cremation. Horvath declined with a simple shake of his head.

When the body was inside and the door to the oven closed, János moved a dial, increasing the intensity of the flames. "Now we wait," he said. "Or do you want me to just take this from here?"

"That would be good," Horvath replied. "What are you going to do with his ashes?"

"We'll process them in the grinder just like anybody else. Then he'll get divided up between the other two jobs we had earlier today. Even the funeral directors don't know exactly how much ash to expect, and anyhow it differs all the time—like four to six pounds. They expect some variance."

"You are very good at what you do, János."

"I have to be. Remember who I do this work for. This work." He spread his hands to indicate the discreet disposal of an occasional corpse.

"I knew what you meant." Horvath wished that he had had this kind of technology available to him in the old days. He could have—it certainly existed then. But neither the Russians nor their subsidiary the Hungarians had been as creative as the Italian family enterprises in New York and New Jersey. "János. There is one thing I must find out before I go. What's your guy's name?" he asked.

"Celli," John replied. "A very simple name. Carter Celli. Tell me, have you ever heard of another Italian named Carter?" He laughed. "He's tough, though. And very smart. He has a law degree and an MBA. These people are not what you see in the movies and on HBO. They are excellent businessmen."

"You told him why I came out of retirement and all about the project I was doing."

"Yes."

"And he told you that his father worked with my colleague?"

"No, no. The old man in Florida is his grandfather, from his mother's side of the family. You remember there was a don who took the family business straight something like forty years ago—he became a deal guy? Investments, securities, venture capital—"

"What's his name?"

"Salvatore Carneccio."

CHAPTER 17

When Rick Yeager arrived, he found a surprisingly big crowd milling about the seventeenth floor atrium lobby of the Tower Club. Most of the men wore polo shirts and sport jackets, the favored summer business uniform for mid-management in northern Virginia technology companies. The women wore summer dresses, all business casual. Few were members of the club, a fact that Rick discerned from the bits of conversation he was able to overhear. The techies were here for a breakfast kicking off a "federal contracting opportunity conference," meaning (in this economy) that everybody was selling with very little chance that anybody in attendance was buying. Before too long the crowd filed noisily into the large front room that the club made available for semipublic functions like this one. Rick was left alone with two other men who were seated, one reading a newspaper and the other intent on an iPad, waiting for their breakfast guests.

He gazed across the wide stairs and out the proscenium window with the expansive top-floor view of Washington, DC, to the east. Rick Yeager's entrée to places like this came through Sanford Tuttle. This was Tuttle's world. He had to admit just how much he normally enjoyed the privilege. The Tower Club was the seat of tech royalty, a well-disorganized group orbiting the nation's capital but keeping its reservation distance. Tuttle served on the club's Board of Governors. The place was designed by Philip Johnson during his most productive years and its building, called Towers Crescent, was his only architecture in Virginia. It stood boldly on a small promontory in Tysons Corner close aboard the Washington Beltway—"outside the Beltway" to be sure, but just barely. It was the perfect place either to be seen or *not* to be seen, depending on the meeting and its participants. This morning Rick was happy not to be seen. He walked back and forth and waited for Sanford Tuttle, who was late. This was most unusual.

Another sleepless night, this time over family. Warren's telephone call came late, after Rick was drifting off, sometime after midnight.

Pop was dying.

His brother was coming apart just like he did after Mom.

Warren would never say so, of course, but Rick could discern that residual adolescent edginess, a quavering tremolo of fear in the timbre of his voice. No one else would be able to hear it. He confirmed just how far over the edge Warren was when his brother informed him that Julia was coming, at his request. They would be meeting this morning. That was the moment when all the worry began in earnest. The anxiety was all over him, as incessant as a dry wind.

The cynic in Rick wanted to scream out at his brother, "Well, at least this time you told me first!" and hang up the phone.

Instead he replied, "I'll be there too, for you and for Pop." They agreed to meet today at the hospital where Dutch had been taken, not far from his elder-care facility. Rick would have left at that moment, but by then it was almost 1 A.M. and he couldn't easily call Tuttle to cancel a 7 A.M. breakfast. Moreover, he definitely didn't want to.

So he walked, waiting, his empty stomach churning, every remembered fit of anxiety in his adult life—and there were plenty of them—coming to a burning point in his gut. He would be on the road northbound as soon as he had eaten, as soon as he could grab a little peace.

"You need some breakfast. You don't look so good." Sanford Tuttle delivered the entry line as he stepped from the elevator as if the Tower Club was a stage. He meant it to tease Rick about being hungry for the world-class buffet here. But as soon as Tuttle took full stock of the way Rick looked he retreated from his bright-good-morning personality and said simply, "I'm sorry. I take that back. Are you all right?"

Rick shook his hand, feeling pretty drawn and empty from the insomnia. He was pleased to be back, if only briefly, touching base with the one consistently optimistic anchor in his life. Tuttle had to see the world that way. This was how he thrived as an entrepreneur.

"No. Not even close. Sandy, my father's had a stroke. I'm headed up to see him today." He immediately scolded himself for leading off with his personal business, which should be of no concern to Sanford Tuttle. "Hey, it's my turn to apologize. I don't want to make this breakfast about my problems. I meant to say that only so you'd know why I'm already distracted."

"This is the trying part of life for anyone, Rick. And you'll manage," Tuttle replied, "because you have tensile strength. You may not see it, but a few of us who know you do." He saw a puzzled look cross Rick's face. "Steel. Toughness. The ability to take stress. You're being tested. Nobody wants it and nobody likes it. But trust me, this isn't going to tear you apart. Come on. Let's get some breakfast, and I want you to start by telling me what's going on with your dad. We'll get to business later."

If only it was that simple, Rick thought.

Over far too many carbohydrates for his new running program, Rick explained briefly what he knew. Dutch was resting after what the doctors said was a stroke. It is medically most difficult to determine the severity of the event in an Alzheimer's patient, especially at his stage.

"I don't know if this is the end or not," Rick concluded. "I'll know better when I see him later today. My brother Warren has been closer to these health issues since the start."

"I talked to him since you and I last met," Tuttle said.

"Warren didn't tell me that."

"You've been more than a little preoccupied yourself, from what I hear." Tuttle's downtown Washington sources, as always, were excellent. Rick had just spent another two days with lawyers, this time at the Department of Justice headquarters meeting with the Public Integrity Section. The subject was the FBI's conduct in his arrest, and the DOJ types could not have been more solicitous. "Are you finally done?"

"Not too likely that I'll ever be," Rick said.

"It may seem like that now," Tuttle replied. "You might be shocked and gratified at how high you've climbed in the general estimation of men I talk to."

"What are you and Warren doing together now?" Rick asked him, eager to change the subject.

"At GT3 we're supporting his current project."

"ViroSat?"

"I wish I had a piece of that deal."

"Get in line, Sandy. That was my intention, too. Not to get a piece of ViroSat, exactly. It would have been nice to do business with Compton Sizemore. Part of the reason that I took the position at Carneccio & Dice in the first place was that I thought I might bring them deal flow."

"Be glad that didn't work out. Did Lois think that having you in her stable would get her into Compton Sizemore's game?"

"She might have. She never mentioned it."

"Trust me. She thought about it. She's wanted to be there for a long time." Tuttle looked at him closely across the table. "So what are you going to do now?"

"Sandy, I'm as close to broke as I've ever been. The short answer is, I just don't know. I start over. It's what I do." Rick was resigned and mildly astonished that he would admit this central truth of his life out loud to Sanford Tuttle, to whom he always attempted to project an aura of escalating success.

"Plus you have that estate to settle."

"I sincerely hope it's only *one* estate I have to deal with. Maybe you can help me with that."

"You want to know about your numbers, right?"

"Right. Were you able to find out anything about that list? I haven't gone anywhere without that will and those numbers since I got them. They're in my briefcase in the car right now."

"The list by itself is meaningless. I did ask some of our mathematicians— the ones who do contract cryptography coding for the Federal Reserve's networks—to play with it. Nothing. Or I should say, nothing yet." Tuttle paused, looked away from Rick, and stared out the window for a moment, then continued. He pulled his leather card holder from his coat pocket and looked at the top page, scribbled thick with notes in blue ink.

"I changed my mind."

"What are you talking about?" Rick asked.

"I had planned on telling you only that and no more. Technically it's the truth. We aren't entirely sure what it is that you may have inherited from the late"—he referred to the note card—"Mrs. Hannah Geller. We really have nothing—and GT3 is extraordinarily good at deconstructing this kind of information. In this case, however, what we *do not know* is of consequence. Rick, you may have stepped into something."

"What have I got, Sandy?"

"You're asking the correct question," Tuttle said, "the question that our team is asking. And, I have to add, the question that your kid brother asked me when I shared the substance of this information with him. It was Warren who suggested to me a working hypothesis. You know how loyal he is to you."

"What was his hypothesis?" At least Tuttle remembered who the older brother was, Rick thought.

"I'll get to that," Tuttle responded. "Stay with me for a moment. Rick, recall what each of my companies has done. I don't mean our financial performance. I mean what we do to earn our money. We manage data and we share data. Then we manipulate data and reorganize it for our customers and clients, which are mostly the agencies of the federal government. When we increase the efficiency with which we manipulate data, we increase profits. Likewise when we increase the speed, agility, throughput, addressability, and interoperability of data transfer, we increase profits. If we don't do any of that, or if we don't do it very well, the market votes and we go out of business. Economic Darwinism. You've heard about how only the strong survive? That's flat-out wrong. Darwin never said that, never inferred it. Only the *adaptable* survive—that's where we make our profit and how we make our mark on society. We sell adaptability. Network adaptability in my case, market adaptability in yours. For your brother it's geoeconomic adaptability on a global scale.

"Now back to data. When do we run into trouble? When is data nonadaptable?"

"You're getting kind of Buddhist on me, Sandy. Philosophy does not become you."

"That's not a koan. It's a question that has an answer: when it's not electronic and it's stuck out of time."

"Meaning?"

"We cannot adapt, manipulate, organize, speed up, or move data if it's *paper* data. That's what you showed me—a piece of paper."

"Stuck out of time?" Rick found it difficult to see the point here.

"Warren suggested a form of bank accounts."

"You said that the numbers weren't bank accounts."

"I said that they weren't like any bank accounts that I've ever been familiar with. That's absolutely true."

Rick was catching on. "But . . . you haven't seen every kind of bank account."

"Correct. There are hundreds, maybe thousands of ways that accounts were organized before national and later international standardization. That fact led to Warren's hypothesis. It's possible that Mrs. Geller gave you some very old bank account numbers. Because they are simply written down, not even typed, they are nonadaptable. They are not the kind of data that we would normally consider at GT3."

"So who would consider it?"

"Our client. Have you ever heard of the Financial Systems and Services Corporation? FSSC?" Tuttle pronounced the acronym *fissick*.

"No."

"Ask Warren," Tuttle said, "when you see him this afternoon. He's very familiar with their operations."

The rest of their breakfast was quick, their conversation concerned primarily with the state of the Washington Nationals baseball team this season—heading into July's All-Star break, they had a decent shot at postseason play. Rick was reminded that Tuttle had led the financial syndicate of local tech leaders who lost the bid to buy the team several years ago, when DC got the franchise from Montreal.

"When I think of it, that's a pretty good example for you to remember in your present circumstances," Tuttle offered.

"You're always telling me something that I don't quite comprehend," Rick responded. "I end up playing straight man and asking you what you mean. You used to do that to me at QUATECH, too."

Tuttle laughed. "Here's your takeaway, Rick. I launched and sold three public companies before I tried to close that baseball deal. It was considered to be a fairly big and fairly public failure, right? You read at the time how I'd lost the magic touch, didn't you? Well Rick, nothing—not a thing I've ever done in business before or since—got me more attention or more investors than cratering that baseball deal. You're going to find the same thing occurring with your ten-minute career at Carneccio & Dice."

"I told the Justice Department yesterday that I was available if they needed a receiver."

"You keep your sense of humor, okay?"

"I will. One more thing, Sandy. You pay more lawyers than anybody I know except Warren, and he won't be any help with this one. Who do you recommend that I should use as an estate lawyer? I have to get a house sold and a will probated."

"Which county did she live in, Fairfax?"

"No. Arlington."

"No contest. Find a lawyer named Dan Ter Horst. Best there is. He used to be a Virginia district court judge. Should I call him for you?"

"That's not necessary. I know him," Rick said, as the burning in his stomach began again earnestly. That slow dry wind was accelerating.

In the Tower Club atrium, Rick said good-bye to Tuttle, who decided to work the crowd of techies attending the big breakfast at the contracting conference. He heard the spontaneous applause build with spirited hoots from the assemblage behind the door only seconds after it closed behind Tuttle. Every small universe has its rock stars, Rick realized, and Sandy is theirs. He waited for the elevator alone.

The path downstairs was a circuitous one that Rick had navigated previously. He took the elevator from seventeen to fourteen, around the small center core of the building to change elevators, then down to the entry lobby. The doors opened. As he stepped out and turned toward the parking lot, he heard a familiar voice from behind—one in which he could almost hear the smile.

Lauren Barr said, "Maybe our third time is the charm."

"Good morning. You really don't do all that well with boundaries, do you?" He was not entirely serious, but the sentiment clearly registered.

"So I've been told."

"And you knew I was here because—"

"—Because Mr. Tuttle's calendar is electronically accessible through-out GT3, to anyone working at the Chantilly executive campus, and the first entry for this morning read '7 A.M., Richard Yeager, Tower Club.' My brother Jonas saw it. We talk all the time and he told me. I thought I'd take unfair advantage of knowing that fact and meet you here."

"You do talk all the time." Rick again found her as maddening as she was compelling.

"Again, so I've been told."

"And you don't have a phone?"

"Would you have answered?"

"Lauren, this is decidedly not the time—"

"I know. You're headed back to the Justice Department one more time. I've figured that out. Let me tag along. I have a few issues to review with you. Please."

Rick paused for an instant, the information volleying around in his brain. He tried to recall if he had shared with Lauren Barr anything con-cerning the conversations he had been having downtown: No. So how would she know? Easy. She's a lawyer, this is still prime gossip for a slow summer, and Washington is the biggest small town in the world. Why would she care? She is interested in me. She wants to see how I manage this, he thought. No. She is not interested in *me*. She is interested in the *outcome*. She needs to know if I walk away clean, as Sandy says, with repu-tation enhanced. I can't get away from her too easily . . . and she is getting perilously close to—

"Could I possibly ride with you and talk to you? I'll catch the Metro back to Maryland once you get downtown?"

"I am not going downtown."

"Well then could I ride with you and talk to you and—"

"I'm driving to New Jersey to be with my father when he dies," Rick snapped at her, venom apparent in his tone. He immediately regretted his words, wondering where that microburst of anger came from.

Lauren Barr could not have looked more intensely pained if he had struck her—which was, to Rick, a disabling thought. Her eyes met his. She turned, walked away from where he stood staring, took about four steps—her short heels clacking on the marble foyer floor—wheeled about, and walked back. Her eyes were wet. Rick wondered whether he or Lauren might lose composure first. He fought the urge to apologize. He said nothing.

"How long will you be in the car?" she asked.

"Four hours, maybe a little more, but I don't see where—"

"Let me suggest a choice to you," she said softly, on the dividing line between bitterness and kindness. "I can walk out of your life for good right now, immediately. Do whatever you want with that estate. The alternative is that you take me with you, as far as any train station. Baltimore, maybe. Wilmington, Philadelphia. I don't care—however long it takes. I'm ready to tell you everything about my Tante Anna."

stress test. She could be imagining Warren's level of distress. What she was not imagining was his pain and sense of dread.

Her mother and father were waiting for her at the breakfast table. It didn't take thirty seconds for her mother to speak her mind.

"Why are you still involved with them?"

Julia sighed. She had been preparing to answer this question ever since she left Washington yesterday afternoon.

"All of us have unfinished business in life, Mom, but that's only part of it. Keeping a promise. Personal obligations. Professional obligations." She needed to be vague. *You can never tell anyone what happened here.* "Most of all, Dutch was always very good to me."

"You aren't going to fool your mother, dear."

"No, Mom, I'm not."

He was pacing, scanning, looking back and forth in nervous anticipation of her arrival. She drove up to the west front of Newark Penn Station, not three miles away from Upper Clinton Hill and her parents' house. Warren Hunter, Wall Street's reigning master of the universe (no one at Compton Sizemore would *ever* use that expression again) stepped into her car, embraced Julia briefly, and placed his forehead on her right shoulder. He either sobbed or gasped very quietly three times, sat upright straight in the passenger seat, and exhaled. The intimate physical shorthand had an immediate effect on Julia. This was exactly the extent—and no more—of physical contact that Warren had permitted during their nine days alone together. *I will build myself back.* Never an embrace. He had never even taken her hand.

"Warren, should we go somewhere and talk?" she asked, pulling away from the train station into the morning rush hour of downtown Newark.

"No."

"You are not exactly the picture of composure right now."

"J.D., you're the only one who could possibly know that."

"You're wrong there. Your brother knows."

"Rick has a few problems of his own to manage right now."

CHAPTER 18

Julia Diana Toussaint awoke very early in the bedroom that had been hers throughout her teen years. She stayed here for the entire time that she commuted from Newark to Teaneck while earning her Fairleigh Dickinson degree. Now a guest room in her parents' house, it had none of the piles of books, the over-furnishing, the wall-to-wall bulletin boards and posters, the clothing, the dolls of her girlhood, and all of the *stuff* that so aggravated her father when she lived at home. As she lay in bed for a few brief moments in the maw between asleep and awake, she remembered that time and felt grateful for its simplicity and its finality. Both of those characteristics made it a good time. Half a life ago.

Warren Hunter had called her shortly after 1 A.M.

"Where have you been? I'm here and I was waiting to hear from you."

"I was in a meeting. Then I went to pray."

"That's a switch."

"You don't know everything about me. Nobody does."

False calm in his expression but deeply rattled within. Warren sounded to Julia exactly like he did on the day of Gloria Yeager's burial—only then she didn't know what was coming. She allowed that she could be wrong, of course. Her perception now was certainly colored by what happened then. Warren, outwardly the rock, came fantastically undone. Those were indeed the worst days of his life. Sharing them with Warren had cost her a marriage. At some level Julia was proud of helping her brother-in-law, pleased with what she had been able to accomplish in nine days of talking and eight nights of crying in a hotel on an interstate highway. Another part of her knew that his measures of psychological recovery were at best temporary repairs, about to head into their worst

"From the way I see things, he's probably doing better than you are." Julia said this with benevolence.

"I spoke to him last night, before I called you. He's on his way. He'll meet us at the hospital."

They drove in silence until she hit the merge onto I-280.

"I'm the brother who takes care of family matters," Warren said.

"Today," Julia said, "is only going to be about Dutch, right?"

"Dutch is dying."

"You don't know that for sure."

"I spoke to his doctor twice this morning. He has no idea how this can be happening. Pop was definitely declining mentally. The Alzheimer's dementia was getting very profound—that's what he called it, very profound. But he was *physically* healthy. Then he has a sudden stroke."

"It was unexpected."

"Absolutely. The neurologist said that in patients who take Coumadin— that's an anticoagulant, a blood thinner, one of the drugs that Pop's cardiologist prescribed years ago—this manner of stroke is unbelievably rare. Again, his words. He told me that the drug inhibits clotting factors. He was at a loss to explain why that did not occur in Pop's case."

"Do you know what condition he's in now?"

"In and out. Do you want to hear the irony? The neurologist says that in some ways, he has *more* mental clarity after this event. Some event."

"I'm sorry, Warren."

"My pop is dying and I can't do a thing about it."

"Warren, Dutch may finally be arriving at the peace he's been seeking for years."

"When you carry around as much rage as he does," Warren replied flatly, "it's not peace that you're seeking."

"You don't know that."

"I do. J.D., you never knew him in his prime. Frankly, Rick and I didn't either. He was such a good man, and he connected to people. That's going to sound strange to you, but he did."

"It's not at all strange. He connected with me."

"It might have been a deliberate contrast to what he did for a living.

Or maybe it was *why* he was successful. You know he was a tax examiner. He could locate anyone no matter where they were hiding, and remember, these were the days long before the Internet. He was considered a national expert on finding people who definitely didn't want to be found. He used to give presentations at conferences about how to go about it, but his skill was really more of an art than something that could be learned.

"Now here's the ironic part, for a tax man, an enforcer. Once he located them, he had an even more unusual skill—encouraging those tax cheats to open up to him. I don't know what it was in his personality. They all told him everything, with no holding back. He could have been a pastor or a cop, the way he got people to confess. What an innate ability—he was a lion in his prime, J.D. I never saw it at the time, but I suppose that a son never does. Not a young son. We learn about it later." Warren was looking out the passenger window as if intent on studying the ragged scenery on the east side of the Garden State Parkway. "The irony was that because of that weird set of skills he had so many people in his life. They all connected to him deeply. And then none of them either stayed or actually got close to him for the long term."

"Warren, are you talking about Dutch or yourself?" Julia asked.

"I'm not in his league, J.D. In some ways his profession and his health issues isolated him. Who goes out of his way to be friends with a tax enforcement agent? My profession is exactly the opposite. Everybody wants to associate with me. Yet I close down to the whole world. Pop wouldn't let anybody inside. He still had people telling him all of their secrets. As far as I know, that has been going on his whole life. These last couple of years, since about the time that you and Rick split, he's been getting in touch with people he met years ago, all at his initiation. Veterans. Men he met during the VA hospital stays. Buddies from World War Two. Even two old guys he helped put in jail for bankruptcy fraud in the sixties."

"It's not unusual for people to get in touch with their lives when they're getting very old," Julia said. "You finally got close to him, didn't you?"

"Yeah. I did."

"Did he forgive you?"

"Of course he did."

"When are you going to forgive him?"

At a dead stop in an unmoving toll plaza clog of traffic, Warren asked Julia, "Did you know that Dutch was a liberator?"

"A concentration camp liberator? That kind?"

"Right."

"I didn't know. How did that happen?" Julia asked. "I thought he was a pilot."

"Not a pilot, a navigator. He and his crew flew into a small airport next to the Bergen-Belsen concentration camp. It was during the last weeks of the war. The camp was in Lower Saxony, between Hamburg and Berlin in northern Germany. It was outside the American sector. The British infantry liberated the camp. There's a famous BBC broadcast about the walking horror they encountered on the day they entered. The ground troops had a radio reporter along with them. It took less than a day for the American air force to start flying in supplies around the clock. Pop got there the night that the British arrived. He was brought into the camp because he spoke perfect German and they needed a translator pretty desperately. He was an eyewitness in real time."

"Rick never told me that. Neither did you, and all you talked about that week was your father."

"I only found out myself less than a year ago."

"Did Dutch tell you?"

"Yes."

"Do you think he waited long enough?"

"He had his reasons."

"Why are you sharing this with me?" Julia asked. "Why is it important for me to know about him?"

"It may explain a few things."

"I knew how much of a tortured soul he was when I met him, Warren. That was one of the first things I heard from Rick, before I met your father. Do you think that it began then?"

"I think it did."

"This is a little delicate, but I wonder if his Alzheimer's dementia has had the effect of reducing his memories."

"I considered that. It might. I also thought it just as likely the opposite could happen—that the cruelty of those memories would intensify and take him over."

"They didn't?" Julia was surprised at how rationally Warren was in describing Dutch's torment.

"That's the worst part," Warren said. "I don't know. I tried the last time I visited him, but there is no getting through. It's vital that I reach him."

"Is it vital for him or for you?"

"For both of us. You have no idea how vital," Warren said.

Past the toll plaza, accelerating to a full thirty-five miles per hour, still in thick traffic, Julia said, "You didn't really need me here, did you?"

"Maybe not. But I couldn't make that judgment until you got here. And I still don't know."

"Today is the first time that you and Rick and I will be in the same place since we stood at Gloria's grave."

"He doesn't believe that anything happened between us, does he?"

"What do you expect, Warren? All he ever knew is that I went away with you. I never got to explain. His reaction told me a great deal, however. It told me all I needed to know about our future."

"How many marriages," Warren asked, "break up without infidelity?"

"One, in my personal experience," Julia said.

"You're the most loyal friend I have," Warren responded.

"That's a remarkable statement."

"Remarkable for its truth."

"You don't deal very often in truth."

"No, I don't."

Reaching Paramus, close to the hospital where Dutch was resting, Julia tried again, seeking safe ground. "You're really going to close the ViroSat deal, right?"

"I'm counting on it."

"A lot of people are. Is it proving difficult for you to hold together?"

"It is. But not out of proportion to the deal itself, which is super-sized. You know all this, J.D."

"I had to hear it from you."

"Why?"

"Warren, there are going to be congressional hearings."

"There always are."

"Not like these. Tenley Harbison chairs the subcommittee on Communications, Technology, and the Internet. She has an incredible interest in regulating ViroSat, especially after that *Washington Post* article. There's a political advance possible now that didn't exist before. I expect that we're going to make an announcement in the next couple of days— oversight and regulatory hearings on the project itself. You should take that as a heads-up."

"A big hearing?"

"Big in importance. The point is to keep it contained, so that it's all Tenley's show."

"And you want me to be there."

"Warren, I want you to be the star of the show."

She saw him smile for the first time this morning.

When parked discreetly, a hearse outside a hospital facility is unnoticeable. Inside, Horvath sat watching. Nothing to do but observe this morning, which was fine with him. A lifetime ago one of his favorite instructors said something that disturbed him at the time. He later came to internalize the observation as great wisdom. Horvath, he said, you may not do as well as you think at this business. You may not be cut out to be a spy. You want to do things. Our value is not in doing things. Our value is in what we see and what we report. Don't be so anxious to take action.

This morning there was going to be no action. He had, however, accomplished much already. Before sunup he had taken the van to the worst projects he could locate, near Elizabeth River Park. He rolled down the windows, left the key in the ignition, and walked away with perfect assurance that the Dominicans' vehicle from Spanish Harlem would be re-stolen in less than an hour. János picked him up two blocks away in the hearse. Their trip to Dover and his trip back here alone took a total of ninety minutes. János had wanted to accompany him. That was out of the question. János had a big mouth. Horvath was still considering what to do about that. He had to tell his partner. They could solve anything together. This was still in perfect control.

Horvath watched the car pull into the lot. Two people stepped out. The white man looked older than the black woman, but not by too much. He was handsome in a man's way and had good hair. She was *nagyszerű*—wait, how did that translate? Gorgeous. Horvath smiled when it hit him. They looked like a morning news team on television.

He continued to watch.

CHAPTER 19

"You are uncharacteristically silent," Rick Yeager said. "I don't know you well, but I've never before seen you anything like this. You're contemplative." He glanced over his shoulder and flipped his left turn signal to accelerate onto the Washington Beltway where the Leesburg Pike cloverleaf tangled at the foot of the Tower Club. Lauren Barr sat in the passenger seat of his four-year-old BMW M3 sedan. She had carried along only a purse and a briefcase, both of which sat in the otherwise useless backseat of the car alongside Rick's briefcase and overnight bag.

"I am finding the right words," Lauren replied, "to apologize for this intrusion. Which is another way of saying that I am considering where to begin."

"Hannah Weiss Geller. You thought it was important to tell me about her, enough so that you're willing to travel with me. Lauren, you are a woman of unusually compelling persistence. This is odd, but I agreed to let you come along. You have no need to apologize. That was my decision."

"Thank you for that."

"For calling you unusual?"

"For respecting how important Tante Anna was to me."

"You've learned more about her."

"Yes. What do you know," Lauren asked, "about Jewish bankers in Cairo and Berlin during the Second Constitutional Era of the Ottoman Empire?"

"Absolutely nothing," Rick Yeager said. He drove and listened, as fascinated by the prospect of history and Providence intruding as he was by her voice and fragile beauty.

*   *   *

"Our great-great-grandparents knew a monumentally different world in the first two decades after the turn of the *last* century, exactly a hundred years ago. We have to begin there. Banking and financial law as we know them were rudimentary. They operated under a structure of private contracts with very little oversight. Governments did not care too much. Banks differed not only from place to place throughout the European continent and the Mediterranean Levant, they differed from bank to bank in the same city. We had an analogous situation here, Rick, especially in New York. There was almost no regulation. Banking was an exceptionally closed society everywhere. Personal associations in the financial industry, such as it was, were more tied to family and clan than they were to any kind of meritocracy. And there was no formal educational preparation for banking. It was all apprenticeship, especially fathers and sons.

"Jewish professionals were marginalized in some professions, integrated in others. Banking was a mixed bag. Culturally this was the era that gave rise to the Zionist movement, and certainly there was an abundance of anti-Semitism and the grossest conspiracy theories—they always seem to come out whenever people are economically threatened, interestingly, as they are today. It was an age of imagining Jewish-Masonic plots, publishing history's most notorious political fraud, *The Protocols of the Learned Elders of Zion*, and latent—not yet overt—distrust of Jews everywhere throughout Europe. In a number of ways, this was a time that prefigured the National Socialist period and the Holocaust. Certainly Hitler could not have risen to power without the strong undercurrents that already existed then.

"Yet oddly and somewhat ironically, along with the ingrained cultural distrust of Jews in Europe that was also a time in which Jewish banks prospered. This was especially true in Germany—Berlin, Hamburg, Cologne, Bremen, Hannover—they all had incredibly successful Jewish banking centers, bourses for equity exchanges, debt financing. It was also a marvelously creative moment in history, from the dawn of the new century until Weimar Germany in the 1920s.

"Along about the time of Germany's November Revolution at the end of the Great War, born in crisis, two events occurred in German banking. One was the formation of a new merchant bank by some very prominent and wealthy financiers in Berlin. They were Jews and Protestants together in the financial business. That was quite remarkable and progressive for 1919. The second was the bank's affiliation with a very old and established firm owned by a Jewish family in Alexandria, in Egypt— part of the waning Ottoman Empire. The family and their bank had been prominent in Egypt for centuries. It was a money-lending institution— basically what we'd consider to be private equity today.

"I know that this is a lot of history, but please listen to the backstory, Rick—it will become important to my aunt's life.

"The Alexandria firm simply bore the name of its family: *Hasab*. It means 'noble' in Arabic. They probably were a form of nobility at some time in the history of pre-modern Egypt, but nobody writes history about financial deals, Rick. They were Alexandria's most respected money-lenders and they provided a necessary service outside the strictures of Islam. Jews, always the outsiders there, filled that role for centuries in that part of the world. While Europe was only beginning to accelerate its cycle of hatred, it seems as though the Hasab organization was at its zenith, trusted and highly regarded. There were Hasab-financed projects all throughout the Near East. The members of the family were in all respects Arabic Jews.

"I know. Today, that would be such a contradiction in terms, but at the time the concept was—in certain slices of Arabic sociology—eminently acceptable. By the end of the Great War, the Ottoman Empire was giving way to tribal dominance and independence movements. Hasab was an institution of stability, but quietly, privately. Are you seeing a pattern, Rick? Not unlike financial practice today, or at least the way financing seemed to work before the economic downturn. Hasab was invested from Alexandria to Cairo, Jerusalem to Amman, and Beirut to Damascus.

"The global financial stresses started shortly after the First World War. Hasab was extremely well-capitalized, but its capital was completely distributed in hard investments, debt and equity. They were not very liquid. At the same time, there were tremendous opportunities beginning to be available to them, especially with the general breakdown in geopolitics and the reordering of the territories being formed from the detritus of the Ottoman Empire. Like any good lender, Hasab wanted to take advantage of an economy that was at the same time stressed and breaking wide open. Real estate, manufacturing, shipbuilding, agriculture, and new chemical technology were all available. We would call it a venture capital environment, but of course no one used that term then. The Hasab family wealth was no longer sufficient for all of the deal flow with which they were being presented. They needed new capital. They knew how to invest. The only new sources of capital were in Europe. It was a great opportunity because no one in Europe was particularly good at making investments in places like Egypt or Palestine.

"Enter a son, Azach Hasab, who was the first member of the family to be educated on the continent. He received a doctorate in mathematics at the Ludwig Maximilian University in Munich. He studied theoretical physics there along with Werner Heisenberg and took a research position in Berlin with Fritz Haber at the Kaiser Wilhelm Institute for Physical Chemistry. He was a brilliant thinker and an inventor, Rick. These were golden years for European science and mathematics. Azach was one of three scientists who traveled with Fritz Haber when he went to Stockholm to receive the Nobel Prize in Chemistry. As far as I know Azach Hasab was the only Egyptian at the Institute, probably the only one in German science. He always called himself an Egyptian, but culturally he had the most continental manners. This fits with Alexandria society of the time. Certainly he was not the only Jewish scientist there— Jews were predominant in German science then. Einstein worked at the Institute before Hasab arrived.

"The Institute, however, was not immune from severe financial pressures. All of Germany was in an economic swamp after that war and the November revolution. Huge financial storms were brewing. So Fritz Haber turned to his Egyptian colleague for help—after all, he was from a family that was one of the Levant's most prominent financiers, and there he was working in his own lab. Have you ever heard of the Emergency Fund for German Science? That was a rhetorical question, Rick.

Of course you haven't. It was an invention of Azach Hasab, who just happened to bridge the worlds of theoretical physics and finance in Weimar Germany. He raised the money that Fritz Haber needed, and he got very inventive along the way. The financing he arranged prefigured all kinds of methods that we take for granted in the law and in finance today—expansion of debt capacity, public-private partnership, quasi-equity, convertible security interests, derivative securitization, risk decoupling . . . all of it seems to have started right there with those German physicists desperate for cash.

"Rick, he was the world's first 'quant.'

"The Emergency Fund salvaged the Institute. Arguably that mild-mannered mathematician saved quantum physics, but I think that's a reach. Inarguably, he found his calling. He would now raise capital in Germany for Hasab projects in the Near East. The Hasab firm could diversify and achieve superior returns by investing in financial instruments in Germany. Even better, Hasab could now take on capital from investors outside the family, all because of Azach's relationships in Europe. Win-win for everybody.

"Now remember the merchant bank I mentioned? Jews and Protestants together in Berlin? It was a near-perfect place for a true outside-outsider like Azach Hasab, and of course he gravitated there. A little less than two years after he raised the Emergency Fund, Hasab was getting mighty restless in physics and chemistry research. The new bank had just been formed and registered by three partners named Meier, Seckendorf, and Böhmer. That's exactly what they named their company— Meier Seckendorf Böhmer GmbH. It was considered very avant-garde of them in that decade of decadence, the 1920s, simply to use the three surnames strung together with nothing else to describe the company. Minimalist in marketing, intense in approach, conservative in management, aggressive in financial operations. There are still people on Wall Street who tell stories about them. Two of the first Harvard Business School case studies in 1931 were about MSB mining deals in the Ruhr Valley industrial region. The three partners, along with Hasab and a handful of carefully chosen associates, set out to build a classic merchant bank along British and German lines. They succeeded magnificently.

The new bank operated with both an investment arm and an advisory arm—and in their deals, a lot of times those lines got blurred. You could do that legally and acceptably in those days. The firm became a model of . . . well, German efficiency and Jewish connectedness. Network finance, if you will.

"I promise that I will bring us to Hannah Weiss Geller, Rick. The whole story from that point on is all about Hasab—the firm not the guy—and Meier Seckendorf Böhmer.

"As I said, the merchant bank was incredibly successful throughout the Weimar recession and later in the Great Depression. They chose investments most carefully. They knew the new technologies—Hasab's years at the Kaiser Wilhelm Institute certainly helped. They encouraged creativity. They fostered an entrepreneurial spirit. They deployed investment capital on strict timelines and harvested it with care. They never initiated litigation but they were ferocious and—what would a Christian call it?—Old Testament judgmental whenever there was any malfeasance or if anyone dared to sue them. As a commercial lawyer I kind of like that disposition. These were tough guys. Good guys but very tough.

"The bank grew and continued to prosper for the next fifteen years. It was one of the brightest lights of Germany in those interwar years. Because it was strictly a private partnership, no one outside the organization was particularly knowledgeable about the profits that MSB was generating. Secrecy and circumspection became important parts of the firm's business culture. At the same time, Germans were losing their life savings, salaries were being paid in worthless paper during rampant inflation, and there were grocery riots. All of the conditions that gave rise to National Socialism were also tearing apart German society. Those conditions were also presenting excellent investment opportunities for Meier Seckendorf Böhmer and of course, for Hasab. Think of it, Rick. Bankers in Berlin and Alexandria, Jewish bankers just like in the wildest anti-Semitic conspiracy fantasies, were building economic society for Germans and Arabs—the people who despise them, the people who very soon are going to become their active enemies. Tolerance, what little existed in Germany and in Egypt, was about to end.

"The bankers at Meier Seckendorf Böhmer had even done business with the German state when the government was run by the Social Democrats, before the establishment of the Third Reich in 1933. Prior to that moment in time, they *were* the establishment, well respected, probably protected somewhat because Seckendorf was the son of a Lutheran bishop in Berlin. But by 1935, the Nazis had harshly consolidated power and were visibly ascendant. That was the year of the Nuremberg Laws, Rick, defining Jews in all kinds of pseudoscientific ways, restricting us with 'laws for the protection of German blood and German honor.' They chiseled Jewish family names off the war memorials and closed public facilities to Jewish citizens. Race was everything.

"As wonderful as their merchant banking business was—profits were outstanding—the environment for the firm was becoming untenable. Seckendorf, that Lutheran? He was married to Meier's daughter. Marriage to a Jewish woman was now forbidden under the new Nuremberg Laws. What do you do when you have such a wonderful business that you cannot operate anymore? Complicating matters, the investment capital from Alexandria—all of it was Arab money—is now spread out in corporate holdings, either loans or stock, in Germany, Austria, Czechoslovakia, Belgium, and the Netherlands.

"So the bankers began quite earnestly to divest. They called in the commercial notes and sold the stock. They did it quietly, methodically, without any announcements, all perfectly in keeping with the circumspect way that the partnership was used to doing business. In a matter of nine months, as the German persecution of Jews intensified, MSB became liquid. All of the merchant bank's holdings were now in cash in German banks. This was excellent timing, because two other factors came into play. The German authorities had already begun looking *extremely* closely at the bank's deals and all of its holdings. At the same time, Germany was making political moves in Austria, Hungary, and Czechoslovakia. The preparation and groundwork would eventually result in all of the extraterritorial gains around Germany before the war began in 1939. Those incursions were making it inordinately difficult for Jewish-owned enterprises to stay in business everywhere in Europe, obviously affecting the MSB investments.

"These were forward-looking financiers. They knew how to read the future. They knew when to get out. Now that they had converted their holdings to cash, the next challenge was getting that cash out and getting themselves out. Make no mistake, the Nazis were closing in.

"Patience, Rick. I'm getting to Tante Anna.

"By sometime in 1936 their plan was set, all worked out ahead of time. Everyone was sworn to secrecy. There were sixty-seven employees of Meier Seckendorf Böhmer in Berlin, another nine at a satellite office in Hamburg. That included Azach Hasab, by the way, who was by this time a full partner in the merchant bank with a German wife and three distinctively non-Aryan children.

"Easter Sunday came early in 1937. March twenty-eighth. The German Reich closed on Thursday afternoon for Good Friday and the Christian Easter holiday. Pesach—that's Passover, Rick—also began that evening. When I first heard about this in Israel, the man who told me the story made the explicit and obvious comparison to the Biblical Jews in Exodus fleeing Egypt. All of the people at Meier Seckendorf Böhmer and all of their families were supposed to depart Germany at the exact same moment. Jews—remember, by now our people were all registered— were permitted at the time to leave Germany, but if they did, they could not come back.

"That was perfectly fine with the partners at MSB. They never intended to return. The plan was to leave the office exactly as if it was closing for three days—desks, papers, the electro-mechanical teletype machines that they used for tracking the markets and trading . . . all of it was left in place. The firm's investment files and the paper records had already been taken away and stored off-site. The plan was extensive and very well thought-out. There were no less than sixteen departure directions from Berlin. Two hundred and forty-six people all told would go— wives, children, parents included.

"Rick, among those family members was a young woman named Hannah Sara Weiss. Her father, a Hungarian Jew, worked for Azach Hasab. He was one of the two primary managers of the Egyptian investments.

"In six months' time, by that fall of 1937, they would reassemble Meier Seckendorf Böhmer in New York. The complete firm was supposed to disappear in Germany and then reappear in New York, with business operations to resume as usual. It was a magnificent plan, and as far as we know, it worked—partially.

"The disappearance of the firm was indeed carried off during that Easter weekend in March. But now a bit of urban legend begins to intrude on the story, because from that moment going forward, no one knows precisely what happened, or why the firm never reconstituted itself in Manhattan. We know about the original plan because some of the extended family members—*some*, Rick, *very* few and not part of the exodus—surfaced after the war, maybe eight or nine years later. The first indication that anyone at all had survived from Meier Seckendorf Böhmer GmbH was in a displaced persons camp in western Ukraine. We know that none of the employees ever made it out of Berlin. Speculation in Israel was that the Gestapo found out about the migration and put a stop to it instantly. That makes about as much sense as every other explanation. The outcome is still the same.

"Every single partner, associate, and employee of the entire merchant bank failed to survive the war, Azach Hasab included.

"Those perfect records from the extermination camps account for two hundred and one out of the two hundred and forty-six people who were supposed to migrate to New York. Because of the ages of the children, it's most likely that twenty or more of them also died in the Shoah. That leaves about fifteen or twenty more from the families that still can't be accounted for.

"I knew about Meier Seckendorf Böhmer, of course. It's such a sad legend among families that have strong ties to the German Jews. But until my mother told me, I had no idea that she was connected.

"Tante Anna was the only one of them that anyone ever found, Rick."

He was well past Baltimore on Interstate 95 northbound by the time Lauren paused.

"Let me make a leap of logic here," Rick said.

"Please. Go on."

"Are you suggesting that I should infer something about the list she left me along with her will? That it has something to do with the disappearance of the Meier bank fortune?"

"Meier Seckendorf Böhmer."

"Right. What you said."

"Not necessarily. No. Not at all."

"Mrs. Geller is going to leave me, an investment advisor, a list of what? Secret numbered bank accounts?"

"That's extremely unlikely. Every commercial bank account in Germany that was in any way traceable to Meier Seckendorf Böhmer was cleaned out during the National Socialist period. They had another nine years to govern the country after the disappearance of the firm. MSB never used Swiss or Austrian accounts, either. Everything was in Germany. Except for a lunatic neo-Nazi fringe and the kind of people who still believe in Jewish-Masonic financial conspiracies, no one could possibly think otherwise. The money is flat-out gone."

"Then what does that list of numbers mean?"

"Maybe nothing," Lauren said. "Possibly everything. There is no enduring mystery left about where the cash went. It was confiscated into the treasury of the Third Reich with recordation. The contemporary reports from the Nazi government's banking overseers were so precise they were scary. The cost accounting within the merchant bank even traced the expenditures for all that never-completed travel to New York. Of course, it took German unification after the Berlin Wall came down before the entire banking history became available. After it did, however, reconstruction of the records was quite perfect. My mother told me that there was even a series of monographs about the financial accounting written a few years ago at the Hebrew University of Jerusalem. They use the Meier Seckendorf Böhmer affair as a case study. There was a civil legal case for restitution brought in the Brandenburg federal state in 1996. I read the case. It was settled."

"Then what is it that I have?"

"A context. That's precisely what you have now. And I sincerely hope that it helps us."

"Lauren, why have I never heard any of this before?"

"Tears in the ocean, Richard Yeager."

"Meaning?"

"There is deepest meaning in two hundred lives, or a single life," Lauren said quite softly with moist eyes, "even among the six million, the countless Calvaries. *Hashem yinkom damam.*"

Rick Yeager drove on, sad and silent, his mind and soul very empty.

"There." Lauren Barr pointed at a sign. "Could we please pull into the rest stop?" The sign read MARYLAND HOUSE, one of the two travel plazas on the highway.

"It's been renovated recently," Rick offered. "I think it used to be the worst in America."

"There's no contest as far as I'm concerned—it still is," Lauren replied as he pulled the BMW to a stop. "I'll meet you back here—and then I guess you can leave me in Wilmington. Are you ready for a second cup of coffee?"

"I am, but let me buy, okay?" Rick punched the remote lock, which chirped back at him.

"Thank you for offering. Grande caffè mocha, please, skinny, have them use two percent milk, but *with* the whipped cream."

Rick stared as she walked off quickly in the direction of the restrooms. He caught himself exhaling.

The wait at the Maryland House Starbucks was much longer than he expected—a full fifteen minutes in line behind the summer's I-95 traffic. This was precisely the apex moment of the morning when the vacation travelers lined up for their caffeine fix. None of them seemed to have made up their minds before arriving at the counter. Rick took it all in stride, an undersized aggravation, as he absorbed Lauren's whole "context" of Hannah Weiss Geller's life.

What a shame for it to end alone on the west bank of the Potomac River.

Surviving the profane means living to die the mundane.

She had a reason for what she left to me.

I don't even drive anymore, Richard.

He squinted in the brilliant sun on the walk back to his car holding

the eco-brown carrier with the two hot cups balanced on the diagonal—
one simple coffee of the week, something called a Pike Place Roast, and
one exquisite skinny caffè mocha with whipped cream.

She should be standing by the car.

Lauren?

Where is she?

He unlocked the car—again, the chirp.

Vanished.

Lauren Barr, her briefcase, and *his* briefcase containing the only copy
of Hannah Weiss Geller's will and a piece of tablet paper with eighteen
lines of numbers. He had another copy of *that*, of course. It was also in
his briefcase.

Gone.

CHAPTER 20

Warren Hunter sat in the sunlight on a park bench. He faced the surface parking lot of the Bergen Regional Medical Center, watching traffic. With a loose fist to the side of his face, he looked introspective and settled. From the hospital's air-conditioned lobby, Julia Toussaint watched him. When she was in high school, Julia planned to be a nurse. She even entered the nursing program when she was a freshman at Fairleigh Dickinson. That was before she caught the political virus, for which she was always thankful. She considered that college epiphany to be one of the most positive developments in her life. For as much as she sincerely enjoyed caring for people, Julia couldn't stand hospitals. During those tumultuous unplanned days alone with her brother-in-law after Gloria Yeager's funeral, she shared her aversion with Warren. Admitting this was not giving too much of herself away—Rick was well aware of it before they were married.

"At the end, Mom got to hate places like this," Warren announced once they arrived at the Paramus campus.

"I remember that."

"And sometimes I think that Pop is more comfortable in a hospital than he is anywhere else."

"Entirely possible, Warren."

After that he walked outside and sat down, alone. They both realized at about the same time that there was nothing else to talk about. Strange and annoying, Julia thought. He pulled me into his life then and now. He is now pushing me away, but not too far away. He wants proximity but not intimacy. He shares that with Dutch.

* * *

Warren Hunter didn't really dream, at least as far as he knew. His dreams, or whatever they were, never strung together in narrative. They swirled. They were difficult to remember. Like many of his wholly wide-awake thoughts, they whipsawed from time to place unhinged from continuity. He sat on the bench in the morning sun enjoying the shallow memories. His head nodded. His hands were loose in his lap.

—Pop laughing loudly scooping up Warren gleeful stumbling toddler tossing him high above his head catching him now rolling him around the back of his neck upside-down then swung by his waist face-to-face with Pop repeating it all as Gloria chuckled with great gentleness and joy.

—Pop's silent unmoving vacant stare Warren more grown but still small under his arm drawn in closely a firm hand on the boy's head television volume far too soft as bombers and flak tent the German sky in black and white movement then soldiers running across the fields soft muffled gulp out of Pop stroking the boy's head.

—Pop already pretty old creaking squatting low fiddling with that impossibly ancient Rolleiflex camera below cap and gowned Warren on the lawn impeccably manicured fronting Old Nassau a little left yes right there right there the tower is perfect wan smile returning his broadest pride with the *schclickt* of the shutter.

He awoke not with a startle but with a deep breath to the touch of Rick's broad palm gripping his right shoulder.

"How long have you been here?" his brother asked.

"I'm not entirely sure."

"Have you gone in to see him yet?"

"No. I was waiting for you."

"Is Julia here?" Rick sat next to Warren and squinted in the sun.

"Inside."

"Warren, before we go to see Pop, I need to thank you for . . . everything you did there in the Carneccio & Dice situation," Rick began.

Warren shook his head and held up a flat palm in Rick's direction. "I had to. It's not just that you're my brother. There was no reason at all for that mess to happen, especially to you. There were also significant professional considerations for me and some pretty serious implications for Compton Sizemore."

"Still, I—"

"We've said all that we need to, okay?"

"You're just as bad as he is, you know." Rick broke into an easy grin.

"You mean Pop?"

"Yes. Neither of you will ever deal with anything emotional, especially personal gratitude."

"I'm learning," Warren replied. "Really. I am." He stood and turned to face Rick, embracing him briefly and tightly as he rose.

From the hearse, Horvath stared at the two brothers and did not move as they walked in the hospital's door.

Rick's reunion with Julia was as wordless as it was affecting. She was standing at the entrance to Dutch's hospital room as the brothers arrived— radiant, sad, kind, wonderful, beautiful, Rick thought. She simply walked up to him and took hold, drawing him close. He kissed the top of her head and stood at the open door, looking over her to see his father asleep, accepting what was certain to come.

Rick was convinced that today was Dutch Yeager's day to die.

They were still holding on to each other, neither releasing, when Warren returned to the corridor accompanied by a small woman in a short laboratory coat embroidered in blue: SHARON ANSARI MD, INTERNAL MEDICINE. She carried a metal medical chart.

"This is my brother, Rick, and this is Julia," Warren said, making the simplest introduction to the doctor. "Could we sit somewhere to talk?" The doctor nodded and motioned the three of them to the bright solarium at the end of the hospital passageway. Rick followed last, reluctant to leave his father's doorway and more reluctant to hear what the physician would have to say.

"He's dying, isn't he?" Rick asked as soon as they were seated, more a statement than a question. "This really is it."

"We can never be entirely certain." The doctor spoke softly. "Overall his condition is not at all good, and it will not be long." Rick heard very little of what she said after that. ". . . systemic shutdown . . . largely unrecoverable . . . multiple organ failure . . . delirium . . . in and out of consciousness . . . the most severe difficulties in cognition . . . very common in the end stages of Alzheimer's . . . this event was a terrible stroke . . . would already have killed a less robust man . . . end stages . . . today . . ."

"You told me that he awoke twice since the stroke," Warren said.

"He did," the doctor replied. "The second time his cognition was much weaker than the first. And both of those times he's spoken."

"In English?"

With a puzzled look she flipped open and referred to the chart on her lap. "I was not with him yesterday afternoon or last night during the times when he was conscious," the doctor reported. "The chart doesn't say anything other than an annotation that he spoke to the nursing staff."

"The last time I visited him," Warren said, "he could only speak in the German language."

Dr. Ansari turned pages deeper into the chart. "I see that in the consulting neurologist's notes from Fair Lawn." She closed the chart and looked from Rick to Julia to Warren. "It is not common, but neither is it rare, for multilingual Alzheimer's patients to conflate their languages. This is apparently what occurred earlier with your father. The situation he is facing now is medically more complicated and much more serious. Mr. Yeager has sustained a massive stroke. There are profound neurological effects. There were no early risk indications of ischemic stroke, but again, that result is not unusual in Alzheimer's patients of his age."

"Doctor," Warren interrupted. "Straight up. Today is the end, right?"

Rick saw it, evident but almost imperceptible. *The tell.* Her eyes blinked much too quickly as she returned Warren's famously penetrating gaze. He did not wait for her spoken answer, but stood and walked away.

At Dutch's bedside Rick was expecting his mind to race. Instead he found himself standing in the weirdest stillness, emotions dampened, steeped not in memories but in questions. He was aware of the slow tap-tap of Julia's shoes on the floor of the hospital room, the touch of her fingers lightly on his back.

"*Ich liebe dich*, Pop," he whispered. "*Du wirst den Frieden jetzt finden.*" You'll find peace now. "*Schliesslich.*" Finally.

First in the haze, then in the darkness, then in the dim light. The clouds were dark, shots of sunlight from the eastern sky. He was looking down through the eyepiece of a Norden bombsight, clouds blending with flak, the preternatural gray spurts of smoke swirling within the billows of white emerging as dawn bloomed. Steady, steady, arrival at the moment he waited for on every run, this one over Pomerania—there it was, utter calm, security.

Das ist mein sohn, der ältere. My son, the older one.

"Pop?"

Ich muss ihm . . . must tell . . . ich muss ihm erzählen.

"Reichard," said Dutch Yeager very clearly.

"Yes, Pop."

"*Sie müssen wissen.*" *Must know.*

"I do know. Ja, ich weiss."

"Nein, sie mussen wissen." *Er kann nicht . . . cannot know, er kann nicht wissen, not yet. Never told him. Nie.*

"Ich sollte was wissen?" Rick asked. "Was ist so wichtig?"

Sehr wichtig, important. The dark-bright flashes of flak were coming closer now, the relative speed of the B-24 through the airspace much more apparent in his peripheral vision. The plane sliced through clouds and flak, ground visible then obscured, then visible again, on track, on point. Something small was wrong though. The voice in his headset was too gentle. No time to consider that right now. The explosions in the sky grew so near that the instantaneous pressure pulses thudded with each flash on the clumsy big bird's skin and his curved window. He could not be— would not be—distracted.

"Alois Stauber," Dutch said, "ist der andere." *The other one, der andere.*

"Pop, I don't know what that means."

"Die Rechnung."

"An accounting. Ja, jetzt verstehe ich. Pop, I understand. You have always been a good man. We are good sons, and today you have nothing but goodness to account for."

He is . . . wie sagt man das auf Englisch—? . . . crying. Weinen. Nein! Nicht accounting, Rechnung, account! Und da—es gibt den jüngeren. My younger one. Warren.

"Beide meiner Söhne." Dutch's voice was clear but weak now.

"Both of your sons are here, Pop." *Die Stimme des Warrens. Warren's . . . was? Was? Voice.* "Rick, can you understand him? You actually speak the language where I can only fake it." *Jetzt weint er auch. He is . . . crying . . . too. Why so difficult, so schwierig—! . . . zu verstehen?*

"Pop?" *Reichard. Out, get it out—bekommen Sie es heraus! Ich muss . . .*

"Weiss. Seine Liste sondern Staubers Rechnung."

"Do I know? No. Warren, I'm sorry, I don't understand him. Pop, I understand the words, but they don't mean anything."

Du müsst verstehen, du must!

"Ägyptisches Reichtum, in ver—ver—"

"Fair, Pop?"

"Vereinig—" *So schwierig!*

"Allesch."

"All, Pop?"

"Alleschan."

"We love you, Pop."

"Tut—Tut—"

"Was sagst du? Es tut mir leid? Pop, no. You have nothing to apologize for."

"Er weiss wer aber nicht wo."

"Warren, he just said 'he knows who but not where.' Gehen sie mit Gott, Pop."

The clouds bloomed awesomely bright in German sunlight at sixteen thousand feet. The antiaircraft artillery rounds arced high from the western Pomeranian fields, close aboard the city, thicker and closer to the plane. There was the bend in the river, the aim point—two kilometers north of the factory. Primary target. It broke beautifully clear and free in his line of sight through the sky. This was the pre-briefed moment for the navigator's handoff to the bombardier, and he yelled, *You got it* into the throat microphone. He barely understood the comeback acknowledgment. The voices on the intercom were far too thin and scratchy to comprehend now, crackling in the static filling his ears. He brushed the furred earpieces off with a brief violent shake of his head down on his right shoulder and momentarily longed for a cigarette. The dunning drone of the big super-turbocharged R-1830 radial engines was deafening to the edge of pain but overridden in volume by the thuds, the explosions of flak. He knew what was coming. He waited for the explosion. It arrived quickly, a solid hit in the back of the big bird. He felt it but never saw it. The curve downward began then in a sweeping wide arc, very fast—not quite a spin but a broad flat outside loop, descending. The negative g-forces as the B-24 came apart had the effect of feeling like he was free-floating. Dutch breathed easy. He smiled as the ground rushed closer and closer, then closed his eyes and mouthed the words, so quietly, that his mother had taught him to say every night before he went to sleep.

"Vater Unser in Himmel, geheiligt werde Dein Name—"

Two good sons wept openly without a bit of shame.

CHAPTER 21

Two mornings later, at the top of page B15 in the *New York Times*, the news obituary spread across four columns.

Dutch Yeager, Liberator, Legendary NJ Fraudbuster
By Anna Glenn

Gustav Adolf "Dutch" Yeager, a liberator of the Bergen-Belsen concentration camp in northern Germany while a first lieutenant in the United States Army Air Forces in 1945 who went on to a public service career uncovering some of the most celebrated financial frauds from the 1960s through the 1980s for the State of New Jersey, died in Bergen County on Tuesday.

The death was announced by his son Warren Hunter, the deputy chief of investment and merchant banking at Compton Sizemore. Mr. Hunter explained that he had adopted the English form of his father's surname. The cause of death was complications of a stroke and Alzheimer's disease.

Mr. Yeager, born in Trenton, was the son of German immigrants. During the Second World War while serving as a first lieutenant in the US Army Air Force, he was a navigator in the 487th Bombardment Group (Heavy) at Lavenham, Suffolk, England. He earned the Distinguished Flying Cross and three Air Medals for combat air action in the European Theater of Operations. During the final months of the war he also worked in military intelligence, an assignment that earned him a footnote in several accounts of the war's end. Columbia University historian Daniel Staunton, in his 2010 book, *The Enemy More Mighty: The Eighth Air Force in Germany,* wrote that his "perfect German brought him to the attention of the Office of Strategic Services in early 1945. Wiry young 'Dutch' Yeager from New Jersey found himself unwillingly seconded to the intelligence service. In this way he became one of the first four Americans to enter the Nazis' Bergen-Belsen concentration camp in Lower Saxony on April 15, 1945, on the day of its liberation by the British 11th Armoured Division and accompanying Canadian forces. Yeager arrived on scene shortly before dusk. He stepped in as the primary translator for British and American intelligence operatives that night, because it turned out that the only translator accompanying the British military forces had but a single year of Oxbridge German under his belt, and it was immediately apparent that the man was inadequate to the task. Speaking rapidly in Niederdeutsch, or Low German, to the few remaining SS guards, Yeager became the first officer among the Allies to comprehend the massive typhus epidemic then raging in the camp and more important, to discern the existence of other killing camps in areas farther to the east still held by German forces. Major General William J. Donovan, Director of the Office of Strategic Services (OSS), later called Yeager 'our first silent hero at the end of the war. His contribution to the Allied cause was unbounded, without measure. What he gave the nation and the world shall never be wholly known.'"

Following the war and a brief career as a production engineer, Mr. Yeager was appointed an enforcement examiner in the New Jersey Department of the Treasury.

His career as a fraud-busting commercial investigator was as quiet as it was legendary, according to former New Jersey Attorney General Anthony Agnelli. "Dutch had a most uncanny ability," he recalled yesterday, "a psychological sense, a capacity of temperance that drew people in and permitted them to tell him their secrets. I think that it was wholly inadvertent, but it was what made him great. The kind of complex tax frauds that he investigated tend to break apart only when you understand human motivations and are able to draw out a few key pieces of information. That was Dutch's gift. He could always locate the core of the conspiracy and then get people comfortable talking about it."

Mr. Yeager pushed doggedly in tax probes, Mr. Agnelli said, citing his work in the Essex Empire public corruption scandal of 1971. In that prosecution, eleven elected officials and fourteen others in Newark and Nutley were convicted of tax fraud, bribery, and conspiracy in a wide-ranging scheme where in excess of $8 million in federal funds were diverted. Mr. Yeager, a notorious insomniac, broke the case after weeks of careful study of the state tax records for three construction firms. They were all subsidiaries of a shadow holding company called Essex Empire Builders, which he meticulously traced through a series of bank accounts back to members of the Newark City Council, all of whom were tied to elements of organized crime. The federal funds, appropriated for rebuilding Newark after the civil disturbance and race riots of 1967, were largely recovered, a first in New Jersey history according to Mr. Agnelli. More than twenty of the Essex Empire conspirators eventually served jail time.

In 1983, then the new chief of tax enforcement for the state, Mr. Yeager was at the center of a joint federal-state task force again investigating organized crime in New York and New Jersey. By this time in Bergen, Essex, and Hudson Counties, the influence of Mafia families had become pervasive and overbearing, especially in the construction industry, labor unions, trucking, and warehousing. Stymied task force prosecutors turned to Mr. Yeager as their expert in tax and finance, said Mr. Agnelli, because that avenue was the only possible way to build a case against dons like "Havana Mike" Lucca and Antonio "Choirboy" Cortale. After months of scouring corporate and personal financial records, Mr. Yeager took a most unusual action. According to a contemporary report in the Newark *Star-Ledger,* he held a lengthy series of meetings alone with "capos" and mid-level "soldiers" in the two New Jersey crime families. In these meetings, he patiently explained the exact amounts and flows of profit and loss in the legitimate or "cover" enterprises in which the Mafia families were involved. "He was a thoroughly serene and enduring guy," said Mr. Agnelli, who served on the task force, "and once the full extent of those old dons' sweetheart deals was understood by the rank and file in their organizations, we thought all hell would break loose." Unexpectedly, calm prevailed because of Mr. Yeager, who found himself in the unusual position of mediator. "He was the only guy they could all trust. Dutch was able to make them see where the money actually went. Even more elegantly, he demonstrated to a whole generation of wiseguys how going straight in business would benefit them financially even more than operating the front companies." The 1983 task force operations resulted in four convictions, including of Mr. Lucca and Mr. Cortale. Among the federal prosecutors was then-Assistant United States Attorney Tenley Harbison, now a United States senator from New Jersey.

Mr. Yeager's marriage to Gloria Alice Montgomery ended in divorce.

In addition to his son, financier Warren Hunter of Manhattan, he is survived by a son, Richard Montgomery Yeager, chief executive officer of a financial services firm in Virginia; and a sister, Maria Eleanora Yeager Biel of Florham Park.

Rick Yeager folded his copy of the *Times* inside-out and lengthwise, placed it on the dining table, and stared at the picture of Dutch in his prime. Scattered clouds and spotty sunshine alternated in the warm steady breeze six stories above Fifth Avenue. The outdoor terrace of the Metropolitan Club overlooked New York's Central Park. This was Warren's club, and this afternoon the two of them occupied the prime real estate, the center spot among the apron of tables on the patio outdoors.

"You did great," he said to his brother. "Pop has a *Times* obituary. Who could have figured? There's not a word about his health issues. This is as much a testament to you as it is to him. How did you manage it?"

"Favors," Warren replied quietly. "Everything's about favors, putting favors in the bank to use in the future. Why should newspapers be any different? Especially when they're as endangered as they seem to be. For better or worse, I have the juice right now. I didn't before, and I have no illusions that there will come a day when I don't have it anymore. So I made two phone calls. The first one was to a *Times* editor. Then I talked to Tony Agnelli—he sends his condolences, by the way, and asked me to tell you not to sweat that whole Carneccio & Dice dust-up. He quoted Winston Churchill to me, something like, 'there's nothing as exhilarating as being shot at and missed.'"

"Pop respected him."

"It was mutual." Warren's voice was uncharacteristically unanimated as he stared at the treetops of Central Park with an air of resignation.

"I'm worried about you. How are you holding together?"

"I don't go in for much introspection, Rick."

"Neither did Pop. Look where it landed him."

Warren squinted in the sun then looked his brother in the eyes. "Did J.D. ever tell you what kind of shape I was in after Mom died?"

"No. But it was easy enough to figure out. You were going to come apart in a million pieces and she was there to keep that from happening."

"I *did* come apart, Rick. And yeah, she was there. I know how much you resented that."

Rick was not sure how to respond. "That's fair."

"You didn't think that I was—"

"At the time I didn't know what to think." Rick was becoming more and more uncomfortable with the direction of the conversation.

Warren tried again. "If that's what broke you two up—"

"It wasn't. Trust me."

"You have to understand, I didn't know what the hell was happening to me."

"And you were afraid that it would happen again. That was why you thought you needed her with us when Pop died."

"I did need her there."

"So my wife was your safety net."

"A hedge, Rick."

"I didn't mind. I really was glad to see her. It had been a long time since we even talked. And if her being there helped you, fine."

"It's very different this time," Warren said. "Of course, I have a lot more to be concerned about than when Mom died. I was counting on sharing so much with Pop, even before his mind started going. That dementia is just a way of tearing apart a man's soul in slow motion. For his part, he had a lot to tell us that he didn't get a chance to. I wish that I could have talked to him more."

"Everybody has that regret afterward."

"No. He was trying to tell us something. Did you understand all of that stuff he was saying?"

"I understood the German. But the substance of what he said didn't make much sense."

"Rick, what does *staub* mean? He kept saying that."

"Dust. Like 'dust in the wind' or 'ashes to ashes, dust to dust.'"

"So that was all about his own mortality? That sure doesn't seem like Pop."

"I agree."

"He had a message."

"You're reading too much into it."

"No, I'm not. I am definitely not."

"The important thing was, we were there, brother. He didn't die alone."

"Yeah, but at the end, I couldn't figure out what he was saying. And neither could you."

"I can think about it some more," Rick said. He tapped his right temple. "You know, I'll never forget it. I stored every word, you know. Right here. English and German. Dust to dust."

"He was saying something. I needed to hear it. I mean, we did."

Rick let it go. He tried changing the subject. "What about your deal?"

"It's progressing. My team is handling what they have to, and our closing is still scheduled for the first of August. It's always the same. The smallest piece comes last and is always the most difficult. I have to close the equity component. It's soft-circled already but nailing it down is proving particularly tough. All part of the limited partnership." Warren simply assumed that Rick was familiar with ViroSat. At this point in the deal, and thanks to Compton Sizemore's readjusted media strategy, it was the primary focus of chatter for all of financial America.

"You're going to make out on this, aren't you?" Rick asked.

Warren looked contemplative. "I am. The beauty of ViroSat is that it's essentially a debt deal. The lenders, especially those big national investment banks in Europe and Asia and South America, are buying in so that they can benefit from the interest on the debt and from the technology. They get to use most of their cash that's been sitting around waiting, basically useless since this economic downturn began. They also get to use the improved telecom infrastructure. My payoff is in the fact that there is so little equity-based cash in the deal. The whole thing is four-fifths debt and one-fifth equity. I bring in that equity, two hundred and eighty-seven billion from my limited partnership. With that, I essentially get to own the deal."

"And . . . that's the part that's proving difficult." Rick let out a slow whistle between his front teeth.

"I was hoping that Pop could help."

"Pop? Warren, come on, at the end he was—"

"Forget it. Let's just say that it's very complicated."

"*You're* complicated. Are you sure that you're holding together right now?"

"Ask your ex-wife." There was more than an edge in Warren's voice.

"I intend to. I'm going to see her back in Virginia."

"I'm glad—you should. For what it's worth, I'm also going to be in Virginia next week. Thank her for me, will you? Tell her I'm back."

"I'm sure that will be most comforting to her," Rick deadpanned.

"I got it. You don't have to put that fine a point on it. I know that this is not about me."

"Decidedly. But I had to speak to her anyway. There's a client's estate that I have to settle, and oddly, the woman knew Julia. Somehow."

"Why is that odd?"

"Everything about her is odd. She died in an accident on the GW Parkway after she told me she didn't drive anymore. Then her niece visits me—three times already—and *that* woman gives new definition to annoying. But it's the kind of annoying that . . . *compels* you, if you follow my meaning. I should probably mention that she's a lawyer. I didn't even know the client, Mrs. Geller, all that well, but it turns out that she named me the executor and beneficiary of her estate. I thought that her niece would be furious with that state of affairs, but instead she just insisted on riding with me when I was driving up here to meet you the day that Pop died. She kept on talking, telling me her aunt's story. We planned for me to leave her at the Wilmington Amtrak station, but then she bailed out on me at the Maryland House on I-95."

"Rick, you lead a weird life."

"Tell me something that I don't know."

"How about this: once my ViroSat deal is wrapped up, this fall at the latest, we're going to concentrate on finding something else for you to do. I'll be on it with you. Do you think that you can have your legal issues and this estate sorted out by then?"

"Yes. Only now there are two estates. That one and Pop's."

"Sure. But I want you to commit to making the leap. I want to do this for you."

"Because right now you have the juice?"

"Because you deserve it." Rick saw Warren smile weakly for the first time since Dutch's death.

He stood in the east-facing window of a magnificent suite in the newly remodeled Plaza Hotel, across Fifth Avenue and a catty-corner block away. Horvath looked up from the angled eyepiece of the telescope on the tripod. The tall thin old man, his partner, stood up from the chair at the round table nearby, placed two hands in the small of his back, and stretched, bending backward. It was evident from his movements that this was one of those times when he detested being old. Technology made the work quite easy now, not like it used to be in Budapest or Prague or Havana. The recordings were all digital. The clarity was spectacular.

Horvath was clearly impressed, surprised at how excited he felt. He was a man who rarely felt emotion and showed it even less of the time. Horvath grinned as he blinked, attempting to normalize and balance out his vision in both eyes after seeing the brothers' conversation unfold in real time. It was thoroughly entertaining to watch them talk at the outdoor table on the roof while listening to them on his partner's electronic equipment.

"Well done," the old man said. "Your placement of that microphone at the club was perfect. It sounded like we were sitting there with them."

"*Köszönöm.*" Thank you.

"*Ön üdvözli.*" You're welcome.

"Is that all the Hungarian you can remember, old friend?" Horvath asked, laughing. "Your pronunciation still sucks."

"So does your diplomacy," he replied, but he was not smiling at all.

"What?" Horvath asked.

"You see our problem now, don't you?"

"I think that I do. You had better tell me. You know I am not good with subtlety. Remember? You said that the first time we ever met."

"I remember. You were drunk. We both were. You told me that you were better at fixing a mess than determining whether one needed fixing."

"So tell me what needs fixing now."

"That part about his never forgetting. How he stored every word, English and German."

"Yeah. I didn't like that," Horvath agreed.

"It's the biggest problem we have at the moment."

"Hey. You said it would only be the old woman and the old man. Then the one with the big mouth. That was okay. We both knew that eventually the guy inside would have to go. But you also told me that we would not have to remove either one of the sons." Horvath curved up one side of his mouth, thinking. "You didn't lie to me?"

"I didn't lie to you. The truth changed. You just heard what I did."

"Okay. I can be fairly inventive."

"See to it that you are. Keep me informed. And Horvath . . . ?"

"What?"

"Warren Hunter cannot close that deal."

"You worry too much. He won't."

CHAPTER 22

There was a moment stuck in Rick Yeager's memory—it was not the only one—that came along with doubts about its authenticity. He was not sure whether he actually remembered the day or if he only remembered it from the Kodak Super 8 film replayed by Dutch throughout his childhood. Fixed in time with Rick barely a toddler, before Warren, the clip was obviously blocked and staged: Dutch had handed his Bell & Howell movie camera to a willing bystander and then produced his own forty-second family reality show.

The shot began with a wide pan, much too fast and jumpy, of the US Capitol building. A gentle U-shaped parking lot with cars at angles to the curb led to the expansive triple-bank of steps at the building's east front. Down the steps, continuing the pan, to a white 1971 Ford Fairlane with New Jersey license plates crawling through the lot. Then came an anachronism even more evident than the old car: plenty of open parking spaces a hundred feet from the Capitol. The Fairlane pulled into one of them. Dutch stepped out holding Rick, lifting him to his right shoulder, hanging onto the child and waving. Gloria was next, a few steps behind, catching up. They walked together toward the camera. Both parents had wide artificial grins. They continued the waves while the child loomed high in constant motion expressing unrefined joy. Tableau scene for ten seconds more as Dutch and Gloria cease waving. Pull back, the Capitol as framing backdrop to the still, then . . . fade.

Rick walked across the east lawn of the Capitol, suddenly struck with a gust of sadness again. A week following Dutch's death, these hits were arriving less frequently but with more precision, he realized, as he compared the flickering home movie scene with what he saw today. The entire block had been rebuilt at least twice since Rick was a kid. The muted gray concrete plaza was offset by white limestone, glass, and red brick, all framed by lush green lawn. The place was full of people. He descended the wide set of stairs leading down and away from the Capitol, just about where Dutch parked in the movie, to join the crowd lined up at the entrance to the visitor center.

Past the metal detectors and X-rays the crowd dispersed. Rick moved forward with the people into the cavernous subterranean atrium. The place was brilliantly lit by the sun pouring through what seemed like a couple of acres of skylights. There—central in the Brownian movement of the tourists, overdressed for the immediate moment in a gull-gray business suit—Julia Toussaint stood waiting. She saw him before he noticed her, and was already walking to Rick when he stepped into the big room.

She hugged him and her embrace lasted much longer than he would have expected. When she kissed him it was very close to his mouth and she lingered. "Fathers and brothers," she said softly, "are always complicated. I am so sorry about Dutch. I am so glad that I was there."

"So am I," Rick said, simply glad to be near this woman again, still holding her, even knowing that he was perilously close to crossing the line between greeting and public display of affection.

Two white families with a half-dozen or more children and teenagers in tow, obviously traveling with each other, stopped and stared, close enough for Rick and Julia both to notice them.

"I don't believe," she whispered, "we've caused that kind of reaction in a long time."

"I don't think we ever have," Rick said. "You'd figure, after Obama—"

"Check the T-shirt," she said, pointing obviously, which was enough of a gesture to make one of the moms begin herding the group.

"Yee hah," Rick called after them lightly. "Roll Tide, Alabama." The discomfiture of the group was now evident. They hurried to turn away.

Julia took his arm and smiled. "Right there—that kind of embarrassment is what my granddaddy worked for his whole life. It's why he moved to Newark from the Delta. Rick, I'm sorry that he never got to meet your father. Come on. Let's walk."

"You made a difference at the end," he offered. "I don't mean for Warren."

"I know," she said, and paused. "Have you and your brother finalized the arrangements?"

"He once talked about being buried in Arlington," Rick said. "Pop was a disabled veteran. His separation from the service in 1946 was because of health issues—"

"You don't have to revisit any of that."

"—so he qualifies for a plot. But there are so many of his generation checking out now that we have to get into a queue. We're not sure what we're going to do. Warren is looking into whether Dutch made any other arrangements. He may have. In any case, it's going to take a month or more."

Julia thought for a moment. "Which will give Warren plenty of time to close his ViroSat deal. And give both of you time to grieve."

"Germans are pretty practical about death. I think that we both inherited that."

"My people embrace it. Homecoming."

"Dutch wouldn't disagree with that."

"And your brother? Is he holding up?"

"I think so. No. I know so. It's very odd. He was so distraught when Mom died and he's trying to be so serene right now. But he's wound terribly tight. I read a lot of anxiety in him—a whole lot—but it doesn't seem to be about Pop."

"Well"—she smiled—"you two are now consuming my time professionally and personally. Not that I mind."

"This is not difficult to guess, Julia. You've landed in the middle of ViroSat."

"Definitely. Hearings are coming up."

"Have you figured out Warren's deal yet?" Rick meant it as a rhetorical question.

"I'll tell you what Tenley Harbison and I know," she replied.

"I'd be fascinated," he said, not entirely sure if they were flirting. If we are, Rick reasoned, we're starting out slowly. If we're not, then this is a good place for us to be. He was quite unsteady about the whole ex-wife thing, which was, if forced to admit it, the principal reason that he'd stayed away from Julia for so long.

"I think that Warren's deal is pretty straightforward, leaving aside the complexities of the country arrangements. The State Department is literally going crazy attempting to untangle those components. And then there are the physics and satellite dimensions. Very daunting. But the finance? When you break it down, the numbers are astounding but the concept is simple elegance itself. Refined. Warren is a genius."

"So I've been told for most of my life."

"I'm sorry, Rick. That wasn't what I meant and you know it."

"I do. Go on."

"The whole price of the deal to Compton Sizemore on August first is what? About a trillion three?"

"One point three seven, according to the *Wall Street Journal*."

"Okay. Now we know that Compton Sizemore has already subscribed debt of more than a trillion dollars. We also know that the public disclosures about that debt say that the leverage ratio is going to be around four to one."

"Where did you learn finance at this level?" Rick was impressed.

"The Congressional Budget Office. The guys there taught me a lot. You'd be surprised how much corporate finance they do these days. Then again, maybe you wouldn't." Julia was clearly on a roll.

"Which means?" Rick was leading her.

"Think about that amount of debt for a moment," Julia said, "especially in this financial environment. Not that long ago everyone was scrambling away from debt—bad loans, toxic mortgages. Business credit is still shut down. Today every significant investment bank in the world, and a good number of foreign governments' sovereign wealth funds, are all invested in ViroSat. Excuse me. They've *loaned money* to ViroSat. The theory is that the strength of this investment is supposed to repair the very foundations of global lending. This deal is going to make everything right again.

"That leaves us with the equity. The ownership." She stopped at the information booth, released Rick's arm, and turned to face him, as if planting her feet to stand her ground—settling in for a good argument, he thought.

"We don't know anything at all about that part," Julia said. "Legally, we don't have to. But there are people around here, Tenley included, who are making noises about the national security implications of Viro-Sat. Warren is being too secretive about ownership."

"Julia, it's far more likely that he's still raising the money. He just about said so to me when we talked about it in New York."

"But how much money? The CBO people—and I know, this isn't their area at all—say it's about three hundred billion, give or take. That's about how much the federal government takes in from corporate income taxes in a whole year. A phenomenal amount of cash."

"Warren's good for it," Rick said. The joke fell flat. Julia was serious.

"Rough numbers. A trillion in new debt. Three hundred billion in equity from who knows where. And practically no oversight of the most complex technological system ever devised. Can you see why Tenley is interested in public hearings before this deal closes?"

"I can see why my brother is distracted."

"Rick, that equity part is all owned by a limited partnership. Your brother is the general partner."

"That part I didn't know."

"You do now. He's also one of the limited partners, a member of the investor group. Whoever else they are, those are the real owners of Viro-Sat. That's where the Department of State says that the national security implications come in."

"I understand. Here's how it breaks down. In this kind of deal, Julia, there are two kinds of investors. There are the straight-return types, the ones where the deal is strictly about the numbers. They're attracted to Warren's proven track record and the technology. They buy into Compton Sizemore's debt structure because they know what a high return they can get on their investment. They know that it's about as secure as risk-based financial products come these days.

"Then there are the folks with a secondary purpose in addition to making an investment return. We see this in all kinds of deals. The best example is green investing—you want to make a good investment profit but you also want to do good. From what I understand, all of that began in the eighties with investors pulling out of South African holdings, in order to end the apartheid system. Investing often has political purposes. Is that what you and the senator are concerned about?"

"Not exactly. I get the whole secondary purpose, but Tenley is more concerned about finding out where, exactly, the government's interest lies in this whole woolly mammoth of a tech deal that your brother's built. She wants to know if we should regulate ViroSat—"

"I can already tell you Warren's answer to *that*."

"—or how we can *use* the system to our own national advantage, especially in national defense. And then there's the 'How secure?' question, which cuts both ways. ViroSat is going to make it impossible for the National Security Agency to read anything transmitted on the system—you know how they call it 'Internet Next'—because it's so far advanced beyond our current technical capabilities. ViroSat makes the cyberworld untraceable. That scares a lot of people in the government, Rick, especially the three-letter agency boys. Of course, they'd also like to use it for their own secure communications, which is what I meant by saying security cuts both ways."

Rick nodded. "Therefore Senator Harbison wants to determine the ownership of ViroSat."

"Precisely."

"Whoever it is, you've ascertained that Warren is part of the group, and he is the public face."

"Again, precisely."

"I doubt that my brother will be too forthcoming."

"Why not?"

"Because of the way this works, Julia. I'm going to bet that he doesn't actually have all of the equity cash in his limited partnership yet. Just promises. The people and the banks that have that kind of money don't simply let it sit around in Compton Sizemore's accounts. They keep it themselves, close by, working for them and earning interest, until the last possible moment before the deal closes. Then it gets transferred. Sometimes it doesn't even have to transfer. It only needs to be secured and available. Disclosure is anathema to those investors. If Warren names names in the senator's hearing, he'll almost certainly crater his own deal."

"The senator doesn't think so. There is a real concern about who's the money behind him. We all know it's not all Warren's money. He doesn't have that kind of cash personally. No one does, Rick."

"The US Treasury does."

"Not now. Not without oversight. You see where this is going?"

"I think so," he said. "Tenley Harbison is going to build support for strong oversight in her hearings. But I'm telling you, Julia, if the investors, whoever they are, want to keep their involvement private, they will."

"Rick, we also have to consider the possibility that Warren has borrowed some of the money inside the limited partnership."

"Leverage on top of leverage? Julia, he wouldn't do that. If he did, he'd be risking an even larger collapse than we had when all the big i-banks were failing. The consequences would be enormous. This one would be global. Unrecoverable."

"Yeah. I thought you'd see it that way."

"He wouldn't do it, Julia."

"But he could."

"Yes, he could."

They walked together through the crowd back to the visitor center entrance. They stepped carefully through the exit, closer than a natural distance but not touching, saying nothing. As they walked outside, the July heat enveloped them. Julia stopped in the shade at the bottom of the granite steps, still underground by twenty feet. She turned to Rick, placed one hand on his chest, and looked at him closely.

"Thank you for coming here. This wasn't a conversation for a telephone, and I appreciate that you could make time to see me. My schedule is impossible."

"You made time for Pop when it counted. And here we're on pretty safe ground, right?"

She smiled. "Something like that."

"Are we going to end up one of those couples," he asked, "who have a better relationship divorced than we did when we were married?"

"I think those are few and far between."

"But not nonexistent."

"No."

"Good. That will give us something to strive for." The two of them began to ascend the steps. Then he remembered. "Julia, there is one more thing I need to ask you. With everything that's gone on in the past couple of weeks, I completely forgot. How did you know a lady named Hannah Weiss Geller? She was a client of mine."

"Was? What happened? Did she fire you?"

This would be intense and very difficult, Horvath figured. The adrenaline coursed through his body. He felt like he was thirty again. He was under no illusions about the challenge. There were too many factors involved. First, he was in a car—not his car, of course. This was a District of Columbia taxicab, stolen from the cab line at Union Station when the driver had the misfortune to urinate at the wrong time. Finding it would be an extremely low priority for the city police, and by the time they did he would be long gone. He crept along slowly in the light traffic on First Street. No one gave a second glance at the cab when he entered the semi-secure zone on East Capitol Street. It's been more than a decade since 9/11, he thought. People get lazy. *Henyélő.* Especially the police. Like most intelligence professionals, Horvath had a very low regard for law enforcement.

With a clear line of sight to the steps leading from the visitor center entrance, he slowed. From under his seat he withdrew an M1911 .45 ACP semiautomatic pistol, standard military-issue in America for decades in his day. The .45 had always been his favorite weapon. This one was a Frankenstein, pieced together, gunsmithed, and then meticulously sighted-in—all by Horvath personally. He grinned. Security would be *incredibly* tight here tomorrow, he was sure. But not now.

Horvath racked the slide of the gun back and chambered a round, checking the safety off as the vehicle glided to a stop. This was his closest point of approach to the entrance stairs. Still it must be sixty meters, he estimated. He put his foot on the brake and pressed down hard and firm, keeping the taxicab in drive, then draped his left arm across the driver's side window ledge and made a loose fist. With the .45 in his right hand he crossed his right wrist over his left and adjusted both hands, shifting his right index finger from the trigger guard to the trigger. He sighted in carefully, both eyes open. Easy, easy, he told himself. There. The two of them were reaching ground level—the woman was very easy to spot. Horvath exhaled and squeezed.

Rick's consciousness of the first shot was the concrete kicking up in front of him, the booming report of the gun somewhere, and the sound of a round hitting the marble fascia of the stairs. He glanced about in all directions. Where did that shot come from? *Was* that a shot? His mind was locked in instant denial, processing information too slowly to react immediately.

The second shot was closer, at his feet. He would later swear that he saw the bullet hit the ground. Time slowed for him. Every neuroelectrical circuit in his body came alive. The shooter was walking the fire in toward him. The next one would find its mark. Rick had to move.

Crack! Crack! Two more shots—or was it three? *Where were they coming from?*

"Julia!" He reached out and grabbed her hand, pulling her roughly in the direction of the grass. They began to run.

Crack! A louder boom this time—or was he imagining that? As they reached the Capitol lawn both dove to the ground. Rick sprawled across Julia, his head up, looking, scanning.

Nothing.

Screams and shouts, at the edge of his awareness.

People running.

Slow motion speeding up.

The wail of a siren.

Running footbeats on the concrete, Capitol police officers, frantic.

More screams.

More nothing.

Julia squirmed beneath him. Rick raised himself slightly, enough to give her some room to turn. When she did, she grabbed him in both arms and squeezed, tight, tighter, and sobbed.

Stuck in traffic, second in line at the corner, Horvath did what all of the other drivers were doing. He craned his neck out of the taxi's window and looked.

"Move! Move!" yelled a Capitol policeman, waving the cars on. "Get out of here!"

Horvath made a right on Constitution Avenue and drove away at medium speed. He would ditch the car a few blocks east and take his time backtracking home. It would be a shame to lose this .45. Horvath was not usually attached to things. You never could be in his business. He made a decision—he could hang on to it for now.

What a mess this has just become, he thought. As he drove Horvath briefly considered all of the options he had remaining. Their number was dwindling. It was always going to be that way for professional keepers of secrets, he told himself. Even at his age, the inventory of secrets kept increasing.

Like the new secret today.

The reason he used the .45. It was almost impossible to hit someone with that weapon at that distance. Horvath knew this, of course. He was an expert.

He meant to miss them.

CHAPTER 23

"Mr. Hunter, I'm sorry, sir, but you are just not going to drive yourself. That is out of the question, for your own security. I have very specific instructions."

Warren stared at the man, incredulous. A moment before he had bounded down the retractable steps of the Bombardier Global 8000 executive jet, the newest addition to the Compton Sizemore air force. Now he found himself in a standoff on the blazing hot tarmac at Signature Flight Support, the private fixed base corporate terminal at Washington Dulles International Airport.

"I made myself clear in New York. Car, no driver."

"Mr. Darlington changed that, sir."

"Call him."

"I can't do that, sir." The guy stood at least six foot four. He leaned on the driver's side door of the black Lincoln MKZ, mirrored wraparound Oakleys staring back at Warren. The man casually slid his hands into his pockets. He wore dark-wash blue jeans and a gray raw silk sportcoat with a miniature gold emblem prominent on his lapel—the "crab" insignia of a Navy SEAL, the eagle, trident, anchor, and pistol.

"Your name's Evans, right?" Warren was steamed more because of the delay than the heat.

"Correct, sir." The guy was unmoved on the surface, but the slightest shift in the way he said the word "sir" conveyed distinct surprise that Warren could recall this information.

Never play these games with somebody who negotiates for a living, Warren thought.

He grabbed his BlackBerry, then punched and held down the number 2. "Jenny," he said, looking right at the security man, "I am on the ground at Dulles Airport. Yeah. Good flight, but that's not what this is about. Connect this call directly to Skip Darlington. Uh-huh." He waited to see if the security man would budge. The guy didn't.

The eponymous Darlington Global Security was formed shortly after 9/11 by a former chief of the Secret Service's presidential protective detail. Only recently a public company (it was a Compton Sizemore deal), the firm had perhaps 80 percent of Fortune 500 corporate market share wherever "personal protective services" were required. Warren Hunter was one of its three outside directors.

"Skip," he spoke loudly, "you now have a significant problem with me. Hey. Don't you dare feed me platitudes. Just listen. What's your contract with Compton Sizemore worth? Wrong. This year we're going to pay you over eleven million. Now what do you think is going to happen when I cancel that contract and resign from your board because I no longer have confidence in your abilities to provide suitable background checks?

"You want an example?" His voice was rising. "How about this knuckle-dragger standing between me and my car at Dulles." Warren could see the slightest movement of the man's cheek. "He checked out, right? A Navy SEAL. Then how come the vaunted Darlington Global proprietary system couldn't figure out what my office did in about eight fucking minutes? Thomas *Rand* Evans is a Navy SEAL . . . and he's still a chief petty officer out in Coronado. Thomas *Randall* Evans, this superlative douche pump whom you pay, was nothing but the doorman at the last DC jack-off strip club that they wiped out to build the Nationals stadium. Aren't you supposed to be about *preventing* identity theft?

"Here's exactly what you're going to do, Skip. When I hang up, you have thirty seconds to make his mobile phone ring and fire him *for life.* Good. Jenny? Let's also create a confidential memorandum about this conversation." He pressed the button ending the conversation without any sign-off.

The security man withdrew his right hand from his pants pocket and reached into his coat, pulling out his mobile phone. He stared at it before answering the insistent buzz. Warren Hunter smiled pleasantly.

"Yes." Wordless listening as the twitches on both sides of the man's jaw accelerated. "Yes, sir. I understand." He pocketed the phone and stepped away from the car, every muscle enraged and tensed in Warren's direction.

"You'd better think real goddamn hard about how I knew that," Warren said to him, "and even harder if you have any idea about following me. You committed fraud when you put *that* on," he said, flicking the miniature Navy SEAL insignia with his forefinger. "You can explain it all in federal court. Welcome to litigation hell. I'll personally see to it that every juror is a veteran. I hate phonies."

He stepped into the Lincoln, adjusted the seat, started the car, and drove off into the Dulles airport traffic.

It felt good to be back.

Back in character.

Still applying leverage in every form it came.

Warren flipped on the radio and relaxed.

From Richmond to Baltimore, from the Chesapeake to the Shenandoah, this is 103.5 FM, WTOP Newsradio . . . Breaking news . . . Reports from Capitol Hill that shots were just fired at the US Capitol building. There is panic on the scene and no word yet about a possible shooter or motive.

CHAPTER 24

The verdant campus of GT3 Corporation in Chantilly was in many ways indistinguishable from the home of any other tech-sector government contractor in northern Virginia. In one way it differed significantly. Behind the three tech-modern office buildings occupied by GT3, practically unnoticeable from any of the driving approaches to the site, a partly subterranean postmodern office building jutted from the trees. Built into a huge berm at the edge of one of Fairfax County's few remaining spots of old forest, it was variously referred to as "Terragreen" (the name that the architect gave it), "the bunker" (its universal name to its own personnel and employees of the adjacent GT3), or simply "FSSC"—always spoken as *fissick*, never the four letters. Pronouncing the letters was a giveaway that you were not an insider. The bunker was the headquarters and the only operating location of the Financial Systems and Services Corporation.

Formed somewhere around fifteen or twenty years ago, the origins of FSSC were just about as murky as the no-man's land that the corporation occupied between federal government and the private sector. Originally conceived as an experimental venture, sort of an academic exercise, FSSC was technically still a public-private partnership. The original start-up capital had come from the federal budget through an incredibly circuitous route usually reserved for the National Security Council—bank-to-bank-to-bank with electronic erasures at every step along the way. This manner of capitalization made sense at the time, because FSSC was the Department of the Treasury's rudimentary equivalent of an intelligence operation. Even the name was selected to be "un-Googleable," as one of FSSC's former chiefs recently suggested, although Google did not exist at the time the venture was conceived.

The cash that built the bunker was actually a loan. It enabled the hiring of the first dozen people that grew into FSSC's present-day cadre of 142. Thirty million dollars was pocket change in the federal budget. That was the entire "public" part of the venture. It was paid back early, with slightly less than market-rate interest and no penalty, within twenty months of the firm's founding. The private part was built by taking on risk, backing numerous technology ventures. They were all quite successful. Each had the distinction of having a measurable direct effect on the financial services sector of a rapidly globalizing economy. FSSC quickly became the economic engine for all of the technology tying together global finance.

By the time the organization matured, its stores of data and deep access to financial records worldwide were unparalleled. Terragreen knew the inner workings of any bank, and any bank *account*, anywhere on the globe.

FSSC was not always the major backer of new financial information technologies. But it was rarely away from the table when they were discussed.

True to its origins, FSSC maintained the strictest secrecy. But it was most unlike the national security operations in a few important ways. In "the community," the secret squirrel universe of the intelligence services, people had to hold exotic security clearances. Facilities needed to be carefully built-out, inspected, and approved. Congress was required to be appeased with constant oversight or at a minimum, its illusion. Here at FSSC none of those strictures applied. The FSSC directors enjoyed the broadest possible autonomy of free enterprise as long as a few key people at Treasury, the White House, and in Congress were kept modesty apprised of the corporation's operations.

That was before the economic mess.

FSSC began its corporate life as the government's way of wading into the waters of financial commerce. Now all of Washington was swimming.

Sanford Tuttle walked across the wide lawn spanning the expanse behind GT3's main building and the forested ridge embracing the bunker.

Every time he made this short hike—a few times a week for the past several years—he marveled anew at its ingenuity and design. The place was green before anybody was even thinking about green. He stopped and waited outside the front door of the building, modestly marked on a pair of frosted glass doors with the stylized green and white four-letter FSSC logo. He didn't have to wait long.

Warren Hunter rounded the corner of the building on the walking path from the discreet parking lot in the woods adjacent to the bunker. He smiled and extended his hand. Tuttle did likewise.

"Sandy, it's been far too long," Warren greeted him.

"I should say the same. I had breakfast with your brother last week and then called him after I read about your father's passing. I'm very sorry for your loss, Warren."

"Thank you. Until the day he died Pop was incredibly important in my life and my brother's."

"We don't often think about how important it is to be a son."

"I know. Or how influential fathers are to our work."

"I couldn't agree more."

"I can also tell you that it hasn't really hit me yet, although it seems like I spent the last two years preparing for the moment. Are you ready to go to work?"

"Absolutely. Come on. Let me introduce you."

They walked into the facility. Sanford Tuttle produced a clip-on badge and signed a paper ledger in a three-ring notebook at the reception station. He was scrutinized by the stern eyes of a middle-aged woman and two armed security guards. Warren noticed that the oval patches on their left sleeves bore the Darlington Global logo. One of them handed him a badge almost identical to Tuttle's with the FSSC logo and the word VISITOR, which Warren slipped into his jacket pocket.

The two of them passed through a long L-shaped hallway brightly sunlit from above by roof windows fitted as skylights. The effect gave the corridor a very open feel. Warren had to remind himself that they were actually underground. As they walked, Tuttle kept up a running commentary.

"They modeled this," he explained, "after the facilities the intelligence agencies use—well, actually the facilities for their contractors. It was the first time that anyone created a 'classified' building for quasi-Treasury activities, banking, the movement of capital, and the incredible information-loading that accompanies those business operations. The big difference is that here, there are none of the bureaucratic restraints that the national security apparatus demands."

"GT3 is the primary contractor."

"Not only the primary contractor. FSSC is the reason that my company exists," Tuttle answered. "I worry about that. The customer concentration problem is huge for us—we can't work for anyone else. On the one hand it's a perfect niche with basically unlimited margins. We write our own government contracts. Every service we provide is sole-source procurement. On the other hand, we don't *have* any other customers."

"Which would explain why you haven't approached me to take out GT3," Warren said, referring to an initial public offering of GT3 stock. He'd wondered about that.

"Precisely," Tuttle replied, nodding. "Everybody here in tech Virginia is expecting me to make this company my fifth IPO. It's not going to happen. I own the whole thing this time, Warren, and my cash flow from these operations is far more than anything I could recover from a sale of stock. That's the reason I haven't sold. It doesn't make economic sense."

"And when it doesn't grow anymore?"

"Please." Tuttle smiled. "Give me some credit. I know your mantra— 'trees don't grow to the sky.' But this is different, Warren. Not at all like the kind of government contracting you're used to. At GT3 we assume risk and we get paid for it. Information technology is at the center of everything. *Everything*. Capital finance is just coming to that realization. Our forte is the federal government's piece. Regulation. Oversight. Massive data-mining in global banks. Ultra high-speed broadband technologies. Anti-money laundering technologies. The SWIFT system for electronic fund transfers. All of it is here in the bunker, all of it is within the direct purview of FSSC, and all of it is built and maintained by GT3. We were fortunate to have two major strokes of luck, the kind of timing that I couldn't create in a million years. First was the economic melt-down. Do you foresee any let-up in banking and financial regulation in the near-term future? Neither do I. Second was ViroSat, and I have to thank you for that, Warren. More than you can know."

"You have a risk position in the deal." Warren smiled admiringly.

"You bet I do. Success fees, based on FSSC's uptake in your limited partnership. And they're significant." Tuttle stopped at a closed door with an electronic pad on the wall.

"I hope so," said Warren, grinning. He also hoped that his famously winning smile and looking Sanford Tuttle directly in the eyes would effectively mask the horrible tightening he was feeling just below his sternum.

With a *clack* of the electronic lock, Tuttle opened the door. The room they entered was square, with a round conference table seating eight. Five were already in place. They rose as Warren Hunter and Sanford Tuttle entered.

"Today," Tuttle said to the evident surprise of the small group, "Mr. Hunter is going to be joining us. Warren, this is the FSSC ViroSat team."

Warren made his way around the table for the introductions. He was puzzled by the fact that there was no evident leader of the team, no clues as to who might be in charge. His response was to crank up the charm, because it was immediately apparent to him that everyone here was quite familiar with him, Compton Sizemore, and certainly with ViroSat. He found that thought more than a little unsettling.

"Now are all of you with FSSC?" he asked as he reached his fourth handshake.

"All of them but me," said the man who took his hand in a firm grip. "Jonas Barr. I'm the contractor. I work for GT3. And I want to thank you."

"For what?" Warren was playing this gregariously.

"I was a senior program manager in the systems directorate of QUAT-ECH, based in Tel Aviv, when you managed the company's IPO. That was the first time I ever had any options, and I hold you responsible for our success."

"Did you do all right?" It was a Wall Street shorthand kind of question, one Warren knew was sort of incongruous here in a semi-federal facility in Chantilly, Virginia.

"More than all right."

"And now you're in charge of ViroSat for Sandy?"

Tuttle answered for him. "Not exactly. Jonas asked me if he could sit in today. He's one of the world's few technical experts on capital collection—putting large aggregations of funds in one place at one time, and then disbursing it. Since that's what we're essentially going to talk about today, it made sense to me that he should be here."

"We need guys like you," Warren said. "If Tuttle here doesn't pay you enough in this gig, you come and see me in New York."

"Do I want to work for you?" Jonas Barr asked.

"You guys do know too much about Compton Sizemore," Warren said, as the room responded with a light laugh.

"Let's get the briefing started," Sanford Tuttle suggested. Warren sat down and leaned back in his chair, still trying to figure out who was in charge.

The FSSC briefer, a chubby, serious, severe woman about Warren Hunter's age, was twelve slides into her PowerPoint presentation when Warren began paying serious attention and interrupted.

"I think that it's time I quit being unnecessarily courteous and got to the point," he said. "You're providing me with far more granular detail about the movement of capital than I need or want. Do any of you even *realize* the scope of this deal?"

No one answered. He looked at Sanford Tuttle.

"No one at Compton Sizemore wastes my time like this. I'm going to give you," Warren continued, "the points of salience surrounding ViroSat that FSSC needs to be concerned about.

"First, this is a private deal. I don't have to disclose anything, especially about the limited partnership. You have a play there—together and quite essentially, FSSC and I are the limited partners. The mechanics of the cash are secondary. Your investment is the primary means of funding the LP. Don't lose sight of that, and don't think that anyone else has to know that information. The whole world is watching the debt side of the financing. We're the equity, and as far as anyone knows, it's a cipher. Keep it that way.

"Second, in order to fund the partnership—and remember, it's almost three hundred billion dollars we're talking about—we're not going to use your capital. Instead, we're going to use your *access* to capital. That's a big difference. Your databases are more valuable than cash.

"Third, I'm the agent of capital. That earns me my limited partnership share and control of the equity in the deal."

"How," asked the briefer, "do the limited partnership shares get distributed?"

"Fifty percent to FSSC, fifty percent to my own private trust—and that's a Compton Sizemore account, in case anyone is wondering."

"And the upside to FSSC?" Sanford Tuttle asked.

"A premium return, fifty percent of the limited partnership gain, and probably far more important, priority access to the ViroSat technology." He let that information sink in.

FSSC would get the keys of the kingdom, prime access to Internet Next. When the entire global financial universe migrated to ViroSat—a movement already underway—FSSC would already be there.

"But FSSC doesn't have anywhere near that kind of capital," the briefer said. "You're talking about one-half of two hundred eighty-seven point seven billion dollars." Her tone was puzzled and challenging. Warren was impressed. The woman had done her homework.

"Truth told," he said, "I don't have it either. And that, my friends, is why our cooperation is now critical."

CHAPTER 25

He was most aware of the dimension of time. Skipping, fractured, pixilated, accelerating and decelerating, nonlinear, ballooning, inchoate time, unhinged time, anything but linear time. Rick Yeager ran for the trees on the north side of the Capitol grounds. He moved toward Constitution Avenue, stumbling, aware that Julia Toussaint, ex-wife and sudden ally in this enterprise of survival, was close to him, so close, following his lead. She gripped his right forearm tightly, a compromise between taking his arm and holding his hand, as if hand-holding was not nearly enough but linked arms would slow them down. They ran silently and panting, both gaining speed as others on the Capitol grounds had the same idea. Head for cover, however sparse it may be.

There were no more shots, but there was much yelling, all of it unintelligible.

Time sputtered and jumped again on its axis of discontinuity. Rick kept moving, across Constitution at the crosswalk to Delaware Avenue and the dense dark green of the park south of the Russell Senate Office Building. He ran faster with Julia keeping pace. Traffic was still moving at a crawl on the roads. He heard sirens, first one or two, then many more in sonic convergence. People began to exit both of the Senate office buildings on the north side of Constitution just as Rick and Julia reached the sidewalk. He slowed to a fast walking pace. Her grip on his arm only tightened.

"Are we safer in with all of the people?" Hearing the tone of her voice he could tell that she was struggling to regain her natural confidence.

"Probably." He had no idea.

Delaware Avenue and its small park—thick with trees and shrubs and therefore quite comforting—were now behind a cordon sanitaire of highly vigilant and nervous US Capitol police. All of them seemed to be alternating between talking into their right shoulders and reaching for their sidearms. As time began to center, reframing, returning to normalcy, Rick watched the closest cop. Hand to shoulder, head turn right and down, click the microphone, talk, head up and jerky scan, hand to service weapon, palm stroke to the thumb-break on the holster, then repeating it all. The small crowd in the park grew. He wondered why they were leaving the buildings.

"It's because of the plan that Homeland Security has for an attack on the Capitol," Julia said.

"What?"

"You asked me why they were leaving the buildings."

"I did?"

"Yes."

Rick shook his head. "I didn't know I said that out loud."

"Maybe that's what getting shot at does to you."

"I was hoping never to find that out."

"Okay, let me see what I can find out," Julia said. She rooted in her purse and withdrew her iPhone. After a few taps on the screen she put the phone to her ear and listened. Rick watched, thinking that in every crisis, we cling to the familiar. For Julia that meant doing her job.

In the Senate Democratic cloakroom, eight attempting-not-to-look-worried senators, two usually laconic professional staff, one incongruous intern, and three tremendously anxious teenage pages stood and paced. They all eyed the flat-screen television and walked back and forth between the two doors each guarded by uniformed Capitol police. Senator Tenley Harbison held her fat BlackBerry in her right hand. She answered it immediately when it buzzed, not even bothering to check who was calling.

"This is Senator Harbison."

"Tenley? It's J.D., and I'm checking in."

"I'm glad you did. We're locked down here in the cloakroom—this is maddening, but I'm told that this is the safest place for us right now. Where are you?"

"In the park on the west side of Delaware, you know, that green space behind Russell."

"Did they evacuate Russell?"

"It certainly looks like that from here."

"Are you with the office staff?"

Julia paused. "No. I was out there, Tenley. At the scene. I was standing on the steps at the visitor center when the shots were fired. I ran over here afterward. There are a whole lot of Capitol police standing around. I think it's all over, but nobody here seems to know anything."

"You were *there*?" The senator's voice raised a half octave.

Julia quickly considered whether or not her boss's reaction was an expression of incredulity or anger. "Tenley, you remember Rick—we used to be married? Well, we met over there to have a private conversation. Part of it was personal, part of it was about ViroSat—"

"Yes, J.D., I remember who his brother is."

"—and I thought that it would be better if he and I talked somewhere outside your office. So we were over in the visitor center. When we were walking outside onto the east plaza, that was when the shots were fired."

"You're kidding. You were *there*?" the senator repeated.

"Rick and I . . ." Julia hesitated ". . . got shot at." With the adrenaline rush worn off and realization setting in, her voice flattened.

"J.D., are you all right?"

"Yes. Maybe."

"We're getting no information at all in here. You have to tell me—what happened?"

"Rick and I were standing at the top of the stairs. We just walked out. We had been standing still for only a short time—Tenley, as I think about it, we were there just long enough for someone to aim at us." Julia spoke haltingly while forming for the first time this profoundly unsettling thought. "Next thing I'm aware of, shots are being fired. At us. *At us*. I don't know how many there were, three or four, maybe more. I could see the bullets hitting the concrete and the marble, and there were streaks on the ground in front of us."

"J.D., you were the target?"

"I think so. I mean, I don't know. It's all terribly confusing." Julia was surprised that she had just blurted out these details to the senator. She hadn't even remembered them until that moment.

"This is very significant," Senator Harbison said gravely. "This does not sound random."

"I agree—but even if we were the target, or one of the targets, I'm pretty sure that we were *chosen* at random."

"You don't know that. There's no way that you can know that. J.D., you cannot go back to the office."

"That won't be a problem—it doesn't look like the police are going to let us back inside anytime soon. Absolutely everybody is locked out of Russell and Hart." Julia looked at the two Senate staff office buildings. "And it's getting more and more crowded here in the park."

"Stay on your mobile," the senator instructed.

"Sure," Julia replied. As if she was ever away from it for a moment on this job.

"And go home. I'll be in touch. Soon. As soon as we're permitted to leave the damn cloakroom." That was about as much profanity as Tenley Harbison ever allowed herself.

"Good-bye, Senator." Julia ended the conversation with a touchstone of formality.

"Bye, J.D. And relax. It's over."

Julia seriously doubted that assertion as she took a deep breath and tapped the screen of her phone, ending the call.

"Metro just closed down," Rick Yeager reported. With Julia on the phone, he had been collecting the kind of information that swirls spontaneously around traumatic events like this one. The news reports were now calling it the Capitol Shooting, with capitalized gravitas. They both looked around the park. Every one of the people disgorged from the two Senate office buildings was in one of two positions: either holding a mobile phone to an ear or furiously tapping away at one in a hunt for information. "It's ironic," he said.

"What is?"

"We're all here smack in the middle of the moment, immediacy and trauma and all that—and nobody knows anything. So they reach out to the Internet for information."

"Hey, I'm perfectly happy," Julia said, "letting the police and the FBI figure out the basic details and then tell me later. Come on, Rick. Let's go."

"You don't want to stay around and talk to the police about how you and I were in the center of all that?"

"No." She was firm and clear. "One of the benefits of senatorial power, and it's very derivative in my case, is that they will eventually find me. Then I'll tell them where to find you. There's nothing we can tell them right now that anyone else can't. Anyone who was there, of course. There were a whole lot of people on the Capitol east front plaza, Rick."

"Okay."

"Did you drive here?"

"Yes. I'm parked at Union Station." They walked slowly in that direction now, farther away from the Capitol building. This time Julia did take hold of his arm tightly.

Neither of them spoke until they were in the car, air conditioner blasting, well on their way to Alexandria. Rick drove an indirect route up Massachusetts Avenue to avoid the federal area and the White House. Traffic crept along, another consequence of high security alert in the shooting's aftermath.

"Do *you* think that we were the target?" he asked.

"Yes," she said without hesitation, as if she had been contemplating exactly this inquiry. "We were, Rick. But the shots were not aimed at *us*, at you and me personally. They were aimed at us as in 'to whom it may concern.' We were the people he kind of aimed at."

"So what do you think brought this on? Right-wing crazies, political anger—"

"Uh-uh. Life is more haphazard than that." She thought for a brief moment. "Rick, do you know who Richard Neustadt was?"

"No."

"Famous political scientist at Harvard. He was a specialist in the

American presidency and an advisor to every president from Truman on. Well, the Democratic presidents, I mean—he was very close to Kennedy and Johnson. Neustadt said that whenever you have a choice between conspiracy and confusion, you should choose confusion. You'll always be correct."

"I don't buy it, J.D."

"You don't have to. This could end up as one of those imponderables. We may never know why we got shot at. But I'm betting that they'll find the shooter in a day or less, and it will turn out to be one more disgruntled and deranged middle-aged white guy who deserves pity as much as he deserves to be in jail for the rest of his life. Unfortunately over the years, this kind of thing has happened a lot in Washington. We were all waiting for something like this to happen after President Obama got elected the first time."

"I would have agreed with you a couple of weeks ago," he said, "but there are just too many coincidences piling up all around us right now."

"Rick, I would have said that you're the least conspiracy-minded person I know."

"Correct, J.D. That's the point. There's an awful lot of confusion piling up." He was stopped in deep traffic at a red light. Rick thought for a moment. "J.D., do you remember that woman named Geller?"

"You mentioned her."

"She died in a car accident while I was in jail." Rick looked at Julia and broke a wan smile, glad that he could finally make light of the federal raid and his arrest at Carneccio & Dice. "She was a client of mine at the personal finance firm in Arlington. She had your business card in her purse."

"What was her full name again?"

"Hannah Weiss Geller." He used the German pronunciation of her family name: *vayss*.

Julia thought briefly. "I remember her. Little old lady, right? Kind of frail, white hair pulled back, stately? Very outgoing. She came to the office asking to see Tenley, and I got to handle her." Rick was savvy enough about the ways of Capitol Hill to know what this meant. Mrs. Geller had come to Harbison's office expecting, like everybody else, to meet with the senator herself. But she had been deflected to Julia, the chief legisla-tive assistant, who no doubt conducted the meeting with respect, alac-rity, and a few white lies about the senator's busy schedule.

"How did that happen?" Rick asked. "She lived in Arlington, Vir-ginia. Why would she want to see a senator from New Jersey?"

"This is coming back to me. She knew our finance guy from Tenley's political organization—he works New Jersey and Virginia and a few other states. You just don't want to get near his work, Rick, but it's abso-lutely necessary to keep getting her reelected. Now remember, I'm one of only two staffers for the senator who is permitted by law to take politi-cal meetings in the Capitol complex. Since the meeting request came in from campaign finance, the scheduler sent Mrs. Geller to me. So I took the meeting. I'm sorry to hear that she died."

"Still, it's more than a little weird."

"She was incredibly nice, Rick. But you're also right. She was slightly strange. She wanted to talk about the banking crisis, like it was fresh in her mind. That was the way she referred to it—the banking crisis. I told her that the 'crisis' was years ago, and that we're deep into a recovery or what-ever this is right now."

"She wanted to meet with Tenley Harbison because . . ."

"Because she could. She did mention that when she came to the United States as a girl, the only family she had was in New Jersey. They had banking interests, so for her that was enough of a connection. Both of the Virginia senators probably gave her the brush-off. She was particu-larly concerned about ballooning deficit spending, the debt, growth in entitlements, and so forth. Nothing new, but I found it sort of surprising, because I wouldn't have made her out to be a fiscal conservative. Maybe that's why she asked to visit Tenley—you know she kind of leans that way. But with Mrs. Geller, the conversation was really quite amorphous. She was all over the place with theories and concerns about government spending. She kept saying that this continuing debt and deficit crisis was not the first one she had been through, and that there was a great deal she could do personally to help us out now. I was kind to her, of course. I told her that the senator was also very frustrated with the state of Wash-ington politics and was actively working for real solutions. You know the speech. Frankly Rick, there was nothing either in her background or anything that she told me to recommend her as any kind of expert. The meeting was just like the last hundred constituent calls and meetings that I've handled. And the next thousand."

Rick was lagging a little behind her as she spoke. "New Jersey," he said slowly.

"Yeah—"

"She told you that her only family was in New Jersey."

"Correct. What's that got to do with anything?"

"Did she say anything about a cousin in California?"

"No, I'm certain about that part, because I was thinking about votes. She was rambling gently. The rest of her promises about a big solution I pretty much graciously ignored."

"Weird," Rick repeated. "Confusion, not conspiracy."

At a conference held at Princeton University's Woodrow Wilson School about four months ago, Senator Tenley Harbison participated in a panel self-admiringly entitled "Media, Government, and Society: The Responsibility Equation." Presenting with her on the panel that day were two reporters, one from the *Washington Post.* She recalled that there was little of substance anyone discussed—much of the usual hand wringing prevailed—but she did learn one important fact: At the *Post*, every telephone desk set and every reporter's mobile phone was required to have and use caller ID. The practice was not necessarily standard in the overstressed newspaper industry, but it was certainly policy at the only paper that mattered in Washington.

That afternoon she had Julia Toussaint change the personal mobile number on her BlackBerry to read "private."

Still in lockdown in the Democratic cloakroom, she squinted at that BlackBerry and scrolled down the tiny screen to select a number. The senator's first call was to the *Washington Post.* Then to the Newark *Star-Ledger's* guy in Washington—an independent contractor, but one she trusted. In rapid succession she also tipped the *Wall Street Journal*, the *New York Times*, of course, and two favored bloggers at BlueJersey.com and NJPolitics.com. Next was the online and visual media: MSNBC, an old friend from Columbia Law now at CBS News, and an overawed young producer for George Stephanopoulos's Sunday show at ABC. Each conversation was very short. Each had the same message and the same information.

It's Senator Harbison. I'm calling to tell you who was the target of the Capitol shooting. And here's where she lives in Alexandria.

The last number she selected was Julia's. The senator grinned as she listened to the tiny symphony of rapidly firing touch tones, then frowned when Julia's mobile rang directly to voice mail. No problem. She could leave a message.

It was high time, she reasoned, for J.D. to step up to the plate. She would be touching and mediagenic, with a politically winning combination of humility, competence, and grace. After all, she had just been literally shot at, battle-tested. But far better that she should hear about her elevation to star status as a fait accompli.

The senator's most loyal legislative aide, she knew for certain, would never agree to play if she actually had a choice in the matter.

CHAPTER 26

Deep inside Terragreen in the small, square, windowless conference room, Sanford Tuttle gripped the arms of his chair and stretched. The chair allowed him about a 20-degree lean-back angle as he stared at the ceiling, clearly working something out. He circled his hands to the back of his head and interlaced his fingers. Staring at the ceiling, he said, "Warren, let me attempt to review the bidding here."

Warren Hunter glanced about the room. The FSSC ViroSat team and Jonas Barr from GT3 all watched carefully, trying to pick up clues from either of the visitors. He said nothing—which he had learned years ago was an incredibly powerful negotiating tactic. Instead of reacting in any way, he simply turned to Sanford Tuttle and nodded. The message clarifying for the FSSC managers: something was going on, and only the two of them had even the slightest clue what it was.

"We all have some enormous stakes in ViroSat," Tuttle began. "Once it's online, GT3—closest to my heart—gets to make new markets beyond FSSC. That goes a long way toward solving my customer concentration problem. And you folks know that I'm not the only one worried about that particular complication." He leaned forward now, and made eye contact again with everyone sitting at the round table. "As for FSSC, the financial returns from this investment are going to give you what you've all desired since the inception of the corporation—enough independence from the federal government to truly stand alone. Who knows? When ViroSat plays out, your organization could achieve what all of the public-private cooperative ventures want but never get. Real privatization. I've heard exactly what you've heard here in the bunker. The executive committee is talking about FSSC becoming a model for Amtrak,

Fannie Mae, Freddie Mac, and every other smaller operation that's become far too reliant upon government funding for its base capitalization, and even for its operations. You're almost private—you're *this* close—but not completely there yet. If FSSC was able to completely go it alone, wouldn't that be bucking a trend? Of course, the act of going all-private may give this place far more visibility than any of us wants, but by then, that will be a very good problem to have.

"And then we've got Compton Sizemore," he said, turning to Warren Hunter, "whose motivations and incentives are obvious."

"I wear my agenda on my sleeve," Warren replied with a broad smile.

"Meanwhile, we're proposing to use the entire resources of GT3"— Tuttle glanced at Jonas Barr—"and FSSC to raise the capital necessary for your limited partnership."

"Our limited partnership," Warren corrected him courteously.

"We're talking about three hundred billion dollars."

"Two hundred eighty-seven point seven billion." Another correction, to which Tuttle nodded this time, appreciating the precision. "And technically speaking, it's really not a 'raise.' We're talking about an 'accumulation.'"

"I know," Sanford Tuttle said. "Permit me to sketch out the deal." He reached for a tablet with the words FSSC CONFERENCE ROOM in muted gray across the top, pulling one from a stack in the center of the table. "Now, ViroSat is worth what, total capital required?"

"One point three seven trillion."

"And of that number, how much is debt?"

"One point zero eight two three trillion," Warren responded, the numbers rolling off instantly and effortlessly.

"Which you've already collected in-house at Compton Sizemore from a few dozen countries, right? Leaving the remainder"—Tuttle wrote $287B *eq* on the pad—"as equity in the deal, coming from the limited partnership."

"Exactly." Warren saw that Tuttle's recap was solely for the benefit of the FSSC people in the room. He was slightly surprised that they were not thoroughly versed in the top-level financial mechanics of the deal.

They were the ViroSat team, after all. They should know the gross numbers cold. Their counterparts in New York certainly did.

"Now," Sanford Tuttle continued, drawing a line on his pad, "before the harvest—the time when Compton Sizemore sells off ViroSat in pieces, including your hundred and twelve enterprise units—the ownership of limited partnership shares is what?"

"Fifty-fifty," Warren said. "Half is my personal holding. Half is FSSC's." His answer was automatic, because he was stuck on the fact that Tuttle knew exactly how many enterprise units—independent cash-generating international companies—there were attached to ViroSat. He smiled inwardly at Tuttle's level of preparation. Not that he should be surprised.

"But that's different from the way that distributions are going to be made after the harvest," Tuttle was saying, this time explaining in a tutorial manner to the conference table how this limited partnership would pay out. "From the proceeds of the partnership, first, there's a premium, ten percent return on the investment, paid to FSSC and to Warren, as the limited partners. But they don't get to keep it. Do the math and you'll see that almost all of it goes to pay GT3's fees and infrastructure costs. Thank you, Warren." He grinned broadly.

"I'd say 'you're welcome,' but you know we're a long way from that payday, Sandy."

Tuttle grunted. "Yeah. I know. We're getting there. So after that premium, the whole proceeds are then divided eighty-twenty. Twenty percent to the general partner. Eighty percent to be divided fifty-fifty between the two limited partners. Warren, you are also personally the general partner, so effectively—"

"Effectively, I'm going to receive sixty percent of the ViroSat equity upside—twenty plus forty, which is my half of eighty—and FSSC is going to get the other forty percent."

A member of the FSSC team, a round-faced bureaucrat who looked to Warren to be between thirty-five and forty, prematurely white-haired, let out a long low whistle. "We really are in partnership, aren't we?" he said.

"We are," Warren replied. "And even better, we have that rare circumstance where our economic motivations are in perfect alignment. Provided, of course, that everyone involved collectively has the sophistication, the understanding, and the risk tolerance to hold up and hold together as this deal progresses."

"Explain that, please," Sanford Tuttle asked.

"Certainly," Warren agreed, turning to address the four FSSC managers. "Sandy, remember the TechniChron deal, the one you had us put together for QUATECH after you were flush with cash following your IPO? Mr. Barr, were you in the company then?"

"Why, yes, I was," Jonas Barr replied, happy for the reference, but unsure where this discussion was going.

"TechniChron was an international holding company wholly owned by QUATECH as a long-term investment. At Compton Sizemore we set up the financial structure and just as important, the international tax structure. The project existed to buy deals—debt interest in small companies— worldwide, in the information technology space. Sandy and I were interested in technology ventures, and eventually we had how many eggs in that basket?"

"Twenty-one."

"We funded intellectual property ventures, marketing plays, new technologies, materials science, and plain old market expansions around the world. The business case was that with a streamlined, centralized, globalized, agile infrastructure provided by QUATECH, the portfolio companies would all benefit. And how many of them did, Sandy?"

"Sixteen."

"Yup. Seventy-six percent. The other five, whose economic motivations were exactly the same as the others—remember what I said about alignment—basically did one of three things. They made idiotic choices. They got too greedy. Or they refused to listen to what I told them to do. They're out of business. Bankrupt and worse. A few of their executives are still in jail in Europe and South America. A couple more of them learned what it's like if you're also dumb enough to sue Compton Sizemore."

"And QUATECH," Tuttle added.

"Right. We locked shields in those lawsuits, Sandy, and then prevailed in every one of our counterclaims. But that's not the main reason I brought up the TechniChron deal. Tell them what happened to the other sixteen."

"All of them are still in business partnership with QUATECH, one way or another, even after a whole lot of corporate consolidation. All of them are still growing and profitable, despite the downturn and a persistent recession."

"Because they held on," Warren concluded, "and refused to panic as the whole pattern developed."

"What pattern was that?" the FSSC man asked.

"I'm glad you asked, because it's the same template or pattern we're about to see here in ViroSat," Warren replied. "Especially in the limited partnership. You have to be comfortable with uncertainty. There will be risks that Sandy and I manage—risks from which FSSC will benefit— that you may not wholly understand. But they're our risks, and our responsibility."

"Nothing illegal, right?" Warren appreciated the guy. He was being thorough, not skeptical.

"Not even close. In fact, international law and regulation have not developed to the point that our counsel in New York are concerned. Now I can't promise that for the next guy that tries something like this . . ."

All of the people at the conference table chuckled. Warren drove on, making his point. "We're all in this together, and I'm navigating. The economic motivations are clear. My financial operations within the deal may not all be totally clear at all times, but you will have to trust me. The companies in the TechniChron project that did are prospering now. The ones that didn't listen to me suffered greatly."

"If I remember right, some of them blame you for their failure," Jonas Barr offered.

"True enough. But I have broad shoulders," Warren said, smiling again, "and all objective observers conclude otherwise. Why do you think I've been so successful in piecing together the debt for ViroSat?"

"Because you have an extraordinary product backing you up," Tuttle answered with pride.

"Yeah. That, too."

"We still haven't talked about the source of the capital. What's buying your fifty percent and ours?" asked the round-faced FSSC man. Warren now concluded that he was the team leader. Just like on Wall Street, real power never shows its hand first or fast.

"You've asked a good question," Warren said quietly. "It goes to the reason that you, my FSSC colleagues, must continue to trust me, and why I am asking you to rely upon my judgment. For your part in this deal, we'll need not only your cooperation. We'll need your infrastructure. Most of all, we'll need FSSC's ability to keep this quiet."

"Warren and I," Sanford Tuttle added, "will be able to assemble the limited partnership cash using those resources."

"Three hundred billion?" asked the FSSC team leader. The question was professional, not incredulous, and clearly went to degree. It was evident that he did not doubt their ability.

"Two eighty-seven seven." Warren corrected him, as he heard that low whistle again.

The meeting broke up in time for a late lunch. Neither Warren Hunter nor Sanford Tuttle was very hungry as they walked back across the Chantilly tech campus to Tuttle's office at GT3 headquarters.

"How did I do?" Warren inquired.

"Spot-on. I know that this is a different world from what you're used to, but believe me, winning over those five people was the most important deal you've closed in ViroSat to date."

"So you think I won them over."

"For now. This is going to work in phases. They definitely believe in your abilities and are willing to let you lead. That's the critical path. They'll support our assembling the cash—and believe me, right now they're meeting with the FSSC general counsel. Two of them there were lawyers, you know."

"No, I didn't know. It wouldn't have made any difference to me if I had."

"I'm sure not." They walked in silence until they reached Tuttle's office building.

"The beauty of the plan is," Warren said, "that all of the cash for the limited partnership is coming from the same source."

"Someone's going to notice when we collect that kind of cash."

"Sandy, no one owns it. You've read the legal opinions. We're on solid ground here. This is new territory to be sure, but we are absolutely rock-solid."

"That's only because there's never been any capital aggregation like it before. Warren, I don't know precisely the origins of over three hundred billion dollars, and right now none of us knows how, again precisely, to locate it."

"That is why I need FSSC."

"You are presenting us with an awe-inspiring risk, my friend."

"And *that* is why there's a real fortune to be made here."

"And why we're headed to this meeting." He opened the door to the main GT3 building and held it for Warren. "You were wise to give them only the broad strokes in the bunker. The technical components of capital assembly, I submit, will prove to be the easy part."

"But you have the means of locating the capital sources."

"I do. With your concurrence, of course." Sanford Tuttle led Warren down the main corridor of the building, up an open flight of stairs in a brilliantly sunlit atrium, reversing course on the upper floor to enter his office suite. Compared to the Compton Sizemore offices in Citigroup Center, it was a decidedly modest place—underfurnished, everything as high-end functional as it was well thought-out. Perfectly balanced, giving off the aura of premium quality with not a bit of waste. Exactly what you'd expect in a top-flight technology company. Warren was about to say that to Tuttle when they stopped in his outer office. "No one," Tuttle asserted, "has been at this longer, nor knows this issue better than he does. And Warren, you can trust him absolutely and unequivocally. Presidents have. If the world could know what he's done for this country in the CIA, in the clandestine service, the world would be astonished."

Sanford Tuttle stepped into his office. Warren followed, his curiosity piqued.

As they entered, a lanky old man unfolded his crossed legs and stood. He was tall, obviously still quite athletic, with rugged features. Warren considered his age and concluded that it would be impossible to guess—he was just old and in great shape. He had a thick head of white hair cropped close, maybe a little longer than old-school military style. His face was expressionless, handsome, and—Warren considered for a moment how to characterize him. Ordinary. That was it. And along with all that, an innate quality within him projected an instantaneous aura of trust. Kind of like Dutch had, he thought. He'd run into that before in deals. There are people who are extremely good at closing mostly because they are inspiring and trusted, deserving or not. This man was definitely one of them. Maybe that quality was what had made him so successful in the intelligence service.

"Warren," Sanford Tuttle was saying, "I'd like you to meet my father."

CHAPTER 27

Past Ronald Reagan National Airport—which Rick Yeager, like most longtime residents of northern Virginia called simply "National"—he slowed the car. Traffic crept in maddening deceleration as the George Washington Parkway bottlenecked down into Washington Street, the main thoroughfare of Alexandria, Virginia. Julia Toussaint stared straight ahead. She was lost in thought, still in shock, or both. At the red light, he reached for her hand. She took a tight grip.

"That was important."

Rick smiled thinly. "You used to do that when we were married. I used to think it was adorable." He paused. "No, that's not right. I still think it's adorable. And you still do it. You were in the middle of a conversation in your own mind—or you're continuing something that we *did* talk about— and I have no idea what you mean."

"I meant that you included me in your life when Dutch died."

"You came with Warren."

"That, too."

"Again, meaning?"

"Rick, we're coming about. This is reconciliation for us, but right now we don't know where it's taking us. When your mother died and I stayed with Warren on that drive back, that was the beginning of the end for us. You and me. I gave your brother my word that I would be there when your father died. When I said that, I was certain we would be together. Again, I mean you and me. I kept my word to Warren, but what I was most worried about wasn't how he would maintain some semblance of control. I was worried about how you would react."

"Did I react well?"

"I would say so." She continued to grip his hand tightly even though the light had now changed to green. He drove forward with one hand on the wheel.

"I miss him already, Julia. If there was ever anybody for whom death was going to bring peace that he never had in this life, it was Dutch."

"I understand that."

"But he couldn't even go out easily, Julia. No sense of serenity. No closure."

"Rick, if he did, that just wouldn't have been Dutch. Or you or Warren, for that matter."

"More Warren than me."

"Yes."

"He struggled right up until the last moment. Pop lived in the past. There was constantly some kind of unfinished business before him. There are times when I believe that's what drove him."

"What's driving you now, Richard Yeager?"

"Not a whole lot," he replied. "Julia, I've never felt more adrift in my entire life."

"Well," she said, "maybe that's what being shot at does to you."

Rick grunted. In response, Julia picked up his hand and brought it to her lips, holding it there as he drove on and choked back tears.

As he turned from North Washington onto King Street in Old Town Alexandria—this used to be his commute home, it occurred to Rick as he realized how automatically he was driving—Julia startled and yelped slightly. "No!"

"Am I missing something here?" he asked.

"Wait a minute," she said. "Please. Just stop here." Julia was fiddling with her iPhone, frantically running her forefinger up and down. "It's from my senator."

She held up the text message for him to read.

attempted call got yr vm. media most interested in yr personal
perspect on shooting & some to meet you @ home in alex. high vis.
I concur w your particip. th

Rick looked from the small screen to the normally sedate street ahead,
where Julia's apartment—what used to be his and Julia's apartment—was
located. There he saw a typical media mob scene. Dominated by the
telescoping television satellite trucks, a remote feed was in the process of
taking shape. No police cruisers were there yet, but they would come.
Cables were being run, a bank of microphones was already in place, and
two radio-remote vans were parking. A couple of laconic still photographers, a guy and a woman both in shaggy clothes, were smoking cigarettes
and talking. They stood at the only entrance to Julia's building—a terrific location for them.

"I do *not* want to do this."

"Then don't."

"Why would Tenley let them know where to find me?"

"Easy, Julia. She saw some political advantage in it."

"She knows that I don't do media."

"She figured that now would be the time to change that. We were
there. This is the story of the moment."

"Rick, I'm *not* going."

"I love it," he said, "when we agree." He turned left onto the next
side street, grateful for all of the navigating of this neighborhood that
he used to do in many futile attempts to find the best ways to avoid traffic. In two minutes he was back on North Washington Street headed the
other way.

"Thank you," Julia said.

"They'll never consider looking for you," he said, "in Reston. But do
you think that Tenley Harbison is going to be upset when she realizes
that you ducked them?"

"That," Julia replied confidently, "I am certain I can handle."

*   *   *

By the time they made it outside the Beltway on the Dulles Toll Road, the main artery to Washington's other airport and the way to Rick's home in Reston, he was thoroughly fed up with traffic.

"You're upset," Julia said.

"Not at you."

"You're steamed at this drive. We've been in the car an hour and a half already."

"Partially."

"It's about Dutch."

"Not at all."

"What else then?"

Rick clenched his jaw, then loosened it. "It's something you told me. One of those persistent little nags to the conscience. That conversation with Mrs. Geller, when she visited you at the senator's office."

"It was nothing, seriously."

"I'm not so certain. Could we talk about it?"

"Sure." She was cool. He judged her reaction more as tolerant curiosity than displeasure.

"Why did she come to you?"

"I told you. The Virginia senators wouldn't see her."

"That's what she said?"

"Wait. No. I assumed that. Rick, I didn't pay that close attention to her—"

"—Stay with me. When did Mrs. Geller come to see you?"

"It was the last week in June, I think. Just before the Fourth of July recess. I'm really not sure what day it was. If you need to know, we can check the calendar for appointments. No one goes in or out of the Russell Building anymore without being registered."

"The important point is, she visited you on the Hill just a day or so before she came to visit me at Carneccio & Dice. The day she was . . . the day she died. She had your business card in her purse."

"Do you think this has any bearing on how she died? You said it was a car accident."

Rick swerved quickly to avoid his own accident, as traffic piled up again approaching the toll booth. He maneuvered into the E-ZPass lane.

"It was. She crashed on the GW Parkway along the Potomac. But that's not what I'm most interested in right now. J.D., what did she say to you about banking?"

"Okay. Let me think. Her father's business had been some kind of banking somewhere. She didn't say where. I got the impression that it was in Europe. But she did talk about how she had family in New Jersey—at least I *think* it was family. They organized banks. They had been through recessionary pressures before. That was the gist of what she wanted to talk about. Solving the banking crisis. I told her that Tenley had just given a speech in Montclair where she'd essentially declared the banking crisis over—it's been a long time since the meltdown, and the Dodd-Frank Act regulations are all being implemented. That's the party line, and even though she isn't running for reelection, she wanted to amplify that message."

"How did Mrs. Geller react?"

"She said that she knew Essex County very well. It was a place in New Jersey where her family had placed significant assets. I remember that. 'Recessionary pressures' and 'significant assets.' It was more than a little strange, I guess, coming from an LOL. She almost sounded like your brother." Julia grinned.

"LOL?"

"Little old lady, Rick. My grandmother worked as a domestic her entire life, remember? That was what she called those oh-so-kindly old white ladies in the family households. To do otherwise—to call them what she wanted to—would have compromised her own dignity."

Rick nodded. "Did Mrs. Geller know where these significant assets were?"

"Hardly. The whole conversation was theoretical, almost in the extreme. That was why I ended it courteously. She kept talking about deficit spending, entitlements, and the federal budget. I felt as though I was giving a tutorial to some high school students. Or maybe getting a tutorial from one of those Ayn Rand people. You know how it is. It was very difficult to keep from becoming patronizing, and I am extremely sensitive to that dynamic. So is Tenley."

"Why did she bring it to you, though?"

"I was the designated stuck-ee," Julia said, using the Hill's colloquial for the staffer stuck with a necessary task. "She came in through the political side, so she had to talk to me."

"Did she say anything at all about that family in New Jersey?" Rick asked. "J.D., here's what's been gnawing at me. Right after I got out of jail"—he surprised himself at how easy it was to say that again—"I met her niece. Well, her sort-of niece. The woman made the funeral arrangements, and she was not at all pleased that I'm the executor of Hannah Weiss Geller's estate."

"You're *what?*"

"Hold on. I'll get to that. This niece, a lawyer, has now come to see me three times, and we've been to Mrs. Geller's house together. The last time she showed up was the day that Pop died, and she rode to Maryland with me when I was driving up to meet Warren and to be with Pop."

"So you're telling me that the niece was from that family in north Jersey?"

"No. She said that Mrs. Geller's only relative was her mother in California."

"That's more than odd. Rick, I'm not sure that Mrs. Geller was talking about family in the blood relative sense. Which one of them do you think was lying? Bet on the lawyer, you'll always be right."

"I just don't know."

"She never told me where they were," Julia said. "Hey, we grew up there, Rick. One of us would have recognized a place in Jersey if she had said something." She paused and crossed her arms, staring at the line of commuter traffic stretching past Wolf Trap on the Dulles Toll Road. "You know, she did bring up a credit union in all of that banking discussion. She said that the senator would surely know it—her words—but I swear, I never heard of it, and my mom and dad have been credit union people in Newark forever."

"Did she say which one?"

"Just initials. ECTFCU. I remember that because I made a lame joke about the 'et cetera' federal credit union. She said it wasn't the first time she heard that."

Rick was silent.

"What?"

"I know it."

"Once again, what?" Julia smiled at him.

"Essex Construction Trades Federal Credit Union. It closed in 1972."

"How would you know that?"

"Julia, you knew my father. He was one continuous flight to obsessions when he wasn't mired in those terrible depressive states that defined his life. You and I weren't the only Yeager marriage to break up on fundamental misunderstandings."

"Misunderstandings like . . ."

"Like my father's years of research into a scandal that he personally broke wide open when I was a baby, even before Warren was born. I always thought that maybe he'd write a book about it. Have you ever heard of Essex Empire?"

"Yes I have. From your father."

"Of course you did. It was one of the many things that he could never let go. Essex Empire was a major public corruption scandal involving most of the Newark city council and three construction firms. I still don't understand it completely, even though Dutch was all over it my whole life. When Warren and I stayed with him, after he and Mom broke up, there were days when he'd spend time with those Essex Empire tax files rather than with us. It was as though he was looking for something long after everyone else forgot about the whole thing. As I got older, I came to see it as therapeutic for him."

"What did the credit union have to do with the scandal?"

"The scheme was a fake holding company that diverted federal funds earmarked to rebuild Newark after the riots. Just like today, government funding was locked down tight but there were rivers of cash available for the 'right' projects. There was very little accountability. This should ring resonantly true for your work now. The fake company was a builder, and the cash was all laundered through—"

"—Essex Construction Trades Federal Credit Union. ECTFCU."

"Right. Dutch tracked it through tax records. He was brilliant at that stuff. But we never knew why he kept at it for years afterward, even as he cracked open bigger and bigger cases. Remember, he even worked with your senator when she was a prosecutor."

"I remember. So does she. Tenley was very moved this week when she was reminiscing about Dutch. I didn't get to tell you that, with everything that happened today. I'm sorry."

"So here's our question, J.D. Why would Mrs. Geller mention a credit union that's been closed for forty years? One that my father from time to time became obsessed about."

"Pure coincidence?"

"Nope. Not this time. J.D., it's not conspiracy, but it's definitely not coincidence."

Two hours and ten minutes, Rick thought as he pulled into the densely wooded parking lot of his condominium complex in Reston. He reflected on the brutality of the Washington auto commute and resolved for the thousandth time not to work downtown—ever.

"I've never been here," Julia said gently.

"It has some advantages over Old Town," he replied, "but there is a lot that I miss there." He walked around the car and opened the door for her.

"You never used to do that," she said, stepping out.

"We all learn and grow."

For too long a moment as they stood in the open passenger side car door, Rick looked down at her—radiant, dark, gorgeous, glowing, her wide brown eyes drawing him in. She smiled quietly, leaned closer to him and halted, then raised a hand to his face. Rick started to speak as Julia kissed him gently, deliberately. Not on the lips, but very very close. Then she kissed him again, lingering.

Rick felt a small storm of emotions as Julia stepped nearer to him and held him in a tight, quick hug, her head tucked into his chest, her face to the side. She breathed deeply. He was considering carefully this moment while in its midst, thinking about the correct response, when he felt her breathing suddenly quicken, gulps of air followed by a low guttural scream—more of a yelp—as she pushed him away and retreated back to lean on the car.

Julia stared and panted, the noise, not words, increasing. "Anghh-hhh . . ."

She went numb.

Rick gazed at her, finally realizing that Julia was fixated on something. There, on the ground next to the only entrance to his condominium, in the center of the small courtyard.

The crumpled body of a woman.

There was no mistaking her for being alive. Her head was twisted obscenely far to the right and upward, almost facing back. Deep bluish-black bruising was already waxing visible on her overstretched neck. Her hair covered her face. She wore a long green skirt and a patterned white blouse. Her legs splayed at the knees. Her waist bent slightly forward. She'd obviously been dropped from a standing position and was now stuck partially on her side in a most unnatural and deeply disturbing twist.

He walked the few steps to the courtyard. He stepped tentatively, carefully, then stopped and bent over.

He touched the body twice and attempted to lift its left arm. She was awfully stiff and would not move. Part of him was afraid to look. All of him was afraid not to. He pushed the hair away from her face.

In shattered consciousness time chattered and disconnected for the second time today. There was no mistaking who she was.

Lauren Barr's cold dead pleading green eyes were wide open and stared back at him.

CHAPTER 28

"Warren Hunter." He extended his hand to the old man.

"Graham Tuttle. You should call me Gray." He spoke that second sentence with the slightest lift in his voice, like the touch of a master actor delivering a line that had been well-practiced his entire life.

"Thank you, Gray." Warren chose to be deliberately deferential. He became aware that Gray Tuttle was studying him closely as he sat back in one of the black leather chairs arranged in the sitting area of the GT3 CEO's suite. That's when it occurred to him. "GT3," he said slowly to Sanford Tuttle, who was seating himself between his father and Warren, "which doesn't stand for anything—"

"—Of course it does. Gray Tuttle's third son. The only company name I ever got personal with." The younger Tuttle grinned broadly. "You now possess a genuine family secret."

His father cracked a thin smile in response. "And, if you'll forgive my getting right down to business, Sanford, that's not the only body of secrets that we're here to discuss."

Warren detected a kindness in the man's voice. It was a kindness tempered with confidence. This was a very different combination of personal qualities from what he was used to in New York, but it seemed to be fairly effective. He continued assessing Sanford Tuttle's father carefully—he was good at this after all, it was a necessary skill in negotiation—but he continued to come up short. That was frustrating. He contemplated this frustration as Sanford Tuttle nodded to him, a signal to begin. Warren was left with a solid intuition that maybe ViroSat's funding was better secured than he knew about before now. And that, he concluded, was okay. He'd play this interaction in the receive mode.

"It's my understanding," Warren began, "that whatever it is you're going to do will supplement the FSSC technical efforts for our aggregation
of certain capital assets. Sandy told me weeks ago that he had retained
an experienced consultant whom we would be working with. He didn't
say that you were his father. I hope that the relationship is relevant."

"All relationships," Gray Tuttle responded, "are always relevant."

Warren held on to that thought for a moment. "Good. Permit me to
explain the scope of our work. We have a specific task to accomplish—
the collection of capital. As you already know, there is a huge and very
diffuse body of what we will call 'unclaimed' capital within the international banking system, whether it's in deposits here in the United States
or elsewhere around the world. The funds are mostly in western banking
systems—the US, UK, and European Union—but especially in the past
decade the money has all gotten even more distributed, particularly in
China and India. No one knows for certain exactly how much cash we're
talking about. The best estimate from my monetary economists at
Compton Sizemore is that the amount is between three and four trillion
dollars worldwide. We, however, are only interested in that portion of it
resident here in the United States. We are not even after all of it. We only
need enough of it to fund the equity partnership of the ViroSat deal.

"Now here is the beauty, and the utter legality, of what we've discovered.

"In the enabling federal legislation that created FSSC, there is a pro-
vision that's unique to its one-of-a-kind public-private partnership. FSSC,
alone among all players in the financial services industry, is able to *keep
and use* any 'unclaimed' capital that it's able to aggregate, as long as three
conditions are met. One, the capital can only be used in an investment
partnership with a private sector corporation—that's specifically my limited partnership, and more generally my investment bank, Compton
Sizemore. Two, the purpose of the investment must broadly benefit the
United States for what the legislation says are 'improvements to the national and international technological infrastructure.' By any test, Viro-
Sat is exactly that. And three, the capital, once the investment becomes
profitable, has to be returned to the federal treasury. Best of all, we have
no statutory requirement to disclose any of this until the time that payment is made to the treasury."

The whole time that Warren spoke, he was aware that Gray Tuttle never moved, and had barely blinked. He had not taken any notes, but Warren was certain that the old man just absorbed every word he said.

"No one," the elder Tuttle said slowly, forming the question as he spoke, "outside of your organization and Sandy's, of course, knows that you plan to use this so-called 'unclaimed' capital to finance your VirtuSat deal?"

"ViroSat. And actually, no one outside this *room* knows it."

The old man smiled—his first real show of emotion, Warren thought. "Good. I like that," he said, "very much."

"Warren," Sanford Tuttle said. "My father needs to tell you what he's been working on. I can't tell you precisely about the extent of his experience in national intelligence. I don't know all of it myself, even after a whole lifetime of being a federal contractor for those guys. But take it for granted that he's among the last of the first."

"Yeah," added Gray Tuttle. "It's hell when you live this long." Warren couldn't tell whether the sentiment was genuine or sarcastic.

"Dad, you ought to tell him why I asked you to take on this project."

Gray grunted. "I ought to," he said. He was thinking hard as he massaged the inside of his right elbow with his left hand, extending his right forearm in what appeared to Warren to be arthritis pain. Then he crossed his arms, and took almost a full minute of silence before he began.

"You went to Princeton, right? Don't act so surprised. Much about you is easily accessible public information. In my life, and for my *whole* life, I've dealt in the currency of information. There's much more about you that I know. Most of it I respect. I mentioned Princeton because it will help you to understand me. I started at Yale in 1940. I finished there too, but that was after the war. Like you, Warren, I was the complete outsider on the day I arrived. Yale had so damn many elitist prep school boys then. That certainly wasn't me. Where I came from is not important. Neither is my family. What's relevant is that I grew up with the harshest lessons you can learn in the Great Depression. Banks were failing. People were losing jobs then losing faith in this country. This is not a complaint. That early toughening in my life, and the way it transferred intergenerationally, gives Sanford and his brothers their drive. They have spirit. I like that. But I'm off-point.

"We knew the war was coming. Pearl Harbor happened in my sophomore year, before finals. I signed up on January fifth. New Haven was a good recruiting ground for Army Intelligence—you could look it up. Long story short, my young friend, I began my career there and, if you consider this financial work for my son to be an extension of those years, well, then I'm still practicing my craft.

"I can read your face. Just a piece of advice. Don't ever play poker with me. You're wondering what any of this has to do with that aggregation of loose capital that I'm supposed to help you with.

"It is all directly related, Warren. I first did this kind of work in 1943.

"Which one of those European philosophers wrote that 'of all the sins of mankind, the greatest of these is forgetting what it is that we are trying to do . . .'? Well, whoever said it doesn't matter. The message is what's important. Sanford, you and I and Warren here had better review what it is we are *attempting* to do. The two of you have in the immediate moment the rarest ability there is in business or government: you can keep and use for your ViroSat project any money you can find and collect. You intend to employ the resources of FSSC and GT3. Let's be frank. GT3 is nothing more than the operational arm of FSSC—and don't deny it, Sanford. You are going to use a massive parallel networked computer system to find all that cash. Back in the day, in the clandestine service we called that 'national technical means.' They probably still do. And I have learned from bitter experience that one cannot rely upon national technical means.

"That leaves us with the resources I am able to call upon. And leads our conversation right back to 1943.

"Warren, this is not the first time that I've been involved in the collection of capital, as you call it. I will bet you that they have been losing track of huge sums of money ever since church and crown invented the concept of a banking system. Although I must confess that by now, with all of our amazing technological enablements, I thought the whole process would be getting better, not worse. This does go to prove my point about national technical means. The problem may be bad now. It may be an opportunity for you. But it was downright terrible during my first war. The big one.

"I finished air intelligence school in Harrisburg, Pennsylvania, and arrived at my air wing in England by January of '43. I was a butter bar then—second lieutenant. My newly trained intelligence specialty was photo interpretation, so naturally I was seconded to a highly classified project involving international flows of capital, especially from Germany. Typical Army efficiency. I didn't know flows of capital from Scapa Flow at the time. The project was a collateral duty. I still had to brief and de-brief all of the bombing missions from our B-24 squadrons. There was a war going on, and that kind of adjunct intelligence operation was not our first priority by any means.

"There you go signaling again, Warren. It's incredibly subtle—I can perceive that you're extremely good at masking your emotions. But you just reacted involuntarily when that question formed in your mind. Hang on. Yes. There is a B-24 connection in which you will be very in-terested. I'm getting to it.

"Loads of money had been fleeing from continental Europe for al-most a decade by the time I was assigned to the trace project. In advance of every expansion of the Third Reich, money simply vanished. Sudeten-land. Poland. The Low Countries. France. That project was a record-keeping nightmare. That's what we're good at in the intelligence community. I was young and enthusiastic and I was learning. We watched where money went. Sometimes we were able to record it, but far more often we watched as the trail went cold. Much of the cash, maybe most of it, went to the United States and Canada. These were the seeds of your present unclaimed capital. I've never worked in finance, but even I know the result of seventy years compounding interest. Contrary to the legends and conspiracy theories, relatively little cash settled in Switzer-land or Liechtenstein. When it arrived here, we noted a trend. The Eu-ropean movers of capital strictly preferred to avoid the national banks or anything with federal oversight and regulation. I can't say that I blame

them, given their own recent experience with strong central governments.

"They placed the cash—we're talking about thousands of accounts, and
unaccounted-for millions—in unregulated financial institutions. Small
community banks. Union pension accounts. Masonic trust accounts for
widows and orphans. Insurance and surety accounts. Private limited partnerships not unlike yours, Warren. Credit unions. All of these institutions,
if you can call them that, were highly unregulated and widely variant in
the quality of their record-keeping. In the late 1930s and early 1940s in this
country, there was no standardization in banking records. There was
barely any standardized accounting. And all of those records were paper
ledgers.

"So why was my beloved United States Army Air Force involved? The
most logical reason is that England at the time was nothing but one
huge US aircraft carrier, and our intelligence resources were, bluntly
put, all that they had available. The project team was full of MI5 men—
counterintelligence and the like. They were woefully unprepared for the
war in '39 and '40, and this capital tracking project was part of the massive catch-up that had all of the British intelligence operatives running
around wild. I found their determination and sense of purpose amusing,
the way you do when you're in your twenties and you watch bureaucracy
at war close-up.

"I've often wondered where most of the cash settled here in the States.
Some of it is the chinking between the cracks of our modern banking
structure, to be sure. Your unclaimed capital for ViroSat comes out of
those cracks. During my years in the company I heard that a lot of it
went into the defense industrial base. Read that farewell speech in 1961
where Eisenhower talked about the military industrial complex. I was
fairly senior, running an office in Langley supporting the White House
then, and General Andy Goodpaster—he wrote that speech—told me
that this was exactly the kind of entanglement that Ike was warning
about. Using that 'loose' money to beef up the Rockwells and Hughes of
the world.

"Men, I'd certainly rather that we use it for your purposes. Our purposes. I like ViroSat. From everything you've told me, Sanford, it is ours to use as long as our friends at the Federal Systems and Services Corporation are aboard.

"Private capital took up residence in the assets of private banking institutions more than seventy years ago. Now we have to find it, and we do not have much time. If I was given over to sarcasm at my age, I'd tell you what a good job of planning you've done. Instead, I need to tell you that your national technical means at FSSC are likely to fall short. You're going to need human intelligence. But you knew that already. That's why you called me.

"FSSC will be only a means to identify our targets, to narrow down the search area. Once again, I've been there before."

Warren watched as Gray Tuttle reached into a leather folder and pulled out a carefully folded-over section of a *New York Times* from last week with the bold italic headline reading "Dutch Yeager, Liberator, Legendary NJ Fraudbuster."

He stared at the page and strongly felt the degree to which Gray Tuttle was observing him.

"Your father helped us on this in 1945, you know. No, forgive me, Warren. You didn't know. I knew him, son, and he was a very good man. I am deeply sorry for your loss."

Gray Tuttle pointed to a section on the *Times* page. "Here. You had the obituary reporter quote Wild Bill Donovan, calling your father"—he read—"'our first silent hero at the end of the war. His contribution to the Allied cause was unbounded, without measure. What he gave the nation and the world shall never be wholly known.' I like that, Warren. Every word is true."

Warren felt a sudden draining, an emptiness, a whole-body exhaling, a profound barrenness of spirit. He missed Dutch deeply in this moment, and felt a whirl of contradictions spinning in his brain. The last time he felt anywhere close to this collapsing passion was on the way back to Manhattan following his mother's funeral . . .

"Are you all right?" Sanford Tuttle's voice.

"I am," Warren heard himself saying, but it was as if he was listening without interest to a disembodied voice that sounded like his own. He could do this. Build back. "Go on," said the Warren voice.

Gray Tuttle was already well into explaining Dutch's darkest days at the end of the war.

". . . tracked a good portion of it for the government's purposes, even going to the extent of following leads to the German concentration camps as they were liberated. That's how Dutch got to Bergen-Belsen, Warren. His German language abilities were far better than anything that MI5 had available. He and I flew in on the first American plane. We landed in the late afternoon and were in the camp while there was still daylight.

"Of course our mission then had nothing to do with that cash tracking project. By the time we saw for ourselves what was going on there, my God, it was all we could do to hold ourselves together. What I experienced that night literally made me resolve to stay in the spy business for the rest of my professional life.

"We failed the world in those years.

"Dutch didn't hold up as well as I did, Warren. I'm certain that you know as much.

"You would never have known about me. Your father did not want to keep in touch with me—not that we were personally close in any event. And no one finds me, even today. This is characteristic of my profession.

"As for the tracking project, it came apart completely in those last months of the war. Somewhere in the intelligence archives there might be some records, but I doubt it. Late in my many years at the Agency we did do some rudimentary capital tracking. These were the earliest days of networked computing and of course we had the best systems—which probably had about the computing power of that BlackBerry of yours. Some of our contractors got involved, too.

"Right. That's the other family secret I was referring to. QUATECH, the first of Sanford's major success in these technology ventures, had this capital tracking task as one of its secondary purposes. Father and son here, we had to be very careful about conflict of interest then. I actually retired from the government just before QUATECH received its first big competitive intelligence community contract. We couldn't have me inside, even in a detached position. It wouldn't look right. It wouldn't *be* right. Integrity is everything, Warren.

"There was a laudable social purpose to QUATECH's operations as well. Sanford, let me brag a bit here. Why do you think that the company had an operating outlet in Israel? Quite simply, one of the things that QUATECH did best was tracking Jewish capital out of Nazi Germany to be repatriated, across continents and generations and lives.

"And they got it all."

Warren Hunter's head pounded hard, irksome vascular beats with increasing frequency. "That is much more background than I was expecting. Thank you, Gray. I appreciate what you told me, and I mean that. But are you certain that the same can be accomplished now, for the sake of the ViroSat limited partnership?"

"I am *reasonably* certain," the old man said. He stood to full height, brushed a palm of spread fingers across his white buzz-cut, and stretched. "We are going to work on two parallel tracks. FSSC and Compton Sizemore are the obvious first track. You and I and Sanford will work alongside them."

"We don't have much time. How can Compton Sizemore and I help our efforts on your track?" Warren asked.

Gray Tuttle faced the window and the parklike campus outside. He pulled back his sport coat and stretched, hands on his hips. Warren was sure that the gesture was for effect, to control the moment. He recorded it mentally. He would use it himself in New York.

"This is more about your personal assistance," Gray Tuttle said. "Sanford?"

His son stood and walked to his desk. From the top center drawer he withdrew a single white sheet of paper, a photocopy. He handed the document to Warren. "Keep it," Sanford Tuttle said. "I got it from your brother. This is a precisely handwritten list of eighteen numbers, with no discernable pattern other than the fact that each line set of numbers is in the same general form as all the others. They all begin with the same three digits. Look."

Warren read a line in the middle of the page.

247347299-01942581897678993304110004

Tuttle continued. "I had our team at FSSC run an exhaustive analysis of the list, looking for any commonalities with bank accounts worldwide. Nothing. We also looked at the whole range of cipher and encryption possibilities, with equally negative results. Then I showed it to my father. He had an idea."

"More of an intuition," Gray Tuttle added. He was still staring out the window.

"The list was fairly close to something he remembered seeing during that period in the Army Air Forces in England."

"This would explain," Warren said, "why it was necessary to go through all of that history."

"Precisely." The affirmation came from Tuttle, senior, talking to the glass.

Sanford Tuttle continued. "We think—my father and I think—that this block of numbers may be the critical path to the capital we are seeking. What we have here, however, is only a part of it."

"Could you tell me where Rick got this?" Warren inquired. "Or should I ask him?"

"He got it from a personal finance client. It was part of an estate. He asked me to look into it and gave me a copy. I did, and now you know the result before he does. You don't mind working with your brother on this, do you?"

"Not in the least."

"Good."

"That was an elderly woman client, right? A tiny estate, if I remember right. What could she possibly have to do with our capital aggregation?"

"I said it was an intuition," Gray Tuttle said, turning around to face them. "I'll know more if you won't mind helping me, and I mean quite personally."

"I'm not sure that I follow your meaning," Warren said.

"If your brother's recently deceased client was who I think she was, we have a clear and shining path, not just a critical one, to everything you're seeking for ViroSat."

"But Sandy, you said this was only a part of what we need."

"Correct." Gray Tuttle answered again.

"Where is the other part? *What* is the other part?"

"I don't know yet," Gray Tuttle said. He paused theatrically—Warren thought it was a bit too much. "Your father might have."

Warren's stomach began to swirl in the black hole again. He was in control, he told himself.

"Where are his papers?"

Before he could control his reaction, Warren burst out in a spontaneous laugh.

Neither Tutttle smiled, but as he recovered, he saw their bewilderment.

"I apologize. The idea of my father having anything like a coherent body of 'papers' is unbearably funny—you are going to have to chalk that one up to a grief reaction, I guess, Sandy. All that Dutch ever kept was a couple of cardboard boxes. His medals and dog tags are in there. Probably his divorce papers. He did have what he called his 'Pearl Harbor File' from the New Jersey tax department, but that must have disappeared long ago—couldn't have been more than two inches thick, and I haven't seen it since I was in college. Whatever he has might be with the stuff Rick and I collected when he went into assisted living. If Dutch left anything, my brother would have it."

"And where would that be?" the old man asked.

"At his condominium in Reston. Not too far from here."

That was the moment in which Warren was dead certain that he detected Gray Tuttle's *tell*. Both sides of the tall old spy's face moved ever so slightly, barely perceptibly.

"I know," Gray said, "exactly where that is."

CHAPTER 29

The room in which they asked him to wait was windowless but surprisingly spacious. Its concrete block walls had an unsettlingly welcoming epoxy-painted finish, green with multicolored flecks, in a pattern complementary to the blue-gray floor. A white drop ceiling bore bright fluorescent lighting. The room was rectangular in shape, quite new, basically unused and still unfurnished. Rick Yeager stood from his seat in one of the three folding chairs at the end of the room. He walked around the bare folding table. There were two doors painted dark green, one on each short wall. He had entered from the door with the long vertical window where, from time to time, people walked past without paying him or the room the slightest regard. The other door was just a simple metal slab with no handle on this side. The place could have been designed as a big conference room or a small community meeting room, a multiuse facility.

There was a one-way mirror dominating one of the long walls.

The moment he discovered Lauren Barr splayed dead on the deck of his condominium—and as soon as he ascertained that she *was* dead—Rick stepped back, silently gripped Julia's hand, and with one stab of his thumb called 911 from his mobile phone. The emergency response took about four minutes by his timing. Within ten minutes there were not less than six Fairfax County police cruisers on scene. Maybe more. He lost count. Yellow tape marked the crime scene. It appeared to him that there were concentric rings being set up. He was successively ushered outside each of them and especially away from Julia. A murder in Reston was an event so rare that it edged mightily against the fortress of impossible, one of the uniformed police officers had told him.

Terrific, Rick thought. I get a poet cop. He wondered at that moment whether such cynicism was an appropriate reaction to the discovery of a body.

Everything they said to him there and here was in the form of a question followed by a justification.

Do you mind if we take the statements of you and your friend separately? We find that we get the best result with that procedure.

My *wife*, he had responded rather forcefully, startling himself almost as much as the detective who made the inquiry.

Could we take you with us to the station? It would help the investigation immensely.

Would you mind speaking to these detectives? They need as much information as possible from you, because the first forty-eight hours are critical in a murder investigation.

That was the second time a policeman had said the word "murder" to him. It was less news than it was affirmation to Rick. He had come to that same conclusion instantly when he saw the earnestness in those open dead eyes, irises rimmed in red.

He was careful and reserved in all of his responses. Two law enforcement interrogations in the space of three weeks will do that to you. There was that cynicism rearing up again. He thought about how his reactions were more like Warren's than his own.

The final question—after the lengthy and internally repetitive conversation in which he recounted his encounters with Lauren Barr and his day right up to the moment when he called 911—brought him to the rectangular room.

Would you mind waiting here? You can be of tremendous assistance to us.

He wondered whether or not he was in custody, weighing this question carefully before concluding that the odds were about sixty-forty that he was not. His greatest concern was not the observation window (for that was surely the purpose of the one-way mirror) but where they had taken Julia. He had not even seen her since they were separated at the crime scene.

He glanced at his watch. Four and a half hours had passed since the moment they arrived at his home, since Julia gasped. Where had the time gone? What had he said?

There is such a big difference between solitude and loneliness. At the moment Rick Yeager was, once again, a very lonely man.

"I apologize, Mr. Yeager." He turned. He had never heard the man enter the room.

"For?"

"We've kept you waiting much too long." The man sat down at the folding table and beckoned Rick to take a seat at right angles to him. "Let me back up. I should begin by introducing myself. Paul Dolbeare. I'm a homicide detective. I was in the group that was observing when you gave your statement. I'm leading this investigation."

Rick said nothing, but he sat down, looked the detective in the eye, and tried to put on the appearance that he was listening attentively.

"Let me bring you up to speed. First things first, you are no longer a suspect."

"No longer."

"That's correct." Detective Dolbeare spoke utterly without emotion, apology, or judgment. "Mr. Yeager, please understand something. An infinitesimally small number of people ever have any interaction with a homicide investigation. When they do, it never works the way you see on television. There's precious little drama. Our best lead, and often our most promising suspect, is the person who discovers the crime, as you apparently did this afternoon. You'll understand that because you knew the victim—"

"I didn't."

"We know that. You've been very forthcoming, for which we are appreciative. Maybe I misspoke. Because you had some previous interaction with the victim, because she sought you out, we were required to begin with you and Ms. Toussaint. Next to you personally, I have the strongest possible motivation of anybody involved to clear the two of you as fast as possible. I assure you, that statement is not what the courts call 'permissible deception.' You see, doing so—clearing you—means that we are able to press ahead to a wider range of suspects and to call on you, with respect, for your assistance. My team and I just spent the last several hours running deep background on you and your former wife. Hence my apologies for keeping you waiting.

"The most interesting part of that exercise, by the way, was a discussion with our colleagues in federal law enforcement about your tangential involvement in the Carneccio & Dice case. In my experience, this kind of connection is no accident. Once you add in today's events at the Capitol, it becomes apparent that something serious is developing around you, sir. It's going to make a fascinating federal investigation, so I suggest that you be prepared for a lot more questions. We've concluded—and by 'we' I mean the FBI and the Fairfax County Police Department—that you are far more likely central *to* the investigation than involved *in* it. Take some small comfort there.

"None of that, however, concerns me at the present moment. I have a murder to solve, and you should take even more comfort from the fact that the preliminary forensic results have knocked you out of the running."

"Out of the running." Rick again repeated the detective's words, his voice dead, drained of emotion.

"Perhaps another poor choice of words. As I said, you are not a suspect. This is for two reasons. One, the medical examiner has fixed the victim's time of death rather conclusively to about a one-hour period, during which time you were busy dodging bullets on the east lawn of the Capitol Building. The footage, by the way, has been running almost continuously since you left downtown. Second, you're how tall?"

"Excuse me?"

"How tall are you?"

"Five-ten in my stocking feet."

"We made you five-nine. Your Virginia driver's license agrees with you. This is relevant information because it's what we call positively exclusionary. A perpetrator who stood at least six foot three or -four killed the woman. Death was caused by a very well-placed choke hold applied by someone who assuredly knew what he was doing. It's done with the crook of an elbow and locking the wrist in the other elbow. Strangling someone this way does not take a great amount of strength. It requires instead a lot of skill. No offense, Mr. Yeager, but there is nothing in your background that remotely suggests you have that skill."

"No offense taken."

The detective nodded, taking that response as a cue to continue. "I know that your guard is still up. Mine would be too if I found myself in the same position that you are in. I know about your recent experience with the US Attorney in Washington. I can neither change nor affect that experience. However, you may rely on the fact that our respectful treatment of you here today is influenced by what we learned about you from that office. You are not detained here. And while you are under absolutely no obligation to assist us in what is about to become a very complex *murder investigation*," he said the words with exaggerated clarity, "we need your help. Please. I am asking you. This is a naked and direct appeal to your sense of civic responsibility, sir."

For half a minute neither of them spoke. Rick broke the silence. "I'm still here. I'm still listening."

"I appreciate that, and on behalf of the county and the commonwealth, *we* appreciate your cooperation. Now what we'd like to do, recognizing that time is still quite critical, is to bear down on a very few areas in your statement. Ms. Toussaint never met the victim, but her conversation with us has validated everything you told us. We have no reason to doubt anything in your statement, but that's just the beginning of the mystery." Detective Dolbeare opened a leather folio and flipped back several pages of tablet paper. "Three meetings, none of them planned, all spontaneous."

"Correct."

"We have video from the morning at the Tower Club, the day that you drove her to Maryland and she disappeared at the rest stop."

"Also correct."

"Please. I'm recounting, not challenging any of this, sir. The Maryland State Police have sent us the electrons already. We have that video, too. Mr. Yeager, she left you deliberately. When you went inside the Maryland House, she departed with this man." He slid across the table a color still photograph bearing a digital time stamp in the lower right-hand corner. "Have you ever seen him before?"

"No."

"His name is Jonas Barr."

"Her brother."

"Did you think it was odd that she would leave you like that? After, as you said, being so terribly persistent about accompanying you on your drive?"

"Detective, everything about Lauren Barr was unusual. That was the morning of the day my father died, and we haven't even been able to bury him yet. I was headed to New Jersey to see him. I barely made it. When she pulled her disappearing act, I had a lot of other things on my mind."

"Understandable. Was there anything else that you knew about her, anything that you may not have recalled when we took our first report with you this afternoon? Sometimes after reflection, and after a witness like yourself knows definitively that he's been cleared of a crime like this, there are other details that he might remember."

"No. I didn't leave anything out," Rick said. "Three times she showed up without calling. That never happens to me. I told your detectives all of this. The first time was after her aunt's death, when we went to the Geller house in Arlington. The second at my home in Reston, right where I found her today. The third was at the Tower Club, another trip, and that was our longest conversation. She works for Kehina Alliance Partners. You know what I know. They're a real estate investment company in Maryland. She's a lawyer there—and I suspect she is a damn formidable one, from the way she behaved at her aunt's house. Sorry. Was."

The look on the detective's face was pained. He nodded again. "I believe you, Mr. Yeager, and several other witnesses and public records bear out much of that account."

"I'm sensing a 'but,'" Rick said.

"You're perceptive," Detective Dolbeare replied. "But the victim's name is not Lauren Barr. There is no Lauren Barr licensed as an attorney in Maryland, and Kehina Alliance Partners—which is quite genuine and now quite concerned—has no record of her ever working there, nor has anyone at the firm ever seen her. For whatever this information is worth, we can find no connection whatsoever of the victim to Mrs. Hannah Weiss Geller, your late client. Other than you, of course. And we believe that this man"—he tapped Jonas Barr's picture—"is almost certainly not her brother. Here's how we reached that conclusion." The detective slid another three printouts of photographs from the Maryland House security camera, time-stamped by the state police, each enhanced just to the point where their pixilation gave way to blurs.

Jonas Barr and Lauren Barr kissed passionately in one, smiled in another. In the third Lauren handed over Rick Yeager's briefcase as Jonas pumped his right fist.

"He is our best lead at the moment."

Rick exhaled deeply. "Who was she?" he asked.

"Mr. Yeager, we have absolutely no idea."

CHAPTER 30

Horvath sat with his back to the wall in the reddening shade, smoking laconically while the sun rays lengthened into the end of day. This time his cigar was a Graycliff, which was far too expensive a stick, but an especially good one. He looked around the empty brick courtyard of the restaurant called Lion and Bull on an open end of the nicely appointed exurban strip mall. Where was this again? Haymarket, Virginia. He rarely ventured this far west of the outer Washington suburbs, but the moment he arrived he understood why Gray Tuttle would choose this location. The development of the shopping center had been arrested by the recession. A third of the stores and restaurants were empty. Foot traffic was thin. It had been easy to park and to walk right into this courtyard, bypassing the restaurant part of the comfortable upscale bar and grill, which seemed to be holding its own during the economic downturn. If he thought about it hard enough, the place reminded him of Belváros, near the city wall in old Pest. In his reverie he wondered whether Tuttle considered that when he selected the meeting place. Probably not. Most important, there were no cameras anywhere. An exceedingly pleasant waitress had greeted him and brought him a beer. American beer. Horvath had to admit after most of his life spent here, that he greatly preferred this to that *brumzol ló*—horse piss. Communist beer. In Budapest when he was young and rising in the state security department that was all there was to drink. He had to hand it to Tuttle. This place was overall an excellent meeting location, miles from anywhere they might be noticed. They needed to talk.

Gray Tuttle was late. From his vantage at the table Horvath watched the old man's arrival. He parked so that it was easy to make eye contact even before he stopped the car. Horvath nodded. As Tuttle moved toward him, Horvath assessed his friend. He watched the walk, the carriage, the way he looked around. Something was off, but he could not yet tell just what. Call it an intuition or an insight. *Éleselméjűség*. Now why would he remember that obscure Hungarian word right now? Horvath did not even think in Hungarian anymore, but words like this were lately making it their habit to surface frequently in his thoughts.

"You're never late, *elvtárs*," Horvath said, laughing lightly.

"Comrade? You haven't called me that in fifty years," Tuttle answered, unsmiling. His voice was uncharacteristically flat.

"Fifty years? It's been longer than that. Sit. Order something. Then tell me what's wrong." Horvath watched his partner as he drew several times on his cigar, which had begun to go out.

The look on Gray Tuttle's face was quite odd, Horvath thought. He did not attempt to deny that something was indeed wrong.

"What happened there?" Tuttle finally asked.

"You mean at the Capitol."

"Yes. Where you rained havoc, it would seem."

"I did everything we agreed upon, old friend. It was rather precise. *Alatt, ki*."

"Horvath, what does that mean? I've exhausted all of the Hungarian language that I still retain."

"'Under, out.' I'm sorry. It's an old shorthand expression from the service. Your side had its nicknames for specific operations too, didn't you?"

"Of course we did. This one means?"

"Put them underground. Get them running. Then take them out."

"But you made them public. That's not exactly 'underground' nor is it very clear-cut."

"Sometimes I am oblique. What I did was to execute the first part, the hardest part. I joined the two of them together. The older son, the quiet and predictable one, he's a caring type. This is both his strength and his weakness. He will never let go of the woman now."

They interrupted their conversation as the waitress returned to the table and took Tuttle's order for a scotch, neat, and a menu. Horvath said nothing until she departed.

"When did you start drinking again?" he asked. His concern was evident.

"I am about to."

"This is not about my part of the operation, is it? Nothing I've done has ever bothered you before."

"No, it's not. Finish what you were saying. You wanted the two of them together. That was a terribly high risk you took."

"It was. But it worked, didn't it? Underground, as I said. They think that they are running and safe so far. It makes my next task so much simpler. We have a good and believable scenario. Her murder followed by his suicide, after experiencing so much trauma from the Capitol shooting. The old tactics are still the best ones. I will bet you anything that they are still huddling scared, reliving it over and over again, at his apartment."

"You would lose that bet."

"What are you talking about? The next move we make is easy. Did you manage to place the weapon in his home? If you didn't, I'll take it with me when I go there." Horvath was beginning to doubt his friend. Now he was sure that his uneasiness was coming through in his voice. He was never one to hide emotions well. This personality trait made him superb at special operations but terrible at the psychology of human spycraft. That was totally Gray Tuttle's terrain.

"I know what we agreed," Tuttle said, "and I know what we planned. I did go there to search his home and to deliver the gun. It would have been period perfect. The weapon is not only accurate for 1945, it is the actual weapon that his father carried into Bergen-Belsen. You'll like it. A forty-five ACP—your favorite. Today it can be traced, but only as far as its issuance to Yeager in 1943. I took it from him on that day we liberated the camp and I've had it ever since."

"Impressive. You didn't tell me that. But I am assuming that for some reason you did not get inside. You said yourself that this part was fairly critical. It would be natural to find the weapon in whatever part of the father's effects that he has. The holster would be there. And you would likely find what we've been looking for."

"Correct."

"So you don't know if the poor old flier's papers are there. Or if he has any papers."

Graham Tuttle scowled. "Dutch Yeager was barely younger than me, you know. And while I was not able to place his gun there for you, I now know that he has some files and yes, they are there. If I am correct—and I am—we can only get partway without them."

"How would you know that if you didn't get inside?" Horvath asked. There were times when he became agitated at his colleague. This was one of them.

"Warren Hunter was very forthcoming when we met this afternoon at my son's office."

Horvath grinned. Tuttle was as subtle as he was skillful. He first formed this opinion in 1956. It was the reason why, after all of these years, this was the only man he would ever consider joining for their kind of partnership.

The waitress reappeared from the door to the restaurant. This time the two old spies slipped immediately and effortlessly into a conversation about politics—Tuttle commenting on a particularly nasty Virginia House race, Horvath disagreeing, but not too much. An old trick, both of them still in practice, and it worked. The waitress placed Tuttle's scotch in front of him and departed.

They stopped talking and looked at the drink.

"Are you going to drink it?" Horvath asked with apprehension.

"Maybe."

"Don't."

"Under, out," Tuttle said, contemplating. "I simply did not think that you would be so dramatic."

"I took an opportunity. The whole nation will believe that the Capitol shots were a random act of terrorism. Or better, that one of the more reactionary elements got excited. The fascists will always be blamed. What do we call them today, the Tea Party? See? We aren't so far removed from the old days and the old ways. There was never any real risk. I am still an excellent shot. Now tell me, please, why we cannot continue with the original plan, and then how we have to modify it."

"I suppose," Graham Tuttle said, "that I have no room to criticize your Capitol drama."

"Okay. Tell me. What happened?"

"I timed my entry to Richard Yeager's home precisely."

"Of course you did."

"But just as I was effecting entry, a woman arrived. I did not see her park. She practically burst onto the patio, intensely vocal, very demanding—who was I, how did I know Mr. Yeager, she was his attorney . . . all of these statements were immediate indicia of falsehood, of course. We know everything about him, including every lawyer he has ever talked to. Her entire manner told me she was bluffing. She was not carrying it off very well. But she was incredibly insistent. And she was loud."

"You eliminated her," Horvath said without emotion.

"Yes."

"Once again, impressive. I never thought that was your specialty."

"It never was."

"But you knew how."

"That knowledge was ingrained and deeply sublimated. Yes, I knew how. At my advanced age I was fortunate that the act took far less strength than skill."

Horvath wanted to inquire how, exactly, but he refrained. He also wondered if that was a first killing by hand for Graham Tuttle. "And then you left her there," he surmised.

"Yes."

"And you went—"

"To that meeting with my son and Warren Hunter."

"You are one cold son of a bitch, *testvér.*"

"You never called me 'brother' before."

"You never *were* this kind of brother before. And at your age." Horvath smiled. Tuttle pointedly did not return the gesture. "Remorse is never productive, you know."

"Don't confuse worry with remorse, Horvath. My worry keeps us alive and on track."

"The death was incidental, like so many before her. So who was she?"

"I could not possibly tell you. But she was in no way incidental."

"What do you mean?"

"Horvath, her last words . . . the last thing she said, with her feet off the ground and just before her throat was crushed in the crook of this elbow, was 'We know all about Meier Seckendorf Böhmer.'"

Rick Yeager said to Detective Paul Dolbeare, "Okay, I accept that I'm no longer a suspect, but here I'm going to stop you until I'm advised by counsel. If she's not Lauren Barr, if Lauren Barr doesn't exist—"

A ringing series of taps on the glass window interrupted his sentence. Both of them looked up reflexively at nothing.

"If that's who I think it is, Mr. Yeager, you have counsel."

As Daniel Ter Horst walked in, Dolbeare rose. "Good afternoon, Your Honor." Rick joined him standing. Two other detectives followed—the familiar first interrogators that Rick had met upon his arrival at the station. Then Julia, accompanied by a scowling young black woman who, like every other detective in the expanding crowd here, wore a gold Fairfax County police shield clipped to her belt. Predictable and mildly offensive, Rick thought. They paired her with their only black woman detective—no wonder the cop is pissed off.

"Paul, it's good to see you again. Thank you for the call." Ter Horst began by shaking the lead detective's hand, and then turned to Rick to greet him and explain. "Detective Dolbeare used to be my courtroom deputy sheriff along about sixteen years ago, when I sat on the Arlington County bench. That was before he went to law school and launched on the trajectory of a distinguished law enforcement career that I can't help but think I might have had something to do with. You are very fortunate, Mr. Yeager. If I had a day like you just did, this is exactly the man I would want in charge. He is not only an ethical officer, but a powerful advocate. Commonwealth's attorneys are routinely intimidated by the few members of the sworn law enforcement community who are also members of the bar."

Julia moved wordlessly to Rick's side and took his hand, interlacing their fingers.

"We'll need a few more chairs," Ter Horst said, as one of the interrogating detectives nodded and departed. "Let's have a seat and get started."

"Obviously my brother called you," Rick said. "That makes sense. You have personal history with the detective, and Warren's the kind of guy who would know that kind of thing. Or rather, his people at Compton Sizemore would."

"No. To the best of my knowledge, I've never spoken to Mr. Hunter or to anyone working for him."

"Then how—"

"We'll get to that. There was a referral, but not from your brother. Please, have a seat." Ter Horst was acting courteously, but clearly taking charge. "Mr. Yeager, first you have to retain me as your counsel. Virginia law does not require this to be done in writing. Your affirmation here is good enough for the commonwealth, and good enough for me. Would you agree to that?"

"Let's say that I do. But Mr. Ter Horst—"

"Dan."

"Why would I want an estate lawyer for this matter? Especially when—and don't take this the wrong way—the last time we met you were less than forthcoming with me."

"There was a reason for that. I was, as you correctly assumed, searching carefully, with the prior written permission of the deceased, for Mrs. Geller's will. It was a will I wrote where you're named both executor and beneficiary. You've read it."

"You didn't write that will. It was downloaded from a free legal services site."

"Freevirginialegalforms-dot-com, right? Mr. Yeager, that's my Web site. Mrs. Geller got all of the basic information there. I modified it for her and then she had it notarized at her bank. Had you been alone when we first met, all of this information would have been appropriately disclosed to you, as per her very specific instructions to me. However, given the present circumstances, I would say that it was wise that you and I did not discuss the estate with Ms. Barr present."

"Jane Doe," Detective Dolbeare interjected.

"With Jane Doe present," Ter Horst corrected himself. "Mr. Yeager—"

"If you're going to represent me, it ought to be Rick."

"Okay. Rick, estate work may be my best legal game, but eighteen years on the bench made me one hell of a good criminal lawyer, too. Until Paul Dolbeare determines who killed Jane Doe here"—he pointed to one of the photographs of Lauren and Jonas Barr together at the Maryland House rest stop—"you and I need to stick closely together and figure out exactly how and why all of this is connected. Including how and why my neighbor Hannah Geller was killed."

Four detectives stared at the former judge.

"I completely agree with that," Rick replied.

"There is one part of this that I would like you to help me with."

"What's that?"

"Who do you know in Dubai?"

"Easy. Absolutely no one. I've never been outside of the United States and Canada. That must have been my brother."

"No, I'm quite certain," Ter Horst said. "The caller was very specific. It was a referral by telephone two days ago. He gave me your complete name, Richard Montgomery Yeager. I knew about your recent federal notoriety, of course. I checked that out after you and I met—you can't blame me. I knew that we'd be having a conversation about Mrs. Geller's will, no matter who you eventually retained as estate counsel. I also knew that your brother was Warren Hunter, from that obituary about your father on the *Times* Web site where you were also mentioned. My sincere condolences, I should hasten to add. But I have no idea why you would know this man in the United Arab Emirates. He was an American, judging from the way he spoke—or at least I am certain that he was educated here. He introduced himself as the head of an Egyptian family office located in the Emirates Towers. He said that he would like to make a legal referral of me to you, personally. Rick, I've been in Virginia law for almost forty years and I've never taken a referral like this one. It would of course have occasioned a phone call to you, but events have now clearly intervened and Paul here called me first."

"Again, I don't know anyone in Dubai. You didn't get his name?"

"I regret that I did not. At the end of the conversation I did write down the name of the family office he represented. It was the Hasab International Group."

CHAPTER 31

Second thoughts raged like wildfire as Senator Tenley Harbison turned the corner and drove into the Denny's restaurant parking lot. This was a bad idea, she kept repeating to herself. Natural risks were woven into the fabric of her political life, but her resignation to that fact didn't mean she had to be comfortable with every kind of risk. She drove forward slowly, found a suitably dark corner of the heavily potholed lot, and swung in wide between the painted lines. She was careful not only for her physical safety but more important right now, for the chance of being seen. The car she drove was her husband's two-year-old Lexus coupe with standard-issue random letters and numbers of New Jersey plates, not those petit-privilege US Senate 1 plates on her own car, which she had left back in Washington yesterday afternoon. She stepped out of the car and chirped it locked with the electronic fob. She looked around briefly and inconspicuously. No one was in sight. The place was an urban desert, meeting her expectation at 4:07 A.M. in Fort Lee. This particular Denny's was walking distance from the George Washington Bridge, literally partway under the last ramp, as close to Manhattan as you can get and still be physically in the Garden State. She checked her reflection in the driver's side window of the car. Hair pulled back loosely, light makeup, rimless backup glasses rather than the contact lenses that she always wore in public, blue-gray designer jeans topped by a simple blue blouse, and caramel summer jacket. She looked undeniably good but remarkably nondescript.

Four people were in the diner when their United States senator entered, blinking briefly at the contrast of the bright interior lights with the city darkness. A round-faced Asian woman sat behind the counter. She was clearly the only waitress out front at this dead hour of summer night preceding the breakfast rush. She glanced briefly at Tenley, eyes up from a tear sheet newspaper dense with Chinese characters, then immediately returned to reading. Two construction types, a robust talkative Hispanic and a pale too-thin white guy, sat in a window booth to her left. Neither noticed her as they continued their conversation, which twice included the words 'higher power.' She scanned the place, now more comfortable with her decision to come here. Her constituents had no idea who she was.

She turned to her right and smiled at Lois Carneccio.

"Do you remember," Lois asked as Tenley slid into the booth and took a seat across from her, "the Forum Diner in Paramus?"

"Of course I do," the senator answered. Typical of Lois, blunt and not a bit of greeting, just thinking out loud whatever's on her mind. Half of the time Tenley Harbison appreciated this distinguishing feature of her cousin's character. The other half of the time it irritated the hell out of her.

"They closed it a couple of years ago, then some car dealer tore it down. A bunch of historic diner preservationists were trying to save it, or at least take it apart and move the whole damn building to Miami or something, but it turns out that it was built too late. Nobody wanted sixties architecture, well, in a diner at least. So look at what we're left with." Lois waved a hand around the Denny's as the waitress walked over with a cup and saucer for Tenley, swirling some awful-looking coffee in an oval glass carafe. "Fill us both up, then give us a minute, okay?" The waitress complied and retreated. She understood the dismissal. They wouldn't see her again.

"The Forum was nice, but there are so many changes going on here and all over the country—" Tenley began.

"—You freakin' bet," Lois interrupted. "Welcome to *Fort Ree*." She laughed a little too loudly.

The senator was thoroughly unamused. "Did you really just make a racial joke?"

"Yeah. Did you really just disapprove?"

"Lois, you are impossible, and yes. I do disapprove."

"Stop it. What do you think they were saying about our people forty, fifty years ago? Did you forget all the shit we grew up with? 'Ayyyyy . . . where do dose Guidos go? Dago here, dago dere, and when deir tires go flat dago *wop, wop, wop*!' And remember how Taddy Sobesiak could tell every Polack joke ever invented by the mind of man? He'd bet beers that you couldn't come up with a new one that he couldn't finish, and he never lost. Same idea. We put up with all that when we were kids, Tenley. So did everybody else. It was no different with the Bohunks or the Windocks or the Dutchies or the Micks. It was the way we chapped each other's asses, and I kind of miss it. It's also my way of telling you that you're spending too much time away from your own kind. Really, what's the possible harm?" Lois did not want an answer.

There were gentler and more decent moments, Tenley recalled as she looked at her cousin, when Lois was not nearly so crude or direct. They were young girls then, children actually, more than fifty years ago this summer. That day of their First Holy Communion at Saint Teresa's they dressed identically and completely in white, with poufy crinoline skirts, veiled in white lace, coiffed in their first—and for both, their absolute last—permanent waves. The photograph Mama took on that Sunday had them looking for all the world like two tiny brides, which was of course the point. Tenley, the smart slightly gawky girl, stood on the left with excellent posture. Lois was the shy one on the right, looking scared, leaning ever so slightly into her cousin. Although both later let go of the Roman Catholic Church, you could never let go of that kind of family bond. This was the reason why Tenley Harbison, United States senator, was here right now meeting with a woman whom all of her judgmental Washington world knew as a financial criminal, or at the very best, a political reprobate and Beltway pariah-for-life.

"Lois," she asked softly, "just how bad is it, and what are they telling you?" "They," of course, were the US Attorney and the Justice Department.

"Bad."

"Bad? That's all?"

"Real bad, then. I *might* be able to avoid jail. But if I do, let's just say you won't be taking me back to the Senate Dining Room anytime soon."

"What are the final charges against you going to be?"

As a former state and federal prosecutor, Tenley knew that Lois Carneccio was in the middle of a critical moment. You start out with the grand jury indictment full of criminal charges and counts, maybe hundreds of them, applied to anyone who's even nearby a broad conspiracy. Then you start to deal. For Lois the outlook was grim. She was charged with violating the Racketeer Influenced and Corrupt Organizations Act. RICO was the biggest gun in criminal law.

"Honestly? I have no idea. But I'm talking, cooperating as much and as fast as I can, and I'm doing it all with a minimum of lawyering. You do what you need to do. You hope for the best."

Bland acquiescence, especially to the prospects of incarceration, did not sound like Lois.

"Lolo, you're going to come out of this whole," Tenley said as nicely as she could. "You have before."

"I only wish, Super-T. I only wish."

The use of those nicknames was not accidental, and certainly not what ordinary girlfriends or even close cousins would say to each other.

The events were ages ago. The traumas were most personal. They were two gorgeous Jersey girls.

One was a year out of Seton Hall handling constituent cases for a liberal Republican congressman from Morristown at a time when the words "liberal" and "Republican" could still be conjoined. The other was working for Ford Models in the City while struggling mightily with her first year at Columbia Law. Both were building portfolios of different kinds. They were seventies women desperate to be taken seriously. Tenley, the model, was booked for a shoot at a designer T-shirt marque called, naturally, Super-T's. Sweet, sexy, wholesome, and twenty-two in a year when being Italian was terrific for a bit of all-American ethnicity in print advertising. The shots were entirely innocent—jeans and colorful Super-T T-shirts— until photo editing added the erect nipples that made Tenley a momentary billboard sensation, regrettably coincident with her second semester as a 1L. Only one person ever got away with calling her "Super-T" to her face.

It was a reminder of love, the sharing of a humiliation that decades of achievement could not wholly erase.

"Lolo," of course, was the very-married congressman's private nickname for Lois, who even today remained uncertain about her degree of willingness or reluctance the first time they slept together. It was the first time shy studious Lois slept with *anybody*, beginning a terribly difficult affair that lasted, off and on, for a year and a half. Only one person, the congressman excepted, ever knew about it. And he never knew the way it hardened her.

There is transcendence in certain connections. They leaned on each other then, creating a sisterhood of the most powerful kind. Tenley Harbison could never set aside that kind of secret sharing.

Plus family was family.

"This cooperating with the government," Lois was saying, "is worse than the arrest was. You read about *that*."

"Everybody did," Tenley replied, instantly sorry for the insensitivity of her response.

Lois shrugged it off. "Look. The core of their case is this complex series of offshore deals. Oil leases, gas rights, petroleum futures, all funded through partnerships in the Bahamas and Panama. I actually do not understand it, and I had nothing to do with any of it, not directly anyway. Marty Dice is our dealmaker. I'm always the connector. You know that. Apparently some of our partners inside and out of the firm were laundering money. I'm now reliably informed that they had a very sweet three-way deal, Panama City to Nassau to Washington, right into my office. From what the Justice Department tells me, they were pretty good at it."

"I think that's all you should tell me."

"No, it's not. Hear me out, Tenley. These sessions with the US Attorney are brutal. I've never experienced this level of stress. Have you ever had a polygraph examination?"

"No."

"Well I've had four so far. Apparently they're satisfied at this point that I'm not at the heart of the whole damn mess, even though I don't know what *that* determination is going to do for my reputation. I suppose it's better to be looked at as a faker and a dupe than to be a fraud and a criminal outright."

"Really not something you should be concerned about right now, Lois."

"The last time I was at Justice, yesterday morning, they started in on my involvement in ViroSat."

"What involvement in ViroSat?" Tenley Harbison's interest was instantly very high.

"None of the bad stuff."

"*What* 'bad stuff'? Lois, what's going on? Now I need to know everything."

"The government is probing a link from my firm to ViroSat and Compton Sizemore that they found in our electronic files. My files. A link that didn't occur to anyone before they read about it at Carneccio & Dice. Tenley, bottom line, I'm pretty sure that I'm going to be offered a plea, and I'll take it if I can avoid jail time. But then I have to go on, and God knows I won't ever again be able to do the only work that I know. Here's the deal, though: I still have a significant financial play in the ViroSat transaction. So I have to preserve both my legal strategy and my upside in the deal if I want to recover from all of this. And that's where I really, desperately, need your help."

"Lois, you're going to recover. In your heart you know that. But needing my help? You still haven't told me what your 'play' is. Reality time. What kind of play?" She sat back, crossed her arms, and glared at her cousin.

Lois Carneccio stared back, as if she was considering just how wise it would be to tell her oldest confidante precisely where she stood in the deal and how she got there. The moment that she exhaled, slumped ever so slightly, and leaned forward, Madame Chairwoman of the United States Senate Subcommittee on Communications, Technology, and the Internet knew that there was more to "Internet Next" than she had imagined.

Her mind was racing with possibilities for the ViroSat hearing as she listened.

* * *

"Tenley, it started entirely innocently with my father, your mama's cousin. Your uncle Sal. Please, please don't look at me that way. I got that look and a lot more from the prosecutors when I told them. I hadn't seen him in—well, forever. A year or more, at least. That's not permissible for an Italian daughter, you know, no matter how old we are. I was in Florida working on a deal. Okay, it was a deal from one of Marty Dice's people, and I had to make sure that we had congressional approval. I was lobbying for it. That's one of the criminal charges, by the way—they say they can prove that I've been acting as a federal lobbyist for our deals, but without properly registering as one. I suppose that's true. It certainly was in this case, but the deal is not what's important. What is important is that I had to meet two congressmen in Miami Beach during the December recess last year, between Christmas and New Year's. And the meeting had to be very discreet. So I didn't check into their hotel—I spent three days in Coral Gables with Papa, being a good daughter.

"Remember, I'm the youngest. Almost nobody from New Jersey—hell, almost nobody from his whole *life*—sees him much anymore. That's what happens when you outlive everybody else you know. He's happy. He exercises, he has new Italian friends retired down there from all over the country, and he also has a lot of Cuban friends. They like to talk to him about the times he spent in Havana before Castro. Papa has them convinced that he was working for the CIA during the Eisenhower administration and they just eat it up. He even sees a couple of ladies—at ninety-three! Nobody special as far as I can tell. And he's still smoking those goddamn cigars.

"Do you remember when my papa got out of the life, Tenley? Around when we were finishing high school and going to college. You said it yourself a couple years ago—you might never have become a prosecutor, maybe not even a lawyer, if he hadn't quit. You and I both owe a lot to that decision. It was terribly hard for him to do. We're too young to remember all of the trips to Cuba before Castro. Papa loved what he did. My mom, God rest her soul, she was a force of nature. She made him leave 'the boys.' That's what she called them. I can still hear her voice in my head yelling at him, especially now, with all I'm going through. 'You can be an Italian *man* without being a *criminal*!' She made it a point to say that in English, so my brothers and sisters and I could understand every word. This was right when all of those Newark politicians went to jail for the building scam after the riots, remember? Federal money? Papa could have had a part in that deal, and that's when he walked away. He was going to be a shareholder in Essex Empire Builders—that was the mob front company where they busted everybody. I'm sure that he doesn't regret getting out, but I'm just as sure that he doesn't forget, either.

"I know. This is pretty difficult for me, too.

"Papa has been chasing deals ever since. That's where I get it. Sometimes they're right on the edge, sometimes a little bit over the edge. I don't know how that makes either Papa or me the slightest bit different from all of 'the boys' on Wall Street. Those guys are the new mob, Tenley—*that thing of theirs* is all legit, all very legal, and more dangerous to all of us than Papa's old associates. You know he never got wealthy. He never said so, but I know how much he and Mom hated the kind of money that Mr. Lucca and Mr. Cortale had while we still struggled. That was why he was so proud of you when you became a lawyer and helped put them away.

"You never knew that? Well, he was. He loves to talk about your career. In Miami, it's always 'My beloved niece, the senator.' The Cubans don't believe him. They believe his CIA stories, but not that.

"So my father, Smiling Salvatore Carneccio is still chasing deals, God love him. And wouldn't you know, this time he actually caught one.

"Then it became exactly like that lame old joke about the dog chasing the car, Tenley. When he caught it, he didn't know what to do with it. Since I was right there, the ever-dutiful daughter, he told me.

"He heard all about it from my sister Gina's oldest, Carter. The construction union lawyer. I know you know him—Gina brags to everybody about how you got Carter Celli into law school. Of course he doesn't practice your kind of law, but he did know all about your favorite project, ViroSat. Papa said that his information came from 'the Hunkie undertaker,' which was either him being very melodramatic in an old man kind of way, or it was one of those don't-ask-don't-tell situations. Either way, I listened. Papa obviously wanted me to benefit. What he was talking about doing was exactly what Carneccio & Dice does. Or rather, did.

"Tenley, please don't roll your eyes—yes you did. ViroSat is a strictly private deal, perhaps the most private deal *ever,* so there was no insider trading going on. Even the federal prosecutors who are my daily working colleagues right now have conceded that point.

"Here's what I learned from Papa: *Tenley, the deal can't close.*

"Everything in its financing is built on leverage, borrowed money that references and builds upon more borrowed money. You have to look very *very* carefully at ViroSat's structure. It's utterly brilliant, but it's all loans, not equity—in other words, there's only a small amount of real money, cash, in the deal. Tenley, when Compton Sizemore started quietly putting this thing together—what?—five, six years ago, that kind of structure was at the outer limits of acceptability. Now its risk is astronomical. You'd never structure a deal like this after the banking crisis. Too big to fail? How about too big to fund?

"ViroSat, your precious Internet Next, is like Oppenheimer and those scientists in the desert at Alamogordo getting ready to cook off the first atomic bomb. They stood there waiting for the blast and wondered if the reaction they were setting in motion would consume the whole world. When Papa told me about the deal, I wondered whether this thing has the capability to consume the whole financial world.

"And there's where the opportunity lies.

"At the heart of the deal is a partnership. The partnership provides the only equity slice of all the financing. Equity is supposed to be a fifth of the deal. But according to Papa and my nephew Carter, they don't have it yet. If the partnership fails, if its component of the financing ceases to exist, the whole thing folds in on itself in a cascading mess. A guy named Warren Hunter controls the partnership. I thought you might know about him. He owns half, from what I know. The other half is the government. Sort of.

"Don't look so surprised. That's the new way we do things, isn't it? Only in this case, it's not *exactly* the government that owns the other half of the partnership. The owner is a public-private venture called the Federal Systems and Services Corporation. FSSC. *Fissick.* Government funded but privately profitable.

"I was just that excited when I found out, too.

"Papa had all of this. But here's the interesting part. The limited partnership is putting up almost *three hundred billion dollars*. Compton Sizemore and Warren Hunter *don't have anywhere near that much*.

"And Papa, old Sal Carneccio, knew just where it was and how to get it.

"You don't just find that kind of money, and you certainly cannot move it around without somebody knowing and the government noticing. Unless you *involve* the government, or a government agency, which is what Hunter did with FSSC.

"And what's FSSC doing to earn its half? Tenley, FSSC is *finding* and *collecting* the money for Warren Hunter and Compton Sizemore. Somewhere out in northern Virginia there's a facility that rivals the capabilities of the National Security Agency. It's real black-budget supercomputer stuff, only they aren't tracking terrorist phone calls and text messages. They're watching bank accounts.

"Papa suggested to me a better way to find the money, because whoever controls that cash will control the deal. Tenley, that's still true.

"After I left Papa, I did three things. First, I invested heavily. I bought into as many of the ViroSat enterprise companies as I possibly could. This thing is huge, it's world changing, and it's only going to get bigger. That took months. Second, I put together every substantive piece of research I could lay my hands on concerning Compton Sizemore, the deal structure, and especially that partnership with FSSC. Here's where you *do not* ask me how I did it—my prosecutor friends are acutely *un*interested in the *origins* of my information. There are thousands of electronic files, texts, and spreadsheets. The *substance* of this stuff is what concerns the prosecutors. Third, I hired Warren Hunter's brother, Rick Yeager. Yeah. It confused me at first, too. They have the same last name, one in English and the other in German. Rick was going to start working for me the day that Carneccio & Dice was raided.

"Tenley, here's what Papa and I—and now you—know that Warren Hunter does not: the cash he's looking for was stashed in the same savings and loan where you and I used to have those bright green passbook savings accounts when we were little girls. Essex Construction Trades Federal Credit Union.

"The money was secreted there decades ago, in the 1930s, when it was Essex Building and Loan. I haven't yet found out where it came from, but it was supposedly big-time European and Middle Eastern money. The beauty of Hunter's plan was, nobody's looking for it and nobody cares about it after three quarters of a century. Anybody who might have a legal claim is either gone or has long since given up.

"The accounts were certainly not worth two hundred eighty-seven billion dollars then. That's the number Warren Hunter needs, Tenley. But they're worth much more than that now—think of the power of interest compounded over seven decades. This leaves us with one problem and one question.

"Problem: the credit union went under in 1972.

"Question: *So where did that cash go?*

"Papa didn't know. But typically, he knew who did.

"Warren Hunter's father found it.

"Yeager, the old man, never said anything to anyone. He was something of a moralist and wasn't too emotionally stable. Conveniently, he died recently—just making Warren Hunter's job more difficult.

"Tenley, are you aware how much unclaimed, unowned, unassigned, and otherwise unaccounted-for cash is on the books of American banks? The amount runs into the low trillions. Yeah. Fact. Absent a credible legal claim, whoever can properly transfer these accounts, by law, *owns* them. It's complicated, but there are several ways in which that can happen. FSSC is only one of them. Nobody pays regulatory attention—as long as the taxes get paid. The trick is in knowing where to go, how to assemble the right accounts, and then collect what's yours.

"That's what Warren Hunter and FSSC are attempting to do. If they pull off the ViroSat deal, then the public-private lash-up is over. FSSC will never need government funding again. More ominously, its capability to see into any bank account anywhere goes right into private hands. Warren's motivation is obvious. Greed. No one has ever scored this kind of wealth in one deal. Compton Sizemore wins by doing the deal, by selling off all those enterprise companies at incredibly high valuations, by brokering the biggest series of bond deals in history, and by collecting interest on all the debt that they're holding in the house accounts.

"Hunter absolutely knows what he's doing. He's using FSSC and its capabilities for financial data mining to locate that cash. He'll then own half of the equity core of ViroSat, and FSSC will own the other half.

"Tenley, here's what I want to do, and here's where you come in. I want to be Warren Hunter. Unlike Compton Sizemore and the FSSC researchers, we know exactly where the money *was*. For us, locating it will be infinitely easier because they're looking *everywhere*. Our search is narrow.

"You can use the same means and method as Compton Sizemore. Prevail on FSSC for a limited, carefully focused exploration. Instead of the private corporation reaping the harvest, make it clear that all benefit and profit will accrue to the federal government. Who needs it more, after all? Our national debt is over sixteen trillion dollars. ViroSat can cover it all if the project revenues simply fold back into the Treasury. FSSC doesn't even have to know what they're looking for—all they'll know is that you want to track down any old moribund accounts from the Essex Construction Trades Federal Credit Union. They certainly have that capability.

"I can take Warren Hunter's place and he won't even know it. I was planning on beating him to the money, but in the weirdest irony prompted by my arrest, this way is even better—I'll have the Justice Department alongside me now, all integrated into my plea bargain. I broached the subject with them as soon as they read through my ViroSat research. They proposed to compensate me with three percent of the partnership, success fee only. Tenley, these are ninety grand a year bureaucrats and they have utterly no idea just how wealthy they are going to make me. ViroSat is a one point three seven trillion dollar deal. They want this thing so bad that they're willing to toss me more than four billion dollars.

"If this works, I come out of it more than okay. The government will own ViroSat outright and will control all of the enterprise companies, selling them off slowly over time.

"You should think of the national security possibilities for Internet Next, Madame Chair. You should think of the political possibilities for yourself.

"Politically you get to broker the whole thing. What could be better? I submit for your consideration a simple substitution play. I step in for

Warren Hunter, but for a whole lot less equity. You and the government of the United States substitute for FSSC.

"Here's where you have to ask me: What makes this plan work?

"You have to expose the guts of the ViroSat deal at your hearings, especially the part where Compton Sizemore is using money that isn't even theirs.

"For you personally, it's all upside. You can only win or break even.

"For me, it's all about redemption."

CHAPTER 32

It had been a brutal week and a half for Rick Yeager. He wanted to simplify his life, to run swiftly past the events swirling around him since the moment he walked into Carneccio & Dice LLC. That was the *Schwerpunkt*, his father would say. The point at which everything changed.

The busier he got, the guiltier he felt about missing Dutch, or more correctly not missing him. It seemed as though he never had a spare hour to grieve.

In the earliest minutes of each morning, when red sunlight began summer days long before he was ready to awaken, Rick dreamed in half-sleep about his father. The blurred snapshots in his memory were always of Dutch Yeager being resolute. They were contemplative moments.

—Dutch sitting on "the glider," a sheet metal monstrosity, a steel couch mounted on free-swinging metal bars, rocking the thing forward and back, again and again, chain-smoking unfiltered cigarettes, staring, and occasionally grinning at Gloria, so young, hanging wash in the small yard of their house in Trenton.

—Dutch standing tall, beaming, his hand on his son's shoulder as a tiny Rick received a badge from his Cubmaster in the all-purpose-room of his elementary school.

—Baby Warren in Dutch's arms as the second-time new father sat in his favorite fat armchair, gazing into the sleeping infant's face with wonder, renewed fear, and a wan smile that conveyed nothing but questions.

In the past eleven days Rick found himself happily spending more and more time with Julia. He drew from her presence a sense of comfort and sad joy—new feelings that were all at one time surprising, settling, and very odd. When they were married their primary shared emotion was passion, human connection. They had never before actually worked together as these strange times now required.

The coincidence of the US Senate's summer recess was particularly accommodating, although Julia did not exactly have a lot of time off. Whenever she was not with Rick she was spending time with Senator Tenley Harbison in preparation for the ViroSat hearings, booked for the day that the Senate reconvened. The senator's new obsession was FSSC's role in the ViroSat transaction. On top of that she had Julia task FSSC with chasing some ancient bank accounts from New Jersey. She called it background. Senators, Julia explained to Rick, got that way whenever they found out about some cool new capability available at a government agency.

After a week of meeting daily at Dan Ter Horst's law office, then multiple times at the Fairfax police headquarters, or at carefully selected neutral locations in Alexandria just to talk, she suggested that they might as well base themselves out of Rick's place in Reston. He wondered whether her suggestion was another step in reconciliation and thought about whether he should just come out and ask Julia about it. She was also becoming increasingly affectionate. This confused him, of course. Touching, laughing easily, kissing occasionally, but always with distance and decency that he never recalled experiencing during their marriage. He decided to say nothing.

If there was such a thing as a good divorce, they now had one. Rick definitely didn't want to screw that up.

The big issue they dealt with was Hannah Weiss Geller's will and estate.

There were no heirs other than Rick. Ter Horst had in his file a notarized affidavit from Mrs. Geller attesting to that fact. There was also a five-month-old investigator's report produced with the full cooperation of Hannah herself. It documented an exhaustive unsuccessful search for heirs in five states, Berlin and three *Bundesländer* (which Rick translated for Julia as "federal states" in Germany) and for good measure, in Austria, Hungary, Slovakia, and the Czech Republic. A very official letter from the Jewish Agency for Israel ("Dear Judge Ter Horst") stood out in the file because it was laser printed on European A4-size paper and hung over the edge of the rest of the documents: Again, no other heirs.

Lauren Barr—Jane Doe—clearly had some motivation and purpose to intrude upon Rick in the earliest moments of this process. Detective Dolbeare now believed, and Rick had to agree, that her interest in him and Mrs. Geller was key to solving her homicide.

One conclusion that he reached by reading Ter Horst's fat client file on Hannah Weiss Geller made him much more troubled.

Every word that Lauren told Rick on that drive to Maryland was turning out to be entirely true.

At the lawyer's insistence Detective Dolbeare opened a second investigation, this one into the circumstances of Mrs. Geller's death. He did not have much to go on. Lauren Barr had claimed the body, ostensibly to prepare for a proper Orthodox Jewish burial.

No one in any of the Orthodox burial societies had ever heard of Lauren Barr or recognized her photograph. When Dolbeare broadened his inquiry and had his team visit every Jewish congregation in the greater Washington metropolitan area, the answer was the same. Lauren Barr was the ultimate cipher. She never existed.

Dolbeare did find her car parked in the lot at Rick's condo. It was registered to Kehina Alliance Partners, the real estate investment corporation in Maryland where she claimed to work—and where again no one had ever seen or heard of her. When he tracked the Prius back to its purchase almost a year ago, the dealer's records showed that Lauren Barr paid cash for it. Not a cashier's check, the detective asked. Nope, the dealer replied. Cash. Folding money. He then produced the proper IRS paperwork required for such an unusual purchase, as Dolbeare shook his head.

Mrs. Geller's earthly remains simply disappeared.

To the detective and the retired judge, that was not the most disturbing disappearance. Jonas Barr was nowhere to be found either, making him Dolbeare's primary suspect in the Jane Doe death—until it was positively affirmed by video that he was either at GT3 or deep in FSSC's Terragreen bunker the entire day of the murder.

Why did he disappear? Where had he gone? *Who was he?*

Rick did his part attempting to figure out those questions. He made two visits to Sanford Tuttle's office at GT3, the second time accompanied by Julia. Tuttle's initial reaction on the day after the murder was concern about what he called "the identity question." He had known Jonas Barr, or thought he had known him, for years. This could not be a deception. Sanford Tuttle was in denial.

The second meeting was at Sanford Tuttle's urgent request three days later, when it was abundantly clear that Jonas Barr was gone—along with any mainframe electronic record of his employment at GT3 or QUAT-ECH, where he and Tuttle had first met.

How? Sandy asked Rick, visibly very disturbed.

It was going to take weeks of serious forensic systems work fully to reconstruct Jonas Barr's trail-gone-cold following its thorough erasure and data-overwriting. This was not an impossible task, but the work would be painful and slow using third-level redundancy off-site backup data storage. Warren Hunter was called and informed of the security breach.

Jonas Barr had been GT3's top systems expert on the ViroSat financing project, with unrestricted access to every facet of FSSC's operations.

Warren was sufficiently concerned to interrupt his twenty-hour workdays in hardcore deal mode as ViroSat approached closing. In New York he immediately involved Skip Darlington. This response did not especially endear him either to Detective Dolbeare or to Dan Ter Horst. Dolbeare had apparently crossed swords before with Darlington Global Security. It was obvious to Rick that the outcome had not been a good one for the lawyer-detective.

Rick smoothed feathers all around and wished once more that he could simplify his life.

There were no witnesses to either death. There were no new leads. Forensics were useless. One missing body. One dead end.

Rick and Julia were interviewed again, separately and together. Eight frustrating days into the investigation they agreed to meet with a consulting psychologist working for the Fairfax County Police Department. The woman spent a perfunctory twenty minutes exploring the conversations that they had had with Hannah Weiss Geller and Lauren Barr and a half hour inquiring about the "strains and elations" of being an interracial couple in "our present age." Rick shut up and decided not to mention the small matter of their divorce. Julia had the good grace to answer the questions and wait until they left her office before laughing out loud.

Rick Yeager had been kept incredibly busy, all of it uncompensated time.

He was also now very broke.

That complication worried him above all else until yesterday when Ter Horst solved his problem by presenting a spiral-bound accounting of the Geller estate. Her house appraised at three hundred and forty thousand dollars and was now listed for two eighty-nine nine hundred, about what the market would bear. There was no mortgage. Ter Horst apologized for how soft real estate sales were, as if it was his fault, reminding Rick that he lived in that neighborhood, too. Then he complimented Rick on his professional cash management skills. The remainder of the Geller estate was entirely in money market issues and would bring in another hundred and seventy-two thousand and change. It was all his, free and clear. That was it for her accounts.

Except for eighteen handwritten lines of numbers. Somewhere.

Julia Toussaint rang the doorbell at Rick's home. When he called out to her, "Just come on in" and she entered, she found him seated on the sectional sofa, feet propped up, arms crossed, staring at an object in the center of the otherwise empty coffee table.

"What?" she asked. Something was off. Ever since their recent reunion Rick had been gracious and attentive, behavior that she rather enjoyed.

"This," he announced, voice flat, "is about four pounds of gray carbon ash, all that's left of Gustav Adolph Yeager." He pointed at the cremation urn, a lacquered rectangular box made of dark red wood.

"I didn't know your father wanted to be cremated," she said softly.

"Neither did Warren and I," he replied. "Dutch made prepaid arrangements immediately after my mother's death. The funeral director said that's pretty common, especially because he was something like twenty years older than Mom."

"They never quit being a couple, did they?" Julia asked.

Rick looked up at her for the first time. "You're fairly transparent."

"Maybe." Julia sat next to him. She leaned close as Rick raised an arm and she curled herself into his body. For minutes neither of them said anything.

Rick broke the silence. "When the funeral director called me, he told me why Pop wanted to be cremated. He said that it was the way he could join the souls of the six million. Pop even talked to him about Bergen-Belsen."

"Did your father ever say anything like that to you?"

"No. He never would."

"This fathers and sons thing gets complicated, doesn't it?"

"Yes." He paused, thinking. "So are you and I complicated?"

"No," Julia responded immediately. "No, we're not." She kissed him on the cheek, lingering, then settling back comfortably into his side.

"I have to ask you for a favor," Rick said. "You need to help me do something that I've been avoiding ever since my father died. I don't want to do it alone. Warren shouldn't help me because I have no idea how he would react if he tried. You know what his life is like right now. He needs this deal. He can't be emotionally distracted. On the other hand, things can't get a whole lot worse for me."

"What are we going to do?"

"We're going to go through Dutch's things. What my father left behind. Other than that . . ." He made a hand motion in the direction of the wooden box.

Julia took a deep breath and nodded. Rick stood, walked out of the living room, and soon returned with two fairly large boxes, one plain brown cardboard with four top flaps folded into each other. Under it was a banker's box with a lid. The lid was sealed, wrapped several times around all sides with thick cellophane mover's tape. Neither box had any exterior markings. He put them on the coffee table and gently removed the wooden box with Dutch's ashes to a bookshelf.

"How long have you had these?" she asked.

"Since Warren and I first took him to the assisted living facility in Fair Lawn. Pop was fairly lucid then. His cognitive disabilities weren't in full flourish yet. When we were throwing stuff out and packing he was very adamant that we had to keep these. He got visibly agitated when Warren almost pitched them. Everything else he had—home furnishings and the like—didn't matter to him. Once I promised him that I'd personally handle these boxes, he calmed down. I took them out to my car and haven't even looked at them since that afternoon."

"And the FBI didn't seize them?"

"They never searched my car."

"What do you think is in there?"

"We'll see. Most probably the totemic things necessary for my father to survive. There was a time when he saved stuff in order to stay in touch with his life. Dutch had significant . . . health issues. You remember that's what we called it, J.D. My mother and Warren and I could never bring ourselves to come right out and say that he was afflicted with a profound depression. Now that he's gone, it's easier to say that to you. Whatever he put in here had to be important to him. And that's another reason why you and I have to handle this. Not Warren."

"I saw Warren come apart, you know."

"I know."

"That's the only reason I stayed with him."

"Again, I know." Rick pulled open the interlaced flaps of the cardboard box.

The first item he removed was a decrepit empty leather pistol holster with the faint letters US burned into the flap. He popped the flap from the metal bud that held it closed and looked at Julia as if to say *Why?* Next were two black photograph albums, one almost exclusively from Dutch's war and his life in Trenton, the other with family photographs—including far more of Rick, the first son, than of Warren.

"I remember these," Rick said quietly.

Dog tags. A deteriorating blue cardboard box housing a Distinguished Flying Cross. A package of letters—V-mail—tied with string, saved no doubt by his Grammy Lotte so long ago. Then the touchstones that he was expecting: a birthday card handmade in crayon and signed "Ricky" . . .

Dutch and Gloria's wedding portrait . . . baptism and confirmation certifi-
cates for both sons . . . a Sheaffer fountain pen with G. A. YEAGER en-
graved in cracked maroon Bakelite . . . the handwritten receipt for
flowers to be delivered to Gloria, from the VA Hospital gift shop in East
Orange, on a date that Rick recognized as his parents' tenth anniversary.
There was more, but he could go no further at the moment.

As he returned the items to the box, he became aware that Julia was
very close, touching his arm with both hands, openly silently sobbing.

"Let's take a look at this one," he said.

Retrieving a kitchen knife to cut the thick tape gave him a moment to
regain his composure. He slit around three sides of the lid to the banker's
box. He peered inside.

"These," he announced, "are Dutch's famous Essex Empire tax files.
I told you about this when—"

"—When we were driving here and you asked me about *my* meeting
with Mrs. Geller. The 'et cetera' federal credit union. Rick, this is also
the place that Senator Harbison had me ask FSSC to examine for lost
accounts just last week. That's what she called them—lost. Do you mind
if I look?"

"You should." He moved the box to the floor and the two of them removed its files, densely packed papers and notebooks, and folded-over
gigantic old green-and-white tractor-fed IBM computer printouts. They
set out silently organizing the material.

"He was an extraordinary man with an extraordinary mind," Julia offered. "In the Senate I've seen hearing materials and evidence for criminal prosecutions, and none of it was organized this well."

"In his prime there was no one better at what he did. I believe he
wanted to write a book about all this."

"No," she replied. "I don't think so. He was doing something else. I
don't know what yet. Can I read for a while?"

"Sure." He stood and walked to the kitchen to set on a pot of coffee.
When he returned, Julia had two of the IBM printouts spread open and
was carefully studying an oddly shaped loose-leaf notebook, long and
thin with about eight evenly spaced rings, its pages mounted vertically.
She had it flipped open and folded back. The heavy cream-colored page

on which she was so intent had handwritten dates and numbers inter-spersed on printed columns.

It was a bank record created sometime in the years before automation. "Who," she asked, "is A. Stauber?" She pronounced the name *staw-ber*.

If he had not just allowed himself to grieve, to take those precious mo-ments of care for his departed father, Rick would never have recalled the name. But in his present state of mind, Dutch's last words in German came back to him in a precise rush of remembrance.

Alois Stauber ist der andere. Alois Stauber is the other one.

Die Rechnung. The account.

Weiss. Seine Liste sondern Staubers Rechnung. Weiss. His list but Stauber's account.

Ägyptisches Reichtum, in Vereinig—the Egyptian wealth, in union—in the United States!

Alleschan—Alexan—Alexander? Alexandria!

Tut—Tut—

Er weiss wer aber nicht wo. He knows who but not where.

He looked up to see Julia leaning over him, her hand on the side of his face.

"You're flushed, Rick. You zoned out on me. What's the matter?"

"Stauber," he said, pronouncing the name properly in German—*schtow-ber*. "When my Pop was dying, he was talking about *Staub*, dust, like dust in the wind, or ashes to ashes, dust to dust. That's what I thought he was saying at the time. I was wrong. He was saying Stauber. It's a name, a family name. That's what he was so intent upon telling me and Warren." In careful detail he walked through Dutch's words with Julia.

"I was so sure that he meant an accounting, a reckoning—you die, you're called to account for your life, that kind of thing. Old country thinking. I should have known better. Pop was Lutheran to the core. He wouldn't have bought into that theology even on his deathbed with his mind in turmoil. He was talking about the accounts. Bank accounts with Egyptian wealth. Julia, he meant the Meier Seckendorf Böhmer accounts."

"The ones that Lauren Barr told you didn't exist. The money was all gone."

"Yes."

"The ones for which there were precise German accountings, both after the war and after the fall of the Wall."

"Obviously not precise enough."

"There are . . ." she counted ". . . eighteen pages here. None of them are sequential. This book has been edited. Or else Dutch saved only the relevant parts."

"There were eighteen lines of numbers with Mrs. Geller's will."

"So how exactly does she fit in?"

"J.D., her father was a banker at Meier Seckendorf—"

"—Wait. Every one of these says . . ." Julia flipped the pages and read the repeatedly typed annotation on the Essex Building and Loan columnar sheets ". . . A. *Stauber has placed in trust for Jakob Weiss and Hannah Sara Weiss, his minor daughter, this personal account.*"

CHAPTER 33

Horvath raked in the shade. When he arrived at the Reston garden condominium complex the Salvadoran crew of five was already working. He
observed that one of the landscapers was even older than he was, and he
grinned at the guy as he simply joined in the work. Nobody said a word
as they regarded him with deep suspicion. This was perfectly fine with
Horvath. They were illegals—of this much he was certain. Horvath had
deeply conflicted feelings about immigration. He had been required to
meet some very stringent bureaucratic requirements in order to enter the
country and become an American citizen. Why should they get a break
that he never got? Of course when he came over he had other motives
never shared with the immigration officials. Now in his advancing age
he was inclined to be more charitable to these men. They were only trying to make a living. Hell, how was that different from the Hungarians
who made steel or dug the mines a hundred years ago? He kind of liked
them. They didn't make trouble. None of them would go out of their
way to talk to a cop either.

For days, completely undetected, he had been trailing Rick Yeager
and Julia Toussaint. For a man of Horvath's talents it was not a particularly difficult task, but this new connection to the retired judge and the
police detective made it both interesting and much more demanding.
He was required to bide his time. He needed to wait for his moment.

Their plans changed when Graham Tuttle had to kill the woman.

Tuttle was always drawn to subtleties and baroque intelligence tradecraft for which Horvath never had any use. If Tuttle had listened to
Horvath in the first place the woman might still be alive. Horvath was
still mulling over whether eliminating her was good or bad for their

operation. Each time he researched this quandary he concluded that he simply did not have enough information to make a determination. This was no different from the way the communists worked. All the time— decision making under conditions of uncertainty.

It was originally Tuttle's idea to put the weapon in Yeager's World War II holster. After Horvath managed the murder-suicide of the older son and the black woman, this would create a credible forensic trail, he said. We can make it appear as though the son planned the whole thing. Police are lazy. They will reach the conclusion to which we lead them. Police also love psychology. Deep motives. They will find that good clean oiled gun had been in a nasty old leather relic. They would inevitably settle on Freudian connotations—a son who could not deal with his dead father's demons left behind.

Bullshit, Horvath told him. You are getting too goddamned fancy. Just give me Yeager's .45 and I'll take care of this.

He was also pretty sure that Tuttle wanted to have a look around the place by himself.

After Lauren Barr's death—which Horvath conceded was unfortunately necessary—Graham Tuttle relented. Horvath now had the weapon. It was wrapped loosely in a silicone cloth in the right patch pocket of the cargo pants he wore while he raked with the Salvadorans. The gun was immaculately clean, absent any fingerprints or epithelial evidence. He prepared it himself to be sure.

There was a risk that Horvath would be seen here, albeit a small one.

He took that risk because he knew how to be invisible. No one ever looks twice at a landscaping crew, and anyone who did would swear that they were all Mexicans or Dominicans or Salvadorans or something. Nobody would remember him.

Horvath reached into his pants pocket, the one without the .45, and pulled out a white wire and two earbuds. The wire came from an iPod, but inside his pocket it terminated at a specialized radio receiver that Gray Tuttle gave him. In Budapest and then later, when he first moved to Washington, they used many devices like this. They were larger then. Getting one would have taken weeks—half of it for the bureaucracy to approve and pay for it. Tuttle bought this one online, along with the seven sensors that Horvath carefully placed in Rick Yeager's condominium.

He fingered the buds into his ears and resumed raking as he listened.

"What do you think is in there?"

"We'll see. Most probably the totemic things necessary for my father to survive."

The quality of the bugs was superb. Twenty-first-century digital technology was a far cry from the shit that the East Germans made during his earliest days in the business. On Horvath's first electronic surveillance operation—simple blackmail, an Italian communist diplomat banging a whore in Buda—the receiver had vacuum tubes.

This unpleasant recollection made him feel very old. He reminded himself that he was doing all of this for his American grandchildren and someday for their children. His family ought to enjoy some prosperity for all that he'd been through.

"Dutch's famous Essex Empire tax files."

Graham Tuttle was correct. If there was going to be an intergenerational transfer of such massive wealth, why shouldn't it be for us?

"There are eighteen pages here. None of them are sequential. This book has been edited. Or else Dutch saved only the relevant parts."

Horvath stopped raking and listened carefully.

"Wait. Every one of these says A. Stauber has placed in trust for Jakob Weiss and Hannah Sara Weiss, his minor daughter, this personal account."

Horvath appreciated once again the beauty and—what?—grace, *kegyelem*, of intelligence operations. You must stay alert, think on your feet.

He would now defer eliminating this son of Gustav Adolph Yeager.

Horvath would enjoy telling Gray Tuttle that he had found exactly what they were looking for.

In exactly where they thought in the first place.

CHAPTER 34

"Azach Hasab was the first 'quant' in finance," Rick said. "The Kaiser Wilhelm Institute. Mathematical modeling. The Emergency Fund for German Science. Meier Seckendorf Böhmer GmbH, investment and merchant bankers."

"But Hasab appears nowhere in the Essex Building and Loan accounts," Julia replied.

"No. He wouldn't. However, Lauren Barr focused on him. Hasab was a Berlin merchant banker—quiet, circumspect. In 1936 you'd have to be if you were an Egyptian Jew assimilated in Germany with a German wife. His family was the connection for the Middle Eastern money invested at Meier Seckendorf Böhmer. Like generations of Hasabs did, he managed capital accounts for Arab families."

"And he invested it in New Jersey?"

"Exactly."

"Why?"

"J.D., the Meier Seckendorf Böhmer bankers in Berlin were distributing cash everywhere. They were getting ready to head for New York. They had a well-thought-out plan. Everybody, families included, would disappear in Germany and then surface to re-form the firm in Manhattan. But first they had to get liquid. Sorry, I mean, they had to convert all of their hard assets into cash and assemble it in European banks."

"Rick, I know about liquidity. I had to get smart on the concept very quickly ever since ViroSat and FSSC became my boss's only political priority."

"Okay. Hasab has significant investments for which he's responsible. He's holding money from his clients in Cairo, Beirut, Jerusalem, Amman, Riyadh, all the way to Baghdad. He not only has a fiduciary duty—I don't know if they called it that then—he also has family obligations and reputation to consider. The Hasabs are respected as money managers going back two centuries. They are trusted. But when the merchant bank first begins planning to decamp Berlin, Hasab's investments are all illiquid. This makes perfect sense. He put the clients' money to work. He's invested in German commercial buildings. Mining deals were big then. He has equity ownership in manufacturing corporations, mills and foundries, service firms, insurance companies. He probably owns agricultural land. If he speculates at all, it's in crop futures. That's the way you professionally managed private equity in those days. Lauren Barr said that Meier Seckendorf Böhmer holdings were spread out all over Germany, Austria, Czechoslovakia, Belgium, and the Netherlands. I have no reason to doubt that information."

"You also have a terrific memory."

"Thanks. I ought to. I've been replaying that conversation constantly ever since we found her body."

"You said that the bank managed to turn its investments into cash while they were planning the big escape from Germany."

"They did."

"And that the commercial accounts were seized by the Nazis."

"They were audited and accounted for twice, in 1946 and again in 1991. It's what you said—after the end of the war and after the fall of the Wall."

"What am I missing?"

"J.D., what does *any* investment manager *always* do? He hedges. Azach Hasab put aside the Meier Seckendorf Böhmer accounts from the Middle East. They were enormously significant. He had two associates working for him. We know that one of them was Jakob Weiss, Hannah Weiss Geller's father. The other had to be Alois Stauber—that was the name my father was trying to tell me. Right there's your paper evidence, in the binder. 'A. Stauber has placed in trust for Jakob Weiss.' In a bank like that, at a time when secrecy meant life or death, Stauber and Weiss would never have acted on their own. The place had far too much integrity. Hasab was the creative one. He would have insisted on a hedge, a backup plan. It makes perfect sense. Why keep all of that newly liquid cash in Europe? So the three of them—Hasab, Weiss, and Stauber, none of whom survived the Holocaust—set up eighteen accounts at Essex Building and Loan. These are what Dutch called the Egyptian accounts—*Ägyptisches Reichtum in Vereinigten Staaten.* Egyptian accounts in the United States. Hasab's headquarters in the Middle East was in Alexandria, not Cairo. Pop said that, too. Half a word: *Alleschan . . .*"

"Rick, there's a part that doesn't work for me. Why would such sophisticated European financiers put their cash into some tiny insignificant building and loan association in north Jersey?"

"I've thought about that," Rick said, his mind racing. "Three reasons. First, there was no regulation. Nobody in government was responsible for oversight of a building and loan association in the 1930s. The concept of regulation was only in its infancy then. A place like Essex was a perfect anonymous American counterpart to Meier Seckendorf Böhmer in Berlin. Essex didn't have anywhere near the same level of esteem and quality, but both of them were small, unobtrusive, and private. That's what counted. Nobody was paying attention except the owners. Why do you think that Essex became so attractive to the Mafia a generation later?"

"That part I understand completely. It was attractive enough that the bad guys put it out of business."

"Right. Second, who actually banked the money for those 1930s building and loan associations? I'll bet if we looked carefully we'll find one of the biggest banks in New York holding the funds."

"Manufacturers Trust," Julia read. "Right here in your father's file. It's printed on the old account cards. By the time Essex Construction Trades Federal Credit Union folded, the bank was Manufacturers Hanover Trust Company. They were also the receiver. Dutch has a whole file here on that."

"Precisely. Stauber would not have placed any significant funds with a small bank. He needed Essex to keep the records—more correctly, to keep everything quiet until the firm could reestablish in New York and recover the cash. The money was always safe in Manufacturers Trust, the big bank. Here's the real beauty of his plan: with the accounts housed at Essex, the only thing visible at Manufacturers Trust—which *was* being watched and regulated—would be an *aggregate* of the building and loan association's holdings. These guys were good. It would have worked too, if they made it to New York. These accounts were their hedge. They hid the Egyptian accounts in the one place that the National Socialist authorities in Germany could never touch. In the United States."

"You said there were three reasons."

"I did. There has to be a family connection somewhere."

Rick sat on the floor. Julia joined him. Together, methodically, they read in earnest. Outdoors the shrill whine of a gas-powered blower increased as the Salvadoran landscapers continued their work.

"I loved your father," Julia said. "Now I admire him. He saved everything necessary to document the Meier Seckendorf Böhmer—"

"—Böhmer," Rick said, drawing out the vowel. "It's an O-umlaut, a sound that we don't normally have in English." He paused and said slowly, "Lauren Barr pronounced all of the German words perfectly. She spoke the language."

"Dolbeare will want to know that. I was saying, Dutch saved all that he needed to prove the existence of the Meier Seckendorf Böhmer accounts."

"Not everything," Rick replied. "We don't have the link to the corresponding accounts at Manufacturers Trust. At the time they were set up, there would have to be a paper record."

"Eighteen accounts, right?"

"Yes."

"Rick, get the eighteen lines of numbers that Mrs. Geller left you in her will. We should compare them."

"I don't have them anymore. Lauren Barr took the original and my copy the day she disappeared in Maryland."

"She can't do anything with it, can she?"

"No one can, J.D. Not without this information right here and knowing what only we know right now."

"Would Ter Horst have kept a copy?"

"No." He thought again. "Wait. I'm an idiot for forgetting. Sanford Tuttle has the list. I gave him one. We discussed it the day I lost mine.

His people were running it through some Federal Reserve algorithms and getting nowhere."

"So all we have to do now is recover that list from him and match it to the Manufacturers Trust accounts."

"Easier said than done, J.D. Where are we going to find them?"

She smiled. "Did you ever hear of Stump and Stumpy?"

"No."

"They were a black lounge act in the forties. My granddaddy loved them. Martin and Lewis, only in Harlem, for black folk only—Jerry Lewis freely gives them credit for his earliest stuff. They had a routine called 'Everything You Need.' The premise is a store with nothing in it—they sell everything you need. If you need it, they have it. If they don't have it, well, you don't need it!"

"What's this got to do with—"

"Dutch left us everything we need." Julia reached for the pile of ancient folded-over IBM printouts. Altogether they stacked up at least seven inches deep, every line printed all the way across. On the top of the first page, written in fountain pen in his father's penmanship, Rick read the words *MAN HAN*.

"Manufacturers Hanover. Used to be Manufacturers Trust. Bank accounts," he said. "And we just have to match them to—"

"Hannah Weiss Geller's list. She had one. A. Stauber would certainly have kept one." Julia was excited. "The Geller numbers exist for one reason—to translate these eighteen Essex Building and Loan accounts into the Manufacturers Trust accounts."

"It makes sense, Julia. Look at the Essex account cards. All of them are numbered and begin with two four seven followed by six other numbers, no letters. So did Mrs. Geller's list. Then there was a dash and a bunch of numbers. All of them were random. They have to correlate to the Manufacturers Trust accounts. Our problem now is, those accounts became Manufacturers Hanover accounts, then Chemical Bank accounts, Chase Manhattan Bank accounts, and JPMorgan Chase accounts." Rick rolled off the names with the exacting knowledge of an outsider who never got to play in those leagues.

"The genealogy of a New York commercial bank."

"Our list, which we don't have, only gets us as far as the first bank before four more successors."

"Rick, can the supercomputers at FSSC track that down?"

He grinned. "Given time, I bet they could. The best shortcut, however, is this stack of forty-year-old computer printouts. Warren needs to know about this, J.D. He and Sandy Tuttle are digging around for accounts that have been renumbered five times since Essex Building and Loan. All of the data mining in the world won't help if the information can't be narrowed down. Warren doesn't have a lot of time. Outside of Dutch's banker's box—the last paper records before automation and information technology took over the financial services industry—the accounts are a million needles in a billion haystacks. Without them, it will take years to locate the money or to claim it."

Julia stared at him. "And you're perfectly okay with this?"

He did not look her in the eyes. "I'm not sure. My brother is always right there on the edge—a lot of time he's working over the edge. But he's my brother. He also knows what he's doing and he is famously in control."

"Except when he wasn't."

"Yes."

"The last time he lost a parent."

"Yes."

"Do you still trust his judgment?"

Rick did not respond.

"Four mergers, right?"

"We're thinking alike, J.D. Bank mergers are a very easy way to lose billions of dollars in the noise, especially when they take place over seventy-five years. So we have to start at the beginning. We need to know how much Stauber put into Essex Building and Loan."

"That will take some math," Julia said. She stood up and walked to the table in Rick's dining area. "Have you got a tablet and a calculator?"

Ten minutes later she produced an answer. "Stauber moved more than fifteen billion dollars into that tiny building and loan association in 1936 and 1937. Look at this number." On the tablet was written $15,010,821,754.

Rick stared at the paper in astonishment while he shook his head. "Hand me the financial calculator." He scribbled a few numbers on the same pad where she had added the accounts, then worked out a future value calculation—seventy-five years of compounded interest at 4 percent. "More than three hundred billion dollars. Enough," he announced, "to fund the entire ViroSat partnership."

Horvath had heard enough. The Salvadorans were wrapping up at this location and he was getting mighty pissed off at the guy with the grass blower. Every time he moved, the kid came close to him. They were poor. They weren't stupid. They didn't want him hanging around. He couldn't blame them. Where they came from they likely had as much experience with secret police as the Hungarians.

He rolled up the white earphone wires and stuffed them into his pocket with the receiver.

Nothing Horvath heard was news to him.

Those two knew. That fact was very significant.

Gray Tuttle would need to hear.

And Horvath was certain that he would not appreciate any of that speculation about family.

"I think I understand why Stauber put the Essex Building and Loan accounts in Jakob Weiss's name," Julia was saying. "That way at least two of them would have access to the cash when the bank reestablished itself in New York. But why 'in trust for his minor daughter'?"

"That part bothers me as well," Rick answered. "It's possible that Hannah Weiss was already safe in New York. Or maybe the accounts were set up that way as part of their overall deception. Or both."

"What kind of deception?"

"J.D., you don't think that Stauber told Essex Building and Loan exactly what he was doing, do you? If he had, what were the chances that some anti-Semite at Essex or at Manufacturers Trust would have taken it on himself to disclose the information to the German authorities? Prob-

ably pretty high. American banking had loads of German sympathizers.
We weren't at war then. A lot of folks here in the late thirties thought that
if there was going to be a European war, we'd back Germany. What's interesting to me are the names—Weiss, Stauber, even Hannah's given
name. None of them are easily identifiable as Jewish names. They're just
regular German names. Jakob is a Jewish name, but a lot of Christian
Germans would have been named that, too. 'Azach Hasab,' on the other
hand, would have been a giveaway. Arabic and Jewish."

"Did people really think that way?"

"Most assuredly."

"And Weiss would have put that much money in trust for a minor
daughter? *Billions?*"

"As a building and loan association they would have considered the
arrangement temporary and the amount unusual—but of course they
were happy to accommodate him. Essex would have assumed that he
was collecting and storing family money. Why else would he have used
so many accounts? This kind of thing was happening everywhere in Europe. Banks around the world were holding Austrian and German money.
My guess is that the first account was set up with Hannah's name. Then
Essex simply repeated the registration information for each subsequent
account. Every time a new Meier Seckendorf Böhmer transfer was made,
a new account was opened. Eighteen of them."

"Rick?"

"What?"

"Ter Horst will say that you own the money if it was in trust for Mrs.
Geller." Julia began to fan through the IBM printouts. "I think that was
her intention. She thought that it might take years to track down the cash,
not to mention the litigation that someone's bound to file. There's also
the not-so-small ethical question of whether you *should* keep it. Here.
There must be a couple hundred thousand Manufacturers Hanover accounts listed in the printouts. How are we possibly going to narrow them
down over four mergers? We're not FSSC."

The printouts stalled with a *flup* as Julia fanned them, so she re-
started. Again, a *flup*: a bookmark.

"It *won't* be that easy." Rick observed. "What is that?"

She pulled a cream-colored note card out of the computer papers. Centered at the top were the letters HWG in block photogravure.

"Dated . . . five months ago," she said.

The handwriting was the same fine European script that transcribed the account numbers and signed the will. The salutation was in German, the brief text in English. They read together.

> *Lieber Herr Jäger,*
> *Thank you. I agree. You are most gracious in your offer. I will*
> *act upon your suggestions concerning both of your sons. I am*
> *grateful for your confidence and know now how to engage the*
> *national interest. Yours is indeed the only way by which we*
> *may do right by all, and in their memory.*
> *With sincere regards,*
> *Hannah Geller*

"This is not," Rick said, stating the obvious, "their first communication. She and my father were writing to each other."

"Before she visited me," Julia said.

"Before she watched me get arrested."

I do have a will, but there is a very serious financial matter that I have to attend to. For several reasons no one but you is appropriate to that task. The words were stinging sharp in his memory. Why had he missed it before? *I am going to need a great deal of assistance with something which will become immensely complicated.*

"She was right," Rick said.

"What are you talking about?"

He told her.

"Immensely complicated," Julia offered, "is never a good thing."

Rick silently agreed.

"What did she mean when she wrote 'both of your sons'? Do you think that's the family connection?"

He shook his head. "No," he said. "I definitely don't."

CHAPTER 35

When a twenty-first-century investment bank shifts into deal mode, theoretical concepts like *calendar, night, day, nutrition, exercise, social life,* and especially *relationships, home, spouse, partner, family,* and *children* are utterly without meaning. They are abstract, highly distracting, and therefore readily disposed of. Nothing matters but the deal. Until the transaction reaches this stage, investment bankers generally favor sexual metaphors for their shared professional preoccupations. They often compete with one another to conceive the most crude and socially unacceptable ways of expressing their work. The marginally few women within the profession—this is a place in America where they remain quite few—often paradoxically win at this element of the dealmakers' game. The shift to deal mode, especially in a big deal, is usually gradual. Sometimes the changeover is abrupt. Either way, upon entering deal mode a transformation takes place in investment bankers' conversational similes along with an acceleration of the work and the personal conflicts thereby engendered. It is the way you can tell that the transformation has occurred. The sexual metaphors, casual cursing, and isolated incidents of personal violence (all of which are tolerated if not officially acceptable for reasons of liability) frequently increase and intensify.

In full-blown deal mode the undergirding allegory is theological.

The deal becomes consuming, all-powerful, omnipotent, and almighty.

The bankers—they constitute the faithful, the high priests and priestesses—are not just reverent. They are expected instead to be fervent, fanatical, and zealous.

There are several gods in the pantheon of a deal.

Greed is the dominant deity in this profane cosmology, but its name may never, ever be spoken. Its closely related petit gods are, however, fine to worship and praise: *equity, piece of the deal, bonus, earnout, payout.*

Every banker at Compton Sizemore bought into the concept if not the precise allegory. Now was the moment for Wall Street's biggest deal—the time for reckoning and resurrection from the Great Wallow. ViroSat would be salvation.

Warren Hunter did not feel anything like a messiah.

You would not have formed that impression from reading the *Wall Street Journal*'s three-day front-page series about ViroSat. The piece was stage-managed to perfection by Compton Sizemore's "ViroSat External Management Group." Warren Hunter gave them firm direction: Leave absolutely nothing to the reporters' judgment. ViroSat, he was dutifully quoted as saying, is a triumph of technology and global corporate social responsibility. The project, unprecedented in scope, would likewise become the worldwide engine of free enterprise igniting the real recovery we have all been waiting for. Creative destruction and innovation would prevail because of the new business created by the enterprise companies, in nation after nation, especially in the developing world. He termed it "a cascade effect." ViroSat networks would rapidly displace what we now call the Internet because of their streamlined new information technology architecture, speed, total security, reliability, and disconnection from any government control. This last comment was widely perceived to be a dig at China—an impression that Warren did nothing to dispel among the *Journal* interviewers—and resulted in a frenzy of new interest in ViroSat enterprise investment among prominent Shanghai financial firms.

Time magazine featured the ViroSat deal in a top-margin headline on its fifth cover of the year featuring a picture of the American president. ("ViroSat: Internet Next's Moment Now.") Two sidebars accompanied the main article, which speculated at length about policy considerations in the upcoming hearings on ViroSat in Washington. The sidebar about Warren Hunter was titled "Trenton Makes, the World Takes," and provided a capsule summary of his career and deal history beginning with running *Business Today* at Princeton then on to the Harvard Business School, JPMorgan Chase, and Compton Sizemore. The other sidebar described "The Ten Biggest Global Conspiracy Theories and Myths" surrounding ViroSat, especially in the European Union. Warren was quoted. He was magnanimous. "Hunter has a ready laugh of dismissal for the wildest of the conspiracy-minded. 'Since about the eighteenth century this has always been how,' he explained, 'a financier knows that he's truly arrived.'"

In all of the new media—twelve ViroSat Facebook pages, a Twitter account with thrice-daily tweets from Compton Sizemore's "ViroSat Social Networking Group" and hundreds of Web sites and blogs—the unifying theme was anticipation.

At Compton Sizemore headquarters the prevailing anxiety was the over-creation of expectations.

Deep inside, Warren Hunter was coming apart.

Jenny Lau stepped off the elevator at the fifty-sixth floor at 5:42 A.M. As the executive assistant to Wall Street's man of the moment her personal reputational currency was never higher. So were the punishing demands on her time—the reason why she was arriving three hours before her usual time to begin work. She glanced at her computer screen. She hadn't bothered to close it last night when she left at midnight. The Outlook calendar showed that Warren Hunter should be concluding his 4:30 A.M videoconference with the director general of the Kuwait Investment Authority, a sovereign wealth fund heavily invested in ViroSat debt. Jenny heard bits and pieces of this conversation going on in his inner office and peeked inside. Six Compton Sizemore investment bankers were participating with three other people she had never seen before. Warren Hunter was talking fast and loud, in charge, A-game engaged. He nodded in greeting and continued, practically manic.

All was right with the world.

Jenny stepped out to the kitchen. When she returned carrying a double espresso for Warren, his office was cleared out and he was alone on the phone. He stood listening quietly with his back to her, the phone cord wrapped halfway around his body. He stared out the south-facing window, framed by the Manhattan skyline. She put the espresso cup and saucer in the center of his blotter. Warren turned around and acknowledged her with a smile of thanks.

"Rick," she heard him say, "you have to begin at the beginning. Play it back to me slowly. In detail. Everything and every word, especially the Meier Secken—right, what you said. Start with that story the murdered woman told you. Then walk me through everything you and J.D. found in Pop's box."

Two and a half years working for Warren Hunter meant that she had absolutely heard it all. Nothing said in that room had the capability to faze her even slightly. "Murdered woman" did get her attention, however. She briefly contemplated if she should say or do something.

She closed the door to the suite and sat down at her workstation. They were troubling words to be sure. Whatever they meant, Warren Hunter had to know what he was doing.

ViroSat now occupied most of Compton Sizemore's real estate on the fifty-first floor. At this point in the deal a "war room" was required. The space was prominently labeled as such, resulting in one verbally violent outburst from an Iraq veteran on the ViroSat military applications group. He protested, "You assholes don't know a fucking thing about war." His objection was ignored and the name stuck.

The place was a human hive of activity this morning. People spilled all over the makeshift offices, mismatched cubicles, cobbled-together conference rooms, and temporary trading floor. Desks were manned for each of the international investment regions and the huge technology section. The fourteen original ViroSat bankers had expanded by now to one hundred and seventy-seven people in the latest "deal census" that Warren had personally approved—and that was only the number working on fifty-one.

He stepped into this highly organized melee ninety-five minutes late for the 6 A.M. daily deal conference, off schedule and off balance when he could least afford to be.

The daily deal conference took place every day including Saturday and Sunday. Those are the first working days of the week in the entire Islamic world, the confidential ViroSat deal book reminded the team. When Warren stepped into the room his arrival was certainly noticed, but the presenter continued without interruption. The immediate agenda item was a technical one, reporting that a major interconnectivity issue had been solved, one affecting most of the enterprise companies. This was excellent news. The development meant that a risk previously expected and accounted for in the market valuations of the companies was now no risk at all. Valuations would increase.

Warren half listened but looked entirely attentive, the way the chief should. His head was pounding. The knot under his sternum tightened in spasms of pain that ebbed and flowed with his breathing. He tried to focus on the presentation—slide thirty-seven of the PowerPoint was up on the screen—and found that he couldn't. He took two deep breaths. This helped a little but caused a high-ebb of the pain in his chest.

"Mr. Hunter, anything to ask or add?" The final slide was up, a white screen with the Compton Sizemore logo centered, the way every briefing here ended.

"No," he said. "My apologies to all for being delayed. Group directors only, please. The people from Chantilly should also stay."

Nothing unusual here. In this environment no one was offended by being excluded. Most of the bankers in the room filed out, back to work, back to the art of the deal. In minutes Warren was alone and again in charge.

"Security first," he announced.

The security group chief, seconded from his position as a senior vice president at Darlington Global Security, stood and got as far as, "Network dailies came in overnight . . ." before Warren interrupted.

"I'll read it. Thanks. Right now I'm only interested in one thing. What happened to the guy who disappeared from GT3?"

"We don't know." The security chief was former Special Forces, an older guy, Vietnam era. He knew that this response was a perfectly good answer. Warren appreciated him because alone among the entire team he never bullshitted.

"Where did his trail go?"

"As far as the parking lot, then nothing."

"Do you have any ideas?"

"I do."

"He was a professional." Warren said it as a statement.

"I believe he was."

"One of ours?"

"Not a chance. Skip and I have been all over this since he disappeared. So has our new colleague." He looked in the direction of the oldest man in the room, Graham Tuttle, silent and paying strict attention at his first daily deal conference.

"Did he ever serve with any of our friends?"

"That depends how you define friends, Mr. Hunter. Again, the answer is no, as far as we can determine—but you know that we'll never get a definitive answer on that point. Skip and I believe that he was purely commercial. Technical espionage. That would fit with the long-term nature of his involvement with the younger Mr. Tuttle."

"You're never going to find him, are you?"

"I can't answer that. We simply don't have enough information to make an assessment. I can tell you that he will not be able to go off-grid. His methods are to manipulate the computer infrastructure, not to operate outside it. That's his strength and also his weakness."

"Thanks."

"There is another security matter."

"What?"

"Dawson McNeil. When he was terminated my guards working here personally escorted him out of this building. He hasn't been seen since."

"I'm not surprised."

"His girlfriend contacted us. Or rather, one of the lawyers at the law firm where she works called. She's filed a missing persons report and they're threatening suit."

"That's a fine result. Send it to legal. I am uninterested."

"I understand."

"Good. Public policy."

The public policy group chief was a Compton Sizemore managing director from the trading side, Warren's eating club buddy from Princeton—

the closest he had to having an actual friend in the firm. He got to the point quickly.

"We're all ready for the hearing," he said, "if you are. Your opening statement has been written and vetted six different ways. We have a preparation team ready and time blocked for you beginning at ten this morning. Think of this exercise like getting ready for a deposition or a negotiation, Warren. The better prepared you are, the less likely it will be that you'll hear a question you haven't already answered and thoroughly practiced. The major difference at a hearing on Capitol Hill is that the senators will all be giving speeches. For them this is right from the ego and all about votes. It's not about the deal, which is the reason why you'll succeed despite operating in their environment. You have the ability to maintain focus. They don't. Stay on point and stay on the facts. Whenever they're lecturing, you're only there to watch the show. You sit quietly and take it all, no matter what they say. When they're questioning, it's almost as easy. You already have the answers and you don't deviate."

Warren nodded. "Do we know precisely what they're after?"

"There's never been a secret kept on Capitol Hill," he replied. "You should know that."

Warren was suddenly uneasy again. He didn't let it show. "View from the balcony, where are Senator Harbison and her committee going to go with me?"

"Four areas. First up are your assurances concerning civil liberties. Manny Velez from Texas, the ranking Republican on the committee, is riding that horse. He wants guarantees that in private hands, the technological capabilities provided by ViroSat aren't going to result in the networks turning into a global commercial Big Brother. You'll hear a full-blown polemic and then you should give him the usual declarations, which he will accept. Second, the Democrats are going to be all over the law enforcement implications of Internet Next, mostly because no one in the federal government understands them yet. They have no idea what ViroSat integration might eventually mean once the FBI, Homeland Security, and the intelligence community are all up and running on our networks. Skip Darlington is going to fly down and be in the hearing room with you, by the way. On this one they're simply frustrated and you have to calm them down. We'll release a ton of data after you're done. You just have to say that you'd like to take the question and provide a more detailed response for the record. Oh, and please don't neglect to mention ViroSat government contracts in California, Nevada, Pennsylvania, and Virginia. The third area is one where you'll hear from senators on both sides. They want to pontificate about the global commercial banking structure of ViroSat. Nothing new, Warren. More fallout from the crash and the continuing economic troubles. When you get this one you should go into your stump speech about the Great Wallow and how ViroSat is going to help us all get back on track economically."

"And the fourth area?"

"Tenley Harbison has been looking much too closely at our financing— and I mean our technical financing. The deal structure. Here you had better be careful. The woman's scary smart, Warren. She's tough and ambitious and she may pull something. You don't want or need a showdown with her. You have to say something while actually giving away nothing. Our deal partners all over the world are relying on Compton Sizemore's privacy and confidentiality, which you cannot compromise. You know better than anyone how skittish and crazy some of them are getting this close to closing day. Frankly, that right there is your biggest risk at the hearing. It's also the part our people in Washington know the least about."

"The hearing is taking place how many days before closing?"

"Two."

"I have been meaning to ask. Who let that happen?"

"We had no control over it. The chairman sets the date."

"Ten minutes," Warren said tersely, "then we reconvene."

His intestines were heaving. His heart raced as he stood and wordlessly walked out, headed for the men's room.

Warren Hunter felt better now.

"Equity capital aggregation group," he announced. This was the newest and least experienced of the Compton Sizemore cross-functional teams. Not one of the members was an investment banker. All six of them—the "people from Chantilly"—were present in New York at Warren's invitation. Three of them were from GT3. The two from FSSC were the project manager and the technical manager, both former government types. Gray Tuttle sat with them, listening and watching as he had been all morning. Warren made introductions, ending with "most of you will remember Sanford Tuttle from one or more of his initial public offerings with this firm. For this project his father has joined us out of retirement as a consultant." It was enough of an explanation for the other group directors.

"Now how close are we?" he asked.

To the bankers in the room, all of them managing directors and senior group directors for ViroSat, it was an entirely unremarkable question. Their assumption, the one that Warren wanted them to make, was that "how close" meant the last-minute legal wrangling over contract language. Each of them had received some variant of the same question at previous daily deal conferences.

What they could not know is that the equity capital aggregation group was still looking for two hundred and eighty-seven billion dollars. A fifth of ViroSat's required capital.

Warren's inquiry continued in this kind of code.

"We're close," said the project manager.

"I agree," added the technical manager as the GT3 guys shook their heads. "Very close."

"You want to give me a percentage?" Warren asked.

"Sixty, sixty-five percent of the way there."

"Not nearly good enough."

"We can't accelerate the process any more. It's too technology dependent."

"You could put additional resources into it. Do you need me to add people from here?"

"No."

"Do you understand that this is a binary proposition? The limited partnership either closes or it doesn't. And on that closing the entire deal hinges. We have all of the pieces of ViroSat scheduled for same-day simultaneous closings. The capital flows all at one moment. That includes the equity piece. Every contract we've signed that even *relates* to ViroSat requires equity to close on or before the debt."

"I understand that." The old man spoke his first words since arriving at the war room. "Did you get the information I asked you about in Virginia?"

The research group director spoke up. "What do you need?" she offered. "I can get you anything at all."

"No," said Warren. "Not this." He addressed Tuttle. "Not to worry. I just found it this morning."

Alone back at his desk Warren checked the flat screen and saw that he had eleven minutes before his next meeting, a settlement conference with a room full of lawyers that would clear the way for a ViroSat satellite trunkline between Portugal and Angola. The sun was brilliant and already at a high azimuth in the unfolding morning. His head hurt mightily, worse than any hangover he had ever experienced, and Warren Hunter was at one time famous for his drinking prowess. Now he didn't have the time or the inclination.

He opened the lower file drawer in his big credenza, the one beneath the southern Manhattan skyline window. The only files he kept in his office were his personal files, and he was looking for one in particular. It didn't take him long to locate it.

The day that Dutch Yeager handed him the two booklets was also the day on which he confirmed the early Alzheimer's diagnosis. Keep them!, his father had exhorted. He'd been angry, agitated, and insistent, extracting Warren's promise.

Sure, Pop, of course I will.

Warren had no idea why Dutch was so insistent or what the books meant. He'd stuffed them in a hanging file that he hand-labeled *Dutch Yeager Annual Reports (?)*.

The first, the smaller one, was bound with two rusted staples. It had a yellow cover with a line drawing of a blockhouse storefront building. *Essex Building and Loan Association* was centered across the top, *Newark–East Orange* and *Annual Report 1939* were printed below. An ancient newspaper clipping made a bookmark. He opened the booklet to that page. On it was a listing of the building and loan association's staff. He read down, searching, until he saw the name and title.

Francis A. Stauber, Jr., Assistant Accountant-Teller, Investments.

He turned over the yellowed clipping. There were no markings to identify the newspaper. The headline read simply "Area Deaths in Service." There. The fourth line down. Stauber, Francis Aloysius Jr. Sgt., Hq. Co. 3 Batt. 358 Inf. Regt. 90th Inf. Div., July 11, 1944, Foret de Mont Castre, France.

A family connection. Those were Rick's words.

The second book was larger, perfect-bound, its grayscale cover bearing no photographs—only square blocks in a simple abstract design and the words *Manufacturers Trust 1945*. Wartime graphic austerity, printed on thin paper. No markings anywhere, but Warren was pretty sure he knew where to look. Page four, Directors and Officers of the Corporation.

Chester Alan Tuttle, Director.

He closed the books and replaced them in the file folder, then returned the folder to his credenza. For the first time in days Warren Hunter felt the resurgence of calm accompanied by resilience and confidence.

"Jenny," he called out, and waited until his assistant arrived. "First, get rid of the Portuguese lawyers. Tell them I said to work out their settlement with legal and when our lawyers approve, so do I. They can use my conference room. Then call the war room. Ask them to locate Mr. Gray Tuttle. It won't be difficult. He's a very tall, very old man. I need to see him here right away."

CHAPTER 36

The day before a summer recess concludes is normally a busy workday on Capitol Hill. This year there were several summer recesses rather than one long one, the result being great consternation and frustration for all Senate staff. Julia Toussaint took it in stride. Legislative affairs, especially when you were one of the only professionals in a senator's office who could handle sensitive *political* matters, were the ultimate balancing act. Your portfolio was all encompassing. The trick was to recognize from the outset that you would never complete everything. Controllers and need-to-know-everything types rarely succeeded here. Flexibility and fortitude were requisite. The best of the breed were as unflappable as they were discreet. She thrived here.

This was the first time in Julia's memory that Tenley Harbison had ever returned to Washington before the Senate reconvened. That was unusual enough. But for days now she had been working out of her secret office in the Capitol building, not even showing up in her public office suite in the Rayburn Building. Julia and the senator's chief of staff were the only ones who knew, and both were sworn to secrecy about Tenley's physical presence on the Hill.

She was therefore unperturbed by, and certainly prepared for, the call to come over and visit.

As she threaded her way through the maze of corridors leading to the senator's unmarked private office door, Julia realized that this was the first time she had been in the big building since the day she and Rick had literally dodged the bullets. While pondering how many times she had used that figure of speech before the incident, she found herself surprised and slightly unsettled that the experience as yet had no lingering traumatic effect. Nonetheless, she was not at all accepting of the reports—she checked frequently—that there was no progress being made in the investigation. Security at the Capitol was especially tight and redundant. Maybe that was why the senator was hiding out here.

Tenley Harbison was alone when Julia arrived. She opened the door with a warm "I'm glad you're here," then sat down on the office's couch surrounded by piles of paper. The mess obviously had some organizational scheme not immediately apparent to Julia. "Grab that chair, J.D.," she said. Senators' secret offices, Julia observed, are not meant for conferences with staff.

"I read both of your background books on ViroSat," the senator began. "Then there were—what?—six batches of PDFs? The technical and legal files. First-rate work on a massively complex project. I'm ready."

"The researchers and the summer interns did the work, Tenley," Julia replied. "I just assembled it. I'll pass on your good words."

"That's not why I called you over. I want to tell you about some additional work I've been doing in advance of tomorrow's hearing. As a result, there's new tasking for you. How familiar are you with the ongoing Department of Justice investigation of Carneccio & Dice LLC?"

"If this is about my ex-husband—"

"No, not in the least. But I will need your complete circumspection on this one. What I'm going to say may not go beyond you and me for now. I would not even be able to share the information with you if it didn't require drafting legislation before I convene the hearing."

"I understand."

"Good. J.D., I had to exercise some long-dormant federal prosecutor chops for this. I admit that it felt pretty good. An associate attorney general and I have been joined at the hip for a week hammering out the details. The gist of the matter is that all of the indictments against Lois Carneccio are going to be dismissed because of some leeway we have in the new federal whistleblower statutes. Charges against the remaining persons from her old firm will remain. Needless to say, this is going to make news. Ms. Carneccio and her counsel are signing documents at the US Attorney's office right now."

"Why would the government allow that?" Julia asked.

"She provided the Justice Department's civil division with volumes of information about Compton Sizemore and the intimacies of its financing for ViroSat. As you pointed out in the background information here, the financing involves equity ownership by a limited partnership. That limited partnership includes the Financial Systems and Services Corporation. So there is prevailing federal jurisdiction over ViroSat."

Julia was skeptical. She was supposed to be. That was her role here. "Did Justice provide an opinion to that effect?" She took notes furiously.

"Not exactly. Because FSSC is a public-private entity, one of a kind, the AAG calls it a massive gray area. That's where you come in. I need to have you draft legislation to the effect that if there's any FSSC ownership or option in any kind of business, then the economic interest belongs to the government of the United States, with complete federal oversight and control. This is an easy one for you. Follow what we wrote in the banking legislation when we did the bailout. Then look at what we did in Dodd-Frank. Only make it stronger."

"Justice suggested that new legislation is required?"

"Not required but highly desired. Justice is certain that the federal case is strong as long as there is FSSC ownership of any part of ViroSat. But Compton Sizemore will litigate it forever and they can afford to. Justice thinks that they'll eventually lose, but nothing is ever certain in civil court. The legislation that you'll write and that I'll introduce tomorrow will forestall any litigation. We move first. Get out in front of Compton Sizemore. ViroSat is too big and too important for the network to remain a private asset. The system is awesome—you said so yourself in the briefing book. It has effectively become a global common resource. Proper ownership and management must now devolve to the public good, not to a base profit motive."

"You'll be announcing this at tomorrow's hearing."

Tenley Harbison smiled. "I like that about you, J.D. We think along the same lines. The simple fact of federal involvement in ViroSat would not particularly draw anyone's attention. So I will also be publicizing some more . . . compelling information, already cleared for release by the associate attorney general."

"Do I get to know?"

"I don't see why not. Ms. Carneccio has provided evidence that convinced the Department of Justice—and me—that ViroSat's partnership deal is incapable of closing. The Wall Street boys don't have the money. J.D., our way is now the *only* way to do the deal. And Compton Sizemore doesn't know it. Yet."

Rick Yeager sat in the car, engine idling and air conditioner on full blast, as he watched the Bombardier jet swing wide, brake, and lurch to a stop. Warren Hunter bounded down the stairs as soon as they emerged from the aircraft, disappeared briefly into the Signature Flight Support building, and emerged at its entrance.

"They'll send my bag downtown," he said as he slammed the passenger-side door. "This time I have the full-blown entourage. Hey, this M3 used to be an incredibly sweet ride. About time for an upgrade, don't you think?"

"Spoken like a man who never budgets anymore," Rick responded, making clear that he neither appreciated the comment nor the fact that he was obliged to point out to his brother the ever wider gulf in their financial circumstances.

"Easy," Warren said as they looped around the wide turn to exit the Dulles Airport complex and sped up. "I meant it as a way of saying 'this too shall pass.'"

"Will it?" Rick asked, not really wanting to hear an answer.

"Yeah. It will. Once ViroSat closes. With what you found, I now have it all nailed down. I owe you a lot. You and Julia."

Rick wasn't in the mood for his gratitude. "Have you considered for a minute," he said sullenly, "that your deal has become Pop's legacy?"

"I've thought about not much else."

"So why did you want me to pick you up?"

"I needed to ask you something, privately. Just you."

"Go on."

"When Dutch died you were trying to talk to him."

Rick shot a puzzled look at his brother.

"You told him he had nothing to apologize for," Warren continued.

"Yeah. He was trying to say he was sorry, in German. *Es tut mir leid.*"

"I don't think that's what he said."

"Warren, your German sucks. I'm rusty but I'm fluent."

"No. It's what *you* said. You were frustrated—just like you are now. You asked him what he was saying and then you said—"

"—*Es tut mir leid.* Right. Where are you going with this?"

"What did *Pop* say? Rick, this is important. I remember it differently from you."

"He was talking in half words, in German. *Vereinig* instead of *Vereinigten* for 'United.' United States. *Alleschan,* which we figured out meant 'Alexandria.' Then he said *Tut—Tut—*" Rick pronounced the German word correctly and precisely, *toot.*

"Wrong," Warren said. "*That's* the difference I meant. Pop said 'Tut—' Like King Tut." *Tuht.*

Rick thought hard. He was silent as he cruised down the highway, accelerating to his exit. "I believe you're right," he said quietly.

"And then he said—"

"*Er weiss wer aber nicht wo.* He knows who but not where."

"Right. What you said."

"Tut. Tuttle." Rick's mind raced.

"Pop was talking about now, not in the war."

"They were looking for Stauber in the death camp."

"Did Pop ever say anything to you about what happened there?

"No. He never would."

"I need to know, Rick."

"*You* need to know? There are two of us." He pulled into the parking area of the GT3 campus in Chantilly.

"I'm ready," Warren said as he stepped out of the car. "You're coming tomorrow, aren't you?"

He glared at Warren and said nothing. Warren slammed the car door and walked confidently to the glass doors of the GT3 headquarters building.

It had been years since he had been this angry. Rick banged the steering wheel hard with the flattened palms of both hands as he drove away. Keep it in check, he told himself. Don't take it out on the road.

His mobile phone rang. He grabbed it from the center console and looked down at a name he hadn't seen in weeks. LOIS CARNECCIO—MOBILE. She always had terrific timing.

He answered the call.

The Tuttles, father and son, were waiting for him when Warren Hunter strode into the CEO's suite at GT3.

Sanford Tuttle beamed. "It didn't take our folks in the bunker forty-eight hours," he said, "after your brother sent these over." He patted the stack of ancient IBM computer paper sitting on his broad desk. Dutch's *MAN HAN* annotation faced him. "Everyone who walks in here wants to know what the heck I'm doing with these. No one working here under the age of forty has ever even seen anything like them. We're a young company in more ways than one, Warren. These kids have heard about the way we used to program and share data, but these printouts? They're like an extinct beast that's come back to life. I'm told that while I've been out they had some field trips arranged to come by and take a look."

"You haven't indicated what they are, have you?" Warren asked. The tone of his voice was light but Sanford Tuttle knew he was dead serious.

"Nope. All secure. Our success was as remarkable as the results. Here." He handed Warren a thin bound report of a dozen pages and a small stick—a computer jump drive with the GT3 logo emblazoned on its case.

The silver GT3 also appeared on the report's cover alongside the green-and-white FSSC logo—exactly the same size—with the words *Account Location* and *Control: Copy 1 of 2, Mr. Hunter.*

"Where were they?" Warren asked.

"Forty-six states, the District of Columbia, the Virgin Islands, and Guam. It's all in there. I asked the FSSC chief economist how much un-claimed capital there is in the United States. Don't worry, I didn't tell him why I wanted to know. He said that all estimates are imprecise, but I finally pinned him down. You're looking at something like twenty or thirty per-cent of it right there."

"And the total?"

"Three hundred and twelve billion," said Gray Tuttle. He was stone-faced, but obviously immensely pleased. "How long are the electronic fund transfers going to take?"

Warren flipped through the report, assessing. "Once we begin the closing, about an hour and a half. No more than two. We can accomplish the transfers and the capital aggregation with incredible speed. We do this sort of thing as a matter of course at Compton Sizemore. Sandy, this is amazing work. You've produced one valuable document."

"It was a team effort. A family project."

Warren looked at Graham Tuttle. "One that you've been working on longer than any of us, Gray. You don't mind if we pick up where we left off the last time we met here, do you?"

The old man didn't blink but he may as well have. Spy or not, Warren had just caught him off guard. Graham Tuttle did not respond.

"There was a reason you were so eager to go into Bergen-Belsen," he said. "You were looking for a Jewish merchant banker named Alois Stauber."

Gray Tuttle stared at him. "That was a reason. But not the only reason. We had very clear orders. We had a mission."

"What you did not have was a German translator. Not before you took Dutch Yeager along."

"Warren, I told you about that. In a long and tough life that I've spent in our nation's service, that is one episode I do not revisit. You could never understand what we went through on that night."

"Help me to understand, Gray. Right now you owe me, and I think I can handle it."

The elder Tuttle considered him carefully and then nodded almost imperceptibly. "I found Stauber," he said simply.

"But you didn't find his accounts."

"No. He was barely alive and had typhus. All he had were the clothes on his back, a shirt and trousers covered in his own excrement."

"What happened to my father?" Warren demanded.

Tuttle's face was drawn. He had less of a frown than an expression of final acquiescence.

"A son," he said, "has the right to know. We had plans for the Meier Seckendorf Böhmer money."

"We did?"

Gray Tuttle did not acknowledge Warren's interruption, but continued. "The OSS and Army intelligence had reports beginning in the summer of 1944 from the camps the Soviet forces overran and liberated on the eastern front. In the intelligence community at least, we already knew something about the precise horrors with which we were going to be dealing. We thought that we understood the effect that going in there had on infantrymen. What the Soviets never expected, and neither did our commanders, was that soldiers, once they saw what the Germans had done to those people in the camps, would just start shooting them on the spot. I heard a rumor about something that supposedly happened in Auschwitz the previous January. Two sergeants in the Soviet infantry collected German sidearms, checked that they were loaded, then handed them out to the Jewish internees who survived. Then they encouraged them to execute their own captors. The incident never appeared in any classified intelligence report. I remembered it, though."

Warren felt the uneasiness swarming into his head and stomach.

Tuttle went on. "We had to get Stauber out of there alive. That was the overriding imperative, in military terms. If we had him we had a fair chance of locating the accounts back in the States. Without him, they would be lost. So I improvised. It's what I do. Stauber and I talked for a while—his English was excellent, which is how I found him—and right then and there, in the goddamned cold and mud in the middle of the night at Belsen, he and I agreed on a plan. He was a brilliant man, but he wasn't a military man. I thought I could rely on his word. I was to hand him my service revolver like the Soviets did at Auschwitz. He was supposed to point it at the German guards. I would grab it back and then arrest him. It was all theater. Scare the shit out of the Germans. Show them some cruelty. Stop it before anybody got hurt. I thought about unloading the piece first, but then why the hell would I give him an unloaded gun? Any deception has to be credible—that's the first rule of tradecraft. For being invented on the spot, it was a fair to good plan—the only possible way I could think of to extract *this one exact prisoner* out of that camp on that very first day the Brits liberated it. We weren't in charge. Some English colonel was."

"Your plan didn't work," Warren said. It was a disembodied voice that sounded like his own.

"I never thought that you had a capacity for understatement, son. You're exactly right. Instead of just waving my gun around, Stauber immediately started shooting German officers. I fucked up—the worst error in judgment in my whole career. I was young."

"What happened to my father?" Warren repeated, his mouth dry. He was inhaling shallow breaths.

"That's the hardest part for me and you," Gray Tuttle said kindly. "Dutch had his service weapon out by the time Stauber got off the third shot. The whole camp was running in our direction—it was chaos in Hell and I caused it. That's when Stauber decided he should shoot your father. Dutch never had a choice, Warren. The guy had just blown the skull off a German with my gun when he turned, intending to shoot your old man."

"My father—"

"Emptied a seven-round forty-five clip into Alois Stauber from about three yards away. Every shot hit. Stauber and the two Germans he killed were buried at Bergen-Belsen that morning. Dutch was in terrible shape after it happened. I got him back to England. Warren, he not only saved my life, he saved my ass."

"I'm going to assume that there was never an intelligence report."

"Please. Not to be unkind, but it was war—the end of the very worst kind of war at that. You have no idea what we buried in those last few weeks before VE day."

"Buried deep," Warren said.

"Yeah."

Warren Hunter stood. Sanford Tuttle, expressionless and clearly discomfited, stared at both of them. Graham Tuttle rose and offered a firm hand, which Warren took.

"All true?"

"Every word."

"But not quite complete."

"It was."

"Except for the old pronoun deception, Gray. I do it myself all the time. We had to get Stauber out of there alive. We had plans for the Meier Seckendorf Böhmer money. You wanted me to assume that by we you meant the OSS, predecessor to your beloved CIA. But it wasn't the OSS or Eighth Air Force intelligence that wanted Stauber's accounts."

"It was—"

"—Chester Alan Tuttle at Manufacturers Trust."

Warren turned to leave the office, grabbing his *Account Location* report and jump drive. "You got my car waiting?" he asked Sanford Tuttle.

After he left, Graham Tuttle put a hand on his son's shoulder. This was as much a gesture of affection as the old man had shown him since Sandy reached adolescence, and the younger man took it as great comfort. "Some of that," he said, "I sincerely regret that you had to hear. Most of it I'm glad you know, especially now. You've just gained a much clearer perspective."

"Did he need to hear all that?"

"Yes."

"And now?"

"Tell me something. Hunter spoke about his electronic funds transfer capabilities at Compton Sizemore. With all of your computing power, do you have the same capacity here at GT3?"

"No, not right here, but Terragreen certainly does. In the international banking system they can do anything in the bunker that Wall Street can do, and more. Faster, too. We built all of the systems, but they are housed over there." Sanford Tuttle smiled. "We can do it, Dad."

"Good." In a single syllable he expressed what a very proud father he was. "That's what I wanted to hear."

Ten minutes later he was walking to his car parked in the most heavily wooded section of the lot that GT3 shared with Terragreen. He had selected his parking space with care. As an invitee of the FSSC security assessment team he meticulously reviewed the video of Jonas Barr's disappearance from this lot. Graham Tuttle therefore knew exactly where the blind spots were. There were only two places where GT3's security cameras didn't cover or overlap. He was parked in the center of one of them.

He had backed in when he arrived for the meeting with Warren Hunter. Now he unlocked the car, sat down, turned the ignition, and lowered the driver's side window.

A Buick LaCrosse was on his left, parked the correct way. Its driver's side window was also down. Gray Tuttle didn't turn his head.

"Our timing," he said, "is now the critical factor. Hunter has to be first. Wait until after the hearing. That gives you two days before the deal closes."

"I won't need that long," Horvath replied. "He'll never leave Washington."

This meeting with Detective Paul Dolbeare was almost pleasant. Rick Yeager had calmed down. It helped that they were meeting in the small conference room of Ter Horst's Arlington law office and not at the Fairfax homicide squad. This will be pretty much a wrap-up, the judge had said. Rick had taken to calling him "Judge" in direct address. Ter Horst did not object.

Today he was late. The detective began without him.

"The best I could do," Dolbeare explained, "was to have Mrs. Geller's death categorized as 'accidental, possibly undetermined.' There is not enough evidence to open a homicide investigation. We don't have a body. There was no autopsy performed because of the initial medical examiner's ruling of accidental death. In Virginia every unattended death has to be investigated, but no autopsy is required unless there is a preliminary determination that it was caused by something other than an accident or from natural causes. Finally, the crash occurred outside of my jurisdiction. If it was me investigating and I'd made the call, I wouldn't recommend to have this one reopened either. Because the crash happened on the George Washington Parkway, the National Park Service Police are in charge. They'll keep a file open as a courtesy to the judge and me. But that's all we can do."

"She deserves better," Rick said. "I hope we find her."

"The Park Service Police agrees with you. I found out that it is not a federal crime to claim a body under false pretenses. Who knew? The disappearance of her remains is, however, something of a major embarrassment for them."

"What about Lauren Barr?"

"Still a Jane Doe. Still an active, open case. And that one *is* mine. I've entered all of her information into the usual law enforcement databases. We included a decent picture of her face all cleaned-up in the morgue. That sometimes helps. But we've got nothing. You and the judge should expect that avenue to be a dead end. There's no doubt that her murder and Hannah Geller's death are related. Proving it, however, is going to be an entirely different matter."

"Tears in the ocean," Rick said.

"Huh?"

Dan Ter Horst arrived before Rick could explain. They both slid their chairs back to stand but the judge motioned for them to stay seated.

"Apologies all around, gentlemen, but you need to hear this. Rick, I misspoke. We're not wrapping up. Paul, I wish you had been with me, I could have used the help.

"I've just returned from the District. The Metropolitan DC Police have the heretofore elusive Jonas Barr in custody. They're holding him on the Fairfax County material witness warrant you drew up. His real name is Yonah Bar-Ilan. He was picked up half a block from the Israeli Embassy in upper Northwest. He ran for the gate and two of DC's finest tackled him. He doesn't look too good. Mr. Barr or Bar-Ilan has stated that he's working for Mossad and is claiming diplomatic immunity. The Israelis aren't buying it—they want nothing to do with him. He's all on his own and right now he's screaming and furious. State, Defense, Homeland Security, Director of National Intelligence, heck, they're all involved.

"When he was arrested he had this in his pocket." Ter Horst showed them a photograph on his mobile phone of a jump drive with a familiar logo: GT3.

CHAPTER 37

The interns that invade Washington every summer are eager, unself-conscious, and intense. Above all else they are intent upon impressing grown-ups. An element of this primal motivation, well honed in the academic environment, is how they notice generational differences in the way people work. The interns like to remark upon these differences. One of the most prominent (which in their inexperience they never notice is geographical rather than generational) is the manner in which the nation's capital consumes printed newspapers. The interns find this characteristic particularly quaint and remarkable. "What's it like," they inquire annoyingly for the sake of conversational opening, "to read three or four newspapers a day *on paper*?"

ViroSat had been a running story in print and online for weeks. With a strong hidden hand, Compton Sizemore's media group ensured that the public understood two major facts about the deal.

One, ViroSat was a difficult financial transaction with higher mathematics involved. It was therefore too involved for short attention span politicians or their enablers, the "party strategists," to take purchase upon. Complexity is always the enemy of scrutiny in public policy. Therefore the illusion of its presence here was essential. Warren Hunter, Compton Sizemore, and Wall Street in general did not desire additional attention for ViroSat. This message was well received.

Two, ViroSat was great for the country and the international economy. Since Wall Street has arrived in Washington, Main Street could trust the C-suite. This message was less well received.

On the morning of the ViroSat hearings at the United States Senate Subcommittee on Communications, Technology, and the Internet, both of these themes were resonant in the newspaper coverage. The media group was able to claim success, two days before the deal's scheduled closing.

Warren Hunter had mixed feelings about his photograph appearing in the *Washington Post*. The ViroSat hearing did not even make page one, which was good, but the news story on page four was far more probative than he would have preferred. That development was less good. The personal focus, including today's hearing, was one he desired to avoid. Despite his recent run of celebrity on the Street, people who knew who Warren Hunter *was* for the most part did not know what Warren Hunter *looked like*. The *Time* profile and now this in the *Post*—a flattering shot, he observed—meant that his picture would be available all over the Web. There was also the national column on page two by a guy Warren knew slightly at Princeton who *did* know math and was unafraid of it. The gist of his piece: "The interconnectedness of ViroSat's financial arrangements amounts to a new risk vista, terra incognita for debt lending at a time when our international economy can afford it least." Warren hoped that the idea would not catch on, but rationalized that it was not worth agonizing over. He had a decent answer prepared if—no, when—he would be asked about the column at today's hearing.

The ViroSat story that did make page one, the lead in large font on both the *New York Times* and *Washington Post* Web sites, was one that no media new or old could have ignored. Two previously unrelated public interest threads were creatively joined.

The first thread was the so-called "public financing" of ViroSat through a previously little-known federally funded public-private joint venture called the Financial Systems and Services Corporation. The second concerned the Carneccio & Dice indictments and how the firm's founding principal, Lois Carneccio, had provided the Justice Department with detailed information about ViroSat's financing through FSSC. DOJ's civil division was appropriately looking into all matters ViroSat. The criminal division, ominously, would be kept apprised. The Department of the Treasury—FSSC's sponsor—and the White House had both declined comment.

Warren studied this news carefully in the copies of the *Times* and the

Post delivered to his hotel room, then spent another fifteen minutes on-line following the story around the Internet. Most of what was presented as fact was entirely and provably wrong, deeply distorted to Ms. Carneccio's advantage, or simple circumstance plus speculation equaling alternate reality.

An accompanying article mostly about Lois Carneccio began on the front page of the *Post*, with a cut to the page where Warren's picture appeared. Indictments against her, it said, had been dropped because of previously undisclosed information that she was a federal whistleblower—the clear implication being that she harbored genuinely good motives throughout.

The article about Lois included a paragraph that caused the knot in Warren's chest to tighten, his familiar low-level headache to commence far too early in the day, and the muscles in his upper back to spasm.

Arrested along with Carneccio in the July 1 federal raid on Carneccio & Dice was Richard M. Yeager, 41, a partner of the firm and brother of ViroSat financier Warren Hunter. Yeager provides the critical link of Carneccio & Dice to investment banking giant Compton Sizemore and ViroSat, according to a source at the Department of Justice who requested anonymity because he was not authorized to speak on the matter pending new court filings. Numerous additional money laundering charges "are certainly part of the equation," the source said, adding that it is too soon to speculate on whether any of the laundered funds are or ever were part of any ViroSat's international debt financing that might have been arranged by Yeager. Reached yesterday, Yeager confirmed that following his arrest he was the only partner or employee of the firm who was never charged in the Carneccio & Dice frauds. When confronted with information provided by Carneccio to Justice, he also confirmed that his team of defense criminal attorneys was retained by his brother, deputy chief of investment and merchant banking at Compton Sizemore, the man who stands to gain the most from the ViroSat deal.

Deep in the Washington paper Warren missed the small story about the arrest yesterday in the District of Columbia of an Israeli citizen named Yonah Bar-Ilan. A State Department spokesperson would say only that charges of industrial espionage were pending under the Arms Export Control Act and the Economic Espionage Act.

Rick Yeager arrived late at the hearing. The line into the Hart Senate Office Building for security checks and metal detectors took an additional half hour. "It's my fault," he said to the puzzled looks of the two women standing in line behind him, who did not ask him for an explanation. When he stepped into the big hearing room the theater had already begun with the boring part well underway. Most of the senators' places were empty behind nameplates identifying the members. The chair, Senator Harbison, was in place at the center, apparently preoccupied while one of her colleagues, a thin and immensely self-important man whom Rick vaguely recognized as a new senator from the Pacific Northwest, read a lengthy speech in sonorous monotone. He counted four senators plus Harbison in their chairs at the hearing dais. Behind them sat a group of earnest young legislative staffers. Rick knew that Julia would not be among them, but that at least one or two of them up there were working for her.

Warren Hunter was alone at the witness table. A gaggle of photographers dressed marginally better than street people occupied the floor space separating him from the senators. Warren rested his chin in his left hand with the most respectfully attentive look Rick had ever seen on his face. He occasionally nodded and jotted a note on the pad in front of him on the table.

The front row of spectators, Rick saw, was filled with Compton Sizemore staff, lawyers, and lobbyists. He took a seat and was forming a poetic image of his brother out in front of a band of—what would you call them?—when Julia slid into the seat next to him.

"I saw you walk in," she whispered, very close.

"Come here often?" he asked, smiling.

"Hmmph. Rick, I *never* attend a hearing. This is unusual for me or for

any legislative director. I practically had to ask somebody for directions
how to find this place. Watch her reaction. Tenley will be shocked when
she sees me here."

"This is very important to her, isn't it?"

"You have no idea."

"How well do you think Warren is doing holding his own?"

"A better question is, will he be able to survive up there?"

"J.D., what do you know?"

"It's over, Rick. I did everything I could."

Senator Harbison pulled the microphone forward. "The chair thanks
the gentleman from Oregon for his timely and penetrating remarks and
takes particular note of his concern for lack of rural infrastructure by-
passed in the ViroSat networks. If our vaunted 'Internet Next' can indeed bring advanced broadband capabilities to the most remote places
on the globe as Mr. Hunter maintained in his opening statement, why
not to the most remote places in our country? I think that's as good a
place as any to begin our inquiry."

"Madame Chair," Warren Hunter began, speaking slowly and referring to a dense page of word-processed notes, "I'd be pleased to address
ViroSat's capabilities in this regard. The senator from Oregon is correct.
I sincerely appreciate the opportunity to address the issue. We have focused more on the international dimensions of ViroSat than on its organic national infrastructure. That's for two reasons. Number one, the
enterprise companies—those are the operating companies that together
make up most of what we shorthand as 'ViroSat'—are almost all tiered
multinationals. ViroSat is truly the rise of the multinationals, senator. By
beginning our growth profile with the international component, we will
be able to significantly reduce long-term costs in America, far below the
level of investment currently required for the initialization of this system. In short, this way we'll be able to build it here faster and cheaper.
Number two, the initial cost of capital for eventual American infrastructure improvements will be far less, because most of our financing is and
will be from overseas debt sources. That's better for everyone concerned

because it spreads the non-systemic risk of ViroSat-based commerce, which I think all of us can agree is a most desirable outcome. It's certainly beneficial for the international banking system."

"Wow," Julia whispered to Rick.

"Impressed?"

"Oh, yeah. Your brother is mind numbing. He has hearing-speak down pat. He had to be prepped by someone who knew what she was doing. Even I don't know what he said. No one could possibly be paying attention." All congressional staff members are to some degree cynics, Julia less than most.

"It would appear as though that's exactly his plan."

"He's a natural, especially when you consider that this is his first Senate testimony ever. And I don't mean that as a compliment." Julia smiled.

"Warren plays any role required to get whatever he wants, J.D. That should not exactly be news to you."

"Tenley won't allow it."

A few people in the audience stood up to leave the hearing room.

"I think that's a great place to begin," Senator Harbison said.

"Excuse me, Madame Chair?"

"You said that most of your financing comes from overseas debt sources."

"That's correct."

"Mr. Hunter, I am interested in that part of ViroSat's financing that does not come from international debt. The other twenty-one percent of your transaction. Two hundred eighty-seven point seven billion dollars at your closing valuation on August first—two days from today."

"If the Chair will permit me—"

"Not yet, Mr. Hunter. Let's walk through this ViroSat financing structure a bit more carefully first, shall we?"

"I'd be . . . pleased to do so," Warren said.

"Simplify a few things for me. I didn't go to the Harvard Business School like you did, and I don't know a heck of a lot about capital finance, so educate me. Debt is when you *loan* money to a company and equity means that you actually *own* a company, right?"

"Yes, senator."

"First let's talk about the debt. On Wall Street you call that leverage, right?"

"Right."

"You said in your opening statement . . ." Tenley Harbison read from her handwritten notes "'. . . ViroSat is backed by national contributions in the form of low-interest or interest-free long-term debt and by commercial bonds, therefore distributing rather than concentrating risk.' Correct?"

"Correct."

"But that's not all the money you need for ViroSat, is it?"

"No, senator, the additional—"

"The additional money comes from a limited partnership. So again, help me understand. Does that limited partnership then *own* ViroSat?"

"The limited partnership holds certain equity interest in ViroSat, senator. Yes."

"And by 'equity interest,' you mean ownership. Have I still got all of this high finance right?"

"Yes, senator, as long as ViroSat is—"

"Hold on, Mr. Hunter. So the limited partnership really *owns* ViroSat. We've just established that. My question to you is this: Who owns the limited partnership?"

Tenley Harbison had been a fearsome cross-examiner during her life as a prosecutor. Warren had not expected that this question would be put to him so directly, but he was prepared.

"Madame Chair, the limited partnership is—and I do not mean to sound disrespectful here—owned by its limited partners, just like every partnership we've ever established at Compton Sizemore. By law and as required by contract, before the transaction concludes and is announced, we are simply unable to disclose the composition of our limited partnership arrangements. The easiest way to think of the limited partners is as investors, but investors who are taking on more risk than the countries and the banks providing the project's international debt." Warren shifted in his seat.

"Okay. Hypothetically, then. In a partnership like this one, would *every* limited partner have to put up cash in the same proportion as his ownership percentage?"

"I'm not sure that I follow your question, senator."

"If I wanted to own a piece of the ViroSat limited partnership—let's say fifty percent of it—would I have to bring half of the partnership cash to the table?"

"Not necessarily, senator."

"So you're telling me that the proportion of ownership in ViroSat is not the same as the proportion of money that the owners invest in ViroSat?"

"No, senator, I did not—"

"Hypothetically, Mr. Hunter. Those foreigners who gave you the debt, they don't own any of the project, do they?"

"Most of them are going to get a return on their investment and all of them will have the benefit of an advanced next-generation network system," Warren began.

"No, let's stay with ownership," Senator Harbison said. "We're still talking hypothetically. You're not sworn here, Mr. Hunter. Speculate for me. If the money for ViroSat was provided by the United States government, don't you think that the United States government should own ViroSat?"

"If that was the case, senator, yes. I'd probably agree with you."

"Well that is the case, isn't it, Mr. Hunter? The money for the equity—what you yourself said is the ownership of ViroSat—is all being provided by the United States Treasury, through a quasi-federal entity called the Financial Systems and Services Corporation or FSSC. A national resource."

"Compton Sizemore has a business relationship with FSSC, like every other investment bank in the country."

"But yours is unique."

Warren did not respond. Rick and Julia watched him closely. Rick saw his neck tighten, the muscles on the side of his jaw flex and release multiple times, and his breathing slow. He was furious. The self-control for which he was famous, the bulwark of his reputation as a financier, was crumbling. One of the Compton Sizemore people sitting immediately behind Warren leaned forward and whispered while reading from a BlackBerry in his palm. Warren nodded.

Senator Harbison continued. "You can tell me whether this information is right or wrong, Mr. Hunter, and please bear in mind that I may already know the answers. The announced date of ViroSat's closing is August first, two days from now, am I correct?"

"You are."

"Without your limited partnership equity, you simply don't get to use all of that international money—what you called in your opening statement 'the debt capital for our Internet Next.' Those debt agreements have some very specific requirements and covenants concerning that point. Ratios and stuff. Don't they?"

"Also correct."

"Did you, personally, visit FSSC recently and discuss that entity *owning* a limited partnership interest in ViroSat?"

"Yes."

"And you've already said that owning the limited partnership would mean owning ViroSat."

"Yes."

"Thank you, Mr. Hunter. You've been most helpful in walking me through these financing issues to get to this point." The senator briefly scanned the audience in the hearing room and smiled. Every eye was on her. The place was silent except for the occasional *clack* of a digital camera from the photographers' gaggle. "ViroSat has developed into a magnificent public resource backed by public funding. I'll leave the mechanics of higher finance to the experts like Mr. Hunter here. What all of us regardless of party can agree upon is that when the United States government pays for a company, or in this case, a broad network of companies, well, then the ownership and benefit deriving from that payment ought to go right to the people of this country. To that end, I will later today be introducing legislation amending that section of the United States Code governing the operations of the Financial Systems and Services Corporation. None of us in the Senate has any objection to the limited partnership arrangements that are the foundation of ViroSat. This legislation simply creates the statutory environment to ensure that when we the people pay for ViroSat, we will also own, control, regulate, and run ViroSat. We made the mistake in the banking crisis of investing without managing our investment. As a nation we simply won't do that again."

"I disagree, senator." Warren's ringing clear voice and courtesy only exaggerated his impertinence.

Tenley Harbison was momentarily nonplussed. She recovered quickly—he was not going to intrude upon her moment. "Your disagreement is noted, Mr. Hunter. I'm sure that you and your colleagues at Compton Sizemore will all make obscene bonuses for your work on ViroSat. You should consider that more than adequate compensation for a job well done. There is, however, one simple and incontrovertible fact. Your only equity partner in this venture is FSSC, in a limited partnership that's two days from closing."

"No, senator, it's not."

"You're admitting to me," she asked with genuine surprise and a measure of elation, "that you can't close the partnership? That you don't have the cash? That you haven't got the foundation on which your entire transaction rests?"

"Not at all," Warren said calmly. He glanced casually at his watch. "I'm enlightening you. FSSC is out of the transaction—uninvolved. Sometimes I close a deal early. Twenty minutes ago in Dubai, the final ViroSat partnership agreement was signed. We have aggregated three hundred and twelve billion dollars in cash, all in the bank. I'm the general partner. Senator, you were very interested in ownership. Now there's no reason to withhold that information. I control half the shares.

"The other half of ViroSat is owned by one of the world's oldest and most respected financial houses—the Hasab International Group."

CHAPTER 38

"You cut out FSSC? *You cut them out!*" Rick Yeager exclaimed to his brother. He was giddy, excited, and grinning broadly as he slammed closed the door to the Lincoln Town Car. The driver took off with them on Constitution Avenue, down the hill, speeding in the direction of Virginia and Dulles Airport.

"I never had any kind of agreement with FSSC," Warren replied. "I did let them assume a lot."

"You used their capabilities, and then you cut them out of the deal."

"I improvised. It's what I do. Like the senator said, FSSC is a national resource. I was simply a citizen availing myself of their services. Their supercomputers were critical to locating and recovering the Meier Seckendorf Böhmer accounts. They have to be angry in that bunker, but I doubt that there's going to be a whole lot of fallout."

"You don't think so?"

"No. Here's why. Even before my meeting at Terragreen it was apparent that Sandy Tuttle was calling the shots. First off, he's a contractor—he has no real role at FSSC. That got me thinking—why would Tuttle care so much about ViroSat? It was never his style to be that involved in specifics. I've done every one of the initial public offerings for his technology companies. Each time, we've had to drag him into the war room—he can't stand detail or finance. He's purely a big-picture thinker, which is his total strength. Now all of a sudden he's calling me, interested in minutiae about the partnership. At first I thought it was the size of this deal. Everybody wants a piece. Then he brought his father in. That's when I knew for sure. Sandy and Gray were running their own play."

"You never planned to let FSSC in the partnership."

"Nope."

"How long were you working on this?"

"Since Mohammed Hasab visited me in New York. That was the same week you came to see me and I told you about Pop's Alzheimer's."

"Wait a minute. His name is Mohammed?"

"Part of the Hasab family is Jewish, part of it is Muslim. That's not as uncommon as you might think in certain parts of the Middle East, at least according to Mohammed. He and I have known each other ever since we were litter mates together at JP Morgan. In the Hasab family, you always have to prove yourself somewhere else before you get a crack at running money for the family businesses. Only a few of the brothers and cousins make it. Mohammed is the best. He's Wharton and the University of Chicago, for crying out loud. He grew up in the Philly suburbs. He's culturally as American as we are. Now he's the wealth manager for the Emir of Dubai and about a hundred other billionaires in the Persian Gulf."

"He told you about the Meier Seckendorf Böhmer accounts."

"Uh-huh. Interestingly, he referred to them the same way that you did when you called me last week—the Egyptian accounts. The Hasab organization has been looking for them for more than sixty-five years."

"So when you and Mohammed Hasab started brainstorming, you didn't have any idea that Pop had already located them back in the 1970s."

"Well, no. I didn't. And Pop only got halfway there. Our original concept was simply to use FSSC to locate the accounts, see what was left of them, and then figure out what we wanted to do. Later on it was my idea to form the ViroSat partnership out of Compton Sizemore and to fund it using the Egyptian accounts. Everybody involved gets better returns that way."

"And if you hadn't located them? Or if you did and there wasn't enough left?"

Warren smiled wide. "You're right about the first part. Highest risk, highest gain. There was an *outstanding* chance that the whole deal could have cratered. Who knows? This deal was always going to be either financial nuclear fusion or financial weapons of mass destruction—I could have blown up the whole world. On the other hand, if we did find the cash, I was very certain that I'd be able to do this deal. Mohammed, you see, is a quant. An extraordinary one. He wrote this sophisticated probabilistic model that predicted a high and low value range for the Egyptian accounts that were likely to be scattered around unclaimed in the United States. The lowest number he gave me was around two hundred and eighty-five billion. How do you think we came up with two-eight-seven as the equity bogey for ViroSat? We started there. Man, I love it when a deal comes together."

"Warren, while you were planning all of this—"

"—Don't forget that I was also building up more than a hundred enterprise units and writing a ton of debt."

"Did you have any idea that Pop and Mrs. Geller had found each other?"

"Nope. Not until much later, when you got yourself involved. I still don't know how Lois Carneccio found out. She definitely knew about the accounts. That's why she hired you."

"Pop and Hannah Geller were trying to break them out just like you were."

"Rick, that's the beauty of what the two of them did. They set the whole scheme in motion for you and me. Nobody but you has any claim to the Egyptian accounts. I simply invested them for you."

"Up until now I followed you."

"The limited partnership shares. Didn't you hear me tell Senator Harbison that I controlled them? I do. The papers are drawn up in trust for you. You finally have some real wealth."

Rick felt immensely drained at that moment. The Town Car swung wide from the Beltway onto the Dulles Access Road around the highway construction. For a long moment neither of the brothers said a word.

Warren reached over and slapped Rick on the knee. "You figure out what it was that Pop and the old lady wanted to do with their money. For me, it's all about the deal."

Rick was still silent, staring ahead, thinking. "Go back to Sandy and his father," he finally said. "They knew, too."

"Yeah." Warren nodded. "There really are no secrets. The Hasabs weren't the only ones chasing that money for sixty-five years."

"You invited Graham Tuttle to New York."

"Sure I did. Making him part of the ViroSat team was how I controlled the information he received. He had people inside Compton Sizemore from the beginning. After I put it all together—Gray had been after the accounts since *his* father found out about them—I simply played to his expectations. I met with him privately to affirm how important the GT3 piece was. The irony is, I wasn't kidding. We had to have that supercomputer analysis to finish Dutch's work."

"That's why you had me give Sandy all of Pop's research."

"I took a major risk but a calculated one. Yeah."

"That old man has to be fuming," Rick said. "He's probably not the kind of guy you should lie to."

"He and Sandy will leave us alone. It's just a deal. People get angry. Then they get over it."

"Warren?"

"What?"

"This money caused Pop's problems, didn't it?"

"No," he said quietly. "No, it didn't. Listen. I need to tell you exactly what happened to Dutch at Bergen-Belsen."

Horvath sat in the sun sweating. Despite all of the hand-wringing publicity about airport security, he found that places like Dulles—big airports with many industrial operations—were the easiest to penetrate. That was true in Vienna when he was a young man and it was true here today. Vienna's airport was where *Allamvedelmi Osztaly* took the new state security men to train. As he waited, Horvath reminisced—surely a prerogative he was permitted at his age. Life was much simpler then. Life was much better now. Vienna was his first taste of the West—the drills, the practice dodging a tail, the following of instructors actively attempting to lose their trainees, and the ambushing. Much of it went on at the old airport, busy, bustling, rude, bearing the scars of war. Some of the training was positively pastoral, at least in his edited memory—dead drops at night in the garden at Schloss Shönbrunn or observation at the old Opera House and the coffee shops. Vienna was where he learned to wait. For Horvath it was an acquired skill. Then and now he had a pre-disposition to action.

He sat in the shade on a bench outside the flight support building, where the private airplanes landed. The residual communist in Horvath was appalled at the excesses of the jets. He thought of them as corporate pornography, vulgar. There were a lot of them here today, but they were all parked. None of them were moving. He wore dark green coveralls, a bright green vest stitched with reflective strips, and a gray baseball cap. No identifying markings. Clipped to his safety vest's left chest pocket was a pack of badges that he had easily lifted from a janitor in the main passenger terminal's men's room.

He studied each airplane, looking for the one belonging to Compton Sizemore.

There. The side number that Graham Tuttle had given him.

Most of tradecraft, his instructor said at the Vienna airport, is look-ing like you know what you are doing. You must appear to belong. Ordi-nary people doing ordinary things everyday do not get noticed. No one pays them attention. When you try too hard to look like you fit in, you don't. That's why this is an art. The instructor, Horvath heard, died young before the end of communism in Hungary. Pity, he thought. He was a good guy.

Horvath walked to the aircraft. He shifted the package in the thigh pocket of his coveralls. It held a loaded syringe. Like father, like son. *Csatlakozott* . . . joined. The generational connectedness appealed to Horvath's sense of order. Why did words like that just keep surfacing in his thoughts? He had to stop getting reflective like this, at least until the operation was over and Graham Tuttle had moved the money.

This time the chemical was potassium chloride in a medical concen-tration. It could be injected deep into any skeletal muscle. His plan was simple and incredibly bold. Hunter would be the first one on the plane— his partner was certain of that. This one always had to be first, always in charge, he said.

Horvath would be waiting, servicing the equipment.

He pulled down the stairs to the Bombardier. No one gave him a second look.

There was one tricky part. The injection had to be delivered in an inconspicuous place on the body. Horvath had used this method once before, on a Russian defector in Munich. He got a medal for that operation. The drug causes the heart to stop by disrupting the electrical signals that keep it beating. The autopsy always concludes that the man died of a heart attack—atrial fibrillation, it was called. The difficulty was picking a spot that the coroner would not notice. Today he planned to use Warren Hunter's calf.

Graham Tuttle liked the plan when Horvath ran it by him. Good method, he said. The banker is a complete stress case. A heart attack will be the most easy and casual conclusion, just like his father's stroke.

Horvath sat down and waited, controlling his breathing.

When the pilots showed up for their preflight inspection and cockpit checks, he stood and began moving around the cabin area, arranging things. They glanced at his badges and greeted him without a second look. Horvath only nodded silently in response.

Warren Hunter would collapse almost immediately once the potassium chloride hit. It stops the heart. Horvath would catch him as he fell, then yell, panic, and run out for help. That was exactly how he killed the Russian in the crowded lobby of the Hotel Vier Jahreszeiten in—when was it?—1962. He just ran out the front door and disappeared on the Maximillianstrasse. He couldn't run as fast now, but the tactic would certainly work here at Dulles.

The pilots were flipping switches and reading checklists. Horvath bent over to look out the small aircraft window, back at the arrival building. No sign of Warren Hunter yet. It wouldn't be a long wait. He turned his back to the cockpit and withdrew the syringe from his pocket.

"Are you okay?"

"I usually ask you that." Rick Yeager was reeling, lightheaded, and wavering between grief and rage at what had happened to Dutch decades ago. "How could he not tell us?"

"In his own way, he did."

"Tuttle caused it."

"So you feel less guilt about the way I cut him out of the deal."

"None at all." This was a strange emotion for Rick, and it made him realize how much like his brother he really was.

The Town Car pulled up to the passengers' entrance door at the private terminal.

"Good."

"Warren, could you have your team look into one more matter?"

"What?"

"Who is Yonah Bar-Ilan working for? The Israelis are denying that they ever heard of him. Who was Lauren Barr?"

"Good questions. What time is it in Dubai? I know exactly how to find out."

When Horvath caught sight of Warren Hunter, he was walking toward the Bombardier jet, mobile phone at his ear, talking with animation and hand gestures. He stepped into the cabin's tiny commode and waited, his back to the cockpit, holding the syringe. He was careful to extend the needle between his fingers. He flexed his hand around the rig a couple of times. His arthritis reminded him of his age. He would have to take some painkillers later.

Focus, he told himself. Have patience. *Türelemmel.*

He wondered for an instant if Warren Hunter believed in God. It was not such an unusual thought for a moment like this one. Horvath had an interest in such matters, especially concerning the subjects of operations. Functionally they made no difference to him, but he had formed an idea recently that if a believer met an unforeseen end, he might get what he expected. A good afterlife. If so, perhaps the same could be true for an atheist—he would get what he expected, which was nothing else. Nothing else was fine with Horvath. Maybe both were right. He shook off the thought. He was an atheist not only because that was how he was raised. He disdained the guilt and remorse that came with belief, none of which he found helpful. Hunter, he concluded, was probably a believer like his father and the lady in the car. He was not sure about the nervous guy in New York City.

Horvath was slightly envious of his target in only one regard. In about two minutes he would know all the answers.

The aircraft engines began to turn up in a deafening whine. It was time.

He watched as Warren Hunter shed his jacket and sat down, all while still on the phone, now shouting over the noise. Horvath moved forward with no effort to be unnoticed. This was not a time for stealth. In four steps he reached Warren's seat and bent down, deftly positioning the syringe at the back of his left leg.

If Warren had not actually been looking down at that instant, he would never have seen the movement of Horvath's hand and swiftly, instinctively shifted his leg. Once clear however, he momentarily froze. Horvath shoved him low in the seat, then jammed and twisted him into the cabin's bulkhead. Despite the difference in their ages, Horvath had tremendous advantages in strength, girth, and surprise. He pressed himself down on Warren hard, full-body, like a wrestler. He continued to push and roughly turned Warren—who was now attempting to yell. So Horvath slammed hard on his back with an elbow, knocking all the air out. This time he would not be deterred. He repositioned the syringe again at the back of Warren's calf.

Horvath already had the needle through the cloth of Hunter's trousers when he felt the gun pressed hard into the back of his head, at the soft spot below his right ear, angled up. He could not see it, but he could tell from the way it felt that it was a big rectangular model, probably one of the Glocks.

"Don't move!" the voice commanded.

Horvath smiled inwardly. He knew this scenario well. They practiced it at the advanced training he attended in the *Gödöllői-dombság*, up in the northern hills. The correct school solution in this circumstance had been drilled into him. The guy with the gun will never fire. He thinks that he can but he cannot. He is too close. His humanity, the heavy anchor of his emotions, and the intimacy of direct physical contact all conspire to prevent him from pulling the trigger. He may believe himself to be in control. He is wrong. You are. You must continue the operation, always. The worst that could happen now, Horvath reasoned in this fervent instant, was that he would be compelled to surrender. So they would catch a crazy old man. Okay. He'd been in prison before.

He shoved the needle deep into Warren Hunter's calf and pushed the plunger hard.

Skip Darlington blew off his head.

CHAPTER 39

From 9 A.M. until noon the following morning a lengthy and quite heated meeting took place in the big conference room at Terragreen. Its participants and observers (most of whom were lawyers) would later describe the atmosphere and interaction there as "toxic," "horrific," and "violent." All manner of legal options possibly available to the Financial Systems and Services Corporation were explored. Frustration reached a zenith after the second hour. There was apparently no acceptable cause of action for litigation against Compton Sizemore, any of the ViroSat entities, Warren Hunter, or the Hasab International Group. Moreover, there was a bigger hurdle. The legislation that created FSSC in its original incarnation required, quite literally, an act of Congress before the corporation could initiate any lawsuit "in any way involving" any banking institution. Much discussion ensued on this point, with FSSC's attorneys several times shouting at each other. The definitions and interpretations of "involving" and "banking institution" were carefully parsed.

The three congressionally appointed directors of FSSC left the meeting during this skirmish and did not return.

The meeting only began to wind down when the CEO of the corporation declared, "If our own attorneys can't even convince each other and us that they have some kind of case, how could any of you ever convince a judge? This matter is *over.*"

Subsequent to this declaration, the attorneys did agree that there might indeed be a "colorable claim" against GT3 and Sanford Tuttle for his deception, and that they could certainly work together in that direction.

* * *

The stock prices of four publicly traded information technology companies including QUATECH Corporation (Nasdaq: QTCH) were off an aggregate mean of 11.42 percent despite solid market gains that day in the Dow Jones, S&P 500, FTSE 100, and Nikkei 225 indices. The analysts following the companies attributed such stunning losses to the *Wall Street Journal* article, carefully and anonymously sourced by the Compton Sizemore media group, that GT3, a private company wholly owned by the founder and majority shareholder of the four firms, had been behind an attempt at derailing ViroSat.

Sanford Tuttle was observed throughout the day sitting quietly at his desk. His principal activity seemed to be staring out his window at the verdant campus. Occasionally he checked the computer screen. At about 3 P.M. he emerged and handed his assistant a seven-inch-thick stack of ancient IBM computer printouts.

"Please shred this," he said, and departed for the day.

He was not seen at the Tower Club for four months.

The war room at Compton Sizemore in the Citigroup Center was in a frenzy. The deal census headcount stood at two hundred and forty-four that morning. This high number was unauthorized by August Compton or any managing director but judged necessary by the group directors at the daily deal conference. There was barely enough room to accommodate the crowd.

At 3 A.M., corresponding to 8 A.M. in London and 9 A.M. in Frankfurt, billions in ViroSat debt began closing and transferring. Closings in the twenty-first century are in almost all cases accomplished electronically, especially when movements of capital in this magnitude are involved. Compton Sizemore's contracts for the debt had all included a carefully crafted clause requiring such movement of capital as soon as equity closed. Yesterday's stunning news from Dubai and Washington about the ViroSat limited partnership triggered the clause, thus earning the investment bank another two point four billion in interest for the extra day.

On the bond markets, where much of the ViroSat debt would be offered for sale, demand for the new debt was strong everywhere, keeping the makeshift trading floor in the war room in constant motion. Prices for the new issues were solidly up. They increased throughout the trading day. This level of activity continued unabated for thirty hours, to accommodate all of the international bond markets, where these results were consistently repeated.

The final number of ViroSat enterprise companies—still called "enterprise units" inside Compton Sizemore—stood at one hundred and sixty. Thirty-seven of them were already being publicly traded on various exchanges throughout the world. It was early evening before the research group was able to provide the first analysis of their performance. A median gain of 12.3 percent was reported, with not one enterprise company posting a loss. "Futures trading," the spot-analysis read, "indicates solid and positive gains into the foreseeable future." This sentence caused the ViroSat equity group director to make a remark about the "department of redundancy department."

Humor was acceptable in the war room on that day.

For the remaining nonpublic enterprise companies, the capital structures group in the war room (the core of which was Warren Hunter's original team) began to reformulate corporate valuations, the determinations of what the companies were worth to investors. As a result of the early closing and surging demand for ViroSat-related issues in hedged portfolios, these valuations increased substantially. The research group later estimated that the propitious launch of the financing was worth another 30 to 35 percent increase in value to Compton Sizemore when these companies were harvested.

It took fourteen hours for the bond closings to conclude, with not one failed closing among all of them.

In retrospect, the only embarrassment of the day (it was very slight) was the heated overuse in all media of the phrase "first trillion-dollar deal," even though in reality ViroSat was an aggregate *series* of many deals. This detail was consistently misspoken.

In the public consciousness, it was one big deal.

*   *   *

At Fairfax County Police Department Headquarters, Detective LaShauna Kent, both the youngest detective and the only African-American woman in the homicide division, took a telephone call from San Francisco, California.

The caller identified himself as a lieutenant in the investigations division at the San Francisco Police Department based at the Mission Station. He asked if Detective Kent would mind if he put her on speakerphone. He had with him one of his detectives and two citizens that he would like to include in their conversation.

He was calling in reference to the recent database entry about a Jane Doe also known as Lauren Barr.

The citizens were named Debra Lund and David Matthias, respectively the mother and stepfather of a thirty-two-year-old woman named Lauren Lund. They had reported the younger Ms. Lund missing three days ago. She had never before neglected to maintain contact with her mother no matter what she did or how much she traveled.

The San Francisco lieutenant spoke compassionately, relating to the Fairfax detective their story. Lauren Lund was a theater and drama major at Berkeley when she first visited Israel. What began with a pleasant summer on a kibbutz continued for six years before Lauren returned to the United States with Israeli citizenship. Since then she had lived and worked both in the Washington area and in Tel Aviv.

She was not married. She had no significant romantic relationship that her mother knew of. No, she was certainly not a lawyer, although she did finish college in Israel.

Her parents reported that she worked in international trade.

They were sure that the morgue photograph of Lauren Barr was their daughter.

DNA testing took twelve days to confirm the identification.

That afternoon a persistent Detective Paul Dolbeare contacted his fifty-first business in the regional funeral industry. The man he spoke to was a funeral director in Solomons, Maryland, a good hour by car from Washington and far removed from the Virginia suburbs on the other side of the Chesapeake Bay. This was the first person in the investigation to acknowledge knowing the name Lauren Barr.

He inquired if the detective knew why she had not yet claimed her aunt's remains.

Dolbeare informed him that unfortunately Ms. Barr was herself recently deceased. He asked if the funeral director had the body stored down there.

"No," he said. "Her ashes."

"I thought Jewish law prohibited cremation," Dolbeare said.

"We do what the family asks," was his reply.

The recovered cremains were interred a month later at King David Memorial Park, the Jewish cemetery in Falls Church, Virginia. They were buried in the ground next to Hanna Weiss Geller's husband, Benjamin. A brief graveside homily followed a beautiful lilting Kaddish, the prayer for the dead. The rabbi remarked that when Jews are cremated against their will, neither God nor his law nor man could hold that against the dead.

His reference was not lost on any of the mourners.

On the floor of the United States Senate, Tenley Harbison gave an impassioned speech about the role of the Financial Systems and Services Corporation and the need for continued federal regulation of the commercial banking industry.

She spoke to the C-SPAN audience, to the junior senator from Tennessee who was sitting in the presider's chair, and to five sixteen-year-old Senate pages—three on the Democratic side of the chamber, two on the Republican.

Lois Carneccio and her legal counsel were on time for their scheduled 1 P.M. meeting at the Department of Justice. They were kept waiting. At 2:15 P.M. a very pleasant young man whose business card identified him as an associate counsel in the civil division told them that unfortunately their conference simply could not take place today. They would be in touch.

It was two weeks until DOJ called again. Lois's lawyer broached a new issue. He wanted to know if Justice would have any problem with Ms. Carneccio selling part of her interest in several ViroSat enterprise companies. In his legal opinion, he explained, there should be none. These were publicly traded corporations and his client was not in possession of any material nonpublic information. But given the current circumstances, and in an excess of caution, he was just checking.

Justice had no objection.

Lois received word that the stock sale cleared by text message from her broker. She was in Coral Gables, Florida, with her father and sisters, where they were all celebrating Salvatore Carneccio's ninety-fourth birthday.

After federal and District of Columbia taxes, Lois Carneccio cleared slightly less than twenty million on the stock sale. She retained significant numbers of shares in each of the companies.

Her legal fees exceeded three million dollars. Her counsel politely declined a discount when she asked.

For the entire day, Dan Ter Horst's calendar was clear. Neither his secretary nor his two paralegals knew where he was.

His undocumented meeting took place in a sensitive compartmented information facility—known by its acronym, a "SCIF"—at the Department of State's Bureau of Intelligence and Research. The location in Foggy Bottom was only a few hundred yards across the Potomac River from Arlington.

When Ter Horst received his security clearance here, the Bureau was described to him as "State's CIA." He was one of two judges in Arlington County to be polygraphed and cleared by INR. A surprising number of cases on the Arlington docket require special access, particularly where foreign intelligence and sensitivities of the diplomatic community was involved. Since his retirement from the bench this was the first and only time he used his clearance.

The meeting concerned Yonah Bar-Ilan.

The main speaker was either a liaison to INR from Mossad or the other way around, a US agent working inside the Israeli intelligence organization. Ter Horst was not sure which. Either way he spoke with great authority. The attendees deferred to him and listened carefully to his briefing.

Yonah Bar-Ilan was not now and never had been attached to Israeli intelligence.

The closest he ever came to Mossad was working in an information technology company in Eilat that held some Israeli government intelligence contracts, none of which he ever personally serviced.

Bar-Ilan was not even his original family name. He changed his name legally, adopting the honorific nom de guerre of a great uncle who fought in the *Irgun* in the 1930s. Militant Zionism ran in his family. He grew up in a now-illegal and quite defiant settlement on the West Bank, the briefer explained. Bar-Ilan believed passionately in a Biblical mandate for Greater Israel. He is our version of a *jihadi*, he explained to nods around the table.

Bar-Ilan had been rejected by every security service in Israel. His fanaticism and psychological instability were cited.

He was particularly obsessed with the Meier Seckendorf Böhmer history. Until very recently, the briefer continued with a dry smile, everyone throughout the Israeli financial establishment thought those lost Egyptian accounts were nothing but urban legend.

Bar-Ilan especially could not stand the thought of all that unclaimed Arab money.

The Department, he concluded, does not have to be at all concerned about him. It's one thing in the United States to pretend to be a former intelligence agent. It's quite another matter in Israel.

No information was provided concerning Bar-Ilan's associate, whom he referred to only as "the woman."

Dan Ter Horst felt a chill when the briefer finished. The safest place for Yonah Bar-Ilan, the judge concluded, was inside a US prison.

His sentence was sixty-five years, well within the federal sentencing guidelines for the hundred and three counts of commercial espionage and Arms Export Control Act violations for which he was convicted.

In prison Yonah Bar-Ilan consistently denied responsibility for the death of Lauren Barr née Lauren Lund.

The issue of his eventual eligibility for parole, vehemently opposed by both US and Israeli governments, became a cause célèbre for Israeli ultraconservatives.

That evening the sun was at high azimuth on the western horizon when the Air Canada Airbus A300 from Toronto touched down at Havana's José Marti International Airport.

At the gate a tall thin old white man stepped out holding a single carry-on bag. He was expected. Two solicitous young men in military uniforms escorted him around to a special customs area. In ten seconds his Irish passport was stamped without inspection.

"*Bienvenidos*," said the first soldier. Welcome.

"*Entiendo que regresa*," added the second. I understand you're returning.

"*Ha visitado Cuba antes?*" the first inquired, simply making polite small talk. You have visited Cuba before?

"*Hace muchos años.*" It's been many years.

He was a man of few words today.

"*Planea quedarse mucho tiempo?*" Do you plan to be here long?

"*Si. Para siempre. Me voy a jubilar acá. Quizás hare algunos*," he said. Yes. Permanently. I am retiring here. Perhaps I will do some business.

The soldiers showed him the scenic route, driving along the beach to his hotel. They stayed in the car as he departed and disappeared inside, precisely as they had been instructed to do.

At 7 A.M. on any workday in Dubai the city center at the Emirates Towers is just beginning to awaken. This is not by any means an early town, a characteristic especially true on the first of August, the beginning of a month-long hiatus for Arabs and the many expatriate westerners based there.

Mohammed Hasab could never shake his American habit of early arrival at the office. He didn't want to.

He quite enjoyed the solitude of an empty office early in the morning.

He carried a venti-sized cup of Starbucks Colombian Bold coffee purchased at the mall thirty-six floors below along with a folded copy of the *Gulf News*, thc English-language newspaper here. Its front page was all about the ViroSat deal. Compton Sizemore was only parenthetically mentioned. ViroSat in this rendering of the story was a global triumph for the Hasab International Group.

He checked in by telephone with the war room in New York, where it was 10 P.M. They were beginning what would be a fantastic trading day in the Middle East bond markets.

No one had heard any other news.

Hasab sat at his desk. He pulled open the center drawer. With a care bordering on reverence he withdrew two thick ancient bound ledgers.

The ledgers were in Azach Hasab's handwriting, the original recordation of the investments made in Cairo, thence to Berlin.

Yesterday, the day that the ViroSat limited partnership closed here in this office, was his last as managing partner and CEO of the Hasab International Group wealth management subsidiary. The family had approved. So had the larger partnership. Mohammed would be forming a new company. In less than two hours he would meet with the first recruits to his hand-picked team.

Base anywhere in the world you like, the directors of the corporation told him. Use any resources necessary. Budget shall not be at issue where the honor and reputation of this family are involved. You must find the heirs of every investor here. *Inshallah*, you shall.

Mohammed Hasab was thinking about starting his new operation in Philadelphia.

But he was thinking more about Warren Hunter and the disturbing noises he heard when their last telephone conversation abruptly ended.

He had not been able to reach Warren or to sleep ever since.

CHAPTER 40

"Observation sucks," Warren Hunter said to his brother. "They took my phone and my clothes."

"You had what they called a 'major cardiac event,'" Rick replied. "Sure, it was forced upon you involuntarily, but don't doubt for a minute how significant it was. 'Observation' only means that they need to keep an eye on you. Your clothes were ruined when Darlington shot your would-be killer. You don't even want to see what you looked like when they brought you in. You were unconscious, flumping around like a rag doll. The emergency room docs were all over you. They thought all that blood and bone and brain tissue was yours."

Warren wore a hospital gown. He was sitting on the bed, his legs over the side. His hospital room could accommodate two patients but he was berthed alone. A uniformed policeman sat outside the door.

"That was bizarre. One minute I'm talking on the phone. Then some madman is on top of me inside the airplane. Next thing I know I'm waking up here."

Rick nodded and said slowly, "He tried to kill you. He almost succeeded."

"Did they tell you what happened?"

"Warren, I was in the men's room at the private terminal when I heard the gunfire. You can understand why I'm a little sensitive when I hear shots now, can't you? Skip Darlington had just walked out to the plane to join you. I was going to head back home with your car and driver."

"I remember up until that point. I was on the aircraft talking to Mohammed Hasab, waiting for Skip."

"Right. He back-filled me last night on what happened. The guy was already in the cabin when you sat down. Neither of the pilots questioned him. They thought he belonged there."

"What did he do to me?"

"He had a syringe filled with a massive dose of potassium chloride. Warren, it's the same drug that they use in executions by lethal injection. In sufficient doses, it stops your heart."

"And he injected me?"

"Only partially. Skip got him at the exact moment he was shoving the needle into your leg. He never completely pushed the plunger down. Your doctor says you took only a very small amount. It was enough to cause heart arrhythmia and for you to pass out. You did not go into full cardiac arrest. I saw how they were working on you in the ER. They gave you drugs to stabilize you and who knows how many sedatives. You were out until this morning."

"You came here with me?"

"I rode in the ambulance."

"Where's Skip Darlington?" Warren asked.

"He was supposed to be meeting with the police again this morning. When he came here last night he said that his attorneys from Darlington Global thought he had nothing to worry about. He certainly appeared entirely unconcerned about himself. He was only worried about you."

"What day is it?"

"August first."

"Wait a minute—ViroSat—"

"All of the debt closed yesterday and the day before. You pulled off the trillion-dollar deal, brother. Face it, you're better at delegating than you thought you were. The war room has been checking in regularly."

"I was out for more than a day?"

"Yep."

"Rick, who would want to kill me? Okay. I know. A lot of people do. I mean who *really* wanted me dead—enough to do this?"

"His name was Sándor Horvath. He was in his seventies, a widower. He lived alone and has two grown sons. He emigrated from Hungary sometime in the 1960s and became an American citizen. I got all this last night from Skip."

"Let me guess," Warren said. "He told you that he 'called a guy.'"

"How did you know?"

"It's what he says when he reaches into the government and he definitely isn't supposed to. Skip was on Clinton's secret service detail. He's better connected than anyone I know because he keeps his mouth shut. That's why he's so good at what he does. What did he find out?"

"Horvath was in the Hungarian secret police under the communists. Skip thinks that the entire time he was here in the United States, at least until the end of communism in Hungary, he was working for AVO. It's the Hungarian version of the KGB. He was some kind of sleeper agent. Horvath used to travel all around the country, maybe as a freelancer."

"And Skip took him out."

"Yes. He wasn't exactly in great shape when he came by last night. Part of it was the police interrogation, I'm sure—I know what *that's* like. He sat right here talking with me for an hour. Did you know that was the first time he ever fired his weapon other than on the range? He was practically admiring of the guy when he told me about Horvath."

"How do you think he fit into our deal?"

"Skip said you'd want to know that. His guy had a theory."

"What?"

"The evidence is circumstantial. Graham Tuttle was the CIA's chief of station in Budapest for two years. He was in charge of our operations there during the failed Hungarian revolution in 1956. Horvath was still in Hungary. Skip's guy thinks they knew each other then and worked together."

"Horvath isn't around to tell us if they did. Why would he say the connection is circumstantial? Can't they question Gray Tuttle?"

"They can't. He's gone."

"What do you mean gone?"

"Just . . . gone."

"People don't disappear, Rick."

"People like Gray Tuttle do. There's also another . . . circumstance."

"Like what?"

"When the police searched Horvath's car they found two semiautomatic pistols, both military-type forty-fives. Skip called them M1911s.

They finished the ballistic tests late yesterday. One of them fired the shots at the US Capitol. Warren, the man who tried to kill you is the same guy that shot at Julia and me. We were his targets."

"Shit."

"Indeed. The other gun looked as if it hadn't been fired but was perfectly conditioned and loaded. It had a hand-etched engraving on the handle. G. YEAGER LT 4572. The way you'd mark your weapon in the Eighth Air Force in 1944."

"Horvath had Pop's gun?"

"Yeah."

"The one he used to shoot Stauber in the death camp."

"Presumably."

"How did he get it? Pop never had a gun when we were growing up."

"There's the other circumstance I was talking about. It had to be Tuttle."

Warren stared at the floor. "We're lucky," he said.

"We are," Rick replied.

"Not the way that you think. We're so lucky we were his sons."

Rick stood, leaned in very close to his kid brother, and put a gentle hand on the back of his neck. "Warren," he said softly, "there was no luck involved."

EPILOGUE

Julia Toussaint easily found a parking place on Witherspoon Street. She locked her car and walked to Nassau Street, glancing at the paper with her scribbled directions. It was a warm overcast Monday in late May. Most of Princeton University was somewhere else during this calm before the storm. Exams had concluded. Graduation was a week away.

This was Julia's first time ever in Princeton. She thought about how odd that was on the drive down this morning from her parents' home in Newark. Born and raised a Jersey girl, college, too. Years with one of New Jersey's United States senators. She should have visited before.

Today would be a good time with a good reason to correct that.

"Excuse me," she said, stopping a lanky beard and backpack on the sidewalk. "Is that the FitzRandolph Gate?" The man could not have looked at her with a stranger gaze if she had addressed him in the Martian language.

"Yeah. What else would it be?" He walked on, shaking his head.

She crossed Nassau Street and stood at the gate, waiting. She was early.

"How was the visit with your folks?" She turned at the sound of Rick Yeager's voice and immediately brightened. Then she hugged him hard.

"It was terrific and they're awesome. Daddy is talking retirement. Mom won't have any of it. My sisters say that she doesn't want him around the house all day."

"I suppose that you don't get to offer an opinion, do you?" He kept his arm around her.

"I did. My vote doesn't count as much. I'm the baby, and I left town."

"And then there was me."

"That, too. Mom is warming to the idea."

"Of me, or of us maybe giving it a try again?"

"Both. She said the money would change you but not as much as if you used it trying to impress a ghost."

"What did you say?"

"You had no one to impress but me."

Julia took his arm with both hands as they walked onto the campus headed east past Nassau Hall, which Rick identified. "That's the only building where I know the name," he said. On the grass and walkways, workmen were erecting platforms and tents.

"Is everything here called 'Nassau'?" she asked.

"I think so. Ask Warren."

"It's beautiful."

"So are you."

"Stop it. Not here," she whispered, although she was very pleased. Together they walked between the library and the chapel, crossed Washington Road, and turned toward the construction.

"Did you tell your mom about the new job?" Rick asked.

"How could I not? That was all she wanted to talk about. I explained to her quite patiently that I was not fired. I'm glad that I could talk to her in person. I went through the differences between being on a senator's personal staff and running a committee's professional staff."

"You should explain the difference to me," he said.

"Easy. Now I have to please twenty-seven senators, not one."

"Tenley Harbison never blamed you."

"No, she didn't. She's a survivor and a grown-up. I'm certain the fact that she was a prosecutor helped. The day I left she likened our whole experience to losing a major criminal case, setting up a very big play and then watching it come apart. She said that it's happened to her before and will again. There are senators—maybe most of them—who would have taken out the repercussions on the staff, but she is definitely not one of them. The fallout is over. She supported me for the new job, too."

Warren Hunter was waiting for them at a construction fence. He wore jeans and a black polo shirt with an orange "P," a backpack slung over one shoulder. No one casually glancing his way would peg him for the new president and chief of investment and merchant banking at Compton Sizemore.

"Muddy boots time," he said in greeting, and grinned. "Neither of you have been here yet." He hugged them both.

"Are you both sure about this?" Julia asked.

"Absolutely," Warren replied. "J.D., this is a joyous occasion." He opened a wooden gate to the construction area and held it for Rick and Julia as they walked in.

The sign was brand new.

Princeton University
Gustav Adolph Yeager Center for International Finance and Industry
A Gift of
The Yeager Family Foundation, Washington
The Compton Sizemore Charitable Trusts, New York
Hasab International Reconstitution Group, Ltd., Philadelphia and Cairo

There was no structure yet. The place was a deep hole filled with catacombs of composite forms for the concrete, rimmed with a line of at least two dozen cement trucks. The mixers were turning. Four large flatbed trucks were being serviced by this parade. From each of them a huge hose protruded—up, across a transverse rig, then hanging straight down. Massive pumps on the flatbeds pushed the concrete through the hoses in thick steady streams. Workmen moved along the edges of the concrete forms, methodically filling them.

The closer they got to the trucks and the pumps the louder the noise got.

"First pour," Warren shouted. "Bottom of the foundation." He led the way to a point about twenty yards ahead of a hanging concrete hose. The foreman of the work crew acknowledged them and gave a thumbs-up sign to Warren. The crew muscled around the hose. Concrete slushed into the set-up forms. The work moved slowly in the mud, taking baby steps toward the three of them.

Warren unshouldered his backpack and opened it. He held it for Rick, who reached inside, withdrawing the lacquered box of dark red wood.

"I've never opened it," Warren commented.

"Neither have I," Rick said. He held the box tightly, top and bottom, and pulled up on the lid. Julia softly placed her hand on Rick's shoulder blade. They all peered inside at the dark gray ash and waited as the *plupsch, plupsch* of the concrete inched ahead.

When the fat hose reached where they were standing the workmen paused. The nozzle operator reached forward and expertly lay in a wet gray base in the trough formed by the standing forms. When it reached a depth of about eighteen inches, he cut off the concrete flow and stepped back. The workers stopped all movement and stood by quietly. In the background all four pumps shifted from high whine to idle. Some of the workers took off their hard hats.

"Do you want to say something first?" Warren asked.

"To his memory," Rick said. "Peace, Pop. *Seelenfrieden*." He hesitated before handing the open box to his brother.

Julia gripped Rick's hand and wept.

Warren carefully spread Dutch's ashes into the wet concrete, dusting them across the length of the form. He gently closed the box and shut his eyes tight as the workers resumed the pour.

ACKNOWLEDGMENTS

As we leave Warren, Rick, and Julia in their gentle healing grief at that construction site in Princeton (trust me, we'll meet them again), I have to express my gratitude to you first and foremost. I mean that. Thank you for reading *The Navigator*—and thank you for *buying* this book. Authors don't say that often enough to readers. More of us should.

Many people have contributed to the making of *The Navigator*. It is a privilege to acknowledge them here.

Stephen Frey, *il miglior fabbro*, gets my loudest shout of thanks. Steve and I have conspired in deals, when we started up the real-world Monticello Capital at about the time that the fictional Compton Sizemore got rolling on Wall Street, and here in this imaginary financial universe where he is the master. I owe him a lot. His perspective after publishing eighteen great novels has made this, my first, a much better book.

If I try to express the true extent to which I am grateful to Kathleen Murphy, I'll start coming across as sentimental, and that's not my style or hers. Kathleen is my literary agent, which is a thoroughly inadequate description. She is a fiercely driven entrepreneur, my business partner, and a creative visionary. I got damn lucky that day Frey told me, "Call this woman. She thinks like us."

Robert Gleason, my chief editor, is a legend and deserves to be. Bob not only writes his own novels in crystalline lucid poetry, he championed this one in the midst of the book publishing industry's economic watershed. Anyone who wants to deny the fine hand of Providence ought to consider just how it is that two guys who both gratefully made it out of steel mills found each other in pursuit of publishing *The Navigator*.

Kelly Quinn, my editor, positively defines what it means to be a rising star in the industry. She embodies the drive of a new generation in literature, possessing enormous intellectual gifts and even greater promise.

Tom Doherty, my publisher and the founder of Tor/Forge, has been unwavering in his support. He put his name on the title page along with mine, and I'm deeply mindful of the respect that action conveys.

By now you should have noticed an Irish theme. You bet. But I'm the one who's been blessed to work editorially with these men and women. I am just as grateful to my exceptional copy editor, NaNá Stoelzle, and my gifted production colleagues at Forge, Brian Heller and Seth Lerner. Patty Garcia and Sally Feller have a genius in the craft of publicity. Linda Quinton especially went the extra mile and then some to position and market this book.

My enduring thanks—

—to Christy Sciscoe and Janet Wilson, my extraordinary partners and greatest supporters, who have been more devoted than anyone else to this novel.

—to the improvers, my not-so-gentle commenters on the earliest drafts, Russell DaSilva, Teo Dagi, John Greathouse, Jim Franklin, Jane Hart, and Beverly Behan, for their perception and critical eyesight.

—to Michael Greelis, clinical psychologist, and Ann Rochmis, psychiatrist, both of them terrific friends who took time to read the novel in its creation and to educate me about trauma, therapy, and how to make the unusual literary convention of next-generation psychological effects ring resonant here.

—to Tony Santore, Seymour Hersh, June Cross, Carlos Campbell, Jim Gilmore, Larry Pressler, Tim White, Jim Thacker, Christopher Hays, Kathleen Stein-Smith, George Shafran, Christopher Nelson, Jack Liebau, Chris Voss, Carl Cox, Steve Hammond, Mark Campbell, Ken Brier, and Michael Adams, for providing me their counsel, experience, and wisdom while I was writing this book.

—to Norb Vonnegut, H. T. Narea, and Margaret McLean for their guidance and enthusiastic encouragement to the new guy.

—to Jim Bloom and Linda Miller, who gave me the humbling opportunity to read from this book publicly for the first time, to an audience of brilliant Muhlenberg College literature majors spanning three generations.

—to Toby Sorensen, Karen Stevenson, Louisa Bennett, Hildie Carney, Julie Ferrell, Ann Fleming, Judy Gartlan-Thompson, Mary Gauthier, Claudia Lewis, Jane McMorrow, Peggy Ryu, and Ginny Witt, literary and gracious women whose book club in Fairfax, Virginia, became my beta test site for *The Navigator* in an early manuscript.

—to my here-remaining-anonymous friends in the Washington intelligence orbit, for providing context and insights to make this narrative more powerful. You know who you are.

—to my wife, Barbara Snelbaker Pocalyko (unsurprisingly, she is my least gentle critic), our son, Jim Pocalyko, our daughter, Katie Pocalyko, and my brother, Paul Pocalyko, for their continuing refinements to my work, and especially for their relentless loving support. I really do have the greatest family. They deserve and here receive my gratitude most of all.

Coming full circle, we end where we began.

For a lifetime I have been deeply influenced by a man who was at Bergen-Belsen as a nineteen-year-old liberator on that darkest night of April 1945. He flew into Germany from Attlebridge, England, a corporal in the Eighth Air Force's 466th Bombardment Group hauling in supplies. *The Navigator* is entirely fiction. But in the prologue when Dutch Yeager saw "the faces of the Englishmen and the other Americans flattened beyond belief in frozen stares," he was looking at Walt Pocalyko in real life. Quietly, nobly bearing into his twilight everything he experienced there, my father is still a lion, a masterful intellect, and ever an inspiration to me.

Peace. *Seelenfrieden.*